TOGETHER ALONE

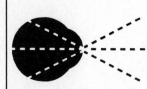

This Large Print Book carries the
Seal of Approval of N.A.V.H.

LT

TOGETHER ALONE

BARBARA DELINSKY .

THORNDIKE PRESS
A part of Gale, Cengage Learning

GALE
CENGAGE Learning·

Detroit • New York • San Francisco • New Haven, Conn • Waterville, Maine • London

GALE
CENGAGE Learning®

LIBRARY OF CONGRESS CATALOGING-IN-PUBLICATION DATA

Delinsky, Barbara.
    Together alone / by Barbara Delinsky.
        pages ; cm. — (Thorndike Press large print famous authors)
    ISBN-13: 978-1-4104-5083-8 (hardcover)
    ISBN-10: 1-4104-5083-X (hardcover)
    1. Empty nesters—Fiction. 2. Domestic fiction. 3. Large type books. I. Title.
PS3554.E4427T64 2012
813'.54—dc23   2012025202

Published in 2012 by arrangement with Harper, an imprint of HarperCollins Publishers.

Printed in the United States of America
1 2 3 4 5 6 7 16 15 14 13 12

*I dedicate this book — again,
still, always — to my guys.*

ACKNOWLEDGMENTS

No writer is all-knowing. For their help in the researching of this book, my heartfelt thanks go to Lt. Jack Hunt of the Needham Police Department, Martha Shepardson of the Rivers School, and all those at the National Center for Missing and Exploited Children. I take full blame for any errors that may have been made in the transition from fact to fiction.

ONE

He wasn't going to like it. He hated the ritual of the formal family picture, but the time was right. In four short days, his only child was leaving the nest, breaking out of her chrysalis into an exciting new world. If ever there was an occasion to mark, this was it.

Starting college was a rite of passage, a beginning.

It was also an ending, one Emily Arkin had been dreading for years. Prior to kindergarten, Jill had been all hers. Then she was gone three hours a day. Then six. Then seven, then eight.

College was twenty-four hours a day, seven days a week. It was a springboard to adulthood and total independence.

"How do I look?" Jill asked, joining Emily's reflection in the bathroom mirror.

Emily lost a moment's breath. She always did when Jill came upon her unexpectedly.

That this striking young woman was her daughter never failed to amaze her. She had Emily's dark hair and fair skin and Doug's height, but the features came from earlier generations, and what was inside was pure Jill. She was sweet, sensitive, and smart. She was innocent, yet sophisticated, the product of growing up in a small town, in a shrinking world.

Emily didn't want the innocence lost. She didn't want the sophistication honed. She didn't want Jill hurt. *Ever.*

"Mom," Jill pleaded softly.

Emily made a helpless sound and reached for a tissue. "Sorry. I didn't mean to do that."

"If you cry, I will, too, and then we'll *both* look a mess. Dad's on the phone." She paused, cautious. "Is he going to be angry?"

Emily forced a bright smile. "What's to be angry about? He's already dressed for the cook-out. In ten minutes, the pictures will be done and we'll be on our way." The doorbell rang, in old age more a clang than a chime. "There's the photographer," she said and took Jill's face in her hands. "You look beautiful. Come."

The sun was falling in the west, gilding the edges of the broad-leafed maples that stood on the front lawn, and the peaks of the white picket fence beyond. Leaving Jill there, Emily went to the door of the small den that was Doug's home office and caught his eye.

He held up a finger and continued to talk.

Stomach jangling, as always when she couldn't gauge his mood, she waited, watching him. At forty-four, he was even more athletic of build than he had been at twenty-two. Then, sheer physical labor had kept his body in shape. Now, daily workouts at a health club did it. His stomach was flat, his back straight, his shoulders broad. He wore his clothes well.

They were fine clothes. He shopped when he traveled, and he looked it. The pleated slacks and open-neck shirt that he wore today spoke more of Europe than of a small town in the northwest corner of Massachusetts.

Emily half-wished she had bought something new to wear for the pictures, to look more sophisticated beside Doug. But she hated spending money on herself, when there were other bills to pay. Better a new muffler for the wagon than a silk something she would never wear again.

Doug hung up the phone. "Who rang the bell?"

She slipped a cajoling arm through his.

11

"Larry Johnson. He's new with the *Sun*. A photographer. He's good, and very cheap. I asked him to take a few pictures before we leave."

"Emily."

"I know. You hate having pictures taken, but Jill's leaving in four days, *four days,* and then our lives will be changed forever."

"Maybe, if she'd been going to D.C. like Marilee. But Boston? It's barely three hours away."

"She won't be our little girl anymore."

"She hasn't been that for a long time."

"You know what I mean," Emily coaxed, but more anxiously now. "This is a milestone, Doug. Besides, she needs a picture of the three of us for her dorm room. Smile for her? Please?"

If he said no, she would send Larry home. A scowling Doug defeated the purpose. But he sighed and produced a vapid smile. Relieved, she led him out of the house.

Jill sat on the swing that hung from the largest of the front maples. With the light dappled by leaves, and a backdrop of rhododendron and white fencing, the setting was bucolic.

Emily was remembering the hours and hours Jill had spent on that swing, the pumping and soaring and spills, when a

12

muted ring came from the house. Doug took off before she could protest. She stared after him in dismay, then resignation. He was home, at least. He had promised to stay the week. It was a concession that didn't come without strings. Taking phone calls was one.

Refusing to be discouraged, she turned back to Jill. "I want a picture of you here," she said and when several shots had been taken, she moved in beside Jill for several of them together.

She covered Jill's hands on the chains of the swing and leaned in close. Cheeks touching, she smiled at the feel of Jill's smile, laughed to the sound of Jill's laugh. History was suddenly pleated, the years juxtaposed, and the laughter was that of childhood again. Emily loved its sound. She couldn't bear to think of the day it would be gone.

Leaving the swing, they went to the backyard and posed on an outcropping of rock by the pond. From slightly above her, Jill draped her arms over Emily's shoulder. Emily held her hands. They leaned against one another, lost their balance and laughed, then tried again, while the photographer snapped away.

"Doug!" Emily yelled toward the window

that marked his den, but Jill had another idea.

"One of my mom alone," she announced.

Emily jumped out of camera-range. "Uh-uh. This is your day."

"But I want one of *you*."

"I want ones of *us*." She looked toward the house. *"Doug?"*

His face appeared at the screen, again a finger raised.

Emily tempered her frustration with a short sigh and the knowledge that he would eventually come. He might be grumpy, but he would accommodate her. It wasn't often that she asked for anything. He knew that.

Returning to the front of the house, they posed on the steps, Emily above, Jill below, then shifted places at the photographer's direction. Emily wore an easy smile. She was good at easy smiles, even when less easy things ate at her mind. Some might call it dishonesty. Emily called it making the best of the situation.

"Hard to tell mother from daughter," the photographer remarked, to which Emily gave a doubtful snort.

"It's true," Jill said. "They'll think you're my sister."

Emily fixated on the "they," strangers in a dorm room three hours away, and felt a hollowness inside.

"Mom," Jill growled, squeezing the fingers laced through hers.

"I'm okay," Emily vowed.

"I'll only be in Boston. We'll talk all the time."

"I know."

"You can drive in and take me to lunch."

"I know."

"We can go shopping."

"I know." But it wasn't the same. It would never be the same again.

Fighting the knot in her throat, Emily gave Jill a hug and held on until she was recomposed. Then, staying close, she faced the camera again.

When the screen door opened behind them, she felt she'd been granted a reprieve. Doug was a distraction from empty thoughts. He was her husband. He had been her world before children had come, and he would be again, once Jill was gone.

"Where do you want me?" he grunted in a way that set her stomach off again.

"Problems?" she asked. He was a business consultant, a troubleshooter hired by small companies to right things gone wrong. At a time of economic anemia, he was state-of-the-art medicine. He had never been more in demand.

He shot her a tired look. "Always."

"Where?"

"Pittsburgh."

Her heart fell. Concord or Manchester, even Boston he might do in a day. Pittsburgh was always longer. "Do you have to go?"

"I don't have to, but if I want to keep the account, I'd better."

"Oh, Doug." He had *promised* her this week. Her heart broke for Jill. Her heart broke for *herself*.

More sharply, he said, "Hell, I can't say no. Money is tight, and universities cost money. I'm still gagging over that check I wrote last week."

"It's okay," Jill said quickly. "We still have stuff to do that Dad can't help us with at all. We'll be busy, Mom. Will you be back before I leave, Dad?"

He softened, touching her head. "Sure, I will. I'll only be gone two days."

The photographer took several shots of them there, with Emily and Jill on the front steps and Doug leaning over the rail. Then he sat Doug on the steps and arranged Emily and Jill nearby, and when he was done with that pose, Jill jumped up.

"I want one of my parents alone," she said, and this time Emily didn't argue. She

16

slid onto the step below Doug and sat between his legs with her elbows on his knees.

It should have been the most comfortable pose in the world. They had sat that way dozens of times, back when they had first met, when life had been simpler.

Emily's life was still simple. It revolved around Jill and Doug, around the small house that needed repairs they couldn't afford, the small group of friends whose loyalty money couldn't buy, and the small town whose wealth lay in its warmth.

Doug's life was the one that had changed. He traveled constantly, power-lunched with power brokers, immersed himself so deeply in innovative management techniques that Emily was hard put to associate him with the unassuming organic farmer she had married. Maybe that was why she felt odd now, sitting between his legs with her elbows on his knees.

"Mother!" Jill cried. *"Smile!"*

Emily smiled. For Jill, anything.

And it wasn't all that hard. Of the many things motherhood had taught her over the years, hiding heartache was one.

Brian Stasek strode into the drugstore with a whimpering Julia on his hip. She wasn't happy, but then, neither was he. He was hungry, tired, and hot. She was hungry, tired, and wet. He had used the last of the Pampers at a rest stop five hours before. They were badly in need.

He found the aisle, found the size, found the sex. Gathering an armload of boxes, he found the cash register. The boxes clattered onto the counter. Julia began to wail.

He jiggled her on his hip while he reached for his wallet. "Almost there. Almost there. Almost there."

"She's a cute baby," said the girl at the register.

Brian grunted. "I thought so, too. Then she became all mine, and things changed. Let me tell you, taking care of kids isn't for the weak of heart. Remember *that*, if you're planning on having one in the near future."

The girl took a step back. Julia cried louder.

"Since Chicago," he muttered.

"Maybe she's sick," came the timid suggestion.

He sighed. "No. Just tired." There was more to it than that, but Brian didn't have the strength or inclination to share the rest, certainly not with a teenaged stranger. He needed dry diapers, warm food, and a solid bed, in that order. So he tucked the change back in his pocket, gathered up the boxes, and returned to the Jeep.

The diaper was changed in no time. After three days, Brian was experienced enough to know that striving for perfection, where an unhappy child was concerned, was absurd. As long as the diaper was in the general vicinity, it would do its thing, give or take.

Give or take was what it had done. So he fished a dry jumpsuit from the depleted clean bag, stuffed the soggy one in the bulging dirty bag, and lifted his repaired daughter.

"Pretty Julia," he said with a grin and gave her a hug.

She began to whimper.

The grin left. "Right. Food." Pausing only to stick an empty baby bottle in the waistband of his jeans, he backed out of the jeep with Julia in his arms and straightened.

She began to squirm.

He held her still and looked her in the eye. "If I let you walk, it'll take twice as long to get where we're going."

She looked back at him with pale blue, unblinking eyes. They were laced with silver, iridescent, almost unearthly — which was how people often described his. They said that his eyes were his deadliest weapon, that one long hard look gave even the meanest man pause. For the first time in his life, he knew what they meant. When Julia looked at him with those eyes that way, it was like she knew something he didn't, like she knew *lots of things* he didn't.

"Yeah, yeah," he said in an attempt to show her that he knew something, too, "you've been stuck in the car for the better part of three days, and you're dying to move."

The eyes held his.

He sighed. "So if you're hungry, you'll make a beeline for the food." He set her down.

She made a beeline for the street.

He caught up her hand with an "Oh, no, you don't, toots," but it was a minute of tugging and vehement, if unintelligible, complaints from Julia before she accepted the sidewalk.

Brian thought of Gayle. She had been the one wanting children, even when he said they should wait. They were both workaholics, he said. They couldn't do a child justice, he said.

She said that they had waited long enough, and that much longer and her ovaries would rot. She said she could do it all, wife, mother, and job.

Then she died, and he was left holding the bag.

And a sweet, sorry, sad little bag she was, he mused, looking down at the bobbing brown curls, the padded bottom, the toddling legs. Julia was used to Gayle being gone days, but the nights were tough, especially now, with four weeks' worth piled one on top of another, and then there was the matter of breast milk, which Gayle had offered morning and night, right up to the end.

He was out of his league on that one.

Maybe on this one, too, he thought, looking on down the street. Then again, maybe not. He dragged in a long breath, then let it out, and when something inside him eased, he inhaled again.

Grannick wasn't bad, if its main street was anything to go by. It was clean. It had the kind of new-old New England charm that was stereotypical of a college town. People strolled in the early evening glow. They looked intelligent and peaceful. They looked casual. They looked countrified. Some of them looked just like him.

He wore old jeans, a black T-shirt that had seen blacker days, a pair of worn sneakers, and a three-day stubble. It was his undercover look. Back home, it was tough. Here, it was camp.

Julia toddled on with the occasional whimper.

Beside the drugstore was a video store, with its long expanse of neon that gave Julia a few seconds' pause, then a bookstore, then, marked by elegant gold letters on a burnished field, the Eatery. Brian felt a surge of energy. "Well, look at that. Right there when we need it. Now, that's a good omen, I'd say."

The Eatery would have been lovely had he been there with Gayle. But Julia was hungry and tired, alternately gnawing on her fist and crying, not at all pleased to be held in one place, and the menu was Southwestern, heavy on avocados, sprouts, and salsa, none of which was her standard fare. He had been hoping for something as pedestrian as roast turkey, mashed potatoes, and peas. Going with the next best thing, he settled for a burger and fries.

The place did have milk, a large glass of which the waitress set before him. It was a breathless minute of pouring from the glass into Julia's bottle, working around her eager arms and impatient cries, before, at last, came a blessed silence.

Brian cornered himself in the booth and settled her in his arms. Her eyes met his and stayed, eerily knowing, daunting in that. He tried to convey confidence, since a confident touch was what she needed, or so his mother had said. She had also said that Julia could stay with her, that it would be easier for him until he was settled, that the trip would be rough with a baby, but he hadn't listened. He had needed to take her then and there, had needed this little scrap of Gayle and him, the best of their old life, the seeds of his future.

Besides, if he hadn't taken her then, he might have lost his nerve.

Which was a joke, given what he did for a living. He was known for his calm under fire, but hell, the police academy hadn't prepared him for fatherhood. As detectives went, he was street-smart and quick, but neither of those things impressed Julia, and as for his shield, she'd as soon bury it in cereal as cower before it.

Brian knew what it was to see the seedy side of life, then go home, close the door, and shower it away. But there was no showering Julia away. She was his for the forseeable future. Taking her from her grandmother in Chicago was the most daring thing he had done in his life.

"A burger and fries," the waitress sang, setting a platter before him. He smiled his thanks, but didn't move. Julia continued to drink. He knew that she was perfectly capable of sitting up, tipping her head back, and holding the bottle herself, but she seemed content.

And so, for that brief moment, was he.

But the moment passed. Julia finished the bottle, sat on the booster seat beside him, and ate pieces of the hamburger he offered, but she was tired. Normally neat, she grew messy and whiney. She rubbed at her eyes with ketchupy hands. She said words that Gayle would have known, but that meant nothing to Brian. He tried to pacify her with more milk, but she wasn't having any part of it — or with the Coke he had ordered for himself — and when she started crying, "Mommmmy — mommmmy," he lost his appetite.

Swinging her into his arms, he paid the bill and started back toward the Jeep, only to set her down again when the squirming resumed.

It was warm out. The air was still, heavy with the ripe smell of trees and grass and so different from where he had been that he wondered if this was an omen, too. He had never particularly wanted to live in the country, but it seemed the best choice, given the circumstances. He needed a sane place

24

to raise Julia. He needed a peaceful place to heal.

Julia began to whimper again.

He swung her up. "What is it, sweetie?"

"Mom-my."

"Mommy isn't here, but Daddy is. Everything's going to be just fine. See? Here's the Jeep, right where we left it." And intact — which was a city thought if ever there was one — but not so dumb, given that the vehicle held the sum of his most precious earthly possessions. Not to mention paraphernalia for Julia, her favorite crackers and juice, and the stuffed rabbit that she refused to sleep without.

Brian's mind lingered on crackers and juice and his own belly, which would undoubtedly speak up several hours hence. Julia's crackers and juice wouldn't do the trick. He had tried the night before.

So he returned to the drugstore and bought a party-size bag of cheddar popcorn, three Heath Bars, and a six-pack of apricot nectar. He was turning to leave, with Julia under one arm and his purchases under the other, when a round of squeals drew his attention to the back of the store.

A photo booth stood there, its half-curtain drawn, and beneath and behind, more legs than he could sort out and count. He grinned. He remembered that fun.

The squeals came again, high laughter followed by a flash of light and the frenzied repositioning of legs. The laughter rang out, the legs froze, the light flashed, then it all began again. When it was done, six preteens tumbled from the booth.

Brian wasn't sure how they had all fit in, but they seemed happy and healthy, and the activity suddenly struck him as such a throwback to an earlier time, such a refreshing change from a world of video arcades and computer massacres, that he couldn't resist.

Tucking the paper sack into the booth, he dug in his pocket for change, and slid in with Julia on his lap. "Grammie will *love* this," he told her, and tried to push her curls into some semblance of order. "If we smile for the camera, she'll see that we're doing just fine. Isn't that a *great* idea, Julia?"

Julia was looking at the innards of the booth as though it were a house of horrors. Her unearthly eyes were growing wider by the second. Tears pooled on their lower lids.

"Oh, sweetie, it's okay," Brian coaxed. "Nothing will hurt you here. Daddy won't let it. Look," he said with pumped-up enthusiasm, "I'll just feed it some quarters

— want to help me — here, hold the quarter —"

It fell on the floor.

He bent over to retrieve it, inadvertently squashing Julia, who let out a wail. He hugged her. He kissed her head. "Shhh. Daddy didn't mean that. Here, let's try again." But he pushed the quarters in himself, because retrieving the thing in such cramped quarters hadn't been easy on him either, and because he figured he had Julia quieted, but not for long. "There. Now we look here," he pointed at the big black circle just as the first flash went off.

Startled, Julia began to scream and didn't stop this time, despite Brian's efforts to console her, cooing his sympathy, holding her cheek to his, begging her to smile. Moments later, standing outside the booth waiting for the strip of pictures to emerge, he figured that, if nothing else, he had that first shot before she had lost it completely. Guardedness was better than terror, he supposed.

As it happened, he didn't even get guardedness. He got three shots of Julia crying her heart out while he held her cheek to his. For that first shot, she had been down on his lap. All that showed of her was a mess of curls on the top of her head.

Wondering if this, too, was an omen, he folded the strip of photos in half and stuffed it in his pocket. Then he set Julia on his hip, snatched up the paper sack, and strode from the store.

Myra Balch sat at the upstairs window of her small frame house, watching the world go by. It wasn't a large one, as worlds went. She lived at the end of a dead end street lined with small frame houses not unlike hers, but from her end, the only house she could see was the Arkins'.

That didn't mean she didn't know what was happening on the rest of the street. She most certainly did. She knew when the Wilsons' weekly oranges came from their daughter in Florida, because the UPS truck turned around in Myra's driveway. She knew when Abel Hinkley got a raise, because the furniture delivery truck did the same. And that funny little truck painted like a rat. The exterminator. At the LeJeunes'. Again.

Of course, there were things her driveway couldn't tell her. That was why she went walking up and down the street every morning at eleven. She wanted the news. And the exercise, of course, she wanted that, too. Frank was a big one for keeping in shape. If she ever got fat, he'd leave her, no questions asked.

The sheers moved, just a flicker. She wished for more, wished for a breeze to cool the house. Frank kept promising her a fan, but he never seemed to get around to buying it, so the air remained still and warm.

She leaned forward. The photographer who had taken pictures of the Arkins was leaving. He was the same one who had taken pictures for Ginny Haist's sixty-fifth birthday, and the pictures were grand. Myra hoped he had done as well for the Arkins.

She had crocheted Jill an afghan for school and planned to give it to her on the night before she left. She knew Emily would be touched.

The photographer backed out of the driveway and drove off, leaving Emily's old wagon looking bare and forlorn. It had seen better days, poor thing.

Doug's car was another matter. It was little more than a gleam of black and chrome in the shelter of the garage. She wondered if it would stay there when they rented out the rooms above. She wondered if the renter would be expected to park on the street. She wondered whose idea it was to rent in the first place.

Probably Doug's. He would want the

money. It wouldn't bother *him* if there were strangers around. *He* wasn't the one who would see them coming and going. *He* wasn't the one whose privacy would be disturbed.

Emily deserved more. Myra did what she could to help — and her lace cookies *were* the best in town — but lace cookies could only do so much.

Flowers helped. Myra always had one bloom or another to give Emily. And, of course, there were things like knitted mittens or an afghan, guaranteed to bring a smile.

Myra gasped. There they were, Emily, Jill, and Doug, climbing into that rusty wagon, off to the Whittakers' cookout. Tomorrow night there was a party at the Davieses', and the next night one at the Eatery, where Jill and her friends had all waitressed.

One party after another. Myra didn't know what it was about people that made them want to make fools of themselves in public. Emily understood that. *She* wasn't throwing a party for Jill. *She* didn't see the girl's leaving home as cause for celebration. Their parting would be a private affair, surely a sad one.

"But I don't talk," Myra vowed as she rose from her chair, "never have, never will. I bake my cookies and knit my sweaters, and keep still. So what do they do? They plan a party for *me*." She started down the stairs. "I don't want a party. *They*'re the ones who want it. They left here the very first chance they could, and they never came back for long, and they feel guilty about that. So now they've brought food for a party, and they've taken over my house."

To her right, at the bottom of the stairs, the dining room table was covered with her mother's embroidered linen and the first of the food her daughters-in-law had brought. To her left, the living room was filled with sons and grandkids, all glued to a baseball game on television.

Turning toward the back of the house, she slipped through the kitchen, let herself out the door, and went down the steps and across the lawn without being noticed. She paused to admire the whole of the huge, pale green weeping willow that stood on the bank of the pond, before settling onto the scrolled wrought-iron bench that sat beneath the veil of its arms.

She plucked bits of fallen leaves — willow lint, she called it affectionately — from the bench, then leaned over and plucked bits from the ground. She worked her way down the bench, grooming the grass beneath the willow until it was neatened to her satisfaction. Then she sat back and admired the pachysandra she had planted and pruned over the years, and beyond that, the impatiens, and beyond that, the lilies. Looking out over the water, she sighed.

Such a beautiful spot. And so well tended. She had done her best. She would continue to, until the day she died.

That thought made her restless, impatient, and frightened at the same time. She carried a dreadful burden. When she thought of death, the burden shifted and threatened to spill. She gathered her strength, steadied it, and vowed that she wouldn't die yet.

But it was coming. She knew it, more and more so, with each birthday that passed. Time was running out.

"Myra?" It was her daughter-in-law Linda, the career woman who believed that all women were sisters, regardless of age, and that "mother" was too formal a name for her mother-in-law. "Why are you sitting out here alone?"

"I'm not alone," Myra said kindly. She liked Linda, actually. Quirks and all, Linda was more tolerant than the others. The others would have argued with her even now, but Linda merely smiled.

"We want pictures. Will you come inside?"

"But pictures should be taken out here. This is the most beautiful spot around."

Linda swatted away a mosquito. "It's very buggy."

"Not for me. I use the right perfume. It's in the bathroom off the kitchen, if you'd like to try some. Not that the boys will like it, but a few bites won't hurt them any. Yes," the idea was growing on her, "if we're taking pictures, I'd like them taken here. But you'll have to call Frank. We can't take pictures without him."

Linda smiled. "I'll go get the others."

Myra returned the smile, and it lingered. A picture-taking session beneath the willow was perfect. So there was something to be said for daughters-in-law, after all. Certainly for grandchildren. Even for sons who felt guilt after years of neglect. Far be it from her to tell them that by the time they had left home, she had been ready for them to go, tired of the fights with each other and with Frank, tired of the cooking and the cleaning. She had been more than ready for a rest.

Not that she would tell *Frank* that. *Lord* no. He would be *furious*. He hadn't liked the boys leaving, hadn't liked it at all.

"Come on inside, Mom," called her oldest, Carl. "We'll take pictures in the living room."

"Out here!" she called back.

"The light is dimming out there."

Indeed it was. Dusk was imminent. But she wasn't as dumb as they thought. "It's still brighter here than it is inside."

"We can use a flash in here."

"You can use a flash out here, too." She grinned. "It's here or not at all, Carl. It's *my* birthday." The grin thinned. "You'll have to tell your father we're out here. Where is he? I thought he was puttering around the woodshed, but I don't see him there. Find him for me, Carl?"

Carl retreated into the house, but only for a minute. When he returned, he wasn't alone. The other sons were with him, and the daughters-in-law, and, trailing dutifully, the grandchildren. Before Myra could do more than pat her hair and check to make sure that her collar lay flat, she was surrounded by family, kneeling in front, sitting beside, standing behind.

In the crush came the thought that maybe this wasn't such a good idea after all, that the grass under the willow would be hurt, but it seemed too late to say that, and then there was the matter of Frank.

"Where's your father, Carl?" she asked,

34

looking around. She didn't see Frank anywhere. "I want him sitting on this bench." She tried to oust the grandchildren to her left, but they were packed in too tight.

Carl put the camera to his eye. "Look here, everyone."

"Where's *Frank?* We can't take a picture without him."

There was murmuring behind Myra and a snicker or two in front. She ignored them, sitting straighter, putting on the kind of starched face that Carl wouldn't care to photograph.

"I want Frank here," she insisted. "It's only right. He's part of this family."

"Take the picture, Carl."

"It's getting darker."

"Mommy, I'm bit!"

"On the count of three," Carl said from behind the camera.

Myra sat forward, looking to see if Frank was off to the side, wading in the pond. He did that sometimes, when the air was warm.

"One . . . two . . . look here, Mom."

"But your father —"

From behind her came a gentle, "Myra," and Linda's hand on her shoulder. "It's all right. He'll be along. What if you smile, and then we can surprise Frank with the picture?"

Unsure, Myra looked back at her. "Should we?"

"Definitely."

"But he may be angry that we didn't wait."

"He won't be angry. He'll be pleased."

Myra wanted that more than anything in the world. Pleasing Frank was crucial. It was the key to her survival. It was what made her steady that heavy load she carried, what made her turn away from death, even those times when she was so tired of fighting that she wanted only to close her eyes and succumb.

She lived on for Frank.

"Look at Carl," Linda urged, and Myra was unsettled enough to do it.

"That's it," came the camera's voice, sounding enough like Frank's to put Myra momentarily at ease. "On the count of three, everyone say 'cheese.' One, two, three —"

There was a collective, "Cheeeeeese," and a flash of light.

Myra neither smiled nor spoke. It wasn't Frank behind the camera, after all, but Carl, and she wasn't sure Frank would like being left out. If he was angry, he could argue with Carl.

But it didn't work that way. She was the one who lived with him. She was the one who suffered.

The count came again, the collective, "Cheeeeeese," and the flash, and then the crowd that had swarmed down on her so suddenly, as suddenly dispersed. The back door slapped again and again, until at last it was still and all was quiet.

Myra closed her eyes. She let the warm night breeze cleanse the space around her. Then, silent as always, she slipped to her knees and began fluffing the grass, combing it with her fingers, caressing the soil beneath. This was the most beautiful spot around. It was right to take a family picture here. This was a place for reunions.

Two

Part of the beauty of having a child, Emily decided, was the reflection it brought to one's own life. Through Jill, she remembered things that would have otherwise been lost — overnights with giggling friends, the fear of being left chairless when the music stopped, the warm, wet flush of a first kiss. As Jill experienced things, Emily relived them.

So, now, she relived leaving home. She relived the frantic shopping and packing, the last teary gatherings with friends, the fear of a faceless roommate, the terror of academic failure. She also relived the excitement, because, in hindsight, going to college had been the single most pivotal point in her life. She had met Doug the first week. They had been married within the year.

It had worked for her. But for Jill, she wanted more. She wanted four years of study and fun, a degree, traveling with friends, sharing an apartment, getting a job, building a name — then coming back to live nearby.

Thinking of Jill's eventual return was one way to fight the sadness of her going away. Another was to keep busy, which Emily did readily in her capacity as laundress, social secretary, and cooker of favorite meals. Still there were times, as Jill whirled through her final preparations, when Emily stood watching her, wondering where the years had gone, wishing them back. There had been a solace in knowing how Jill spent her time and with whom. There had been a luxury in determining it.

Now she was losing her grip.

It had to be, but that fact didn't ease Emily's dread. The time was too short, four days gone in a flash. Before it seemed at all possible, Emily found herself behind the wheel of the wagon, with Jill's eyes fixed on the turnpike ahead, and every inch of spare space behind them filled.

Emily tried to think of what might have been forgotten. "Do you have your bank check?" It represented Jill's summer's earnings and would be her spending money at school.

"In my wallet."

"Your tuition receipt?" She had to show it

39

to get her dorm key.

"In my pocket."

"The campus map?"

"Right here," held aloft in the tightest of grips.

"Careful. Don't crush it."

Jill relaxed her hand.

As they passed Springfield, Emily tried to think of last bits of advice. Time was running out fast. "You should be able to pick up curtains and a carpet at stores on the edge of campus."

"I know. I have a list of places."

"Go with your roommate."

"Of course."

"Don't wander around alone."

"I'll be fine, Mom."

They passed Worcester. As straight as the road was, Emily's stomach swerved.

"Say no like you mean it."

"Huh?"

"If some boy tries to pressure you. Be firm. Use your knee."

Jill sighed loudly.

When they passed the Weston tolls and Boston materialized on the horizon, Emily felt a crowding of emotion, overlaid with hollowness, shot with dread. Then Jill took her hand.

They said little more for the rest of the

trip, holding hands that way until they pulled off at the Cambridge tolls, and then life switched to fast-forward. They found the dorm and unloaded the car. They met Jill's roommate and the girls across the hall, down the hall, and around the corner. They put things in drawers. They filled the closet, made the bed, spread Myra's afghan. They set up a desk lamp and the answering machine and Jill's computer.

Fast-forward ended abruptly, with the room as neat as it would probably be for the rest of the term, and nothing else for Emily to do. So they sat on Jill's bed, just the two of them plastered side by side, and looked at the pictures Jill had brought. There was one of Jill and five friends, crowding together in laughter at the Davieses' party, one of Jill and her two best friends, Marilee and Dawn, one of the same three girls and their mothers.

"I like this one a lot," Emily remarked. The other mothers, Kay and Celeste, were her own two closest friends. She had a copy of the print on her kitchen corkboard. "And this one a *whole* lot." It was a montage of five of the Larry prints, with Emily and Jill in varying states of connection.

"My sister," Jill teased.

"Your mother."

"They'll never guess. Just think of all that you won't have to do with me gone."

Emily gave her a look. "Are you kidding? I'm spending the next month cleaning your room."

"Don't *touch* my room. I want everything the same when I go home. I'll clean then. It's only seven weeks 'til fall break, less if I get lonesome. Maybe I'll take a bus home and surprise you some weekend."

Emily's throat tightened. She was losing her daughter. *Oh God.* "I want you to have fun here, Jill," the rational side of her said. "These will be an incredible four years. I just know they will."

"What about you, Mom? Will you be okay?"

Emily felt a thudding inside. She put an arm around Jill. "I'll be fine."

"I don't like the idea of your being alone."

"Your father will be home at the end of the week."

"Yeah. For two days, before he leaves again. Can't you get him to stay home more? It isn't fair to you that he's gone all the time."

Emily swallowed her agreement. Loyalty to Doug made her say, "He has to work. He wouldn't travel so much if it weren't important."

"I know, but you've always had me before, and now you won't."

"I'll have Kay and Celeste, and John, and all the other people I know around town. I'll have Myra, who loves to sit and talk, and if I can't clean your room, I'll clean the rest of the house, and when I'm done with that, I'll do the room over the garage."

"My playroom?" Jill asked in dismay.

"You haven't played there in years. It has the potential for being a great little apartment."

"My friends and I loved it. Can I live there next summer?"

"Not if someone else is paying for that privilege."

"You'd really rent it out?"

"Why not?"

"Because it's *ours*." Which was just what Emily had told Doug when he had first suggested it. As though hearing the thought, Jill said, "Daddy's the one who wants to do it, isn't he?"

Emily wondered if Jill resented Doug's not being there at the dorm with them. Plenty of other fathers were. "Why do you think that?"

"Because he isn't home enough to *care* whether some stranger lives in our house."

"It's the space over the garage," Emily

43

argued, as Doug had, "and it's a good thirty feet from the house. It has a separate entrance, not even on the house side. We won't see a thing."

"*Was* it his idea?"

"I don't remember whose idea it was," Emily lied, because whose idea it was didn't matter, "but it does make sense. The money will come in handy. Maybe then your father could stay home more." She raised the last picture. It was another from the Larry batch. Doug was sitting on the front steps, Emily one step lower with her arm around his thigh, Jill one step higher with her arm around his neck.

Emily had the impression that they were restraining him, deliberately holding him there, which wasn't all that absurd, given that he had run back to answer the phone again, shortly before the shot had been snapped.

"Nice picture," Emily said, but suddenly she wasn't thinking of Doug. She was thinking that the time had come, the inevitable last few grains of sand through the hourglass. She was hearing freshman sounds in the hall, knowing that Jill should be out there, not in here with her. *Oh God.* "I should go," she whispered, and the tears came then, helpless tears that flowed with love. "You be good."

Jill threw her arms around her neck and held on tight.

"Be good," Emily repeated in the same choked whisper, "and have fun, and study, and call me."

Jill was crying, too. Emily could feel the sobbing rhythm and hated it, *hated* it, but loved the warmth and the closeness.

"Call me," Emily repeated.

"I will. I'll miss you. I'll worry."

Emily held her back, startled by that. "Worry? About me?"

Jill nodded, but she didn't elaborate, and Emily was on the verge of an all-out deluge, knowing that the longer she stayed, the worse it would be. So she stood quickly, gave Jill a last hug, and ran from the room.

She was barely out the door when she turned right back. She shouldn't have done it, because Jill hadn't had time to move. She was sitting alone on the bed, her face teary, looking forlorn.

"Oh God," Emily whispered, then said, "I'm going straight to Grannick, but I may stop at the market before I go home. If you call and I'm not there, just leave a message, and I'll call back. We may have to do that for a while, until you start classes and things settle down. I'll be in tonight, but not

45

tomorrow morning. I'm having breakfast with Kay and Celeste." She caught her breath. "Oh God," she whispered again. She ran to the bed and gave Jill a final last hug. "Want to walk me down?"

"*Go,* Mom."

"It was *awful*," Emily cried at the Eatery, emotional even twenty hours after the fact. "I have no idea how I found my way back to the car, and then I could barely see the road, I was crying so hard. She looked so *alone* sitting there on that bed."

Celeste grinned. "And two minutes after you left, she was probably out in the hall having a grand time. Did you talk with her last night?"

Emily searched her pockets for a tissue. "Uh-huh."

"And?"

She blotted her eyes. "Uh-huh. A grand time. Great girls, hot guys, quote unquote. How about you? Have you heard from Dawn?"

"Not a word, but that was the deal. She agreed to go to college in Grannick in exchange for my pretending she's miles away. I can't call her. She calls me. And she hasn't."

"That should only be my problem," Kay

mused, catching the eye of the waitress and pointing at her coffee cup. "Three times the first day, twice yesterday. The books say that's normal. What they don't say is that it costs. I was forewarned about tuition, room-and-board, and textbooks, but none of them mentioned the phone bill. I'll have to pay it before John sees it. He'll hit the roof. He still thinks she should have gone to UMass."

"Hah," Emily said. "John may make noise, but he can't fool me." She knew him well. She had been his friend before Kay's, and both of those, before the girls were even born. "John is proud as punch that she's in Washington. You wait. He'll be looking forward to those calls."

"Three times a day?" Kay asked and looked impatiently around. "I need caffeine. You do know that if I didn't love you guys so much, I'd never be here this early."

Emily knew about that love. Monday meetings with Kay and Celeste, sans spouses or offspring, were therapeutic. They had breakfasted through the summer and would switch back to dinners once Kay, who taught eighth-grade English, returned to work. "When does school start?"

"Thursday. Ahhh. Here she comes." She extended her coffee cup to the waitress with a grateful smile, then, declaring a pre-school splurge, ordered a hearty breakfast.

Emily and Celeste ordered more modestly.

Celeste watched the waitress leave. "Seems like yesterday our kids were taking the orders."

Emily knew what she meant. "It was, almost."

"It's weird waking up to an empty house. I keep looking into Dawn's room, just to make sure she's gone."

"Do you miss her?" Emily wanted to know she wasn't the only one who felt all hollowed out.

"She just left."

"So did Marilee," Kay said, "still I miss her. We've been separated before, and for longer periods of time than two days, but college is different. It's significative."

Emily thought that sounded right.

"It's also about time," Celeste avowed. "Dawn's been my responsibility and mine alone — which is nice, when you think that I haven't had to pander to her father all these years, and not so nice when you think of the work. I'm the one who's had to nag and pester and bribe her to keep studying. That's the down-side of single parenthood."

Just as Emily was thinking it, Kay said, "It's the down-side of *motherhood.*"

"Do I miss her?" Celeste asked. "Emotionally, yes. Practically, no. I feel relieved, like I got her where she is, and now someone else is sharing the responsibility."

"Who?" Emily asked, eager for reassurance. She trembled to think of Jill alone in Boston.

"Whoever — the school, the adviser, the RA. *Her. She*'s responsible for more of her life. Finally."

"Do you think she'll do okay?" Kay asked, with good cause. Of the three girls, Dawn was both the brightest and the most impulsive. More than once, Jill and Marilee had kept her from doing things she would have come to regret.

Emily hoped she would find new friends to guard her like that. She worried about it even with Jill, who was eminently sensible. Jill thrived on being surrounded by friends. In the rush to align herself with a group in college, she might make a mistake. For all Emily knew, the girls on her floor, who had seemed so nice, might have been waiting for their parents to leave to show their true colors. For all Emily knew, they might want to drink themselves drunk every night, buzz-cut their hair, and snort coke. For all Emily knew, the guys would be cute and polite and thoroughly lecherous. For all Emily knew, serial killers staked out the cafeteria lines.

Celeste didn't seem worried. "Dawn will be fine. She knows what I expect. God only knows I've drummed it into her enough. Actually, her father is making noises now. Isn't that a hoot? The shadow takes form, after all these years. She got her brains from him, and now he's footing the bill. Little did he know when he agreed to pay her college tuition in his rush to be free of me, what it would cost."

"Little did any of us know," Emily remarked. "It's tough."

Celeste eyed her strangely. "Doug does well."

"Doing well barely meets the cost of the tuition."

"But he's a single-practitioner. He markets his mind and works out of the den. He has no overhead to speak of."

"He has huge travel costs."

Celeste remained skeptical. "To look at him, you'd never know he's anything but loaded. He was like something out of a magazine the other night."

"Clothes are his weakness," Emily allowed. "Clothes and cars. But he doesn't gamble, and he doesn't come home with lipstick on his collar."

"He doesn't come home, period."

"Sure, he does. He's home most week-ends."

"Will he come home more, now that you're alone?" Kay asked.

"How can he, with Jill's bills? He has to work harder than ever."

Celeste made a noise. "Doesn't it get you down, that he isn't there more? At least I have an alimony check to warm my cold hands."

Yes, it got Emily down. She and Doug had been inseparable, eons ago. But she couldn't dwell on the past. "It's not so bad," she said. She yawned and stretched, then set her elbows on the table and grinned. "I have the bathroom all to myself. Besides, things will be different with Jill gone. For the first time in years, weekends will be just Doug and me. Good quality time, *fun,* like the old days, just the two of us." The prospect gave her hope.

Kay sighed. "I'm envious. John knows nothing about fun."

"John is wonderful," Emily argued.

"He's a cop. Life is one long investigation."

"He is decent, upstanding, and honest."

"Oh yes," Kay granted. "He's also a master worrywart. He sees the underside of a lettuce leaf. Why do you think I pour

51

myself into my work? If I listened to half of what he says, I'd be a basket case. I don't even have Marilee to distract me now. I'd die without a job." She focused on Emily. "You need one."

"Doug doesn't want me to work."

"If he isn't here, what difference does it make?" Celeste asked. "If he isn't here, you can do what you want."

"But I respect his feelings. We've discussed it. I've offered, but he says no. It's a matter of pride."

"Pride? Hah! He feels threatened."

Emily laughed. "He does not."

"He's worried that if you get a job, you might succeed at it and eclipse him. It was that way with the book."

"No, it wasn't. I did that book as a favor to John. It was never intended to be anything big."

"You wrote a book," Celeste argued, "and it was published. That's one hell of an accomplishment."

But Emily didn't see it that way. "I ghostwrote it. Sam and Donnie were the ones who did the police work. They told me their story. All I did was take down their words and neaten them up."

Kay started to speak, stopped when their food arrived, resumed the minute the waitress left. "You did more than that, Emily. John knows it, Sam and Donnie know it, and I'd warrant Doug does, too. You listened to Sam and Donnie's ideas, you interviewed people and verified facts, then you put everything together. You were the only one who sat at that typewriter, night after night, after Jill was in bed. It always bothered me that your name wasn't on the cover."

"I didn't need it on the cover," Emily protested, laughing again. She picked up her spoon. "It was inside. That was enough."

Celeste stared at her. "If it was me, I'd have milked being a published author for everything it was worth."

"But the work meant something to me. I didn't do it for the money or the acclaim. Believe me, I was perfectly happy with the mention I got. I don't aspire to be in the limelight."

"You may not," Celeste said, "but I do." She raised a piece of English muffin and held it daintily, though she wasn't first and foremost a dainty woman. She was tall and slim, with a direct gaze and a fresh mouth. She rarely wore makeup, couldn't bother with much more than a French braid, and made so little attempt to attract men that they were invariably attracted. While Kay leaned toward blouses and skirts and Emily toward tunics and leggings, Celeste was more comfortable in jeans and a simple white shirt. "Ladies," she declared now, "my time has come."

Emily exchanged a bemused look with Kay. "Your time for what?"

Celeste set down her muffin. "Living. Without Dawn to nag, I have undirected energy."

"She just *left,*" Kay said, as Celeste had moments before, but Celeste ignored her.

"I've been looking at my life, really looking, turning it inside out and looking at it that way, too. I've been waking up with the sun, in a stone-gray empty house, thinking about what I want to do. For starters, I'm getting my nose fixed."

Kay's jaw dropped. "You're kidding."

"But *why?*" Emily asked.

"Look at this nose. It's an ugly nose."

"But you've had it forever. It's part of who you are."

"Not anymore. As of Thursday morning, it'll be narrowed and shaped, along with this."

Emily couldn't see what she was pointing at. "What's that?"

"My double chin."

"I don't see a double chin." To Kay, she said, "Do you see one?"

"No. You're nuts, Celeste."

But Celeste was insistent. "I see the double chin, and I see the ugly nose. The fact that you two don't is irrelevant. I'm the only one who matters. It's my self-image."

Emily couldn't argue with that. Still. "You really don't need any of it, Celeste."

"But I want it. And when the swelling's gone down and the stitches are out, I'm having streaks put in my hair."

"Gray ones like mine?" Kay cracked, though Emily was hard put to differentiate between sandy and gray in Kay's hair.

"Blonde ones," Celeste said. "I'm going with a lighter brown as a base color and blond streaks. Lighter is younger. Except for you, Emily. You always look sixteen."

Emily's sable-colored hair was thick and glossy, blunt-cut an inch below her earlobe. Two minutes with a blow-dryer and the ends curled under. She had worn it that way since she was, well, sixteen.

"And after my hair is done," Celeste announced, "I'm buying clothes."

"New jeans?"

"Only if they have gold studs running up and down the legs, and even then, only if there's a matching top that buttons down to here." She pointed to a spot below her breasts, then added in an undertone, "Or unbuttons. Whichever."

"That isn't you," Kay said.

"Why not? Why can't I change?"

"Why would you want to?"

"Because I'm *bored* with me."

Emily was wary. "Where are we headed, here?"

Celeste grinned. "Men. I'm starting to date."

"Celeste," Kay chided, "you already date."

"I go to dinner or a movie with friends who happen to be male. I wouldn't call them dates."

Emily humored her. "If those weren't dates, how will these be dates?"

"They'll be romantic, for one thing. I'm putting an ad in the paper."

"You aren't."

"Celeste."

"I am. I want wine and roses and music and poetry. And sex."

"Not healthy," Emily warned. "Things have changed since we were kids."

"Physical needs haven't. Mine's been on hold for seventeen years. A few more, and I'll be too old to care. The way I see it, it's now or never."

"Are you looking for a *husband?*" Emily asked in search of a method to the madness.

56

Celeste made a face. "Are you kidding? And let Jackson off the alimony hook? No way. I want some fun. That's all."

Kay folded a rasher of bacon into her mouth. Emily pushed a blueberry around with her spoon.

"You guys disapprove," Celeste said.

Emily set down the spoon. "Putting an ad in the paper is dangerous. You won't know what you're getting. The personals are an invitation for crazy men to prey on lonely women."

"What if I put an ad in a reputable publication, like something for Harvard alums."

"You didn't go to Harvard."

"So?"

"So, someone responding might not have gone, either."

"Come on, Emily. There are ways to cull out the bad ones. I've researched this. Trust me. And anyway," she said more smugly, "if *you* guys help me cull out the bad ones, I can't go wrong."

"Whoa," Kay said, "do you know what John would say if he heard you were doing this? Do you know what he would say if he thought I was helping you?"

Emily agreed. "The idea of this makes me uncomfortable."

"That's because you're married. If you'd

been single like me all these years, you'd be excited. Come on, you two. I've been good. I waited for a winner to waltz into town, and when he didn't, I settled for driving the church van on Saturday nights. Dawn is gone now, so it's not like I'm setting a bad example."

"But the *personals?*"

"Well, look, what are my alternatives? You know this town as well as I do. There aren't any eligible men here, at least not any with spirit, and I want *spirit.*"

"John hired a new man," Kay offered. "He just got here."

"No good. Our uniforms stink. Now, if our guys wore jodphurs and helmets, and rode motorcycles like the Staties —"

"This guy won't be in uniform. He's a detective. From Manhattan."

Emily hadn't heard anything about a new man on the force. "A detective? Is he here on a special assignment?"

"No. We lost one of ours to the FBI. John is simply appointing a replacement."

"From Manhattan?" Celeste asked. "Is he single?"

"Uh-huh."

"How old?"

"Early forties."

"What's wrong with him?"

Kay laughed. "What do you mean, what's wrong with him?"

"If he's in his early forties and still single —"

"Who do you think your ad will attract?" Emily asked, still upset by that idea, but Celeste wasn't done with Kay.

"If he's in his early forties and still single, and he's leaving New York City for a place like this, something must be wrong with him. He must be up on charges of misconduct. Or he's burned out. The last thing I need is a has-been."

"He isn't a has-been," Kay insisted. "John says he's at the top of his field."

"Then why did he leave New York?"

"Because his wife was killed in a hit-and-run accident, and he has a young child to raise, and he didn't think he could handle doing that in New York."

"How awful," Emily said, imagining well the havoc in his life. "How old is the child?"

"Little. Under two."

"How *awful.*"

"I'll say," said Celeste. "Hell, I've just gotten my freedom. I'd be crazy to get involved with a man with a child."

Emily felt a stab of annoyance. "If he's just come off the death of his wife, and he's changed jobs and moved to a strange place for the sake of his daughter, I doubt he'd want to be involved with you, either."

"Gee, thanks."

She let out a breath. "You know what I mean, Celeste. Anyway, you're right. He isn't thinking freedom the way you are. Score one for him. You make me very nervous."

"Not to worry," she said. "The surgery's being done Thursday. Will you guys visit me?"

"Come Thursday, I'm a career woman again," Kay reminded her. "It'll have to be after school."

"And you, lady of leisure?" Celeste asked Emily.

Emily smiled. "Lady of leisure. Cute."

"Well, aren't you?"

"No more so than before. There are things around the house that I've been putting off until Jill left."

"Don't touch Jill's things," Kay advised.

"I don't dare. She was very clear on that."

"Well, she's right. The books say kids need to know that their personal space is secure."

"It's just her closet. It's a *mess*."

"No matter. When she comes home the first time, everything should be exactly as it was when she left."

Emily sighed. "Fine. I won't touch hers,

but there are other closets to clean. And the basement. And I want to repaper the bathrooms."

"Let Doug do that," Celeste said.

"When? I'm the one with the time."

"I think you should do another book," Kay decided. "Does your editor still call?"

"Every few months, but just to talk. We're friends."

"I read the note she sent along with that bottle of champagne. She loved working with you. She didn't need to say that."

"Okay, so we got along, but that doesn't mean she wants another book, and even if she did, what would I write about?"

"Open the newspaper," Celeste suggested. "Pick a crime."

"True crime is hot," Kay added.

But Emily shook her head. It wasn't only Doug's pride that kept her from looking for work. "I really do want to fix up the house. And when that's done, I'll tackle the room above the garage." She would be busy for months.

"You really are renting it out?" Celeste asked.

"The space is just going to waste."

"Talk about inviting strangers into your life."

"We could use the money."

"For God's sake, Emily, you aren't indigent."

"Jill's school bills make Doug nervous."

"Yet he won't let you work?" Kay asked. "I don't understand him."

"He knew this day was coming," Celeste complained. "He should have had her tuition all stashed away."

"How could he do that?" Emily asked. "We've always used his income to live on." She defended Doug out of habit, though she was annoyed herself. They lived frugally. His business had grown steadily. She didn't understand why they were so strapped.

But if the money wasn't there, it wasn't there. She sighed. "It's only the room above the garage. It won't be so bad." With a sheepish smile and a one-shouldered shrug, she said, "It might actually be nice. Beat the silence. You know?"

THREE

It was a silence filled with voices she couldn't hear, an eerie quiet barely breeched by the smooth slur of the jazz sax wafting from the stereo in the den. She turned up the volume and listened, with the small of her back to the doorjamb and her arms crossed. Closing her eyes, she let the beat take her away.

But not for long, never for long. This was where she needed to be.

Peeling her spine from the wood, she began an aimless wandering from room to room. Earlier, she had talked with Jill, who was on her way to a dorm dinner and sounded excited, and with Doug, who was on his way to a client meeting and sounded rushed. She had heated the beef stew Myra delivered. She had watched the evening news. She had folded Jill's freshly laundered sheets — there was a line to be drawn on the leave-her-room-alone rule — and put them back on the bed.

After arranging the pillows neatly at its head, she had stood for a while holding Cat. Its fur was matted and its whiskers sparse, one eye gone, its tail shredded. She remembered reading *The Velveteen Rabbit* dozens of times, with Jill close by her side and Cat close by Jill's. No doubt about it, Cat was as loved as that rabbit.

Surprising, that she had left it home. Kids brought stuffed pets to college. Hadn't Jill's roommate — "she's *so* cool, Mom" — brought two? Then again, if Jill wanted her room at home preserved, there was no better watchdog than Cat. So Emily had gently placed it on the pillows, making sure that its time-worn body was securely propped.

She went down the hall now, past one closed door, the bathroom, and the bedroom she shared with Doug, to the stairs. The runner was worn. Emily remembered when it had been new. The thought made her feel old herself, absurd, given that she was barely forty. But she didn't have children at home anymore, which meant that she was, in theory, semiretired, which was an *awful* thought. She had always been highly directed.

Discouraged, she sank into the living room sofa. It, too, was worn, though not worth recovering. She and Doug didn't entertain often. He wasn't home enough.

She sighed as her gaze settled on the mantel. She picked out photos from the crowd there, recalling when each had been taken, and the memories kept her company for a time. Then they faded, and she was alone.

She thought of taking a bath. She had rarely had time for that, raising Jill. Or she could read a book. She had a stack on the dresser, four good ones to choose from.

The windows were open to the late-August night, to the chirrup of the crickets and the slurp of the pond. Earlier, there had been the drone of a lawn mower, done now, though the scent of cut grass hung thick in the humid air.

Sitting in the dark of night, so quiet and still, she felt as though her life had come to a screeching halt. In quick succession she had been daughter, student, wife, and mother.

What was she now? A wife without a husband? A mother without a child?

But Doug would be home at the end of the week. And she talked with Jill on the phone.

Rising from the sofa, she rubbed her damp palms together and peered out the window.

She tried to see if anyone was coming, but the night was too dense to see anything from here, so she straightened her T-shirt behind the overall shorts that hung loose from her shoulders, stepped into a pair of sneakers, and slipped out the door.

The neighborhood was still. From the front gate, she looked down the chain of neat picket fences. No two segments were exactly alike in style, height, or state of repair, but they coalesced to form a ghostly trail that beckoned in the inert night air.

She started down the street, leaving behind Myra's house with its tiny nightlight glowing from an upstairs window, then the Wilsons', the LeJeunes', and the Hinkleys'. She studied the shadows as she walked — front yards, side yards, wooded thickets between — but nothing moved, nothing cried.

At the end of China Pond Road, she turned right onto Walker, then left onto Sycamore until she came to LaGrange, where, at the high stone wall of the Berlo estate, she turned right again. A light mist had begun to fall, but her feet knew the way and weren't stopping. Her eyes slipped between the elegant old Victorians she passed. She counted down as she had, pushing carriages so long ago — eight, seven, six, five — until she passed the last house and reached the corner.

To her right, on the next block, was the hulk of the fire station, and tucked beside it, like a holstered weapon, the police station. She passed it by, then passed two blocks of stores. At the curb, heart pounding, she stopped.

The post office was ahead, a pretty brick building that glittered in the mist, with a parking lot so roomy and open as to invite patrons to visit, and beyond the post office and the block of stores used by all yet considered no man's land, was Grannick's college half.

Turn back, came a cry from inside, but her feet wouldn't move. She was riveted to the sight of the students who, even in the mist, came from the campus for a late night cappucino or pizza.

With a cry of raw envy and an even deeper sorrow, she whirled around and half-ran, half-walked back in the direction from which she'd come. She distracted herself by ticking off the stores she passed, one after another, one block, then the next. She was approaching the police station when a cruiser came from behind her and drew to a stop just ahead. She slowed as she reached it, then, with a breathless little sigh, stopped.

"Hi, sweetheart," came a kindly voice from the driver's window.

"Hi, John."

"Out for a walk?"

She tucked her hands behind the bib of her overalls, looked out across the street, and shrugged. "Guess so."

"Startin' to sprinkle," he said in that same kindly voice, more friend than cop, more father than friend. "Climb in. I'll give you a lift home."

Brushing the dampness from her eyes, she rounded the cruiser and slid into the front seat. Once they were on their way, she said, "It was too quiet at home. It made me think."

He drove slowly down the street. The wipers arced intermittently, allowing for a blurring before reality came clear.

"Hard, with the girls gone," he said.

"Mmm. The days before they left were so busy. Now, nothing."

"Where's Doug?"

"Chicago."

"When'll he be home?"

"Thursday night." The cruiser turned left off LaGrange at the Berlo estate, onto Sycamore. John studied the road ahead. Emily studied him. He wasn't in uniform. "Why are you out so late?" she asked. He normally worked days, leaving nightly rounds to his deputies. "Is something wrong?"

"No."

"Are you sure?"

"I was restless. My place was quiet, too."

"What's Kay doing?"

"Reading."

Emily smiled fondly. "I shouldn't have asked."

John made a right onto Walker and drove along at an exemplary pace. "She likes to read. Says it's important. For school."

Kay had a successful career. Emily didn't envy it exactly. But there was something to be said for having a whole other life. "She's very good at what she does."

"Huh." He turned left onto China Pond and cruised until he reached the house at the end on the right.

Self-conscious now that she was safely home, Emily said, "Thanks, John. I'm glad I didn't have to walk all the way home."

"You'd have got wet."

"Probably."

"Think of that next time. Better still, call us next time. We'll meet you halfway."

"Not if Kay's reading."

"Then I'll meet you myself."

"I really am okay," she insisted. "I don't

want you worrying about me."

"If not you, who, now that Marilee's gone?"

Emily opened her mouth to argue, but the words didn't come. The truth was that she treasured his watchfulness.

Leaning across the seat, she kissed his cheek. Then she slid out of the car, closed the door, and ran through the drizzle to the house.

Kay called first thing Tuesday morning. "John said he gave you a lift last night. Are you all right?"

"I'm fine," Emily said. It was a new day. She felt better.

"Want me to come over?"

"No need. Things just crowded in. But I'm okay now."

"When's Doug due home?"

"Thursday night. I want to do some baking, actually."

"Strawberry-rhubarb pie."

"How did you guess?"

"It's the first one of yours I ever tasted. Doug's favorite. You were making it for him way back when. Hey, I have some shopping to do before school starts. Why don't you make your pie, then come with me. We'll do lunch."

"I'd better stick around here, in case Jill calls."

"Did she say she would?"

"No, but I'd hate her to get the machine and think that I'm suddenly out running around now that she's gone. I want her to know I'm here if she needs me."

Kay was quiet for a minute before saying a soft, "Don't do this to yourself, Emily. Jill will love school."

Emily anchored nervous fingers on a fistful of the huge T-shirt she wore. "I hope so. But I worry."

"So do I. More about you than the girls. You need to get out of that house."

"I'm fine. Really."

"Well. Don't panic if you see a police car pull up. John may stop by."

"Oh, Kay. He doesn't have to. I'm *okay.*"

"You know how he is. He may just have to see for himself. You're his new personal cause, now that Marilee is gone. He's a little lost, without her here to wait up for at night. He's driving me nuts, hovering around."

Emily caught a movement at the kitchen window. "There he is, just pulled into the driveway. In the cruiser. In *broad daylight.* How can he *do* this to me? Myra will be out in two seconds wondering what's wrong. She sees *everything.*"

71

"That's good."

Yes and no, Emily thought. Mostly yes, when Doug was gone. Like John watching out for her by night, Myra did it by day. She would be terrified when she saw the police car.

"I'll catch you later," Emily told Kay and hung up the phone. She pushed open the screen door to find John mounting the steps. "I was just on the phone with your wife. I really am fine. You two worry for nothing."

"Good. But that isn't why I'm here. Tell me about the space over your garage. Is it really for rent?"

Emily frowned. "Not yet. Not for a while. Why?"

"I may have a tenant for you. He's been looking all over and can't find anything he likes."

"He's not about to like this. It's still months away from being livable."

"Can we see it?"

We? Emily glanced at the cruiser. A man was twisted in the back seat, behind the screen designed to restrain dangerous criminals. "John," she cried, "what did you *bring?*"

"He's a good guy, Emily. You know I'd only bring around the best. Come meet him." He had her elbow and was drawing her outside.

"I can't. I'm waiting for Jill to call."

But he drew her on. "This'll only take a minute."

"If I don't hear the phone —"

"I'll be listening, too."

"I'm not wearing shoes."

"You never do."

"But this is totally premature. There's weeks of work to do up there. I'm not looking for tenants yet. *I'm* not looking for tenants at all. Doug's the one who wants to rent."

"Figured that," John murmured just as the man from the back seat slipped out and straightened. "Ignore the stuff on his face. He says he doesn't have time to shave so he's growing a beard. That'll change, once he gets organized. Emily Arkin, Brian Stasek. Brian's joining the force. Detective."

The new detective from New York. Emily tried to remember what else Kay had said, but all she could think was that he didn't look like a detective. He looked tired and more than a little disheveled. He also looked vaguely disreputable, thanks to the stubble on his face, a wrinkled shirt, and torn jeans. But if John trusted him enough to have hired him, Emily supposed he had to be okay. He certainly had incredible eyes.

"Nice to meet you," he said in a civilized enough voice.

"Same here, but I'm afraid John should have called before he brought you over. The space I have won't be ready for a while."

"Let's take a look," John said.

"But if he needs something now —"

"The other things he's seen have been pits."

"Trust me. This is worse."

"Can I see it?" Brian asked quietly, and something about his tone brought her around. It was weary. She almost imagined he didn't have the strength to raise his voice more. And then there were his eyes. They were the palest of blues, with silver flecks and shards of sheer desperation.

Relenting, she said, "I have to warn you, it needs work."

He ran a hand through his hair, which was dark blond and thinning on top, though not unattractively. "At this stage," he sighed, "I'm looking for potential. Nothing else has even come close."

A sound came from inside the cruiser. Moaning, he ducked back inside. When he emerged this time, he held a child.

Early forties, Emily remembered now. Dead wife. Young child.

She caught in a breath at the sight of that child, who was young indeed, and looked nearly as disheveled as her father. Emily's heart went out to them both, but it was the baby to whom she was drawn. She was a beautiful child, disheveled and all, with clear skin, delicate features, and tousled brown curls so like those Jill had had that Emily felt a pang of longing.

"What's her name?" she asked, coming closer.

"Julia. Julia, say hello to Emily."

Julia chewed on her fist and stared at Emily with the same pale eyes as her father — only hers weren't so much desperate as somber.

Emily smiled and touched her cheek. "Such a sad little face."

"She's not very happy with me."

"Uh-oh. What did you do?"

"I mean, overall. She wants her mother, but her mother's dead."

"I did hear that. I'm sorry. It must be hard for you, too."

"It wouldn't be so bad if I could find a place to stay." Pale pleading blues pinned her to the spot, releasing her only to focus on the garage.

Emily sought John's help, but his expression was one of benign complacency.

75

Clearly, he liked Brian. Clearly, he liked the idea of Brian living over her garage.

"It really is awful," she warned. "I don't know as you'd want a child there."

"Jill and Marilee used to play there," John stated.

Emily jiggled Julia's hand. "Not at this age, and there's a difference between playing there and living there."

"Does it have heat?" Brian asked.

"Yes."

"Plumbing?"

"Of sorts. The outlets are all there, but there aren't any fixtures other than in the bathroom. The people who owned the house before us were in the process of building an apartment for their son when they moved away. We haven't added a thing."

"How many rooms?"

"One big, one small."

"Kitchen?"

"Along one wall of the big room. But it's unfinished, no appliances, no cabinets. Take a look. You'll see. It's light years away from being habitable."

"Emily?" came a cry from across the street, followed by Myra scurrying over. "Why is this police car here? Has something happened? Is something wrong? Why is Chief Davies here?"

"It's all right," Emily assured her. "They're just here about the garage."

Myra glanced uneasily at Brian. "What about the garage? Is there a problem with the garage?"

"I want to look at it," Brian said.

"But there's nothing there," Myra cried. "How *could* there be? It's just a shell of a place. You'd have to take up the floor to put anything there."

Emily touched her shoulder. "He's looking to rent it, Myra. He's new to John's department."

"A policeman?" Myra asked, lighting up. "Oh, *good.* There's never any crime on the streets where they live." She frowned. "But Frank won't like it."

Emily said softly, "You don't have to tell him."

"No. I don't. Do I?"

Julia began to whimper.

Brian shifted her on his hip. "She's impatient. Her attention span is limited. Can I see the apartment?"

Emily swallowed. His eyes were startlingly direct. They spoke of exhaustion, of needing to be somewhere but not knowing where, wanting to do something but not knowing what.

Emily knew how that was.

"Myra," she said, "do me a huge favor? Go into my kitchen, pour yourself a cup of tea, and listen for the phone? I don't want to miss Jill if she calls."

"But they won't find anything in the garage," Myra protested.

Emily smiled and steered her off. "I've been telling them that, but they'll have to see for themselves. Will you wait inside so I can take them up?"

"If it will help you out."

"It will. Very much." She waited until Myra had gone in before leading the others to the far side of the garage. The door there opened to a comfortably wide staircase. "For starters, we need new locks. These are nonfunctional." She started up the stairs, placing her bare feet with care on the occasional rough tread. Brian followed with the whimpering Julia. John took up the rear.

At the top, a second door opened into a large room. Kindly speaking, it had wood floors, papered walls, and a vaulted ceiling. More accurately, the floors were scuffed and dusty, the striped wallpaper was faded into spectral cords, the high ceiling was webby, and the air was stale.

Acting on the last, Emily opened two of the windows. They were too narrow to offer much by way of relief, but they gave an illusion of openness. Not that she wanted Brian to like the place. But it was hers, and she did have pride. She also had fond memories of times she had played here with Jill, times Jill had played here with friends. Once, there had been a tiny table and chairs, a small chalkboard, a bookshelf, a bin filled with toys. Those things had long since been cleared out to allow for Jill and her friends to spend the night in sleeping bags on the floor. All that remained of those parties were panels of notes written in different colored markers for all of posterity to see, and punch stains on the floor.

"Pretty sorry sight, huh?" she asked, brushing dust from her hands.

Julia was whimpering more insistently, but Brian only smiled. "There's nothing here that a little elbow grease won't fix."

"A *little.* That's optimistic."

"It's a nice size." He started walking around, rubbing Julia's back as he went.

Emily watched. Large hand, small back. Long, blunt fingers that looked like they would be all thumbs with a diaper pin but that moved in a gentle, soothing motion.

She wondered whether he was a good cop or a bad cop, industrious or lazy, curious or bored. She wondered what kind of work he had done in New York and what kind he would be doing here.

When he set Julia on her feet, she took off.

He looked like a nice guy. But Emily really wasn't ready to rent out the space. She slid another silent plea John's way, only to find him reading the writing on the wall.

"There's nothing shocking there," she said. "It's typical teenage stuff."

" 'Sean Potts carries an assortment in his back pocket,' " John read aloud.

"Well, didn't you, when you were in high school?"

"They didn't have assortments then. I carried one. For show."

"So now they carry an assortment. For show."

"Doesn't that worry you?"

"It *panics* me. I'm not ready to have a sexually active child. But I'm even less ready to have one with AIDS." She turned to find Brian studying her. Julia was across the room, with her tiny fingers on the window sill, trying to make herself tall enough to see outside.

"You don't look old enough to have a child in college," he said.

She supposed not, what with her huge T-shirt covering all but the frayed cuffs of her shorts, her face and feet bare, and her

80

hair in its sixteenish bob. "I am. Forty last month."

"Same here. But look at me." He hitched his chin toward Julia, who had settled onto the floor with an unhappy plump and was puckering up to cry. With a weary sigh, he scooped her up.

"It goes fast," Emily said, half-wanting to take Julia from him and give her a hug. Arms were made for holding children. Hers felt bereft. "Anyway" — she cleared her throat — "you can see that this place has problems. Once the appliances are in, and the furniture, it'll be pretty cramped. And stuffy. And dark. The windows are too small."

"But the view is great," he said. "It's all woods. I wouldn't even need drapes."

"I have to strip the walls, scrub the windows, repaint the woodwork, sand and varnish the floors, repair the stairs," the thought of it all left her breathless, "and then there's the matter of appliances. They'll take weeks to arrive."

"Nah. We can find some quickly." He had returned to where she stood and was passing her, heading into the second room.

Emily followed. "Small, huh? You couldn't possibly fit a bed *and* a crib in here."

"Just a crib. I'd use a pull-out sofa in the

main room for myself. This is perfect for a child." He shifted Julia in his arms. "What do you think, toots?"

Julia began to cry. He cradled her closer, to no avail.

"I'm sorry," he told Emily over the baby's head. "She's not always like this." He fixed a stare at the wall. "Wrong, Bri. She *is* always like this. You can sweet-talk a stoolie into ratting on his mother, but you can't get a goddamned smile from this kid. Not a one."

Emily stroked Julia's head. "She's been through a trauma."

"You don't know the half. She was there when it happened."

"When your wife was killed?"

"Gayle was jogging, pushing Julia in one of those special carriages joggers use for their kids." His words came hard and fast over Julia's sobs. "She had run through the park and was back on the streets. She thought she could catch the end of a WALK. She didn't want to break stride, never wanted to break stride, damn it. She was always like that, determined that she could beat every odd, and she did, until this time. She gave the carriage a shove a split second before she was hit."

"Did Julia see?"

"No, but there were the sounds — brakes, screams, sirens — shhh, sweetie, it's okay, Daddy's here."

Emily's heart broke for the crying child. For the father, too. She sensed the panic in him.

Desperate to do something, she reached over, took Julia from Brian, and settled her in her own arms. The crying continued, but the fit was comfortable. Oh yes, arms were made for holding. They were adjustable in ways nothing made by man could be.

"When did it happen?" she asked softly.

Brian looked relieved to be spelled for a bit. "Nearly five weeks ago. My mother had Julia with her for the first month, then I insisted on taking her. I thought I was doing the right thing — I mean, everyone says fathers are supposed to be able to do it. Only no one tells them how."

"No one tells mothers, either."

"Mothers are born knowing how."

She sent him a dubious look.

"No? So how do they manage?"

"Trial and error. Common sense. Okay, a little instinct. But lots more luck." She peered down at what she could see of Julia's face. The sobs were slowing. A thumb was inching toward the mouth. "She's tired. When does she usually nap?"

"Whenever. Wherever. She goes nuts when I leave her with a sitter, so I've been taking her with me — I'm trying to line up things like day care and a pediatrician. Mostly she falls asleep in the car."

"Jill always needed more of a schedule. She depended on regular naps. She dropped the morning one when she was about this size, but she stayed with the afternoon one for a good long time. She looked forward to it. After hours of constant vigilance, so did I."

Julia's cries had shrunk to hiccups. Her eyes were closed.

"Ahhh," Brian whispered. "Peace."

Emily thought the same thing, but for different reasons. Julia was a dream to hold. She cuddled. "She needs to be settled. That's why this place is no good."

"But I like it. It's on a quiet street —"

"With a pond," Emily cautioned. "That's the constant vigilance part. But you need a place now. This one won't be ready for months."

"I could have it ready in two weeks," he said, those striking eyes now strong and hopeful. And compelling, and confident, and contagious.

But she didn't want a tenant. Yes, Brian Stasek would probably be a fine one, but *she didn't want a tenant.* Doug did. He said they needed the money. He said the space was wasted. He said that turning it into an apartment would enhance the value of their house.

But she didn't want a stranger so close.

Then again, Brian was an impressive stranger. He was alone and living with pain. He was polite, articulate, and gainfully employed, and he had Julia, whose sweaty little cheek felt like heaven against her.

But she wasn't *ready.* "John, he can't work on this place if he's working for you."

John was bent over, squinting at the wall. " 'French kisses taste best with Chunky Monkey.' What in the hell's Chunky Monkey?"

"Ice cream. Answer me. How can Brian work on this place if he's working for you?"

"He's not working for me for another two weeks."

She stared at him. "You're just saying that." She shifted her stare to Brian. "This is a conspiracy."

Brian was looking calmer. "I really like it here."

"But it's too small."

"Not for my furniture. It's in the back of my Jeep."

She couldn't quite believe that.

"Okay," he conceded, "so I'll have to buy a bed and a few basics, but I left everything else behind. The simpler the better. Less to dodge, less to clean. You're looking at a guy who's not used to living alone."

Emily was looking at Julia, who had settled more deeply into her arms. "You're not living alone."

"Technically, no. Practically, yes. I have responsibilities now that I've never had before, so the less complex my life is, the better. Honestly. This place is perfect. I can't handle anything more. What do you want for rent?"

She turned to John in a last ditch attempt to slow things down, but he was disappearing into the other room. Open-mouthed, she faced Brian again. She closed her mouth. She shrugged. "Beats me."

"Emily," John called, "Myra says Jill's on the phone."

She caught in an excited breath, let it out in a grateful sigh, and with nothing but a short, "Excuse me," gently transferred Julia to her father's arms and left the garage apartment.

Jill sounded wonderful. The girls on her floor were awesome; the freshman boys living upstairs were okay; the upper-class boys who were helping with orientation were hot.

She had registered for her courses, told Emily what they were and when they met. Her tone grew less sure only when she asked how Emily was doing.

"I'm great," Emily said, and actually meant it. She felt better than she had earlier. No doubt it had to do with holding Julia.

She could see John and Brian talking in the driveway. Brian was shorter than John's six-five by several inches, but something about him made up the difference. She wondered if it was the easy way he held himself. Or the stubble. Or the fact that he was from Manhattan and worldly wise. Or, simply, his eyes.

"Is the house lonely?" Jill asked.

Tough call, how to answer honestly without upsetting her. "Yes. When I stop to think about it. But I'm keeping busy."

"Have you heard from Dad?"

"Last night. He asked for you. I gave him your phone number, but he'll be on the run for the next few days." It was a lame excuse. Public phone booths were a dime a dozen, particularly in hotel lobbies and airports.

"Where is he now?" Jill asked.

"Today, Baltimore. Tomorrow and Thursday, Philadelphia."

"And he's coming home from there?"

"Directly. I'm hoping to have the bathrooms done before then. I want us to do something nice this weekend — go off for the day or on a picnic or something. We'll definitely call you while he's home."

"I miss you, Mom."

"Me too, sweetie."

John and Brian were still in the driveway when she hung up the phone, but her time with Jill had been a breather. When she rejoined them, she felt more together. "The fact is," she told Brian, who wore sunglasses now as he held a sleeping Julia, "that I have no idea how much the rent will be. I'll have to talk with my husband. It's his decision."

"When will you know?"

"He's on a business trip. He should be calling tonight."

"I'll give you a deposit now."

"No need."

"Can I come by tomorrow, then?"

"If you'd like." If she had to have a tenant, she could do worse than renting to a detective. "And you think the work could be done in two weeks?"

Though sunglasses hid his eyes, his voice held conviction. "Easy. Julia and I can be sleeping there in less time than that."

"No way."

"We can," he insisted. "I'll do the basics

in the little room first and set up her crib there so she can nap. Regularly. Afternoons for sure. On weekends, at least. Maybe she'll start liking me more."

"I'm sure she will," Emily said. "But what about you?"

"I'll be sleeping on the floor anyway until I buy a bed."

"The bathroom isn't even functional. The tub was never installed properly. You can't bathe."

John spoke up. "One of my men can fix that in a day." When she shot him an incredulous look, he said, "Well, hell, Doug wants you to rent, and Brian needs a place, and I'd rather he live here than someone else. I may just help you strip the walls, myself. Did our kids really write those things? Knowing you'd see them?"

"That was the whole point," Emily drawled. "The extent of their rebellion. We got off easy, I think." She paused. "Unless there's more to come. No," she waved the thought away with a self-scolding, "don't even think it."

"Huh," John grunted in agreement and gestured Brian toward the door. "I got work to do."

So did Emily. If she was to spend the next two weeks working on the apartment with

89

Brian, she had baking to do now. Doug was coming home Thursday night. For the first time in twenty years, they would have the weekend all to themselves. She wanted it to be perfect.

FOUR

Not only did Emily bake Doug's favorite strawberry-rhubarb pie, but she baked a loaf of the walnut bread that he liked and three dozen congo bars to mail to Jill. She southern-fried several pounds of chicken and froze it, thinking that if she and Doug did decide to pack a picnic, it would be perfect. Finally, she made carrot soup for herself and had it for supper.

Doug wasn't wild about carrot soup. He had been once, when they were first married. Anything that was simple and healthy had appealed to him then. Suppers often consisted of fresh soup and home-baked bread, as tasty as it was politically correct. Doug was, after all, an organic farmer.

In those early days, he and his partner worked a piece of land on the far side of town, and while they weren't setting the world afire, they managed to bring in enough of a profit to make for a comfortable life in Grannick. Then the public caught on to the idea of organically grown produce, and the farm began to thrive. Adjacent land was purchased. Production increased. They hired more hands. Doug set up an office, ditched his jeans and work-boots for khakis and loafers, and immersed himself in management and marketing. He began to travel. He met savvy entrepreneurs. He graduated to suits.

Eventually he sold the business to his partner, invested his take in his own consulting firm, and was on his way.

He was still on his way. Gone, wherever.

Emily waited for him to call, but he didn't. Several friends did, wanting to know how she was doing without Jill. But Doug was apparently tied up.

He was very bright, his success no surprise. He applied to his business the same foresight that had prompted him to buy their house at a time when they could barely afford it but when it was dirt cheap. They owned it free and clear now.

Emily wished he had been as wise in planning for Jill's education.

But that was water over the dam, come to mind only because she was idle waiting for him to call. She preferred being busy. Then she didn't think about things beyond her control.

Determined not to repeat the fiasco of the night before, she put John Coltrane on the stereo, aimed the speakers toward the downstairs bathroom, and began stripping wallpaper. It was a small half-bath. Two nights' work would be all, she figured, and if matching the pattern took longer than she expected, she could always work late. She had nothing better to do.

Pulling off the last of the strips, she stuffed them into a garbage bag and set it outside with the trash. Returning, she sanded rough spots on the wall and spackled cracks, with one ear on the music and one on the phone.

Doug usually called before dinner, since his meetings often ran late. Occasionally he called during a mid-evening break. Some nights he didn't call at all.

She was worried that he wouldn't call this night. But she had to speak with him. So, when nine o'clock came without any word, she phoned his hotel.

The front desk informed her that he wasn't there, had never been there, had never even made a reservation.

She didn't understand. The last thing he had told her on his way out on Sunday was, "You know where I'll be."

93

Well, she didn't. And she wanted to reach him. Apparently he was staying somewhere new. She had no idea where.

She returned to the bathroom and worked a little longer, but the more she thought about it, the more disturbed she was. Thinking that maybe the person on the phone had made a mistake, she called again. She spoke with someone different this time, but the end result was the same.

In an attempt to find but what hotel Doug was at if not at the usual, she tried calling the travel agent who booked his flights, but the office was closed.

On the chance that he had left Baltimore and gone to Philadelphia a day early, she called his hotel there, but he wasn't expected until late the next day. She hung up the phone, feeling unsettled and alone.

Within seconds, she snatched the phone back up.

Kay was stretched out on the lounge in the screened-in porch at the back of her house, luxuriating with a biography of Jenny Churchill and a tumbler of iced lemonade, when the phone rang in the den. She slid her glasses to the top of her head and listened to the rumble of John's voice. When he didn't immediately call her, she assumed it

94

was for him.

Then again, it could be Marilee, though Marilee usually tried to call when John was out. John was a stickler of a father. He asked questions in a way that suggested he wasn't getting the truth.

Well, hell, sometimes he wasn't. But when it came to Marilee, who did confide in Kay, what he didn't know wouldn't hurt him.

"It's Emily," he said now and passed the phone to her.

"Emily. Hi. What's up?"

"Can I run something by you?"

Kay heard worry. "Sure. Go ahead."

"I didn't tell John. You know how he gets. But I can't reach Doug. He's supposed to have been in Baltimore for the past two days, but the hotel has no record of him."

Kay sat up. "He must be at another hotel."

"Would he do that without telling me? I have no way of reaching him. What if there were an emergency here? What if something happened to Jill and I needed to contact him?"

"You'd call other hotels. You'd call the police. You'd go to his desk and get his client's number. I'm sure it's an innocent mistake."

There was a pause on the other end. "Must be. It's frustrating, though. The one time I try calling him, he isn't there. It's not very considerate of him."

Kay didn't think so, either, but was surprised to hear Emily say it. She usually defended Doug to the hilt. "He left on Sunday, just when you were getting Jill ready to go. In the rush and emotion of that, he may have been distracted. When did you talk with him last?"

"Last night. But I have to talk with him tonight. Did John tell you that he brought his new detective by to see the garage apartment?"

"Vaguely." John's specialty was asking, not telling. He far preferred investigation to benign chitchat. What news he did bring came in single, simple sentences.

"Well, Brian Stasek wants to rent the place," Emily was saying, "and I need input from Doug."

"What did you think of him?"

"Brian? He seems nice. His daughter is adorable."

Kay smiled. "I figured you'd fall for the kid."

"What's not to fall for? The poor thing just lost her mother, and her father is slightly bewildered. He offered to help get the place ready, but I can't do a thing until I talk with Doug."

"Why not?"

"Because this is Doug's project."

"Seems to me you're the one doing the work."

"But he pays the bills."

"So?"

"So, he has to tell me what he wants for rent, and how much I can spend on appliances and all. It's his money."

"It's yours, too," Kay argued. "It's everything you weren't paid all these years while you were raising Jill and coddling him. You have a right to take some credit for his success."

"Well," Emily mused, "that's neither here nor there. The fact is that I need to talk with him tonight, but I have no idea where he is."

"Give him a little longer. Maybe he'll call."

"If not, I will track him down. You're right, through his client. He may be annoyed."

"Tough. He should be embarrassed, not telling you where he is."

"He's busy. That's all."

"He's self-centered."

"He's under a lot of pressure."

Sensing that Emily would counter each accusation with an excuse, Kay offered a few last words of encouragement before ending the call. She was surprised to find

John still at the door.

"She okay?" he asked.

"She will be. Doug wasn't where he said he'd be. It's probably just a mix-up, but it's too bad it happened this week. It's a raw time for Emily."

"Where's he supposed to be?"

Kay told him the story in crisp answers to the questions he fired, but when he threatened to make some calls, she objected. "Don't, John. Please. Emily won't want that. Doug's not missing, just momentarily displaced." She collapsed the antenna and handed him the phone. "Will Brian Stasek be a good tenant?"

"Yup."

"Not that they really need one. Doug's making good money. If he's feeling pinched, he could let Emily work."

"This will be easier for her. Once the apartment's fixed up, all she'll have to do is sit back and collect the rent."

"Now, that sounds exciting," Kay mocked. "Instead of doing something to stimulate her mind, she can sit around collecting rent."

"She was good with the baby."

Kay had an awful thought. "You're not setting her up to babysit, are you?"

"It would keep her busy. And he'd pay."

"But she's been a babysitter for the last twenty years. It's time she moved on."

"Maybe she doesn't want to."

"Maybe she does but won't say it."

They stared at each other, but Kay wasn't backing down. She rarely did, where women and work were concerned. Not that it did much good. John was still most comfortable thinking of women safe and sound at home.

"Anyway," he said without quite conceding the point, "Brian will keep an eye on her." He turned to leave. "When did Marilee call last?"

"Mid-afternoon."

"What's she doing?"

"Having a ball," the devil in Kay said.

"What does that mean?"

"It means she's doing what she's supposed to be doing."

"She's supposed to be studying."

"Classes haven't started yet."

"Then why is she there? How long does orientation have to run? Give kids time and freedom in a big city, and there's trouble." He glared off through the screen. "There's a perfectly good college right here in town."

"She didn't have the grades to apply, much less get in."

"Then UMass. Why isn't she there?"

"Because half her graduating class is

there. She wanted something different."

"Did she have to go so *far?*"

"It's only an hour's flight."

"UMass would have been an hour's drive."

"And if she'd been there, what would you have done? Gone down every night and patrolled the campus? Kept her under surveillance? Really, John."

He shot her a frown.

She sighed. He wasn't ill-meaning, just old-fashioned. More gently, she said, "It's possible that she chose Washington so that you *couldn't* do any of that. She's a big girl, John. She's a *good* girl. She knows right from wrong. She won't be doing anything you didn't do yourself when you were her age."

"That's what worries me."

Kay thought of the John she hadn't known, the bachelor who had lived some, not only at eighteen but at twenty-five, twenty-eight, thirty-one. Twelve years her senior, he had been ready to settle down when she arrived in Grannick, and in all the time since, he had behaved to the letter. If not, she might have run in the opposite direction. She had been an innocent when they first met, and no beauty. She couldn't have competed with other women. She wouldn't have tried. But John had been

100

sweet and attentive, and after anticipating spinsterhood, she had been snowed.

"Marilee will be *fine*," she insisted now. "*Jill* will be fine. Dawn, on the other hand," she mused, "may need a little watching." Taking the phone back from John, she pulled up the antenna.

Celeste was in her bedroom when the phone rang. Her back was cushioned by the huge down comforter that was piled high, summer-style, at the foot of the bed. Before her on the pristine white throw were the contents of the small cigar box that contained the sum total of her childhood pictures.

The box had belonged to her father, dead since she was sixteen, but even now the scent of him lingered. It conjured images of kindness and simplicity and a love so pure that ugly noses didn't matter. He had loved her, ugly nose and all.

It struck her now, looking through these pictures for the first time in years and with a deliberately critical eye, that he had the same ugly nose and, incredibly, the same double chin.

Funny, but she hadn't been aware of his having either, until now. No doubt because she loved him. And because men could get away with a lot more than women.

She had taken her nose and her jaw from him. Now she was about to obliterate them. For the first time, she felt a twinge of doubt, and the more she stared at her father, the greater it grew.

The phone was a welcome reprieve. During the few seconds it took her to put down the pictures she was holding and stretch across the bed to reach it, she imagined someone tall, dark, and handsome, with her father's kindness and love, on the other end.

"Hello?"

"I promised Marilee that I'd get Dawn's number. Do you have it handy?"

So much for tall, dark, and handsome. Celeste reeled it off. "She called before. I lectured her on everything I hope she's doing right."

"Ah. The power of positive thinking. Have you told her about your nose?"

"No. I don't want her getting any ideas."

"She'll see it for herself."

"Not for a while. She swore she wouldn't be home until fall break."

"She might drop in unannounced."

"Only if she needs something."

"She'll be angry you didn't tell her."

"If it's over and done and healed, she might not even realize what's happened.

She'll think I look great to her because she hasn't seen me in a while."

"Celeste. She has your nose."

Celeste felt a moment's panic. "This is true." She glanced at the pictures on the bed. "Kay, am I doing the right thing?"

"I can't tell you that. You're the one calling the shots. It's your self-image, remember?"

"Yeah. But it's also my heritage. I'm feeling guilty about erasing it."

"Then don't."

"But I *want* to. I don't like this nose. I don't like seeing it in the mirror. I don't like walking around with it. I want to be able to hold my head high, but I can't now, and that only accentuates the double chin. I want a new face to go with a new life."

"Then do it."

"But will I live to regret it?"

"Celeste, it's only your nose. It isn't *you*. *You* won't change, either way. So flip a coin."

"But what if I lose? I've been wanting to do this for *years*."

"There's your answer," Kay said. "Listen, it's getting late. I want to finish this book tonight. When do you go in?"

"Tomorrow night. Emily's driving me. The surgery is first thing Thursday morning. Will you come see me?"

"Thursday night. I told you I would."

"You won't laugh if it looks awful, will you?"

"I won't laugh. And it will look awful, at first. Then it'll look gorgeous."

Hearing it from Kay, who wasn't into vanity, made Celeste feel better.

"Do me a favor, Celeste? Give Emily a call. She's waiting to hear from Doug. She tried calling him at his usual hotel, but he wasn't registered there. She's feeling rattled."

"Well, of course, she would," Celeste said with a measure of disgust. "What's wrong with the man? Would it have hurt him to give her the *right* hotel? Doesn't he know how much he means to her? Is he *blind?* Or just male. Insensitivity is such a male thing. Same with irresponsibility. And they say *we*'re flighty. Hah!"

"Uh, forget calling Emily. You'll only rile her up."

"No, I won't. You just got me going. Men really are rats. What's yours doing?"

"As we speak? Mine is sitting in the other room, thinking about all the dirty little things he did to girls when he was eighteen, and imagining some randy guy doing them to Marilee."

Celeste was intrigued. "What dirty little things did John do?"

"You'd have to ask him that. He never did them to me. Where I was concerned, he went by the book."

"If the book was the *Kama-sutra* —"

"Celeste. Please."

"Okay. I'm calling Emily. Catch you later."

Emily had a roll of new wallpaper unwound on the living room floor and was on her hands and knees, measuring off strips, when the phone rang. The paper arced and curled when she jumped up, but she didn't give it a second thought over the rush of relief she felt. She had been waiting forever for Doug to call.

"It's not Doug," Celeste said without preamble. "Still no word?"

Emily let out a disappointed breath. "Not yet." She glanced at her watch. It was after ten. "He may, still. I just wish I knew where he was."

"Do you know who he's with?"

"No. He has five accounts in Baltimore. He could be with any one of them. I should have asked before he left, but my mind was on Jill. Same thing when he called last night. I should have showed more interest in what he was doing."

"Oh no, don't go blaming yourself, Emily. This isn't your fault. If Doug had any inkling of what you're going through this week, he'd have volunteered that information and more. He should be pampering you a little."

"I don't need pampering."

"Every woman needs pampering. Every *person* needs it. I actually think men get it more than we do. Some irony, them being the stronger sex and all, yuk, yuk. But there must be some strong ones out there. Maybe I can ferret out a few. Want one?"

"No, thanks. I'll stick with Doug. If he ever calls."

"He'll call."

"But I wanted to talk with him tonight." It was strange, when she thought of it, the urgency she felt. She was the one who didn't want a tenant. Now she was rushing to cement the deal.

She guessed it was because of Brian Stasek and his daughter. They were lost souls. If the garage apartment could help them gain their footing, something good would come of renting out the space.

"I think," Celeste was saying, "that men have a sixth sense that tells them when we most want something. Then they know not to give it. Jackson always hit it right on the nose."

"Doug is not Jackson."

"And thank God for that, though I do think you should tell him off, Emily. He should tell you where he's staying. He should give you a detailed itinerary each time he leaves home. My dream guy will definitely do that. No. I take that back. My dream guy won't travel. He'll be here every night."

"Mmmm. That does sound nice." The call-waiting clicked, sending her stomach jangling. "There's the other line. It must be Doug. Let's talk in the morning." She touched the phone. "Hello?"

"Hi, Emily."

"Doug." She let out a breath. "*Doug.* Where *are* you?"

"In Baltimore. Why?"

"Where in Baltimore?"

"What's wrong?"

"I tried calling you."

"Is there a problem?"

"Yeah," she said, annoyed. The problem should have been obvious to him. "I couldn't *reach* you."

"Is there a *problem?*" he bit out.

His sharpness took her back. "You mean, with Jill? No."

"Then why were you trying to call?"

Because you're my husband and I miss you. Because my only child is gone and I need your voice to remind me that I'm not as alone as I feel.

But she didn't want to sound like a whiner, or a clinger, so she simply said, "I wanted to talk with you about the garage apartment. I found someone to rent it, a man who's joining our police department. He was a detective in New York, but his wife just died, and he has a little girl to take care of, so he's looking for something quiet." She assumed he was also looking for an escape from memories. Maybe a new start. She envied him that.

"Isn't the garage too small for a man with a child?" Doug asked.

"He says that something small will be easier to take care of. He's also willing to help get it ready. He doesn't start with the department for two weeks. He claims he can have it done by then."

"How many months' free rent does he want, in exchange for doing the work?"

"He didn't mention anything about that."

"I'm sure he had it in mind."

Emily wasn't so sure. She really wasn't. "He asked how much the rent would be, and I didn't know. How much do you want?"

"Nine hundred."

"A *month?* You're kidding."

"There's no harm shooting high. Besides, we have to go out now and buy a refrigerator, a stove, cabinets."

"Nine hundred is too high." She would choke on the words, before she got them but of her mouth in front of Brian.

"It's a one-bedroom apartment."

"It's little more than a studio, Doug, that second room is so small. Grannick isn't Boston. It isn't even Worcester."

"Eight hundred, then."

"Five. I can't gouge the man." She pictured Brian and Julia, and *knew* she couldn't. "If I asked anything more, he'd laugh in my face. He isn't a hayseed. He's from Manhattan. He knows what a fair price is, and even if he *did* agree to it, I'd feel like a piece of dirt every month when he came to hand over the check. We can live nicely with an extra five hundred a month."

"We have to pay for appliances."

"That's a capital investment — like taking the proceeds from the sale of the farm and putting them into your business. It pays off. So even if every cent of that rent for the first few months goes for appliances, at the

109

end of the time we'll have a fully equipped apartment bringing in rent free and clear."

"What about utilities?"

"Okay. He can pay for those himself." She couldn't imagine they would amount to much in such a small space. "But the rent should be five."

"God, you're a lousy businesswoman."

"Maybe. But I'm not charging a cent more."

"Fine. So why did you need to talk with me?"

She opened her mouth, then shut it, stunned, after the fact, by her boldness. What did she know about setting rent? Only that nine, even eight, was too high. "I, uh, just wanted to verify it, I guess. Before I put it to Brian."

"Brian."

"Stasek. The detective." Why did she feel guilty using his first name? Because Doug had a way of *making* her feel guilty. It was nothing new. "I also wanted to know about a budget for appliances and fixtures and things."

"You had the answer to the rent. You must have the answer to that one, too."

He was annoyed. She softened her tone. "I haven't really thought it out. It's been a long time since I've bought major appliances. I have no idea what prices are like."

"Well, find out. I can't. I'm too busy. It's been one hell of a week, meetings running overtime, people uncooperative. I won't even make it to Philadelphia until the day after tomorrow. I don't see how I can get home before late Saturday."

Emily was crushed. *"Doug."*

"It's not like I have control over this."

"I've been telling myself Thursday night, Thursday night, Thursday night. I've been baking. I've been planning."

"Planning *what?*"

"A picnic. A hike up Bee Hill. Antiquing in Great Barrington."

"We don't go antiquing."

"We used to go all the time, when we first moved here."

"That was when we dreamed of buying one of the Victorians on LaGrange and furnishing it with antiques, but that dream is dead, Emily. We own a perfectly good house. We're not going anywhere."

"Not even antiquing just for the fun of it?" she asked. She didn't want a new house. All she wanted was to spend time with Doug.

"If I were doing anything just for the fun of it, I would be playing golf."

She nearly laughed. "You don't play golf."

111

"Yes. I do."

"Golf?"

"It's a business tool. There's many a CEO I've brought around to my way of thinking over the span of eighteen holes."

Emily was dumbfounded. The image ran counter to the one she had always held of Doug in a borrowed executive office, with papers covering the desk, people running in and out, and secretaries typing up his ideas as quickly as he could spew them out. "But you don't know *how* to play golf," she argued, perhaps stupidly, but she was feeling bewildered.

"I learned. It's not hard to pick up."

"What about golf shoes, clubs?"

"I rent, or borrow."

"I'm stunned." It was a whole other side of him that she hadn't known about. "You never said a word."

"I never had cause. It's something I do for business. Like I said, if I had free time I'd do it for fun, too, but I don't have free time, and, anyway. Grannick doesn't have a golf course, so it's irrelevant."

"Not to me," she cried, hurt enough to say, "I don't know who you are sometimes, Doug."

He sighed. "Look, it's been a long day. I have to be at work by seven in the morning.

Can't we discuss this when I get home?"

"*When?* If you're not coming home until Saturday night and you'll be leaving again Sunday afternoon, when do we talk?"

"Sunday morning. Okay?"

He sounded more irked than conciliatory, making her feel guilty again, like she was a nag. But it was the first time she had asked. It was the first time she'd had to. Always before he had been around more.

Well, maybe not much more. But when Jill was home, she hadn't minded so much.

It was only one weekend lost. She supposed she shouldn't panic. Still, the vision came to her of an endless string of months and years, with Doug stopping in to have his laundry done one, maybe two days a week. Not much of a marriage. Not much of a life.

"Emily?"

She felt like crying. "Sunday morning. Okay."

"I'll call you when I get to Phillie."

"Fine." She hung up the phone, only then realizing that she still didn't know where he was, which meant she couldn't call him back, even if she wanted to, not that she did. He burned her each time they talked.

She didn't know what his problem was.

She did know that he hadn't asked about

113

Jill. Or about her.

And she still didn't know how much to spend on materials for the garage apartment.

FIVE

Emily attacked the walls of the downstairs bathroom not to please Doug, since he wouldn't even be home to see until Saturday night — *Saturday* night — but to keep herself busy. She didn't want to think, didn't want to brood, didn't want to fear. She didn't want to go out walking, either. So she piped in Thelonius Monk and pushed herself until the last strip was up, squeegied, and wiped clean, and when all that was done, she covered the light switches.

By then it was three in the morning, and her body was tired. So she took the long, hot bath that she had rarely had time for before, even threw in a capful of the scented bath oil Jill had given her on the occasion of wishful thinking.

She slept for all of two hours, waking with the sun, needing to be busy again. By seven in the morning, when Doug would be getting to work, she was in the apartment over the garage with pen and paper, making a list of what she was going to need.

At the top of the list was a cordless phone. Doug had a separate business line with an answering service, so she didn't worry about his calls. She did worry about calls from Jill. She didn't want to miss one while she was working on the apartment, and when the work was done, well, she could talk on the phone sitting with Myra under the willow.

Everyone else had a cordless phone. It was high time the Arkins did, too — and to hell with any protest Doug might make. He had told her to make decisions regarding the apartment. Well, she would.

She listed cleaning supplies. She listed appliances and kitchen cabinets, and took measurements for each. She listed a sander, which she could rent, and varnish. She listed a ceiling fan, because even this early in the morning, with both windows open, the place was hot. Besides, a ceiling fan mounted high in the center of the large room would be a nice touch.

She listed paint for the woodwork and walls, and flooring for the bathroom. She listed light fixtures for each of the rooms, because the bare bulbs that had sufficed up to now were harsh. And she listed new locks.

She bought the phone and the cleaning

supplies on her first trip into Grannick, and on her way home, stopped for coffee. While she waited in line with workmen, most of whom she knew from years of going to Nell's, she snagged an electrician and a plumber to stop by the garage later in the day.

Pleased to have already accomplished something, she returned home and, by eight-thirty, was at work.

Across town, in a small room in the Grannick Lodge, Brian Stasek rummaged through his duffle bag. He was sure he had a clean pair of jeans. He had done the wash two days before — had spent half the god-damned night running back and forth to the laundry room doing four mammoth loads — and was *sure* he had washed some jeans. He tossed T-shirts, socks, and shorts out of the duffle. He turned to the dresser and rifled through the drawers, then tore into the closet.

The jeans were on the top shelf. He grabbed them down and swore when the motel's spare blankets came with them. "Not my day," he muttered, stuffing the blankets back up. At least Julia was quiet. She was a little lump amid a scattering of Cheerios in front of the television, stoned

117

on a sippy-cup of juice.

She had fussed most of the night. She was beat.

So was he. He had worried most of the night, convinced in turn that she was sick, in pain, or dying. He had finally fallen asleep to dream that he had left the room to do more laundry and returned to find the place engulfed in flames. He could hear Julia screaming, but he couldn't get through the fire, couldn't do anything to save her.

He had bolted awake in a sweat, heart racing, nerves raw. He didn't need a psychiatrist to tell him that he was feeling helpless about Gayle's death. When it came to Julia, he was feeling helpless about most everything.

They needed to be settled. He planned to give Julia a bath and dress her up so that she looked too pretty to resist, then clean himself up so that he wasn't frightening, then drive over to Emily Arkin's house and beg for mercy.

Gayle would have said the place was too small, but Gayle wasn't here — and, besides, Gayle had always gravitated toward sleek leather, chrome, and marble. She wouldn't understand his desire for wood, or the warmth he had felt in that little, unfinished, over-the-garage space. It was different enough from his previous life to speak to him of new beginnings. He needed things warm and fresh. He needed that apartment.

When a knock came at the door, he snapped his jeans and drew it open. The manager, a reedy sort, peered nervously past him into the room. "Is your daughter all right?" he asked.

"She's fine."

"I had reports that she was crying last night."

Something of an accusatory nature made Brian wary. "Who did you hear that from?"

"People in other rooms. We had some calls, but I told the night manager not to disturb you." He gave a thin laugh. "I have children of my own. They just won't shut up some times. These are cramped quarters. How is your apartment search coming?"

"It's coming."

"Have you found anything?"

"Maybe."

"Well, that's good. When will you be checking out?"

Brian's wariness grew. He didn't like being rushed. "I'm not sure. Is there a problem with my staying here?"

"Well, this isn't a good place for a child so young."

"The Grannick Lodge is billed as a family motel."

"Most of our children are older."

Brian started to burn. He was paying dearly for this room, and in ways other than the green. "I've had to listen to their older noise every night for a week. It keeps waking up my daughter. Maybe you ought to be talking with them."

"They don't stay more than two or three days. You're staying longer than most." He looked beyond Brian again. "It's too bad we can't get in here to give the place a good cleaning, but with clothes and toys all over the place, well —" He shrugged.

Brian fixed the man with a stare that wiped the smarmy smile from his face. In a low voice, he said, "As long as you take my money, you'll make my bed, put fresh sheets on my daughter's crib, clean the bathroom, and vacuum the rugs, and you'll continue to do it until I check out, or you'll have a discrimination suit on your hands so big and so fast that you won't know what hit you."

The man backed off. "No need to make threats."

"That isn't a threat. It's a promise. Now if you'll excuse me, my daughter and I have places to go." He shut the door in the man's

120

face, turned, and leaned against it for an angry minute. It was another minute before he realized that Julia was staring at him.

He grinned. "How was that, toots? Impressed?" He pushed away from the door and scooped her off the floor. "Your old man knows the words, all right. He knows the tone of voice. He knows the look." His voice fell. " 'Course, it doesn't work much on you, does it?"

Julia continued to stare.

"How about a smile?" He pushed at the corners of her mouth. "Just a little one? I mean, hell, we're in this together, aren't we?" He gave her a pleading look, then sighed. "Okay." He looked around the room. "What'll it be? The pink overalls? The red dress? *We* are going to impress Emily Arkin today. Right?"

Emily was taking a mid-morning break, sitting in the middle of the floor drinking the last of her cold coffee, when Brian's voice rose from the bottom of the stairs.

"Hello?"

"Up here!" She had been wondering when he would come by, or even *if*. It had occurred to her more than once during the long night just past, that he might have seen another place or changed his mind. She

121

wondered now if he was coming to tell her that.

She hoped he wasn't. After the to-do with Doug and her own taking-the-bull-by-the-horns, she felt committed. Besides, she liked Brian. She liked the thought of his being close.

His footfall told of his climb, moments before he filled the doorway with Julia in one arm and a bag in the other. "Morning," he said.

The first thing she noticed was that he had shaved. The second was that his eyes were as striking as she remembered them to be. The third was that Julia looked precious.

Emily crossed the floor. "Hello, Julia. You look so pretty." She took her from Brian and, in a private little voice, said, "I *love* your jeans. Did you pick them out yourself? And your sneakers. And the bow in your hair." It was red and lopsided, but it matched her jersey. "*Who* put that bow there?"

Julia regarded her with solemn eyes.

"This is the second time you've done it," Brian said. "She won't let anyone else hold her. Screams every time I try."

Emily shrugged. "I love little ones. She must sense that."

"But she screams for me sometimes, too.

Can't she feel *my* love?"

"Sure, but if you're tired or tense or uncertain, she feels that, too." She fingered Julia's curls. "She may feel my experience. Or my desperation. It's been too long since I've held a little one this size. It's delicious. In another year or two, she'll refuse to be held, so this time is *really* special."

Brian cleared his throat. "Not exactly the adjective I'd have chosen. I could use a little more self-sufficiency. I could use a little speech to tell me what she wants."

"Julia doesn't talk yet?" Emily asked Julia. "I'll bet she thinks all kinds of things, but just isn't ready to share them. Is that right, Julia?" Julia rubbed an eye. "My daughter didn't say much until she turned three."

"How did you survive?"

"I knew what she wanted."

"How?"

"I knew her. I knew what pleased her."

Brian sighed. "Maybe it'll come, then. After I've been with her more. Want some coffee? I stopped at a great place."

"Nell's. I recognize the bag. Half the town hits Nell's at some point during the day."

"You, too?"

"Very early this morning. But I'd love a refill."

Brian hunkered down by Emily's empty

cup and began unloading the contents of the bag.

"Oooh," Emily cooed to Julia. "I see something good. Is Julia hungry?"

Julia had spotted what Emily had, and made a wanting sound. Emily set her down and watched her run to Brian, who put a donut hole in her hand.

"Little ones for little people, big ones for big people." He took several full-sized donuts from inside the bag.

Emily sat cross-legged on the floor. "Buttercrunch. My favorite."

"Really?"

She nodded. "This is a treat."

"It's actually a bribe," Brian said, sitting nearby. "I want this apartment."

She grinned. "It's yours."

"How much?"

"Five a month, utilities not included."

"It's a deal."

She took a bite of the donut, feeling inordinately pleased. In addition to being a detective, he was a nice guy. "Are you still willing to help get it ready?"

"You bet. It's right down my alley. My dad was a carpenter. I spent summers working with him, before I joined the force."

"Your parents live in New York, then?"

He shook his head. "Chicago, and it's just

124

my mom, now. My dad died a few years ago." He uncapped a coffee and handed it over. "I went to school in New York and loved it, so I stayed on to work. After a while, I met Gayle. She was an architect with a career in the city. There was no way we were going to leave." He rubbed an eyebrow. "Funny, how things work out."

"How long were you married?"

He uncapped the second coffee and took a drink. "Ten years. We worked hard at it. We each had time-consuming careers. Could go for a week at a stretch doing nothing more than sharing a bed for a few hours a night." He drew in a breath. "But I miss her. We had an interesting life. A grown-up life, compared to the one I lead now. My days have been consumed with interviewing babysitters, finding 'Sesame Street' on the tube, slicing bananas, and changing diapers."

"It gets better," Emily said with a smile.

"When?"

"Soon. She'll eat the banana whole."

"Swell."

"Any luck with babysitters?"

"Hard to tell. I wasn't kidding when I said you're the only one who can hold her. Anyone else comes near, and she loses it.

One woman in the center of town has potential."

"Janice Stolski."

His eyes lit. "Do you know her?"

"She's lovely. She limits the number of children she takes so that she can give personal care. Will she take Julia?"

"She says so. But will Julia take her? That's the question. I'll give it a try tomorrow while I'm working here. It'd be dangerous to have Julia underfoot, and besides, I'd better give it a test run. I have to find the right person before I start work."

"What will you be doing with the department?"

"Whatever needs to be done."

"What did you do in New York?"

"Homicide. Not at first, though. I started in uniform. But I was good with people. I could get them to trust me, and when they trust you, they give you information you need. So I moved up."

"It's your eyes," she said. "They have a trust-me quality." Other qualities, too, but she wasn't elaborating. If she said they were compelling, or intriguing or sensual, he might take it the wrong way. "They're hard to miss."

"That has a down side. I wore tinted contacts when I went undercover." He was studying Julia. "It's probably just as well I left. Contacts or no, someone on the street catches on after a while, and the next thing you know . . ." He pulled an imaginary trigger.

Emily flinched.

"Anyway," he went on, "Grannick will be tamer."

"We have crime."

"But not like New York. Nothing's like New York." He helped himself to a donut.

"There was a kidnapping in town several years back," Emily offered. "A coed from the college. She was from a wealthy family in the Midwest."

"Was she ever found?"

"Uh-huh. By two of our own doing fancy footwork, but not before one baby finger and two million dollars were exchanged."

Brian grunted. "Motive?"

"Revenge. An employee let go. Have you ever worked on a kidnapping?"

"Yes. They're tough. In most murders, the victim and the perpetrator know each other. That's less true in kidnappings. The victims are often innocents."

"Children."

"Not always. But often. And then there's the heartache of the parents."

Emily nodded. She turned to Julia, who

was squatting between them. "Is that good, sweetheart? Oooops. That half got away. Here it is." She secured the crumbly piece of donut in Julia's little hand, and looked up to find Brian focused on the back wall. "Having second thoughts?"

"Not on your life. This is the place. It's homey even now."

"Needs lots of work."

"The work will be therapeutic — for me, at least. I apologize for rushing you into this. You may have had other things to do."

"No, the timing is actually fine. My daughter just left for college, and my husband travels a lot. I like keeping busy."

He smiled and popped his brows, hinting that this would keep her busy enough, then he raised his eyes to the vaulted ceiling. "Any chance of getting a paddle fan up there?"

"It's already on my list."

His eyes returned to the back wall. "How about a window there? A tall arched one, covering the space where those two small ones are and then some. It would make the room huge, open it up to the woods."

Emily pictured it instantly. But she hadn't anticipated doing anything quite so grand. "Wouldn't that involve structural work?"

"Not really. I've done this kind of thing

128

before. It isn't hard. If you spring for the window, I'll provide the labor for free."

She couldn't argue with the offer. The window would remain long after Brian was gone. Labor was the expensive part.

She remembered what Doug had said. "That sounds fair enough, but the rest isn't. You're giving two weeks of your time."

He looked puzzled.

"What would you like in return?"

"I'm getting the apartment in return."

Hah! Doug was wrong! "I'll waive the first month's rent," she offered.

"I'm not asking for that."

"I know, but it seems only right."

"Why? I volunteered to do this work. I'm looking forward to it."

The more noble he was, the more so she wanted to be, herself. "But you ought to get something for it." She had an idea. "I could babysit."

"No," he said quickly and, sheepish now, scratched the back of his head. "When I stopped at the station before, John warned me about that. He said his wife would divorce him if I used you that way."

"You're not using me. I'm offering."

But his eyes said he wouldn't be moved, and those eyes weren't to be doubted.

"Well," she said, "I feel awkward about

129

this. I'm getting something for nothing. It isn't right."

"There is something."

"What?"

"You could let me use your washer and dryer. I've had one hell of a hassle doing Julia's wash at the motel. If I could just sneak into your basement once in a while."

Emily smiled. "I have a better idea." She looked at the wall where the kitchen would be. "I'll put a vertical set in that corner and close it in with louvered doors."

"Not necessary."

"But it's right," Emily said, pleased. "Doug wanted this to be an apartment, so it should be an apartment, and apartments nowadays have washers and dryers. At least, most do." She paused. "Don't they?" But her mind was made up. "I want it done."

"Yoo-hoo. Emily?"

"I'm here, Myra," she called. To Brian, she said, "Myra makes her rounds of the neighborhood every morning. No doubt she sees your car and wants to know who's here." She had a thought. "You're not driving a cruiser are you? She panics when she sees cruisers."

"No cruiser. Just the Jeep."

"Well, hello again," Myra sang in a way

that suggested she knew very well who was there.

Emily figured she had been sitting at her window when they arrived.

Myra bent over. "It is Julia, isn't it? Hello, Julia." She straightened. "And her policeman father. But you're out of uniform, officer."

Brian smiled. "I haven't started working yet."

"He's a detective," Emily said. "He won't be wearing a uniform."

"No uniform? Oh. But that is good. Less upsetting." To Emily, in a confidential undertone, she murmured, "I haven't said anything to Frank yet. If there isn't any uniform, he may never have to find out." Her eyes flew to Brian. "Unless you put those bright lights on the top of your car."

"No bright lights," Brian assured her. "Not coming down this street."

"Then why are you here, if not to come down this street?"

"He's here," Emily said softly, "because there was an opening in our department just when he needed to get away from New York. His wife died recently. He wants a quiet place to raise Julia."

Myra clucked her tongue. "What a *sad* story. But don't be fooled," she told Brian.

"Grannick isn't so quiet. Things happen here, too."

"That's why I'm here."

"Now, I *knew* that. See, Emily, I *knew* he was here to solve things. But who's taking care of Julia while he does that?"

"He's arranging for day care in town."

"Well, that's a silly thing to do." To Brian, brightly, she said, "I can take care of Julia. I make the most lovely tea parties under my willow. Don't I, Emily?"

Emily touched her arm. "Julia needs to be with other children."

"Not if she's sick. She can't go out then. I don't like the idea of day care. Frank doesn't either. He says children should be at home." Myra turned a stern look on Brian. "If Julia is sick, you come get me and I'll stay with her. Do you promise you'll do that? It's the least I can do for you, after you've come all this way. I make *wonderful* lace cookies. And mittens. I've taken *good* care of Emily — haven't I, Emily?"

Emily put an arm around her shoulder and guided her toward the door. "Very good care. Did I tell you that we put the afghan you crocheted for Jill right on her bed at school?"

"Did you really? How nice! I miss Jill. If I make her some cookies, can we send them to her?"

"You make them, I'll send them. Deal?"

"Deal."

Emily waited until she was down the stairs before turning apologetically to Brian. "She is a very sweet, very harmless lady, and she does make wonderful cookies."

Brian completed her thought. "But I shouldn't let her babysit Julia."

Emily felt disloyal. Still, she shook her head. "She isn't batty, exactly. She's perfectly lucid when it comes to most things. Her family wants to put her into a nursing home, but that would kill her — and there isn't any need. She is entirely capable of taking care of herself. Unfortunately, she lives with Frank."

"Is he a problem?"

"Depends on how you see it. He's been dead for six years."

"Oh."

"For whatever reasons, she can't accept it. She cooks for him, sets a place for him at the table, refers to him in conversation."

"Were they married a very long time?"

"Yes."

"And very close?"

"I suppose." Emily had never quite understood the appeal. "Frank was a difficult man. Not terribly social. He drank. I don't

133

know if he ever hit Myra, but he was verbally abusive. I heard it more than once. He held a power over her. She was terrified of him. Quite honestly, I thought that when he died she would be freed, but it's like she can't let go."

"Sad."

"Very." She met his gaze. "But don't let Myra scare you away. She's a wonderful neighbor. She's always looked out for Jill and me, brings us food, little gifts, in exchange for our sitting with her under the willow. That's all she wants. She isn't dangerous."

"I never thought she was. She won't scare me away. I'm sold on this place, especially" — his mouth quirked endearingly — "if you let me put that window in."

The window was as done a deal as the lease itself. All that remained was to sign the papers.

The paperwork was done by the end of the week, both for the lease and for the materials placed on rush order, and in the meantime Emily and Brian lent elbow grease to the apartment in anticipation of those soon-to-arrive goods. By Saturday afternoon, years of dirt had been wiped away, and every wall in the place stripped of paper, spackled, and sanded in preparation for the simple coat of white paint that Brian wanted. The electrician had installed the overhead fan, which immediately improved their working conditions, and had wired for increased lighting and for the washer/dryer that hadn't originally been planned. The plumber had rendered the bathroom fully functional with the ease John had predicted. The telephone company had installed a line.

Aside from the time she spent with Celeste, who emerged from surgery bandaged and bruised, and in dire need of encouragement, Emily spent her waking hours working in the apartment.

Doug called from Philadelphia on Thursday night and didn't spend long on the phone, but she was busy enough not to mind. She was also uneasy enough not to mind. *I don't know who you are sometimes, Doug.* The words kept echoing, refusing to fade. On the telephone, he was a stranger, wrapped in his other world. When he got home, she told herself, he would be her husband again. They would talk then.

Saturday morning, she took the chicken from the freezer in anticipation of an evening picnic by the pond. She took the pie from the refrigerator and set it on the counter to reach room temperature. She bought fresh corn from a farm-stand on the edge of town, and Boston lettuce, radicchio, sliced black olives, pine nuts, and sprouts. She stopped at the record store for the new Streisand tape that Doug had been wanting. She chilled the bottle of champagne that her editor in New York had sent upon publication of her book and that she had squirreled away at the time. Champagne was festive. Doug didn't have to know its source.

As it happened, he didn't arrive home until eleven at night, after Emily had, item by item, hope by hope, returned the food to the refrigerator and dismantled the picnic makings. By the time he arrived there was no sign that she had been expecting him earlier. Nor did she clue him in. After all, he had said Saturday night. She was the one who had assumed he would make it for dinner. She had simply assumed wrong. It was her mistake.

He gave her a perfunctory kiss, then rolled into bed and fell promptly asleep. He was still sleeping when she woke up the next morning, and while she might have liked to rouse him, to do the kinds of things Sunday mornings had meant once, she resisted. He clearly needed the sleep. Waking him when he was exhausted was more apt to invoke annoyance than desire.

Sunday brunch seemed the next best thing. She mixed a coffee cake from scratch and put it in the oven, fixed a bowl of berries and kiwi. After tiptoeing back into the bedroom, gathering his dirty clothes and putting them in the wash, she assembled the makings of a three-cheese omelet, put the pan on the stove with a wad of butter inside, and, thinking that breakfast could be a celebratory occasion, too, set out fluted glasses for mimosas.

Doug wandered into the kitchen at ten-thirty, took one look at her preparations, and put a cautionary hand on his middle. "None of that for me. My stomach's been acting up. I think it's too much rich food. Hotel eating's like that."

Emily was set back. "Some fruit, then," she urged, trying to be understanding, and he agreed. She put away the omelet makings and the champagne. "Coffee?" She had the beans ground and the water in the machine.

But he shook his head. "Maybe later. Just fruit for now."

Just fruit for now. Okay. She wanted him to be happy to be home. She could accept just fruit for now, if that would make him happy.

She filled two bowls and sat down beside

him at a kitchen table made festive by glass dishes, linen napkins, and Myra's contribution to the homecoming, apricot marigolds. She didn't push him to talk right away. More considerate, she thought, to let him relax for a bit.

In time, he set down his spoon. "What's the word from Jill?"

"She's great. She calls every day. Classes start tomorrow."

"Good courses?"

Emily had run them past him when he had called on Thursday. He must have forgotten. Patiently, she repeated what she had told him then. Moving along without comment, he asked, "How's her room-mate?"

"Nice, apparently."

"That's good." He picked up his spoon and resumed eating.

Emily studied his face. He didn't look tired, exactly. But weary, somehow. "Are you okay, Doug?"

"Of course. Why do you ask?"

"You seem far away."

He jabbed at a berry. "I have a lot on my mind."

"Want to share it?"

"Not particularly. I've been living with it all week. I want a break."

That was fine and dandy for him, not so fine and dandy for her. He needed silence, but she needed talk. "Is it the Baltimore account?"

He shrugged.

"The problem wasn't resolved by the time you left?"

He set down his spoon. "We're making progress." He reached for the Sunday paper.

"What about Philadelphia?"

He unfolded the paper with a snap. "What about it?"

"How did it go?"

"Fine." He focused on the front page.

She waited. She watched his eyes move, but she wasn't sure if he was actually reading. "Talk to me, Doug," she said softly.

He turned down the paper only enough to meet her eyes. "This is the first day in a week that I've been able to relax over breakfast with the morning paper. It really is a luxury. Indulge me?"

Put that way, she felt guilty. He was the one on the road, the one working all week, the one feeling pressure to produce and earn. She supposed that if she were in his position, she would find reading the morning paper a luxury, too.

"Can we have lunch out by the pond?" she asked. That seemed a fair compromise.

"Lunch. I can't think of lunch. We're just having breakfast."

"Only fruit. That's not much. I have fried chicken and fresh corn and salad. And strawberry-rhubarb pie."

"Strawberry-rhubarb?" At last, an inkling of interest. "Yours?"

She nodded, feeling pleased.

He searched the counter. "Where is it?"

"In the fridge."

"Can I have a piece now?"

"What about your stomach?"

"It's worth it, for a piece of that pie. It is *the* best."

Relieved to catch a glimpse of the old Doug, she left the table and cut him a piece. Then she watched him eat every last bite. The instant he was done, she reached for his hand. "Come. I want to show you something."

"What?"

"The garage apartment. You won't recognize the place."

"Let me get dressed first."

"No need." He was wearing a knee-length terrycloth robe. It was comfortable and familiar to Emily. The urbane business consultant was miles away. She didn't wish him back.

She led him out the kitchen door, down

the steps, and across the driveway to the far side of the garage. She pointed at the locks when she opened the door. "They're new. And I've ordered a runner for these stairs." They started up. "It'll be safer for a child."

"Jill did fine without."

"Jill wouldn't have sued us if she fell."

"And this guy will? Maybe it's a mistake renting to a cop."

"No mistake. He's a nice guy. I'm just thinking landlord thoughts." She led him into the room and smiled. "Different, huh?"

She waited for an answering smile. What she got was something akin to dismay. "The walls look raw."

"We'll be painting next week."

"Well, I suppose anything's an improvement over that dingy wallpaper and Jill's awful scribbles."

Emily didn't think the scribbles were awful. "I saved them for her. She'll laugh hysterically over them someday. They're like a chronicle of her adolescence. John was appalled."

"When was John here?"

"When he brought Brian over," she said, but she was sorry John's name had slipped out. Friends once, Doug and he had drifted apart. Aside from the girls, they had little in common. At times Emily sensed an animosity in Doug toward John. She didn't ask its cause, didn't want to know.

"What are the markings over there?" Doug asked.

"We're putting in a round top window."

"My God, it's a huge space."

"It'll be charming when it's done."

"Is it necessary? For five hundred bucks a month? And the ceiling fan's new. This guy's getting one hell of a deal."

"So are we," Emily said defensively. She was proud of what she had done here. She was tired of being put down. "He's installing the window himself."

"Paying for it?"

"No. Providing the labor."

"I thought you said he was a cop."

"He worked as a carpenter when he was younger. I told you he offered to help finish the place."

"This isn't finishing. It's reconstructing. Does he know what he's doing? Have you seen his work? How do you know you won't end up with a collapsed roof, or a window that leaks?"

"I don't know for sure," she argued. "I wouldn't know for sure even if I hired a contractor."

"At least a contractor is bonded."

"A contractor is also expensive, whereas

Brian comes cheap. I've worked with him for three days now. I've heard him talking with the electrician and the plumber. He's knowledgeable. And anyway, if he does it wrong, he's the one who'll have to live with it."

"We're the ones who'll have to fix it."

"I trust him, Doug," Emily insisted. "You would, too, if you met him. Why don't I have him stop over later?" She liked that idea. She wanted Brian to meet Doug.

But Doug gave an impatient wave. "I can't waste time meeting a tenant. I'm leaving at three. I have to be in Atlanta tonight for an early morning meeting tomorrow."

"Three," Emily cried in dismay. She had been hoping for four or five, at the least. "That doesn't give us much time."

"For what?"

"To *talk.* You promised we would."

He stared at her, then put his hands on his hips. "Okay. I'm here now. Talk."

Time, place, atmosphere — all were wrong for what she wanted to say. She had been hoping for a warmer mood, a more intimate setting. But if her choice was between this one or none at all, there was no contest.

So she blurted out, "Jill's gone, and I'm all alone in this house. I was counting on our being together Thursday, and when that

143

didn't happen, I was counting on Saturday, and now that's come and gone, and we've done none of the things I was hoping we would. I want us to spend time together, Doug. I want to *do* things together, to have *fun* like we used to."

"Yeah, well, that would be nice. I could retire. But then who'd pay the bills?"

"Not retire. Just make home time."

"Emily, I have a business to run."

"So do other men, but they manage to make time for their wives."

"Are you saying I don't manage my time well?"

She thought to pull back, but the words spilled out. "It's a question of priorities."

"And you think mine are screwed up? You are *unbelievable.* I'm out there working my tail off so that my wife and daughter can live comfortably, and you stand here and complain? What's *with* you?"

Ahhh, the guilt. "I'm lonesome."

"Well, so am I, stuck alone in strange cities, but I'm not paying a bundle to have you tag along."

"You could call more often. You could tell me about your day and I could tell you about mine."

"We do that."

"Not every night, and it's mostly me doing the telling. There was a time when you used to do it, too."

His voice grew slow and pedantic. "Life was simpler in those days. We used to talk about the weather or the lettuce harvest or a new piece of machinery I'd ordered. My work is more complicated now."

"I'm not dumb. I can understand it."

"But why do you want to know?"

"Because it's your work and it interests me."

He gave her a cold stare. "You're making things very difficult."

"How?" she argued, stung. "Is *talking* to me difficult?"

"You're pressuring me."

"All I want is a little time."

"I don't have it to give," he ground out. "Christ, Emily, life is tough enough. Don't make it worse."

She studied him for a disbelieving minute, then let out a defeated breath. "That wasn't my intent."

"Yeah, well, it never is," he said.

"What does *that* mean?" she cried.

He made for the door. "You're such an innocent."

"Is that bad?"

"Deathly." He started down the stairs.

"Doug?" She ran to the door. *"Doug."* But

he didn't look back, and in seconds he was gone, leaving her vaguely shocked and wondering what in the hell had just happened.

Emily remained in that same vague sense of shock through the few hours that remained of Doug's stay at home. She didn't try to talk with him again, but was simply, sweetly there, as she had been for most of the last twenty-one years.

That seemed her role in their marriage. She hadn't thought twice about it, what with Jill such a major player in her life, but Jill was gone now, back for vacations but moving toward an independent life as surely as the sun moved east to west.

Emily's future was with Doug. If this weekend was indicative of what that future would be, she didn't know what she would do.

So she didn't dwell on it. She folded his clean clothes and packed his bag while he busied himself in the den. To show that she understood the importance of his work, that *she* could compromise, she brought him lunch there. It was an inside version of the picnic that wouldn't be, and when he finally took a break, she called Jill.

She wanted Jill to hear their voices together. That seemed just as important as leaving her bedroom intact.

Six

Bright and early Monday morning, Brian dressed Julia and drove her to the baby-sitter's house. His stomach was tied in knots in anticipation of her crying.

She didn't let him down. The crying started the minute he took her out of the car.

The fact that she clung to him as though she adored him to pieces and simply couldn't bear parting with him was small solace. He felt like he was an ogre, turning her over to an executioner, rather than to a woman who had impressed him both with her knowing ways and her references, and he had certainly checked those out. Every last one. Emily's endorsement was representative of the lot.

"Shhhhh," he whispered while Julia screamed against his shoulder, "no one'll hurt you here. You'll have lots of fun, and

I'll be back to get you later, I will, I'll be back."

Janice pried her from Brian's arms. "Once you're gone, she'll be fine. This isn't unusual, especially at first." She started off toward the other children.

Julia's screams rose. Her little arms reached around Janice for Brian. They touched air and Brian's heart, which was breaking. He couldn't take his eyes off her. "Maybe this isn't such a good idea," he called, feeling a touch of panic. "We've been together every minute for days now. Mine is the only face she's known. We're inseparable. I'm all she has."

"She'll be fine once you leave, Mr. Stasek."

"Loud noises frighten her. Bursts of activity. She still misses her mother. She doesn't understand what happened to Gayle. She'll think I'm going for good, too. Maybe I should stay."

Janice was kneeling beside several children who were playing with oversized plastic bricks. "Look, Julia, see the pretty blocks. What do you think they're building? What are you making, Adam?"

Julia kept crying, kept frantic eyes on Brian, who was feeling more cruel by the minute. "Should I stay?" he called.

"Definitely not. As soon as you leave,

she'll be fine."

"I put two changes of clothes in the bag. Is that enough?"

"Plenty."

"And her rabbit. She can't sleep without it."

"We'll make sure she has it."

"I'll be right here in town. You have the number. I can be over in five minutes. Should I come by at noon to see how she's doing?"

"Not unless you want her to start crying again."

That was assuming she stopped crying now. Brian wanted to think she would, but she seemed caught up in one of the snowballing fits that made mockery of his street smarts.

She used to smile, used to look up from whatever she was doing and beam at Gayle or him. Now her little face was scrunched up and red. He wondered if she would ever smile again.

"If you can't reach me at my number, call the police station. They know where I am. They'll come right out and get me." He figured the reminder of his connections didn't hurt.

Janice continued to talk softly to Julia, saying things about the toys and the other children and what they would be doing that morning. Something must have sunk in, because while Julia continued to cry, she dared take her eyes off Brian.

He slipped out the door and walked to the Jeep feeling cowardly, traitorous, and frightened.

It occurred to him that the references might be wrong.

But the other children weren't crying.

So maybe something was wrong with Julia.

But if so Janice would call him. Assuming she was on the up and up. But hadn't Emily had good words for her?

That thought brought him a measure of calm. Emily did that to him, and not only where Julia was concerned. From the minute he had met her, he had felt something peaceful. She was straightforward and honest, settled at a time when his life was anything but. She was the embodiment of the simpler life he needed just then.

By midday, the spot in the apartment over the garage where the arched window would be was halfway to being a gaping hole, and Brian was feeling better. Physical work always satisfied him, all the more so when it required concentration. Breaking through a wall so that the hole fit the window required both brawn and brains.

It took his mind off Julia, for small stretches at least. But he couldn't forget her for long. She was his responsibility.

Just when he was wondering what she was having for lunch and thinking that he could use some himself, Emily produced a platter of leftover fried chicken and a pitcher of lemonade, set both on the floor along with a pile of napkins, and gestured for him to join her.

"This is above and beyond," he protested, though the chicken looked more appetizing than anything he had eaten in weeks. It also smelled a damn sight better than he did. Most anything would, he supposed. Emily sure did. "I could've gone in town for sandwiches."

She smiled. "If we don't eat this, it'll spoil. I made it for the weekend, but my husband was in and out so fast he couldn't eat much."

Her husband was an idiot. "Is he always so busy?"

"It's worse lately." Her smile grew sheepish. "I should be grateful. So many people are out of work, and Doug is deluged."

She passed him a glass of lemonade. He drained it and hunkered down by the chicken. "Gratitude is nice, in theory. I was grateful that Gayle had a career. I had all the pride and respect in the world for her, but I hated it when she wasn't home when I was."

"She must have felt the same about your career."

"Maybe yes, maybe no. She was self-sufficient in nearly every respect. She didn't need me."

"But she married you."

"Not from need. From want."

"All the nicer."

Brian wasn't so sure. "She was on the go all the time. Marriage stood for something settled in her mind. Same with having a baby. She was raised in a traditional family that said marriage and children were musts. Her career didn't allow much time for them, but without them she would have felt like a failure."

"Was it the same way with you?" Emily asked.

He reached for a piece of chicken. "My career wasn't any more generous than hers. I've been known to work round the clock for days in a row."

"On murder investigations?"

"Mm." He bit into the chicken, salivating even before the meat hit his tongue.

"Did you have to have a body to launch a murder investigation?"

He shook his head and finished what was in his mouth. "But we needed some evidence of foul play. It didn't have to be physical evidence. In the case of a missing person, it usually wasn't, not in the sense of blood-stained somethings. But there were other things that could get us involved."

"Like what?"

"Like a car abandoned where it shouldn't have been. A wallet thrown in a trash can. Appointments missed. Those cases were always a challenge. Like finding pieces of a puzzle, one by one, and putting them together."

"How successful were you?"

"I had a pretty good batting average — but it took time, which meant time away from Gayle and from Julia." He wondered if Julia was taking a nap. He would never forgive himself if she cried herself to sleep. Not that he would ever know, since she wouldn't say.

He felt discouraged. "There are times when I wonder if we're going to make it, Julia and me. I'm groping blind on hostile turf."

"Not hostile, just new. My husband would have felt the same way if he'd had to jump in all of a sudden and mother Jill."

"He wasn't a do-it-all father?"

"Not quite," she drawled, then held up a contrite hand, "which was okay. He had his business, and I was perfectly happy mothering Jill. I didn't want him worrying about her. So if anyone's at fault for his not having been involved, it's me."

"He's lucky to have you. Full-time mothers are few and far between these days."

"I have that luxury because he works."

"So when will I get to meet him?"

"Soon. He'll be back."

"John said he was a business consultant. Does he have an office here in Grannick?"

"In our den. His computer has a fax and a modem, and programs that do incredible things. Several times a day he accesses his mail and messages. It's ingenious, really. But you must know about all that. Aren't the police using electronics much more?"

Brian shrugged. "We can match fingerprints, trace license plates, pull up rap sheets faster than we could before. But nothing substitutes for good old-fashioned legwork." He thought about legwork while he ate, thought about someone changing Julia's diaper, putting her rabbit in with her to nap, rubbing her back for a bit. "Like raising kids. Computers can't do it."

"She's fine," Emily assured him, reading his mind. "You've called twice. She wasn't crying either time."

"She probably cried herself into a stupor."

"She's probably intrigued by the other kids."

"She's never been with others much. We always had a sitter at our place."

"Then this is good."

He figured she ought to know, since she had raised an only child, herself. "Hard to imagine Julia interacting with other children."

"She won't yet. But she sees them. She imitates them. She learns that she can't have every toy the minute she wants it. And she learns that even though her father leaves her, he always comes back to get her and take her home."

He remembered the nightmare of leaving her that morning. "It kills me to think she's feeling abandoned."

"You give her too much credit. Not that she isn't bright. Not that she isn't the brightest one there," this said, with a knowing half-smile, "but kids are fickle. They're easily distracted. Show them a new toy and they're fine. She may cry each morning when you leave —"

"That doesn't stop?" he interrupted, appalled.

"Eventually. Jill cried for the longest time when I left her with her playgroup. We were very close, even then."

"I'll bet you miss her a lot."

Emily studied the broken-down wall. "Six weeks and counting 'til fall break. That's why this is good. It distracts me." She frowned at the window. "What if it rains tonight?"

He willingly leaped from parenthood to carpentry and the surer footing he had there. "We'll stretch a tarp over the hole before we leave. Two guys from the station are coming by first thing tomorrow to help with the window. We'll have it in by noon."

Shortly after noon on the following day, Emily sat in the very same spot, feeling awed. The arched window looked spectacular. She was starved for the sunlight and the cheer it added. Doug hadn't called last night. After the fiasco of the weekend, that hurt. She had hoped he would want to apologize, or mend fences, or simply see how she was. Apparently not.

"So, what do you think?" Brian asked. He stood tall above her, regarding the window with a well-deserved pride.

She let the sight of him lighten her mood. He was so different from Doug, so positive, so *earthy* in a clean, sexy way. "It makes the room into something special. Jill will be angry we didn't think to do it when she was around." She offered up a sandwich. "Roast beef on rye, with Russian dressing."

"I thought it was my turn to buy lunch."

"Tomorrow," she promised, figuring that otherwise he would argue. Lunch was a small price to pay for his help, not to mention his company. He was easy on the mind. She liked him.

He sat down beside her and unwrapped the sandwich. "How is she doing — your daughter?"

Emily sighed. "She isn't as wild about classes as she was about orientation, but she'll be fine." At least, Emily kept telling herself that. Jill had suddenly realized there was more to college than parties. She was feeling intimidated and lonesome. And she kept asking about Doug.

"You two ought to plan a vacation," she'd said. "A real going-away kind of trip, now that I'm gone. My roommate's parents just got back from Bermuda, kind of to celebrate their freedom. They loved it."

"Your father travels all week." No *way* would he spring for a weekend away, what with the other expenses they had. Emily knew enough not to ask. "Staying home is his vacation."

"But it's not much of one for you."

"I'm fine."

"Really, Mom? Are you okay without me?"

"How are you doing without her?" Brian asked.

Emily was a minute in separating his question from the one Jill had asked, and another in deciding how honest to be. She could gloss over the loss and say she was fine. But she was tired of doing that. It wasn't the truth, not really. "I miss her." She patted her heart. "There's a big hole where her presence has always been. She's been my world for a long time." She took a breath. "But I'd better get used to it, right? This was what I raised her for, to let her go." She had read that on a mug once. It sounded good.

"Did you ever work?"

From another mug. "Every mother works."

"Outside the home."

"No. Not formally. I dropped out of college to marry Doug. When Jill got old enough for school, I started taking courses down the street, but more for my own sake than for that of a job."

159

"Did you get your degree?"

She nodded. "In English. I've always loved to write. I write for the local paper sometimes. Fill in for the regular reporter."

"Do you really?"

"Yup. It's fun."

"I'll bet."

"While I was getting my degree, I got to know the professors. I grade papers for them sometimes, or help organize their research, like their own personal editor. It's a loose arrangement. We swap — my work for a free ride taking extra courses. I've taken some good ones. Criminology. Abnormal Psychology. People interest me. Their motives. Why they go wrong or crack up or do bizarre things. Why a gunman randomly opens fire in a crowded subway. Why a motorist plows his car into a crowd of Christmas shoppers. What really happened to the Lindbergh baby."

"He was kidnapped," Brian said.

"Some say his father took him as a prank, then the prank went awry." The thought of it gave Emily a bone-deep chill, still she had read it, had taken in every last argument for and against the theory.

Brian was thoughtful as he ate. Finally, he shook his head. "There was the ladder used in the kidnapping, the ransom note, the money — all traced to Hauptmann. He had a record. He had escaped from a German jail."

Emily was delighted that he knew the case. She certainly couldn't discuss it with Doug. "But there were no witnesses. Hauptmann's wife protested his innocence to the end."

"What about the later threats against the Lindberghs? Did Lindy make those?"

"He could have," she said, because anything was possible when minds were warped. "I'm not saying he did. But he was a complicated person."

"Many people are. There aren't always answers to why they do what they do. Motive is right up there with murder weapon in making or breaking a case. That's most often what the all-nighters are about."

"Have you ever been involved in the search for a missing child?"

"In New York? Sure. Kids disappear there all the time."

"Do you find them?"

"Depends on the situation. If a kid is just lost, separated from a parent, he'll show up. If he's abducted, things become more dicey. We usually get them back if there's money involved, where the intention all along is to make an exchange. If the abduction is the

161

result of a custody battle, it could go either way. If perversion is involved — sex or insanity — it's not good."

"Because the family isn't contacted, so there's no trail?"

"Partly. And because we're dealing with crazies. They can be brilliant covering tracks. They can lie convincingly."

Emily swallowed. It was a harrowing thought. "Did you ever work on a case where the victim was gone for years?"

"Six years, once."

"How did you crack it?"

"We got a tip."

"Hey!" came a bark from downstairs. "Is anyone home?"

Not now, Emily cried silently, resenting the interruption. But then, that was foolish. Her discussion with Brian would hold. There was no urgency, after all.

"Must be the floor man," she sighed and rose. "He's doing the bathroom this afternoon."

By late Tuesday, the flooring was in, a simple brick pattern in a pale gray faux-marble that Emily assured Brian wouldn't show dirt. She also convinced him that bathroom walls papered with vinyl would withstand both moisture and a child better

162

than bare paint, and that a child's room papered with vinyl had greater potential for excitement. She drove into town and found several rolls of a handsome navy and gray plaid, and several rolls of primary-color paint streaks on a glossy white field, and began measuring out strips for the bathroom and for Julia's room, respectively, while Brian put the finishing touches on the arched window.

By Wednesday the bathroom was done and the kitchen had arrived. By Thursday the cabinets had been installed and the appliances were delivered. By Friday the appliances were functional, as were new, bright, modern light fixtures.

"Not bad for a first week," Brian decided, looking around.

Emily agreed. They both looked vaguely worse for the wear, slightly dirty, generally sweaty, and more than a little tired, but they had plenty to show for it. "We may finish next week, after all," she remarked.

"Doubted me, huh?"

"Maybe a little, at first. But I'm learning."

"We'll start the walls on Monday."

"I may start tomorrow. Doug's been delayed." She tried for nonchalance, but she was upset. He had called last night, apparently for the sole purpose of telling her,

163

since he hadn't had anything else to say. He refused to talk about his week, and when she told him about work on the apartment, he answered with bored uh-huhs. Five minutes, and he'd been off the phone with what she guessed was relief.

"Is everything all right?" Brian asked. He was studying her with those iridescent eyes that saw too much.

"Yes," she said, smiled, frowned, shook her head. "No. I wanted to have both nights. I'm disappointed. It's scary with him gone so much."

"Scary staying alone?"

"No. Scary —" she gestured, hard put to say the words aloud — "his work. No free time."

What was scary was the thought that this was her life. Doug wasn't apologizing. He wasn't saying things would change. Whenever she alluded to loneliness, he got angry, as though it were her fault, something she had brought on herself.

Maybe it was. But that didn't ease the hurt, or the confusion. If she couldn't get through to Doug, where were they *headed*?

"Want to come shopping with Julia and me tomorrow?" Brian asked. "We're buying furniture."

Something inside her lifted. It was a better offer than Doug had made her in weeks. "When are you going?"

"We're flexible. When's good for you?"

She and Kay were spending the morning pampering Celeste, but otherwise she was free. "Noon? One? Two?" She was without pride.

"Noon." He grinned. "See you then."

They bought a long oak-framed sofa that opened to a large bed, and two matching side chairs. They bought a low coffee table, a large wardrobe, several bookshelves, and a table and chairs, all in the same warm oak. They bought two large impressionistic landscapes for the main room, and two small circus prints for Julia's room. They bought a rattan coat tree.

Everything was scheduled for delivery the following Friday.

Doug came home in time for dinner Saturday night. Emily served a rack of lamb that had been absurdly expensive, a *Silver Palate* pasta dish that had been absurdly complicated, and fresh broccoli. She had made an English trifle for dessert.

It was an ominous choice.

Doug took a bite, chuckled softly, and announced that he was going to London for two weeks.

Emily was startled. "Two *weeks?*"

"This is a new account. A good one. There's a whole day of travel at either end."

"But that's twelve days there. You *never* spend twelve days straight working on one account."

"This is London, Emily. It's a new door opening to me."

"That's wonderful," she said, trying to see his point. "But where does it leave us?"

"A little more comfortable financially."

She felt a sudden fury at his insensitivity, his *blitheness.* "Damn the money. Where does it leave *us?*"

"What are you talking about?"

"Us, Doug. You and me. Our marriage. The time we're supposed to be spending together now that Jill is away."

"I don't know who told you about that time." He tossed his napkin on the table and rose. "It's a fantasy." He walked off.

"Wait! Let's talk about this!"

He turned back with a long-suffering look. "What's there to say? It's my business. What can I do?"

"Change it. Shorten it. You don't need to go so far." She sounded desperate. She *was* desperate. Her husband was growing less and less familiar to her, more and more distant. She felt that if she reached out to pull him back, he might just slip through her fingers and dissolve.

"Are you kidding?" he countered. "I've been waiting for years for this kind of contract to come through. I'm not giving it up."

"Can I come?"

"No."

"Why not?"

"It isn't appropriate."

"Why not? I can spend the day at museums."

"And then what? What'll you do at night when I'm working with people over dinner?"

"I'll listen in. I can be a pleasant dinner companion."

"Now, what would you have to say to those people?" he asked, stopping just shy of a belittling laugh. "Absolutely nothing. Your world and theirs are light-years apart."

"And yours?" she asked, thinking of the man who had once lived in jeans, an honest smile, and a healthy sweat.

He was slower in answering, but no less confident. "Mine is somewhere in the middle. I want it to move closer to theirs in the course of this trip. Don't you understand," he pleaded, "this could be a breakthrough for me. It could mean the beginning of an international reputation. Do you know what that's worth?"

It struck Emily then that he wasn't hearing her. He had no idea what she was trying to say, and, worse, he didn't care. They were at opposite ends of a marital spectrum. She might as well be his maid, given his level of involvement with her.

That thought shook her from head to toe.

"I'll be in the den," he said.

She carried the dishes to the sink, loaded the dishwasher, then turned back to the table, where the English trifle sat. It was a beautiful creation, a froth of berries, sherry-soaked cake, and whipped cream, as artistic as it was indecently good.

Lifting the bowl by the stem, she upended it in the sink and washed the lot down the drain.

Monday morning, she was back at work beside Brian, painting the walls while he labored over the woodwork. She tried not to think about Doug — thinking about him brought a pain she couldn't do anything about — but the thoughts were as stubborn as her emotions. They ate at her, monopolizing her mind.

"Emily?"

She jumped, startled to find Brian beside her.

"You look like you're about to cry. Is something wrong?"

She shook her head. "Just thinking about things I shouldn't."

"Like what?"

She sighed. "Like getting old." It was true, in a sense. That was what life after kids was about, deciding how to spend the rest of one's days.

"You have a while to go."

"Thanks."

"Don't thank me. I said it for my benefit, seeing as I'm the same age as you."

He gave her a sweet smile and returned to work, leaving Emily to wonder why Doug never smiled at her that way. But then, Doug was her husband. They had been married for twenty-two years. They had a life together, had shared a major trauma.

Traumas either brought people together or drove them apart. Since she and Doug remained married, she had always assumed the former. Now she wondered.

By dusk Wednesday, the painting was done. Early Thursday, they sanded the wood floor. By the end of the day, they had lacquered the planks and left to allow them to dry.

"This calls for a celebration," Brian said. "Got any beer in your fridge?"

Emily did it one better, uncorking the bottle of champagne that had come so long ago with her book. Since Doug didn't want to drink it, much less acknowledge its existence, she saw no harm in sharing it with Brian.

He raised his glass. "To a job well done."

She took a sip, then sat back against the rocks. They were in the backyard by the pond. The late afternoon was serene.

"This captures what I first saw in that apartment," Brian said, looking out over the pond. "The peace. It's what Julia and I both need."

"I'm glad. I hope it works for you."

"And you?"

She looked at him, bemused, but only for a minute. His eyes — those penetrating eyes — said that she couldn't fool him. "Maybe for me, too, some day," she confessed and felt a lump form in her throat.

"Not now?"

She waited for the lump to shrink. "Now's a difficult time. Things are changing."

"With Jill?"

"And Doug."

"Are there problems between you?"

Problems? She sighed and looked up at

170

the leaves. "I suppose you could say that."
The lump in her throat returned.

"Want to talk about it?"

She didn't look at him, afraid that if she
did, she would cry. He was such a nice man.
He was gentle and understanding in ways
she hungered for.

"You don't have to," he said. "We haven't
known each other long. But we have the
makings of a friendship. I respect what
you've done with your life."

She had no idea why. "I haven't done
much."

"You don't call making a home much? Or
raising a child much? Or waiting around for
your husband much?"

"It's not like having an occupation. Not
like what your wife did."

"There was a trade-off. She wasn't a
mother or wife like you are. She didn't have
the patience for it, or the self-confidence."

Emily did look at him then. "Self-
confidence? From what you've told me, she
could handle herself in any situation. If *she*
was invited to London for two weeks, she
would have had plenty to say at dinner."

"She needed a paycheck. That was the
only way she could judge her success. She
wanted a child, but she couldn't give up the
other. She didn't have the self-confidence

to say to her colleagues, 'Okay, guys, it's family time.' " He paused. "No self-confidence. No desire." He rubbed his eyebrow. "No desire. The bottom line."

Like Doug, Emily thought, and sure enough, looking at Brian, whose face was a work of kindness etched in strength, she felt her eyes fill. Doug didn't want to spend time with her. No desire. The bottom line.

She looked away.

"I'm a good listener," Brian coaxed.

She nodded.

"It's gotten worse as the week has gone on," he remarked.

"Just thinking more," she managed to say.

He grew quiet. She knew that he wouldn't force her to talk, if she didn't want to. And she did. But it was hard.

"I'll be moving in tomorrow," he said on a lighter note. "It's kind of exciting."

Yes. It was. But after two weeks in a flurry, the work was done. She didn't know what she would do with herself come Monday.

The upstairs bathroom, probably.

But why? Doug was never there. She had picked out paper with him in mind. If the bathroom were hers alone, she would have made a different choice.

She could choose different paper now. And put it up. Then see what Doug had to say about it when he deigned to visit.

Fuck you, probably. No, that was wrong. More likely, he wouldn't even notice. He was past caring about bathroom walls. He was past caring about *her.* He had moved on.

So where was she? she cried and felt a catch deep inside. She put her head to her knees and tried to erase the thought.

She felt Brian's hand on her shoulder. "Things work out," he said, but it wasn't his voice she heard. It was John's, saying the same thing nineteen years before, only it was a crock. Things hadn't worked out. Things hadn't worked out *at all.*

She pushed up to her feet and away from Brian. "I have to go." She took off across the grass.

He was beside her in an instant. "I want to help."

But she couldn't talk, couldn't think. Guilt, fear, despair resurged inside her. Why now? she cried fleetingly, and though she didn't have the wherewithal to formulate the answer, she felt it.

With Jill gone, she was alone.

An hour later, Brian marched into the Grannick Police Station, strode through the squad room, and burst into John's office

173

without so much as a knock. Julia was on his hip, utterly silent, seeming to know not to fuss, just as everyone he passed knew not to speak.

John looked up in surprise.

"Tell me about her," Brian ordered.

"Who?"

"You introduced me to Emily Arkin. You went along with the idea that I could get her apartment ready, and you knew I'd be working with her. Well, I have, and I've seen sad, even haunted looks. There's more to her than meets the eye, but I don't know what it is. I want you to tell me."

John stared at him. His mouth was tight, but it was the sorrow in his eyes that made Brian uneasy. "Did you ask her?"

"I've been asking her all week. Her prick of a husband is abandoning her, and that's part of the problem, but my gut says there's more. I want to know why he doesn't want to be with her. I want to know why she only has one child, when she clearly makes children her life. I want to know why she's so interested in my work. She asks direct questions, always around the same theme. My gut tells me you know what that theme is, plus a whole lot more. I could turn this place upside down looking for answers, but that'd be pretty messy, and it would take a hell of a lot of time. Spare me the effort, huh?"

John stared at him for a minute longer. Finally, looking sadder than ever, almost defeated, he curved his hands around the edge of the desk and pushed off from his chair. He went to a corner file cabinet, opened the lowest drawer, and pulled out a folder. It was inches thick. He tossed it on the desk. Brian was staring at it, his heart batting against his ribs, when a book landed on top.

"Might as well take that, too. It'll tell you where she's at." When Brian raised his eyes, he added, "If you get any suggestions, I'm all ears. It's been a guilty time for me, too."

For a split second, Brian wasn't sure he wanted any part of either the folder or the book. Then he thought of Emily and the promise of serenity that she had come to epitomize in his jumbled life, and he knew without knowing a goddamned thing else, that if he didn't try to save the promise, he would be guilty, too.

SEVEN

Emily Arkin was nineteen when her first child, a boy, was born. He was named Daniel, after his paternal great-grandfather, and she and Doug doted on him. Doug, who owned a farm on the outskirts of town, often stopped home midday to see him. For the rest of the time, Daniel was his mother's constant companion and, as such, became well known around town.

A reluctant napper, he often fell asleep in the car while Emily did errands. Such was the case one October day when the boy was two. She pulled into the parking lot outside the local post office, saw that Daniel was sleeping, and, knowing that she wouldn't be long, left him in the car while she ran inside. She was there for five minutes. When she returned, she found the straps that had held him in his car seat neatly unfastened and Daniel nowhere in sight.

The local police arrived within minutes.

While Emily swore that Daniel couldn't have freed himself from the seat on his own, they searched the parking lot and the surrounding areas on the chance that he had done just that, and had wandered off. They questioned the other patrons at the post office, as well as those who had emerged while Emily was inside. They canvassed the local shops. They combed the center of town and fanned outward.

Daniel was gone.

The police dispatcher phoned the state police and the neighboring police departments to alert them to Daniel's disappearance, but without description of either a vehicle or a suspect, there was little to go on. Photographs of Daniel were passed around. The FBI was notified.

John Davies, the officer assigned to the Arkins, questioned Emily and Doug extensively. Whatever dubious leads emerged from that questioning were thoroughly explored and discarded. Meanwhile, the Arkins held vigil by the telephone for a ransom call that never came.

In the weeks that followed, largely at Emily's prodding, appeals were made in an ever-widening radius of towns, cities, and states, but with nothing more than Daniel's picture, the case grew cold as ice. After a time, other matters were occupying the Grannick police, and though the Arkin case remained open, it slid into inactivity.

Brian read the "Dear Chief" that John had written, both the short report filed immediately after the child's disappearance, and the later, more lengthy one that detailed the investigation in its entirety. He studied the pictures of Daniel, one alone, one with his parents. He pored over the questioning of Emily and Doug, their neighbors and friends, Doug's employees, the owners of the shops Emily had visited that day prior to stopping at the post office. He waded through a cataloging of the efforts of other law enforcement agencies that the Grannick police had contacted.

Then he opened the book Emily had written and read it from cover to cover. It was about the case she had mentioned to him, the kidnapping of Susan Demery, a local college student, by a disgruntled former employee of her father. The girl had been taken from her dormitory room late one winter night and stashed, bound and gagged, in a tool shed on the grounds of the local estate where one of the kidnappers worked.

The Demery kidnapping had taken place five years before, fourteen years after Daniel's disappearance. The handling of the case was a study of the advances in investigative technology that had occurred during those fourteen years, from computer hookups between police departments, to fingerprint matching, to fiber analysis of the carpet in the dormitory room from which the girl was abducted.

The book was well-organized, the case clearly presented, the writing itself no less than brilliant, given the pain Emily had to have experienced in its course. Brian couldn't begin to imagine that pain, or the pain she felt thinking of Daniel even now.

He slept for a brief hour before waking to the sounds of Julia talking to her rabbit. Moaning, he threw an arm over his eyes and cursed whatever it was about childhood that began at dawn.

Then he remembered all that he had spent the night reading, and his pique vanished. He pushed himself up on his elbows and watched his daughter play, and as he did, he saw far more. Since Gayle's death, his feelings for Julia had been dominated by anxiety over her care. He had been preoccupied with minutia, blinded to the larger picture. He had forgotten that children were miracles — and it didn't matter that he had originally wanted to wait longer before having a child, he had been in the delivery room when Julia was born. He knew the awe that came with the emergence of a fully formed, perfectly functioning, miniature human being that he had helped make.

He had forgotten that awe. He had forgotten the pride, the possessiveness that had been a recurrent swelling in his throat during those first few weeks of her life, before the demands of his work had made him swallow it away.

It returned now in spades. With the image of Daniel Arkin wavering in his mind, he watched Julia with a new appreciation.

Her play was innocent. She was trying to make the rabbit sit, but succeeded only until she let go. Then the rabbit's legs popped straight and it toppled over. She picked it up again, sat it down, watched it fall.

She did it again and again, her cheeks pink, her tiny mouth moist, her hair a mess of curls, and all the while she was talking, saying things he couldn't understand. Then again, maybe he could. He listened. He caught the repetition of sounds. Yes, indeed, there was a slurred "bunny" in there, a vague "sit," and lots of *ooooo*s of appreciation.

Leaving the bed, he hunkered down beside the crib.

She looked at him. Her eyes were softer in the morning, more baby blue than silver. He fancied she was pleased he was up.

"Hi," he said softly. "Playing with bunny?" He reached through the slats of the crib, picked the toy up, and sat it down before her. "Hi, Julia," he bunny-voiced. "Want to play?" He hopped the bunny forward and tickled her tummy with its head.

She scrunched herself around the tickling and giggled. It was a heavenly sound. He moved the bunny back, hopped it forward, tickled her again. The giggling was precious, both in its lack of guile and its spontaneity. He was amazed at how easily it had come.

But that, like dawn risings, was what childhood was about. When Julia hurt, she cried. When she was tickled, she laughed. Her responses were impulsive. Nothing about her was intellectualized.

But she did take cues from those around her. What was it Emily had said — that Julia could sense the tension in his arms when he held her? And he was tense. He was terrified when he thought of raising a child alone. He wondered if Julia sensed that, if her unhappiness had more to do with his own upset, than with Gayle.

Needing to hold her close, he brought her out of the crib and into a hug. "I love you,

181

Julia Stasek. I may be a bungling idiot when it comes to parenting, but I can learn." He shifted her so that she could see him, and grinned. "We can both learn. How does that sound? Daddy screws up, you tell him. Julia screws up, I tell her. Either of us does good, we celebrate. Fair enough?"

She didn't smile, but there was a warming in those knowing eyes of hers, and she said something sweet.

"Fair enough," he interpreted. Then, feeling buoyant, because she was safe and sound and relatively content in his arms, he said, "Know what today is? Today's moving-in day. I'm going to drop you at Janice's — no, now don't pout, because you *know* that you're starting to like her. Didn't you do finger painting yesterday? Wasn't that fun? Didn't you play in the sandbox? Didn't you have an *ice cream cone?* Yes, you did do all of those things, and I have the dirty clothes to prove it, which I am going to wash tonight in that brand-new washer-dryer at our own brand-new place. I am very excited about that. Just think. No more running to the laundry room while you're asleep, and shoving quarters in, and timing myself to be back before some no-good son-of-a-bee takes off with them. 'Course, I don't know what any no-good son-of-a-bee

182

would want with your sleepees, do you?"

He kept up the monologue through a diaper change, and it worked. Julia was listening intently, seeming to understand everything he said. She was less pleased when he started to dress her. The jersey he chose had shrunk something awful in the wash — he didn't know why — but it wasn't fitting over her head, so he pushed and pulled, getting it half-on before he realized that it hadn't shrunk at all, but was buttoned at the neck. He fought with the buttons, wondering how he'd gotten it *off* her, and by the time he realized that Janice must have taken it off and rebuttoned it, Julia's hair was tangled around a button.

The pulling started her crying. He fiddled with the tangled curls for a minute, but he was all thumbs, and in the end, for want of a scissors, he used his razor to cut her free.

They never quite recaptured those earlier moments of communion, but Brian wasn't discouraged. Once he and Julia were settled in the apartment, their lives would gain a semblance of order.

This day, when he left her at Janice's, he held her tightly for an extra-long minute before handing her over.

Fifteen minutes later, he walked into John's

183

office. The hollow feeling that had lumped in the pit of his stomach for most of the night was back. He slid into the chair by the desk. "I want to talk."

"Figured you would," John said, tipping his own chair back. "Did you read the file?"

"Every sentence. Same with the book. Were you the one who suggested she write it?"

"I was the one who put the possibility into words, but it didn't take any brains. From the minute word spread about the Demery girl, Emily was here. She watched the investigation unfold, and it wasn't like we could kick her out. We all knew what she'd been through. I swear she kept us on our toes without saying a goddamned word."

"Did you know her before Daniel's disappearance?"

"As much as any small-town cop knows of people in his town." He paused, self-conscious. "Well, maybe a little more. We'd had our troubles with the kids at the college protesting this and that, and then these two come along looking like hippies, wanting to grow alfalfa sprouts without chemicals. We watched them close. It wasn't until the boy's kidnapping that we learned they were nice people."

"Then you don't think the husband had

anything to do with it."

John recoiled. "Are you crazy? He adored the kid. You read the file. The guy was out in the fields at the time. Three separate people confirmed it. Why would you think he was involved?"

Brian thought it because he didn't like Doug Arkin. "The man's strange, how he treats his wife, being gone so much. Besides, there was something Emily said, when she and I were doing the apartment. She mentioned the theory that Charles Lindbergh kidnapped his own son. She knew all the arguments in favor. I was wondering if there were parallels."

John shook his head with conviction. "If there was a ransom demand, I might have said Doug wanted the money to bolster his business, but there was no insurance, and there wasn't any money in either of their families, so where was the money to pay a ransom supposed to come from, and besides, there wasn't ever any ransom demand."

Brian remembered clearly what Emily had said. "The Lindbergh theory holds that Lindy was a prankster, and this was a prank gone wrong. Could that have been the case with Doug?"

John was shaking his head even before he

185

finished. "Doug isn't a prankster. Doesn't have much of a sense of humor, leastways not that I've seen, and Kay and I've been friends of theirs for a long time. Maybe he had a sense of humor before the kidnapping. Maybe the kidnapping changed him. But that'd be another argument against his involvement."

"Most kidnappings are parental."

John stood his ground. "Not this one. I don't like the guy, but he isn't a kidnapper."

"Why don't you like him?" Brian wondered if their reasons were the same.

They were. "Because he's lousy to Emily. She's one of the nicest people I know. Good-hearted. Generous. She'd give you the shirt off her back, and then iron it for you. She was a second mother to my daughter. She picked up the slack when Kay couldn't be there. I owe her a lot."

"You like her, then."

"I just said I did."

"Do you see her much?"

"I see her around town."

"Are you anything more than friends?"

There was a pause, then a cautious, "Come again?"

"Is it purely social — you and your wife, and Emily and Doug?"

186

A chill replaced caution. "What are you saying?"

Brian knew it sounded wrong. He wasn't sure why he had brought it up — yes, he was. John said he had gone through a guilty time. Brian wanted to know what that meant. "You have feelings for Emily."

"Damn right, I do. For all the reasons I've already given, and then some."

He looked furious. For an instant, Brian wondered if he'd blown his new job.

Then John went on. "The fact is that it's none of your business." He paused, brooding. "But since you've read that file, and since you're living in her garage, and since you'll be in a position to see for yourself and maybe even help, I'll tell you. Once, and no more, and if you bring it up again, you're out on your can." Eyes and voice both leveled. "I got to know Emily during the search for Daniel, and after every lead turned cold, we became friends. She was newly pregnant when the boy was taken, and so was my wife. Our girls are best friends. So are Emily and Kay. They see each other a lot, in de pen dent of anything the four or six of us might do. I'm a long way from being as close to Emily as Kay is, but I like her, and I feel bad for her. I also feel responsible."

"Because you couldn't solve the case?"

"Well, what did I have to work with?" he burst out, betraying his frustration. "You read that file. There's nothing. It's like someone waved a wand and the kid vanished." He grunted. "I don't know why I even mentioned leads turning cold. There were never any leads to speak of. In the whole of my career, it's the damnest case I've ever seen."

So much for anything juicy going on between Emily and John. Brian could sniff out lies. He hadn't heard any yet. There was guilt, but not from sex. It didn't matter that the FBI had been involved, or that John had been a mere patrolman at the time. He had been the officer assigned to the Arkins and had taken the case to heart.

"All things considered, Emily seems surprisingly normal," Brian remarked. "She must be a very strong woman. Either that, or a religious one."

"She's not religious. I don't know if she was before, but after, well, what kind of God would do what He did to her?"

"Still, something is holding her together. Unless I'm missing the boat. Will she freak out if I mention Daniel?"

"No. She doesn't freak out."

Brian heard a catch. "Go on."

John did so with clear reluctance, as though hating to betray a confidence but wanting Brian to know. "For months after Daniel disappeared, she would walk around town, up one street and down the next, looking, listening for a cry, like he might be hiding in the bushes. She stopped doing it when Jill was born, but I caught her at it again a couple of weeks ago. It was right after Jill left. The boy would have been twenty-one and at college, too. This must be a tough time for her."

"Her husband's no help."

"Never was. I don't think he ever understood what Emily was feeling. Maybe that would'a been too much to ask. He was suffering. Then he changed. Like he got tired of suffering."

"After how long?"

"A few years. We kept the case active as long as we could, until there just wasn't anything more to do. After that, Doug just wanted to forget. He made Emily put Daniel's pictures away."

"That's very cold."

"No," John cautioned. "Think about it. Think about how you'd feel if he was yours, if you didn't know if he was alive or dead, healthy or maimed, happy or sad. Think of grotesque things happening to him. Think of him crying and crying for you and not understanding why you won't come. Then realize that you can't do a fucking thing about it. It's eating you alive, but you're totally helpless." He looked at Brian in a humbling way. "You might want to forget and start over, too."

Brian thought of Julia. "I could never forget."

"Wrong word. Try fill-your-life-with-other-things. Emily filled her life with Jill and her friends and their kids, and making a home for Doug. Doug filled his with work. That was when he got involved in the management and marketing end of his business, and started to travel. Awful to say, but he would never have built the farm to what it was when he sold it, or have the business he has now, if that little boy hadn't disappeared."

"Emily would have been better off without any of it," Brian believed. "She lost the child, then the father."

"He supports her financially. It's more than some men do."

It struck Brian that as a husband, he hadn't been much different from Doug. Uncomfortable with that thought, he tried another. "Was Emily overprotective of Jill?"

"At times. But she knew she couldn't

smother Jill. Mind you, she never left that child alone in the car. She never left the child alone *anywhere* for the first few years of her life. She wasn't risking it. And she struggled later on, too. When Jill got so she wanted to walk to a friend's house, Emily was dying, but she knew Jill needed to do it, so she let her go. You have to respect her."

Brian pushed himself out of the chair. "Yeah. Well, I do, but that doesn't help her much, does it."

"Sure does. She needs support."

"She needs more than support. She needs a crystal ball to tell her what happened to the boy. She needs closure." He ran a hand along the back of his neck.

"Got any ideas?" John asked.

He had a few, but they were longshots. The case had been cold for years. It wasn't like new leads had suddenly popped up. Not now. Not before. Not even *bogus* leads. "Let me think about it. There may be a few things we can try. Can I hold on to the file for a while?"

"It's yours. But do me a favor. Don't say anything to her. Chances are pretty slim. Y'know?"

Emily was reading the morning paper when Brian arrived. She heard the Jeep pull into

191

the driveway and started to rise, intent on hiding — making the bed, doing the laundry, dusting the living room — anything to avoid a conversation, should he stop by on his way to the garage. She was feeling foolish, having aired her dirty laundry in front of a stranger.

Well, he wasn't exactly a stranger. At least, he didn't feel like one.

With that thought in mind, she slowly sat herself back down. She looked at the paper. She waited. She didn't look up, even when she heard him climbing the stairs, and when he knocked, a wave of renewed embarrassment held her still.

"I can see you," he sang through the screen.

Slowly she set down the paper.

"I have buttercrunch donuts."

She smiled at his shamelessness.

"And coffee. And time to talk, if you want."

Did she want? No. Yes.

She looked up finally and gestured him in. He promptly set a bag on the table, removed and uncapped two coffees, and unwrapped the donuts.

"You can't keep doing this," she said then.

"Why not?"

"I'll get fat."

He took the chair beside her and slid one of the coffees her way. "I doubt that."

She wrapped her hands around the cup.

"But you're right. I can't keep doing it. I start work Monday morning."

He was darling, striking a light note, but she couldn't forget their last discussion, which hadn't been a discussion at all, or a celebration, for that matter. She had run off in tears.

Awkward, she said, "You're feeling sorry about last night. But you shouldn't. I get down sometimes. It passes."

"I know about Daniel," he said softly.

Her eyes widened.

"I read the file," he explained.

Oddly, she felt relieved. She wanted him to know. Daniel was part of who she was. "It happened a long time ago."

"But it was never resolved. That has to be hell."

"Only when I think," she said with a crooked smile. "I try not to. It won't get me anywhere. If he isn't dead, he's certainly gone. I accept that." She studied her coffee cup. "I used to dream that someone who was desperate to have a baby walked by, saw him there in the car, snatched him up, and walked off, and that whoever it was, raised him well and loved him the way I did." She couldn't look at him. "Silly, huh?"

"No."

"But not likely. What kind of person would take someone else's baby? Not someone who knows right from wrong. How could that kind of person possibly raise my son the way I would?" She could feel the old panic rising inside her and took a steadying breath. "There was another dream. It had two possible endings. Daniel was taken by his kidnapper across the country to a remote part of Montana, where he was abandoned at a rest stop. The first ending had him being picked up and raised by a well-meaning soul who assumed he was abandoned by his parents."

"What was the second ending?"

"He wandered away from the rest stop and was raised by a pack of wolves." She looked up with a self-mocking smile.

But his eyes didn't mock her. They were silver-soft and sympathetic. "I'd be dreaming the same things, if it was my child. What does Doug say?"

Emily felt a catch at the sound of his name. When she was thinking about Daniel, she wasn't thinking about Doug. Two sources of pain and confusion. Room for only one at a time.

She considered lying. But only for a

194

minute. Brian was her friend. She wanted him to know. "Doug says nothing. He deals with Daniel's kidnapping by pretending he never existed."

"How can he do that?"

Since they couldn't discuss it, she could only guess. "Daniel was the first child, the son. He was handsome and responsive and quick, everything a father could ask. Doug can't cope with the pain of what might have been."

"Does that bother you?"

"Sometimes. On Daniel's birthday." Her voice cracked. She stared at her coffee for a minute before swallowing and continuing. "I can't forget giving birth to Daniel. My body knows it happened. It remembers the contractions. It feels them again."

"Was Doug in the delivery room with you?"

"Yes. But he's never home on Daniel's birthday."

"Geez."

"It's okay. I mourn by myself."

"Does Jill know about Daniel?"

"She does now. But for a long time I couldn't say anything. I didn't want her fearing that the same thing might happen to her. I taught her the rules — tell us where she's going, go with other kids, run fast and yell loud if someone threatens her in any way — but I tried to make it sound like a standard precaution."

"Remarkable that you were able to be sane about it."

"The alternative was to make her neurotic," which Emily had refused to do. It was bad enough that she had left Daniel alone and unguarded in the car. To screw up Jill because of it would have compounded the error.

"How did she react when she learned about Daniel?"

"She kept saying there had to be something we could do to find him. I tried to explain that everything had been done, and that too much time had passed. She accepts it now, like I do. You can't keep living with something like that, day in, day out. I go through periods when I don't think of Daniel at all — like Doug, I guess — then something hits me, and I'm back there again, in that police station, reporting his disappearance, reliving the horror of it." She was reliving it now, feeling the jangles that came with total panic. "I thought they would find him. Really, I did. I wasn't in the post office for more than five minutes. He couldn't have gone far in that time."

She stopped. She did drink her coffee

then, for the warmth, and when she set it down, Brian took her hand. She clung to it. "I shouldn't have left him alone in the car. It was my fault. It wasn't like I was in a strange town," she reasoned. "If I'd been anywhere else, I never would have left him. But it was *Grannick*." She held his hand tighter, caught up in dismay. "No one saw a thing. John and the others interviewed half the town, but no one saw *anything*. It's bizarre. This is a provincial place. If you get a new car, people see it and spread the word. Same if you have a baby or get divorced. Gossip spreads fast. But no one was looking that day. No one saw *anything*." She caught herself and took a breath. She sat straighter. She gave Brian an apologetic smile and reluctantly drew her fingers from his. She tucked them in her lap. "He would have been twenty-one."

"Yes. John said that."

"Things are different today. Today, there's the National Center for Missing and Exploited Children, and networks like CJIS and NCIC. They circulate reports of kidnappings nationwide in no time flat. If Daniel disappeared today, the FBI would be crawling over the car picking up the tiniest traces of fingerprints and fibers. Photographs would be circulated by the millions.

The story would be carried by the networks, talked up by Oprah, written about in *People,* plastered on milk cartons. None of that happened back then."

She had been been driven wild by the frustration of it, wanting to do more when there simply wasn't more to do. She had pushed and pushed, until the pain of hitting that brick wall again and again and again had finally numbed her. Only then had she ceased.

"Want to see his room?" she asked. When Brian's eyes went wide, she stood. "I dust there, but I haven't touched it otherwise." Nor had she shown it to anyone else. But it seemed right that Brian should see.

Knowing that he would follow, she set off. She didn't stop until she had climbed the stairs, and gone down the hall to the only door that was closed.

She opened it and stood aside to let him in, then leaned against the door frame staring back down the hall, and even then the pain hit her, a wound unbandaged, raw and inflamed, even after all this time. She didn't have to look to see the lineup of tiny matchbox cars, the stuffed animals, the Lego blocks. She knew when Brian was looking at the picture books lined up along the bookshelf, and when he opened the closet door to see the little boy clothes that hung there, and when he lifted one after another of the many pictures that had graced the living room mantel before being banished by Doug. As she stood against the door frame, looking away, she was enveloped in the baby smell that had been Daniel nineteen years before, and though she knew that it couldn't possibly still exist, her memory brought it back and made it real.

She pressed her fingertips to her forehead, determined not to cry, but the emotion rose in her and wouldn't be quelled. Daniel had been so small, so helpless, so innocent. She had played with him when she dressed him, singing, laughing, hugging him afterward, all chubby little belly, arms and legs wrapped around her. Then he was gone.

She cried softly, unable to help herself, and when Brian drew her to his chest and wrapped his arms around her, she continued to weep. She couldn't remember when she'd had the luxury of crying over Daniel in someone's arms. So she indulged herself, until her tears slowed and she pulled back.

Leaving an arm around her shoulder, he guided her away from the room. She heard the door close and felt a weight lift from her chest. Freed, she drew in a long, shuddering breath.

He led her back down the stairs. At the bottom, she took an in de pen dent breath, wiped the tears from her face, and stepped clear. She threw him a self-conscious smile. "Now you know."

He had his hands in his pockets. His eyes were silvery warm. "Now I know." Voice and expression were both so gentle she nearly started crying again, not for Daniel, this time, but for everything she didn't have with the one man she should.

She told herself there was still hope. But with Doug in England for another full week, she felt helpless.

So, later that morning, when the small apartment over the garage suddenly filled with the newly delivered furniture and the contents of Brian's Jeep, she helped unpack. She loved arranging furniture. She loved hanging pictures on the walls, helping set up Julia's crib, putting bright little toys on shelves in her room. She loved going with Brian to buy plants and lamps and food. She loved watching the apartment take on warmth with each little touch, and when he invited her to join Julia and him for a dinner to christen life there, she couldn't turn him down.

EIGHT

Emily arrived at Celeste's on Sunday morning with her arms filled.

"What did you *bring?*" Celeste cried in dismay when she opened the door.

"I'm making brunch."

"Not for me. I'm dieting. I need a thin body to go with my face." She turned her head for Emily. "What do you think?"

Emily studied her face, one side to the other. She had liked the old Celeste. This one was still a little strange. "The swelling is definitely down."

"Emily."

Emily smiled. "It's an adorable nose."

Celeste turned so that Emily could see behind her jaw. "The stitches came out yesterday. See how thin the scars are. They'll fade to nothing. Same with the black eyes. Actually, the green eyes. Yellow's next." She rubbed her hands together. "Everything is going according to plan. By the time I'm looking human, I'll be getting responses from my ad. The deadline's tomorrow. I want you to help me with the wording."

Emily was more inclined to try to talk her out of placing it, and was about to say so, when Kay pulled into the driveway.

Celeste grinned. "Ahh, good. Three heads are better than two."

Leaving her at the door, Emily went back to the kitchen. She was making brunch whether Celeste ate it or not. It was an exercise that Emily needed to perform.

The two joined her moments later, Kay with an agenda of her own. "Emily, has Jill talked with Dawn?"

Emily removed fresh bagels from the bag. "Not for several days. She keeps getting the machine."

"Same with Marilee. What's she doing, Celeste?"

"Beats me," Celeste said.

"Hasn't she called?"

"Oh, yes."

Emily set a melon on the counter. "And?"

"She says she's fine. When I ask what's happening, she says she's really busy and that everything's great. When I ask for details, she gives me the details of something totally irrelevant."

"Wily child," Kay remarked.

"She says I'm too controlling. Am I too controlling?"

Emily busied herself slicing the melon. She had never thought of Celeste as controlling. Fixated on grades, perhaps. But only because she wanted Dawn to succeed.

"Am I?" Celeste prodded when Kay, too, remained still.

"No more so than us," Kay said with tact. "But you have more to control. Dawn's wild streak is wilder than Marilee's or Jill's."

"Well, Dawn will be fine. Trust me. If she doesn't study, she'll flunk out, and if she does that, she's back home with me." Celeste made a sound. "Don't know who that would punish most, her or me." She cleared her throat. "Moving on to important things." She opened a folder. "How does this sound. 'Sexy blond DWF —' "

"You aren't blond," Kay said.

"I will be. 'Sexy blond DWF —' "

"Not 'sexy.' It's too flagrant. You have to be more subtle. Think of the kind of man you'll attract leading off with that word."

"Precisely," Celeste admitted. "I don't want a eunuch. I want a red-blooded American male. Besides, if I'm subtle, my ad will just fade away. Trust me, bold is the way to go."

"Use 'intelligent.' It's more classy."

Celeste sighed. "Okay. Intelligent. 'Intelligent blond DWF.' " She made a face. "Doesn't have the same ring."

"Maybe you ought to tell more about yourself," Emily suggested in a half-hearted attempt to join in. "You could say you're slim and witty —"

"Let me finish. 'Intelligent blond DWF whose second life is just starting is looking for tall knight in shining armor to share Montrachet, Harley, and Tanglewood.' "

"Harley?" Kay cried. "Celeste, you'll get *bikers.* You'll get leather and tattoos and group sex."

"I will not. I'll get someone like me who thinks young."

Emily began cutting the cantaloupe. "You haven't mentioned your age."

"Should I?"

"Yes."

"You certainly can't hide it."

"Kay," Celeste protested.

"What she means," Emily said, turning around, "is that unless you decide to hide Dawn, whoever you date will know you're older than thirty. You wouldn't have had her when you were twelve."

"I could have. I might have been a child bride."

"That's John's latest line of worry," Kay

said. "He asked how I'd feel if Marilee got pregnant. Like I haven't taught her the facts of life. Like I haven't *drummed* safe sex into her."

"How would you feel?" Emily asked. She much preferred talking about the girls to talking about shopping for men, though either was preferable to thinking about Doug.

Kay considered the question. "I wouldn't be thrilled. I like to think she's saving herself."

"Realistically."

"Realistically? John would have the old shotgun out. Not that I think he'll need it. Marilee wants an advanced degree. She knows she can't get it if she does anything irresponsible. How about you? What if Jill had a baby this young? How would you feel?"

Emily didn't have to give it much thought. "Worried. I think eighteen, nineteen, whatever, is too young."

"You were married at eighteen."

Oh, yes, she had been indeed, and look where she was now. "Maybe it was wrong."

"Wrong?" Celeste asked. "How?"

Emily wrapped her arms around her middle. "We were very young. We've grown up into different people."

"Different from each other?" Kay asked.

Very different. Irrevocably different. Emily had pretended it wasn't so for weeks, months, maybe longer — but it was too obvious to be ignored anymore. She ached when she thought of Doug, ached from the realization that her marriage wasn't right and never would be.

She wanted her closest friends to tell her she was wrong. "Jill was our link. With her gone, there isn't much else."

"There must be."

"You're just feeling blue about Jill."

"No," Emily insisted. "I've made allowances for that."

Celeste threw a hand in the air. "Well, damn it, you and Doug might have something if he was ever around!"

"I don't think he wants to be."

"Why do you say that?" Kay asked.

Emily smiled sadly. "I can fool myself all I want — I can let myself be fooled by what Doug says — but he doesn't have to travel as much as he does. He has an office at home equipped with state-of-the-art electronics. He could cut the travel time in half and still pull down the same income."

She paused, waiting. She looked from Kay to Celeste. "No one's arguing."

"Have you told him this?" Celeste asked.

"No. I haven't admitted it to myself until now."

"Will you tell him?" Kay asked.

"I guess. At some point. Unless things suddenly take a turn for the better." When neither Kay nor Celeste said that they would, she made a pained sound. "It's a lousy situation."

"What do you want to happen?"

"I don't know."

"I think you should confront him," Celeste declared, and that was fine and dandy. Celeste was already divorced. She wouldn't be threatened by a confrontation. She had nothing to lose.

Emily did. "I don't know as I'm ready to face the consequences," she admitted. "I'm barely able to *think* of them. Anyway, that's why I don't want Jill to get married so young. I want her to be older and wiser. Same with any potential husband."

"Doug was older than you were."

"Not old enough. We were kids then. We've grown into different people."

"I feel so badly."

"Is there anything we can do?"

She shook her head and managed a smile. "One of these weekends, Doug will be home for more than a day. We need time together. That's all. One good talk could clear the air. I'm not throwing in the towel yet." She cleared her throat, ready to change the subject, since she hadn't heard any miracle cure for her woes. "In any case, I want more for Jill. Your turn, Celeste. How would you feel if Dawn had a baby so young?"

Celeste didn't answer.

Emily could tell from the look on her face — from Kay's, too — that they were reluctant to leave the subject of Emily's marriage. "There's not much more to say," she told them softly. "I don't know what's happening, I just don't, and it hurts to dwell on it. I need you guys to cheer me up. So answer me, Celeste. How would you feel?"

Celeste was another minute in putting the issue of Doug aside, and then she was subdued. "I'd hate it. I'm too young to be a grandmother."

Kay pointed out, "At forty-three, you're young enough to really enjoy a grandchild."

Celeste shook her head. "Not yet."

"Have you told Dawn that?"

"In no uncertain terms. I've also told her — God only knows how many times — that she has the brains to do great things in life, assuming she doesn't mess up. She says she may not want to do great things in life."

"What does she want to do?"

"She doesn't say."

"Doesn't she want a career?"

"Who knows."

"Haven't you asked?"

"Dozens of times."

"Aren't you curious?"

"Kay, *enough,*" Celeste complained. "I can't answer your questions. Good God, you're starting to sound like John."

Kay looked from Celeste to Emily. "Want to hear the latest? He suggested we fly down to Washington next weekend. To sightsee." When Celeste barked out a laugh, she added, "He said we could stay at a nice place and make a romantic weekend of it."

Emily felt a pang. She had been planning romantic weekends for Doug and her not so long ago. At the time, Kay had expressed envy. Now the tables were turned. "And you thought he wasn't a romantic," she chided, but she was distracted, wondering whether Doug was enjoying London, whether *he* was sightseeing, whether his client was pleased with his work and what that would mean for her marriage.

"John isn't a romantic," Kay was saying. "Nor is he interested in sightseeing. Monuments and museums bore him to tears, and then there's his back, which acts up whenever he has to do something he doesn't like. No, he doesn't want to sightsee."

"He wants to visit Marilee," Celeste suggested.

"*Spy* on Marilee," Kay corrected. "He must be bored with work. Or going through a midlife crisis ten years late. In any case, Marilee told him she was worried about Dawn — knowing, I'm sure, that he would get on Dawn's case — and he's been grilling me ever since, so if I sound like him, indulge me. No doubt he'll meet me at the door wanting to know what you know."

Celeste sighed. "Dawn is eighteen years old. She says I'm controlling. Well, I'm done being controlling. She's on her own, all of ten minutes away."

Emily wished Jill were that close. Then again, maybe it was just as well that she wasn't. Emily needed time before she saw Jill to figure out what was going on with Doug.

"You aren't nervous at all?" Kay asked Celeste.

"Of course, I'm nervous, but she's at a top school, with top kids, and she's no longer a minor. She's free to make her own mistakes."

"But if you can help her avoid —"

"How?" Celeste cried. "I can't *be* there. I *can't*."

In that instant Emily realized that Celeste

210

wasn't as ho-hum about Dawn as she acted. It was reassuring.

"So," Celeste said in the same, frustrated voice. "Is the ad okay?"

Kay scowled at her, then snatched up the paper. "Take out the Harley part. It may discourage a great guy who drives a Porsche."

It was a brilliant tactic, Emily thought.

Celeste crossed out the Harley part.

"Better still," added Kay, "make it generic. Say fine wine, adventure, and song. And give your age."

"Okay," Celeste said in a mollifying way. " 'Sexy blond DWF —' "

"I thought you changed 'sexy' to 'intelligent.' "

"Not if I'm cutting out 'Harley.' It'll be too tame. 'Sexy blond DWF, 40 —' "

"You're forty-three."

"Why don't I say forty-ish?"

"Because then they'll think you're forty-nine."

"No, they won't."

Kay skimmed the personals Celeste had clipped from the paper. "Most of them list their ages. Here's one who doesn't. She says she's looking for a doctor between the ages of thirty-five and forty-five. How old would you guess *she* is?"

"Forty-five," Emily said.

Celeste didn't answer.

"Why not thirty-five or younger?" Kay asked Emily.

"She would have listed her age if she were younger."

"Bingo. Without specifics, people assume the worst."

Celeste threw up a hand. "Okay, okay. I'll list my age, but it goes against my grain. My age shouldn't matter. I may be forty-three in body, but I'm twenty-five in spirit."

"Yes, well, that may be true," Kay conceded, "but men don't look at things that way. It's the in-body figure they're most concerned with."

Emily thought of the weeks it had been since Doug had reached for her with anything remotely akin to passion. She had chosen to blame it on exhaustion, but many an exhausted guy wanted sex, and then there were the mornings when he wasn't exhausted at all. It was like he had outgrown her physically, too.

She didn't understand how that could be. She had turned him on once. Wasn't chemistry a constant? She hadn't gained weight. She wasn't lined or gray or stooped. Okay, so everything hung a bit lower than it had twenty-two years ago, but she was still attractive.

Wasn't she?

"Emily."

She looked up to find Kay and Celeste standing before her.

Kay touched her arm. "You look tortured. Maybe you should spend a few days here with Celeste."

"I'd love it," Celeste coaxed. "I have room."

But Emily wanted to be back in her house, in case Jill called, in case Doug called. Like the plates beneath the earth's crust at the time of a quake, the underpinnings of her life were shifting. All she could do was to take shelter under the most stable structure she knew, and wait it out.

She drove home after brunch, with the best of intentions. Having spent all of Saturday with Brian and Julia, she was determined to leave them alone today. Julia needed to bond with Brian. Brian needed to grow more comfortable with Julia. They needed to make the new apartment theirs without Emily's intrusive presence.

She had no sooner entered the kitchen, though, when she spotted Myra coming around the garage from the direction of the apartment. Curious, even a bit concerned, she went outside.

Myra instantly veered her way. "I've just had the nicest visit with Detective Stasek and his daughter. What a lovely man he is. I'm afraid I caught him before he'd had a chance to shave, though. I hope I didn't embarrass him. Did you know that he grew up in Chicago? Imagine, Grannick having someone so worldly on our own police force. I brought daylilies from the garden, and when Detective Stasek didn't have a vase, I went and got one of mine."

"That was sweet, Myra."

"It's the least I can do. I still can't believe that he's living right here on our street. The police department has been needing someone new. Chief Davies has been here too long."

Emily defended John. "He does a wonderful job."

"He's too old. He doesn't see things. No, we need a fresh eye. Detective Stasek will be good for us." She frowned. "Funny, you'd have thought his wife would have had a vase or two. Most women do."

"I'm sure she had some, but he left most of their things behind."

Myra nodded. "Because of the memories. I can understand that. But it's good to preserve them, sometimes. That's why I tend the ground around my willow. Willows can be messy things, growing so large, what with all that pond water to drink and that moist earth to spread their roots in. Did you know that the upper portion of my willow nearly exactly duplicates what's underground? Nearly, mind you. Not exactly."

Emily let her ramble. Myra was a bit weird when it came to her willow, but she was a kind woman. It couldn't have been easy for her, living with Frank, who had been mean to the core. Emily had heard him roar many a night.

She had never suffered anything like that with Doug. He rarely raised his voice, certainly never raised a hand. She was lucky, in that sense.

Maybe she was being too sensitive. Maybe it was the Jill-leaving blues, after all. Maybe she was being selfish, expecting him to be around all the time. Maybe she expected too much, period.

"You know," Myra was saying, "I remember what you said about the detective not wearing a uniform, being a detective and all, and since that's the case, I'm going to have him over for tea with Frank. Do you think he would clean himself up if I invited him? Frank doesn't like beards. He says he wants to see a man's face when he's talking to him. He wants to know what he's up against. When he doesn't know, he gets angry."

Emily put a hand on her arm. "Myra, Frank is dead."

"Yes, but I think we should be cautious, anyway. Frank's anger is a frightening thing." She set off for her house.

Emily was watching her cross the cul-de-sac when Brian came quietly around the side of the garage. Indeed, he was unshaven and disheveled, nearly as much as the first time she'd seen him, but he didn't look at all desperate now — or disreputable, despite Myra's worry. Emily actually thought he looked wonderfully male, with bedroom eyes and a warm, welcome grin.

"Myra brought flowers," he said, letting the grin grow crooked and fun.

Suddenly, Emily wasn't brooding about Doug or longing for Jill. She felt oddly anesthetized. "So she told me. I hope she wasn't a bother."

"Nah. She's sweet, if eccentric. She wanted to tell me that the LeJeunes have rats. She's worried they'll spread to her place, or worse, the pond. She asked me how she would know if they did, and if maybe I would come over and take a look.

She worries about her willow."

Emily fought a smile. "Her tree is perfectly safe. The pond doesn't have rats, and neither do the LeJeunes. What they have is an exterminator who does his preventative thing every three months. His truck is shaped like a rat. Myra jumps to conclusions."

She let the smile come then, because Brian was smiling, and it was impossible not to catch his good mood.

He stuck his hands in the pockets of his jeans. "I came looking for you earlier. Julia and I were going for a walk in the woods. I was going to make you come so we wouldn't get lost."

"Obviously, you didn't. Get lost, that is." Though she would have loved to have gone. "Is Julia sleeping?"

"Soundly. The exercise wore her out."

"Sweet."

"She is."

Emily liked feeling happy. "Want a beer?"

"Sure."

She gestured him into the house, pulled two bottles from Doug's stock in the fridge, and handed him one. "This is my husband's last vestige of an earlier life. When we were young and poor, we preferred beer to cheap wine. Doug is into better wine now, but when he's watching a football game, he still wants a beer."

"When's he due back?"

"Friday."

"For the weekend?"

"Longer, I hope," she said in a nonchalant way that made her almost believe it. And why not? She had been making believe for years. "Let's go outside. We can sit in back and hear Julia if she cries." She grabbed the phone on the way out and led him to a shady spot beneath a gnarled oak. It was wide enough for both of their backs, with space to spare.

"This is nice," he said, settling against the bark. "Different from where I was. We had Central Park, but it wasn't like this."

"Did you take Julia for walks there?"

"Sometimes. Gayle did it more than me. The nanny did it more than Gayle." He snorted. "Was I ever a lousy father."

"Your work kept you busy," Emily offered.

"Yeah, well, that sounds good, and it was the truth, but it didn't have to be. I pulled my share of overtime. I didn't need to do that."

"You were conscientious."

"About work, sure. But what about Julia? My priorities were screwed up."

Emily shrugged. "Tradition says that since

218

you're the man, you're the breadwinnner, rather than the child-rearer."

"So look at me now."

She was doing just that. "You look pretty together to me."

"Right now, sure. I'm sitting here with the baby asleep and a beer in my hand and a beautiful woman beside me, but pretty soon the baby'll wake up and I'll have to find something for her to do."

"Why? She has toys to play with," Emily said, though she might have dwelt longer on the beautiful woman part. She was *starved* for comments like that.

"Toys aren't enough. You have to *do* things with kids."

"Uh-huh. Show them how to play with those toys. Read to them. Take them to the park. Mostly *be* with them. You could do whatever you'd normally do on a Sunday, and take Julia right along."

"She wouldn't appreciate the Mets."

"Well. Maybe not. But you could take her along for most else."

He was looking like he wanted to believe her. "What about kids' things. Like ballet."

Emily tried not to smile, he was so serious. "She has a while to go yet."

"But what'll I do when the time comes? I don't know anything about ballet. I wouldn't know the first thing about putting her in a tutu. I wouldn't know the first thing about buying one."

"There's a ballet store in town. They'll answer your questions."

He was frowning at the grass, then at her. "I don't know the first thing about buying her clothes, period. Okay, she's set for now, but pretty soon she'll be outgrowing the things she has. I haven't ever bought her clothes before."

"It's easy."

"Fine for you to say. You're a woman. You've been through it all. But it won't be easy for me. I have enough trouble buying my own clothes."

"Brian," she insisted, "it's *easy*. You'll drive to the nearest department store, go to the children's section, and tell the salesperson what Julia needs."

He was skeptical. "How will I know what she needs?"

"You'll know. When winter sets in, you'll know that she needs something warm, so you'll look at the snowsuits, and the one-piece suits are going to look much easier to put on."

"What if Julia doesn't like it?"

"Tough," Emily said gently. "She'll wear it anyway. By the time she's older, the two of you will walk into the store, and she'll tell you which one she likes. Before you know it, she'll be shopping for herself."

"What about her hair?"

"Most snowsuits have hoods."

"I mean, what about haircuts and braids and bows and other things little girls like?"

"I've seen your bows. They're good."

He made a doubtful sound and looked off.

She touched his arm. "You'll do fine. Look how far you've come. Look at all you're doing for Julia that you weren't doing a few months ago."

"Necessity is the father of invention."

"Isn't most of life that way? When it gets so that you can't do anything with Julia's hair, you'll go to a hair shop and have it cut. When you start having to cram her feet into her shoes, you'll go to a shoe store and get her new ones. When her teeth start rotting and falling out —" He shot her a horrified look. She squeezed his arm. "Just kidding."

"When do I have to start with the dentist?" he asked weakly.

"When she's three."

"What about toilet training?"

Emily sat back. "That depends. Jill was ready when she was eighteen months. Daniel couldn't have been bothered even at

221

two." Thought of Daniel brought an old, familiar ache. More quietly, she added, "Maybe he was punishing me ahead of time for leaving him alone in that car."

Brian faced her. "Did you know that, statistically speaking, there are more abductions in small towns than large ones? People in small towns live and breathe trust. It may not be wise, but what's the alternative? We can't live like we're under siege. Hell, that's why I left New York and came here. You weren't remiss, Emily. My guess is you were a better mother than most." He sighed. "No parent is perfect. You sure have answers to things that drive *me* to a cold sweat in the middle of the night, and I've seen you with Julia. You're a natural."

He seemed genuine — not at all patronizing, like Doug had always been. She had never completely believed Doug's denials. Brian, she did believe. She figured it had to do with his being a cop. And an impartial observer. And having eyes with an eerie power.

They were truly stunning eyes — shiny in the way of steel, without the hardness — and, yes, otherworldly. If he said she hadn't done wrong, she hadn't.

"Maybe I should open a day-care center," she said only half in jest. She knew Doug wouldn't hear of it, much less guarantee a loan. "I was counting on the apartment taking several months of my time. But it's done now, and the work I want to do in the house won't take long. So, who will I be then?"

"You're a writer."

"That book was a once in a lifetime thing."

"Did you enjoy doing it?"

"Yes. It was therapeutic. Writing's always been that for me." She studied the grass. "I kept notes after Daniel was taken. They kept me sane." She tugged at the sleek green blades. "Maybe I'll do more writing for the *Sun.* Or for friends at the college." Doug didn't have to know about either. "Of course, Jill will be home in three and a half weeks, then for Thanksgiving, then again in December, and it'll be for a whole *month* then. And long before that I'll have Doug."

"Next weekend."

"Uh-huh. That's right."

Doug had little to say. He arrived Friday evening, professing to have eaten on the plane, and after briefly allowing for Emily's questions about London, left to work out at the health club in town. When he returned, he sank down in front of the television, where he stayed until after she had fallen asleep waiting for him. When she awoke in the morning, he was the one who was asleep.

She studied his face, looking for softness, familiarity, hope, but felt distanced. She didn't know why. In sleep, certainly, his features were no different from before.

She tried to put herself back several years, lying like this, looking at him when things had been better between them, but the only such memories she had went back to the time when they were newly married. And, perhaps, when Daniel was a baby. She remembered the three of them lying in bed, remembered looking from Daniel to Doug and back, marveling at how lucky she was.

She couldn't remember lying in bed with Doug and Jill. But Jill had come after Daniel. Emily had done far less lying around feeling lucky and far more running around — trying to please Doug, wanting to mother Jill, needing to compensate for her one tragic lapse, which they never, ever discussed. She had learned to follow Doug's example and keep her thoughts to herself, about Daniel and, increasingly, about the rest of Doug's life.

She assumed that was the distance she felt now. She wished she were imagining it, but as the weekend passed, it became more and more clear. She and Doug rarely discussed anything. Nor did she confront him on it.

He was home for such a short time that she didn't want any unpleasantness. So she watched him push aside his orange juice, saying that he preferred pineapple juice, and she nodded sweetly when he asked if his shirts would be ironed on time, and when she suggested going out to dinner on Saturday night and he opted for a movie instead, she didn't argue.

Something inside her snapped, though, when she saw him with Brian. She had been wanting them to meet. But the juxtaposition was too much, the differences between them too stark. There was Brian — wearing jeans, a sweatshirt, and no shoes, carrying Julia, who was dressed the same — talking with Doug, who wore pleated pants, a pressed shirt, and polished loafers. Brian smiled more, skillfully directing the conversation from the apartment, which he took Doug to see, to the fiscal management of Grannick, to the horsepower of Doug's precious car.

Beside Brian, Doug looked one dimensional and stodgy. Brian looked warmer and kinder and far more attractive to her. And that infuriated Emily. She was angry at Doug for being so strange and superior and aloof, and angry at herself for making the comparison to Brian. Excusing herself, she fled into the house.

Minutes later, Doug joined her and said with enthusiasm, "He's a nice guy. I'm glad you have someone like him here with you, while I'm away. I worry about your being alone."

She gave him a sharp look. "I've been here alone for years, and you've never worried."

"You've always had Jill."

"Jill's my daughter. It's not the same as having you around."

He stared at her, then at the wall. "Don't start in."

"What's happening, Doug? We see less and less of each other at a time when we should be seeing more and more."

He rolled his eyes. "We've been through this before."

"But I don't understand it. You talk like the money you may make tomorrow will be the difference between staying afloat and going under, but it doesn't make sense. Your business is thriving — and yes, we have bills," she said before he could, "but they aren't any greater than anyone else's."

"I have a child in college."

"So do millions of other people, and they survive. We aren't spendthrifts. We lead frugal lives. At least, I do."

"What is *that* supposed to mean?"

"All it means," she said with a sigh, "is that we should have more than enough money to keep us comfortable, college tuition and all, so why can't you stay home more? You did, before Jill left."

He put his hands on his hips and faced her. "Business has picked up."

"Turn some down. Take time off."

"But I like the direction my business is going."

"You like being on the road five days a week? Six, sometimes? You don't want to spend time at home? *Ever?* Or will you just do it when Jill is home? For show."

He sighed. "What are you suggesting now?"

For a split second she considered backing off, but she had come too far and was too upset. Her sole concession was to lower her voice. "What do you want from our marriage?"

"A place to come home to." He looked around. "This house, this town, you, Jill."

"What do I do for you, besides wash your clothes?"

"You're my wife."

"Do you like being with me?"

"Of course I do."

"Eight days a month."

"Emily, what is *wrong* with you?"

227

She squeezed her eyes shut, touched her forehead, shook her head. Maybe it *was* her. Straightening, she dropped her hand. "I don't know who I am. I don't know what I'm supposed to be doing or where I'm supposed to be going. How am I supposed to fill my time? I can only fiddle around the house so much. After a while everything's done, and then what?"

"You want to work." He threw his hands in the air. "Christ, Emily, we've been through this one, too. You're not qualified to *do* anything. All you'll do is bring in a piddling amount that will raise our taxes and make a mountain of paperwork for me." He headed for the door. "Why can't you just — just watch television?"

She went after him. "I am *not* unqualified to do anything. I got my degree."

"Yeah. In English. That degree, plus two bits, won't buy you a cup of coffee."

She reeled, but only for a minute. Then she was following him up the stairs. "That isn't true, Doug. There are lots of things I could do. But you don't want me to work."

"For reasons I've explained a dozen times. Why don't they sink in?"

"Because they don't make sense. And they aren't fair."

He swore under his breath and turned into

the bedroom.

She hung on the doorjamb. "I need to do something. I can't just sit around here."

"Why not? My mother did."

"She had a husband."

He glared at her. "Her husband didn't do the kind of work I do — *or* make what I do."

Finally, an acknowledgment that he wasn't on the verge of bankruptcy. "But what good is the money, if we're not happy?"

"I'm happy. I'm perfectly happy. At least, I am when you're not on my back." He shot her a withering look. "Ease up, huh?"

Emily did draw back then. She went outside to the pond, and stayed there until Doug came out to say goodbye. Nothing had been solved. She felt worse than before.

But she feared that if she pushed he wouldn't come home at all, and if he didn't, her marriage would be well and truly over, and if it was, Jill would be hurt.

That worried her most — which was interesting, since there were so many other things that should worry her, too, like what would become of the house if her marriage ended, how she would pay for food and clothes, what in the devil she would do when her failing car fell apart.

Only then, sitting by the pond with Doug off and gone again, and the whole of her future looming ahead, did she realize just how dependent she was.

NINE

Emily sat by the pond until it grew dark. For the first time, she wasn't concerned about missing a call from Jill. She didn't know what she would say if Jill did call. Lying about having a lovely weekend with Doug was growing harder, and Jill, bless her, always asked.

Jill was Emily's best friend. They could hug each other. They could cry on each other's shoulders. Emily was desperately in need of both a hug and a cry just then. But she couldn't tell Jill what was happening.

She thought of calling Kay or Celeste. They came in second to Jill in the best-friend category, and she was sure they would be wondering how the weekend had gone. But she didn't call them. She felt too bottled up, even for that.

For the first time in years, she wished she had a mother who would come and hold her and not demand a word. That was what

Emily did for Jill when something upset her too much for talk. The holding helped loosen the congestion inside, and the talk inevitably came.

But Emily's mother had been dead for a long time, and even in life, she had been cold. Widowed early, she'd had to work to support herself and her daughter. She never let Emily forget it.

Emily had no siblings. Contact had long since been lost with what few aunts, uncles, and cousins there were. There was no one at all to call.

So she sat for a while in the dark. When the night air cooled, she went inside and made a cup of tea. Then she sat in the dark again, this time in the living room with the haze of a smoky clarinet rising from the stereo.

The phone rang several times, once from Jill, once from Celeste. She let the machine take both and didn't move, other than to curl more tightly into herself.

The music was long done when she finally rose and went upstairs. From the bedroom door, she studied the remains of Doug's stay. The closet and a bureau drawer were open. A shirt was thrown over the arm of the chair, a stray sock lay on the floor by the bed. Miscellaneous change was on the nightstand, mostly pennies.

Like a tip! A *lousy* tip!

Wheeling away, she raced down the stairs, threw on a jacket, and slammed out the door. She hit the sidewalk at a savage pace, kept it up to the end of China Pond Road, down Walker, down Sycamore, and onto LaGrange at the Berlo estate. She didn't see much of what she passed. Her mind roiled with anger at Doug.

Don't start in — when she said she wanted him home more. *What is wrong with you* — when she tried to pin him down about his feelings. *You're not qualified to do anything* — when she broached the topic of work. And when he was tired of talking — *Ease up, huh?*

He didn't listen, didn't understand, didn't care. She had to get through to him. But she didn't know how, which was pathetic. They had been married for twenty-two years. They had a daughter they loved. Emily didn't want a divorce.

The question was whether she could survive, alone this way. She had so much to give, so much love and caring that she was choked by it sometimes.

She passed through the center of town, crossed the street, and started back. Her pace grew more sane as her anger wore itself out. In its place was a deep, dark, familiar hole that took away all the warmth, the hope, the pleasure of life. She had always thought it had Daniel's name on it. She wondered now if it didn't have Doug's.

She zipped her jacket, tucked her hands in its pockets, and pulled up the collar. Even then she shivered.

Shadows lurked on either side, but she didn't look as she passed. She kept her eyes straight ahead, her thoughts focused on reaching the house, climbing into bed, and burrowing under a mountain of blankets. She figured she might stay there forever.

Foolish thought. But she couldn't think of a better one.

She tried to clear her mind by concentrating on breathing in, breathing out, relaxing the muscles of her thighs, her arms, her back as she walked, but the chill fought her, tightening everything she tried to loosen. By the time she reached China Pond Road, she gave up the struggle. Eternity under a mountain of blankets was sounding less foolish with each cold step.

She was nearly home when she saw him, sitting on her steps, rising when she approached. She slowed. Her knees were startlingly weak, given the stiffness of her legs, but they managed to take her to where he stood.

"I saw you leave," he said. "Are you okay?"

"Oh, God," she breathed in a sigh. "I wish I knew."

When he opened an arm, she moved into it. She felt it close around her, felt a large hand press her head to his chest, felt intense relief. If there was impropriety in the embrace, she didn't care. He was warm and strong. She figured that absorbing even a teeny bit of either quality would be an improvement.

She didn't know how long they stood there, he with his arms wrapped around her, she with her eyes closed and all responsibility for herself and her life momentarily forgotten. She relaxed as she hadn't been able to do on the walk home. She inhaled his warmth. She made a small sound of pleasure, then one of protest when he started to pull back.

"You're freezing," he said in a half-whisper. "Let me get you inside."

Inside was his place, and she didn't argue. The apartment was pleasantly messy, but peaceful. It didn't hold the memories for her that the house did, now that it was renovated and filled with Brian's things.

The hot chocolate he gave her felt good going down. So did his presence. He was wearing a sweatshirt and sweatpants, and he wore them well. So she simply sat and let the sight of him do for her what his arms had outside.

He settled beside her on the sofa. "Better?"

She nodded. She held her hot chocolate in both hands and kept her eyes on him.

"Julia said 'Daddy' tonight. Screamed it actually, in protest. I was changing her. She has a diaper rash. I wasn't sure what to do."

"Try zinc ointment."

"Zinc ointment?"

"It's messy, and it smells, but it usually does the trick."

She wondered what it was about Brian that she found so appealing. Feature for feature, he wasn't as handsome as Doug, but the overall package was far more appealing. It was masculine, yet approachable. More than approachable. Hard to resist.

Not sure about the direction of that thought, she hitched her chin toward the folders that were strewn on the coffee table. "What are you reading?"

"Files of all the juvenile offenses committed in town in the last few years. John wanted to wake me up. Kids here aren't as innocent as I thought."

"You're talking about the vandalism." In

recent months there had been a rash of minor incidents — spray-painted graffiti, broken windows, even a cemetery desecration.

"Vandalism seems to be in vogue right now, but there's still the occasional truck race at the quarry and the more than occasional orgy on the railroad bridge. The races and the orgies are the work of the trade school kids and coincide with their school schedule. The vandalism is more random, a little something here, a little something there. Individuals may be behind it, rather than a gang. I'll see what I can pick up at the high school. I work pretty well with kids."

"And to think you're afraid of Julia," she teased.

"Julia's mine. That's one difference. Another is that she can't communicate."

"Many high school kids can't either," Emily said, and felt instantly hypocritical. She wasn't communicating with Brian about what had sent her out walking. Her reason? She liked being with him. She didn't want to taint that time with her problems. She didn't want to dwell on those problems, period. "Have you been to the school?"

"Not yet. I needed a cop's view of the town first. Sam Webber's been taking me with him on patrol."

"I haven't seen Sam in a while. We were together a lot while we were doing the book. How is he?"

"Fine, I guess. Wary. I'm the new guy on the force." He waved the problem away. "But it'll get better." His hands fell between his knees. He regarded her expectantly for a minute. Then he sighed and smiled.

In that instant, Emily wanted to set down her drink and return to his arms.

Thinking better of it, she set down her drink and rose. "I'd better leave you to your work."

He was beside her before she reached the door and followed her down the stairs. At the bottom, she turned back and focused in the general area of his chest. "Thanks."

"I didn't do much."

"You did. Believe me."

"I wish I could do more."

She closed her eyes against the torment of having Doug distant and Brian close, Doug cold and Brian warm. It was a complication in what had become for her a terribly complicated world. She didn't need it.

Ah, but she did. When Brian drew her close, her arms went around him. She breathed him in and thought improper thoughts, and when a humming began inside, she enjoyed it — but for only a brief, forbidden minute. Then she drew back and with a guilty little smile, let herself out.

Early Monday morning, Brian strapped Julia into the back of the Jeep, tossed his files into the front, and was about to follow them in when he glanced at the house. There was no sign of life, unusual for Emily, who customarily had the kitchen door ajar. Granted, it was a cool morning. But she hadn't brought the newspaper in either, and she usually did that before seven. After last night, he was concerned.

He fetched the paper from the front walk, climbed the steps, knocked, and waited with a hand on his hip and his head bowed. When there was no response, he knocked louder. He shaded his eyes and peered inside. Everything was neat. There was no sign of mayhem.

Not that he expected it. Not from Emily.

But then, he hadn't expected Gayle to be hit by a car. He had shown up too late to do anything about that, but if Emily's upset of the night before had taken a turn for the worse, and if he walked off just like her asshole husband and came back too late, he would never forgive himself.

He tried the bell, though she must have

239

been roused by his knock, because he had barely removed his finger when he saw her making her way through the kitchen, tying a robe. She ran a hand through her hair, opened the door, and gave him a groggy smile.

He felt suddenly foolish. "Hey. I'm sorry."

She shook her head. "Not your fault. I was the one who overslept. I had trouble falling asleep."

Brooding about her husband, no doubt. "I'm sorry for that."

She repeated the headshake, repeated, "Not your fault."

"Well, I'm sorry, anyway." A noise came from the car, but he ignored it. Emily was more needy than Julia just then. "Certainly sorry I woke you. I was worried. I hate seeing you down."

He wished she would tell him about what had happened with Doug. It couldn't have been rewarding, not with her clinging to *him* the way she had last night.

But she didn't betray her husband. All she said was, "I'm better, I think." She gave him a tremulous smile. "Thanks for caring."

"I do." What to blame it on? The vacuum left by Gayle's death? The inherent unfairness of Emily's situation? The fact that she was his landlord or that, as a homemaker, she was an endangered species? Or, simply, that she was small and vulnerable-looking? Whatever, he felt protective.

So he handed her the paper. "Go back to bed."

"I might." Her gaze dropped a notch. "Neat tie."

It was a garish thing, toned down by a white shirt, jeans, and a venerable corduroy baseball jacket. He was about to say something about establishing his identity in the department, when Julia cried again.

"Your fan club calls," Emily said with a glance at the Jeep.

"We're stopping at the drugstore. Zinc ointment?"

She nodded, then waved when he pulled out of the driveway. Holding the image, he headed for town.

Content now that the car was in motion, Julia was a pretty picture in his rearview mirror. He had tried something new this morning, letting her play in the bath while he shaved, then rinsing her off with him in the shower. She hadn't loved the shower part as much as the bath part, but he figured she would get used to it. It sure had saved time.

"How ya doin', toots?" he called back. "Feelin' good? So am I." He kept picturing

Emily waving him off. "Look at those trees!" They were red and orange, vibrant in the autumn sun. "They didn't look like that in New York, let me tell you, not even in the park."

He wondered how much she remembered. "Mom-mee."

Lots, apparently. "Mommy's not here. Just Daddy. He's going to take you to the drugstore, then to Janice's. Where's bunny?"

He breathed a sigh of relief when she waved the rabbit in the air. Yesterday he had forgotten it and had to turn around and go back. He had been late getting to work, which hadn't bothered John any, but Brian sensed that the others had noticed. Sam wasn't the only one wary of him. They all were. Not only was he the new guy on the block and from *New York City,* but he was a detective lieutenant, answering only to John.

Brian wasn't desperate for the approval of the others on the force. He wasn't looking for tight friends, didn't have time for them, what with Julia. But good rapport would make for a more pleasant work environment, and in the absence of heart-pounding, adrenaline-pumping, sweat-popping criminality, a pleasant work environment would be nice. Showing up late two days in a row wouldn't help.

He nosed into a space in front of the drugstore, jumped from the car, and was halfway across the sidewalk when he heard Julia's protest. Backtracking, he pulled open the door and leaned in. "Zinc ointment. That's all I'm getting. Two seconds. It'll be easier if you stay here."

"Ah-kahhh."

"You don't want to keep bunny company?"

"No."

He sighed and reached for her. "Okay. Let's make this quick." Tucking her under his arm, he strode into the store. The owner and his wife were in their daytime places. "How are you, Harold?"

"Not bad, Detective."

"Zinc ointment?"

"Last aisle over."

Brian went to the last aisle over and found the ointment in a snap. Figuring that between the ease of that and his brilliance in putting Julia in the tub earlier, he might just be on a roll, he headed for the photo booth at the back of the store.

Digging into his pocket, he pulled out a handful of quarters. "Let's give it another shot, toots. One good one. That's all Grammie wants. You, me, and my neat tie. She'll be thrilled." He slid into the booth. "No, no, baby, don't stiffen up. Just take it easy, take it easy while I get these things in." He fiddled with the quarters, but Julia was arching her back and twisting, and just when he finally managed to get the first quarter into the slot, a loud buzzer sounded outside the booth.

Julia broke into a wail to rival the buzzer, which went on and on and on.

Brian ducked out of the booth. Muffling her cries against his shirt, he unsnapped the service revolver holstered under his jacket, and stole around the back of the aisle for a view of the cash register.

Harold was there, calmly talking with a teenaged boy. The buzzer stilled. Harold's wife, Mary Elizabeth, joined them. Neither Harold nor Mary Elizabeth seemed threatened.

Straightening, Brian relaxed his hold of Julia, whose cries subsided into sniffles. Snapping his revolver back into place, he approached the front of the store.

The boy looked to be seventeen or eighteen and, judging from his clothes, well-off. He wore tan bucks, designer jeans and shirt, and a jacket whose butter-soft leather oozed style. His backpack was high-end L.L. Bean. It lay open on the counter, having disgorged the large bottle of vitamin C that had set off the alarm. Harold held it now, along with two candy bars.

"I must have dropped it in there when I went for my money," the boy was saying, sounding neither apologetic nor embarrassed.

Harold spoke quietly. "Do you want to buy it?"

The boy dug into his pocket and pulled out a twenty.

"Everything all right here?" Brian asked.

Harold shot him a quick look as he rang in the sale. "Just fine. No problem."

Brian wasn't sure he believed that and glanced around, wondering if the boy had accomplices, if a greater threat lay beyond the immediate action. He didn't see anything more suspicious than a shiny new sports car waiting at the curb.

When the boy pocketed his change and headed for it, Brian put the zinc ointment and a five in Mary Elizabeth's waiting hand. "Was it an accident?" he asked Harold, who shrugged. "Has it happened before?"

This time the shrug was more a quirk of the brows. "He isn't a bad boy."

"What's his name?"

"Richie Berlo."

"Berlo, as in the walled-in mansion on the corner of Sycamore and LaGrange?" Brian passed the place every day on his way into town. Sam had given him a rundown on the money behind it, which would easily explain the car and the twenty.

"The same."

"Does the father know the boy has a problem?"

"It isn't really a problem."

True, the boy didn't have a rap sheet. Brian would have noticed if there had been a file among those in the car. Still. "Shoplifting is against the law. Why else do you have this alarm system?"

"Look, Detective," Harold said lightly, "I know what you're thinking, and you're right, the alarm's there to catch thieves, but Richie Berlo is the son of Grannick's biggest donor. Nestor Berlo has built us a library and a senior citizens center, and he's a major donor to the college, and the college means business for us." He chuckled. "It was only a bottle of vitamin C, and the boy did pay for it. I'm only sorry the alarm upset your daughter."

Brian took the tube of zinc ointment and his change. He wasn't worried about Julia, who had quieted nicely. "You may not be doing that boy a favor by looking the other way. It's sending him a bad message."

Harold only smiled and shooed him out

the door.

Brian might have stayed to argue if he had more time, but he had already spent longer at the drugstore than he intended, and by the time he left Julia at Janice's, picked up coffee at Nell's, and drove to the police station, his mind had moved on.

The department had two computers. He had hoped to use one to type up the notes he had made after reading the juvenile records, since John wouldn't ever be able to decipher his scribbles. But both computers were in use when he arrived, so he picked up the report from the night before.

There had been one drunk driving arrest, one suspected prowler, one heart attack, and one stolen car — a tame night, by Brian's standards, a typical one by Grannick's.

Setting the report aside, he checked the computers again. When he found them still in use, he went to John's office. "Got a minute?" he asked from the door.

John waved him in.

He wandered along the side of the room with his hands in his pockets. "I reread the file on Daniel Arkin. I take it you weren't in charge of the case at the time." He wanted to know how freely he could speak without insulting John.

"I was assigned to Emily and Doug. Chief called the shots. Say what you want."

Brian accepted the invitation. "The investigation left some holes. There were people in the post office at the time of the abduction who were never questioned."

John wasn't fazed. "They were inside the whole time. They said they didn't see anything. Chief didn't see the point in pursuing them as witnesses."

"Sometimes people see things without knowing it. One of them might have gone out for a smoke, or seen something out of the ordinary inside but thought nothing of it. There were also people in the stores across the street who weren't questioned. The owners were, but not their customers."

"Chief felt that in a town like Grannick, if any of those had seen something, they'd have come forward on their own. He didn't want to badger."

Brian stopped at the desk. "Christ, John, a little boy disappeared. It might have been worth the badgering."

John held up a hand. "I'm just telling you Chief's rationale. Most everyone knew Emily. Most everyone liked her. Chief assumed that for her sake alone, anyone who knew anything would have come forward."

Brian sighed. "Well, that sounds good, but

you and I both know it doesn't always work that way. What if someone saw another person, a friend, or the friend of a friend, doing something suspicious, and didn't want to implicate that person?"

"Emily talked with some of those others who were in the stores. She was asking questions long after we stopped. She couldn't let it go. Not that she was loud about it. She just kept after us in her own quiet way. I did some extra questioning on my own. Once I got to know her, I had a personal stake in it. But there was only so much I could do then, once Chief said enough, and now, well, a lot of them are gone, moved on to other places."

"Why didn't Emily?" Brian asked. "You'd have thought she would want to go someplace where there wasn't a painful memory around every corner."

"She can't leave. This was the only home Daniel knew. As long as the case is unsolved, she'll stay here."

Brian felt the pain of it. "She's a prisoner, then. That's doubly why I should question whoever I can find."

John remained skeptical. "Memory fades, after all this time."

Brian disagreed. "It's not like we're asking about a random day on the calendar. Everyone who was living in town at that time knew when Daniel Arkin disappeared. My guess is that anyone who had a potential lead hasn't forgotten a thing."

"Do you think the boy might still be alive?"

Brian dropped into the chair. "No. But I don't see the harm in questioning the people we missed the first time around. I'd also do a computer enhancement of Daniel's picture, to come up with something of what he might look like today, and I'd do a fingerprint match."

"Huh. Where you gonna get a fingerprint." It wasn't a question.

"From one of the little boy's picture books. They're still in his room. Fingerprints spread as they get larger, but the points and loops stay the same. I'd also do a computer cross-check on kidnappers who were at it when Daniel was taken. And I'd work through a list of Grannick's sex offenders."

John drew back.

"Doesn't it make sense?" Brian asked.

"We weren't thinking that way in the seventies."

"There were sex offenders then."

"Sure. But we didn't blame them for every crime, and we didn't put their names on a list. Not in Grannick. Not until two years ago."

Brian was astounded. "Why not?"

"Because these are our people. We don't like compromising them. If one of our own does something wrong and serves his time, we feel he has a right to come back here and start over with a clean slate."

"So why'd you start doing it two years ago?"

"Had to. The college appointed a professor who had served time for rape, the locals learned about it, and made a stink. Personally, I had no problem with him. He'd been five years at another school before coming here, and his record was spotless. Stayed spotless, too. But a lot of people were nervous. So the right to public protection took precedence over the right to privacy."

"I take it your list is confidential."

"Sure."

"So the right to privacy is respected, too."

"Except if guys like you want to dig up the list and start questioning the people on it."

Brian couldn't *not* look at that list. "If someone abducts a little boy and never sends a ransom note, you rule out greed as a motive, right? So what's left?" He thought of Emily's dream. "It'd be real nice if it turns out that someone just wanted a baby to raise, but the chances of that are slim. The truth is that among kids abducted by strangers, the majority are sexually violated."

"He was just a baby."

"No matter, to a crazy."

John was scowling. "Have you mentioned this to Emily?"

"Christ, no."

"Don't. It'll make her sick."

"You think she hasn't imagined it?" When John didn't answer, he said, "You can be sure she's following every missing child case that gets coverage, and what she doesn't imagine on her own, the media paints in living color."

John was quiet.

"Let me give it a try," Brian urged. "I'll be subtle. There doesn't have to be a formal reactivation of the case."

"Start questioning people," John warned, "and word will spread. It always does, in Grannick."

"I'll say we're cleaning up loose ends, tidying up the files, and in a sense that's all we are doing. I'll say I'm new here, that the case fascinates me, and I thought this would give me a chance to meet some of the townsfolk. They'll buy it."

"What about Emily?"

"Not a word. She accepts that he's dead. I can't raise her hopes, what with the odds against us after all this time."

John looked torn. Finally, he grumbled, "Keep it quiet and unoffensive. If word gets back to me that you're antagonizing people, I'll call it off. Hell, it's not like something new just came up. It's not like we suddenly have a concrete lead. It's just you, falling hard for Emily Arkin."

Brian held up a hand. "Hold on. The lady's married."

"Try to remember it, huh?"

It was one thing to remember that Emily was married, and another to stop thinking about her. Brian liked her a lot. Something about her made him feel calm, even now, when he knew that her life was as unsettled as his. When he saw her, or thought about her, he felt a deep, curling warmth.

It wasn't sexual. At least, he didn't think it was. He doubted he could be thinking about sex, with Gayle barely cold in her grave and Julia a full-time occupation on top of the other.

If he was ready to be interested in sex, he could be interested in Emily. But he wasn't ready for that. Just for friendship. And as

Emily's friend, he was worried.

That was why, with Julia happily chasing dandelion fluff beside the white picket fence, he rapped on the kitchen door on his way home from work that night. Oh, yeah, a deep, curling warmth. There it was, when she opened the door.

"Hi," she said softly.

He studied her face. "You look better. I wanted to make sure."

"I went back to bed after you left."

"And slept?"

"And slept," she acknowledged.

Her smile lingered, toying with the corners of her mouth in a way that heightened the deep curling warmth he felt, and at that moment it struck him that the attraction was sexual after all — unless he was misinterpreting what he was feeling down low, the pooling that came from her smile, or from her petiteness, or from the hint of breasts under her sweater, or from the memory of their feel against him the night before.

"So." He cleared his throat. "What did you do, today?"

"This and that. Lazy things mostly. I talked with Jill. She sounded good. That always gives me a lift."

"When will I meet her?"

"Two and a half weeks and counting."

Julia ran over, holding up a partly denuded dandelion.

"Ohhhh, pretty," Emily said, going down the steps, dropping to her haunches, and drawing her close. "Did you blow?" She gave a noisy demonstration, then moved the flower close to Julia's mouth. "You try. Blow. No? Okay. How about we shake it?" She gave the flower a sharp shake. When the fluff flew in all directions, Julia squealed in delight, reaching, jumping, squatting. Emily laughed at her, then gave the flower another shake, setting Julia off again. When the flower was nothing but a stem, Julia ran off for more.

Brian was smiling when Emily stood. "It's good to hear her laugh. Good to hear you laugh, too. Are you meeting your friends tonight?" It was Monday, after all.

"Uh-huh."

"Will you talk with them?" He meant, about the weekend, about Doug.

The waning of her smile said she understood. "I think so."

"It helps to share," he said, and because she was a friend and he felt the need, he drew her into a quick, close, bolstering hug, before returning to Julia.

Myra saw the hug from her dining room

window and couldn't have been more pleased. She didn't for a minute think that Emily was doing anything improper — not Emily — but the closer she and the detective grew, the better.

He was the key. Myra just knew it. She could feel it in her bones, along with the arthritis that kept reminding her of her age and frightened her no end, given all there was still to do.

Back in the kitchen, the table was set, the ham ready. She cut a neat slice for herself and two for Frank, and arranged them on plates, put a small potato on her own and a large one on Frank's, then added green beans and a dribble of raisin sauce. Pleased with the pretty picture, she put the plates on the table.

"Dinner's ready, Frank!" she called and began to eat. "This is very good. What a perfect size ham. I'll be able to make a package for Emily and one for the detective." She took another bite. "And I'll mash the potatoes for the little girl. Children love mashed potatoes."

She wondered when Julia's birthday was, thinking that a party under the willow would the *most* delightful thing. But something told her that the birthday wasn't until spring. She couldn't possibly wait that long.

October was already here. If she didn't do something soon, the ground would freeze and the snow would come, and then all hope would be gone until the thaw. But she *couldn't* wait that long.

A tea party wasn't right. The detective wouldn't be interested in that, any more than her sons had been, and she had certainly invited them often enough. Dinner, perhaps. Or a cookout. Yes. A cookout. Emily would bring the grill, and Myra would do the rest.

But it had to be soon. Fall was here. The leaves were changing.

She glanced out the window toward the pond, and in the next instant was jumping up from her chair, scurrying out the back door and down the steps.

"Shoooo! Shooooo!" she cried and watched the Canada geese fly off. "Messy little pests," she muttered, "doing their business under my willow." She scrutinized the grass there, relaxing marginally when it appeared to be clean. She bent to pluck up the few bits of lint that had gathered in the short time since she had last been out. Then she sat down on the scrolled wrought-iron bench and envisioned the day when she could relax completely, when she would be unburdened and safe. She ached for that day, ached so badly sometimes that she terrified herself, thinking that she was having a heart attack, or a gall bladder attack, or an arthritis attack that would paralyze her for good.

A cookout. That would be just the thing. A hamburger would lure him if he was anything like her sons, and then once he was here, he would know. She wouldn't have to say a word.

That was the way she wanted it.

TEN

Another long week passed. Emily was plodding along in a state of limbo when she arrived at the Eatery Monday evening. After being buffeted in turn by highs and lows, she was emotionally bruised, and there were no answers in sight.

Grateful, at least, to know where she was headed at this very moment in time, she zeroed in on Kay and Celeste and headed their way, only to stop when she found Brian and Julia in a booth along the way.

Her heart skipped a beat, then resurged with a spill of warmth. Brian affected her that way. He was the one most often responsible for her highs.

"Hey," she said, smiling. Two pairs of pale blue eyes touched her, both mellow and warm. "How are you guys?"

"Not bad," Brian answered for the two. "Thought we'd eat out tonight." He shot a look around. "I figured this place would be empty on a Monday, but half the town's here."

"Recuperating from the weekend," Emily said. When Julia offered up a french fry, she took it. "What a sweet little girl. Thank you." She took a bite. "Mmmmm. This is good. Are you sharing with your daddy?" She smiled when Julia pushed a fry toward Brian's mouth, and kept smiling when he sucked it in like a piece of spaghetti.

Oh, he was bad, and sexy, and dangerously attentive, looking into her with those appetizing eyes of his. She half-wished she could scoot in and have dinner right here.

But she had more proper plans. With a glance over her shoulder, she said, "My dates are waiting. See you later?"

He nodded, and as she turned away, she thought about twists of fate. The tenant she hadn't wanted was turning out to be a lifeline for her. Brian was easygoing, understanding, and appealing — for which reason she should be keeping her distance, but she couldn't. She awoke each morning looking forward to seeing him.

Proper? No. Exciting? Definitely.

Still high when she reached Kay and Celeste, she slid into the booth with a grin. "Hi, guys."

"Is that Brian?" Celeste asked.

Emily slipped out of her jacket. "Uh-huh."

"Nice-looking guy. Very masculine."

"He has a child," Emily reminded her. "You're not interested."

"He has great eyes. I saw them on my way in. They stop you in your tracks, know what I mean?"

Did she ever. "Heeey, lookin' *good*," she said, scrutinizing Celeste's face.

"Well, *I* thought so," Celeste complained, "which is why I agreed to eat out again." She shot a disparaging glance at the Eatery's clientele. "Would you believe no one's noticed?"

"Isn't that good? You don't want them to notice. You want them to think you look wonderful but be too shy to say so, lest they imply that you didn't look good before."

"Emily's right," Kay said.

But Celeste remained doubtful. "There's still some swelling. They're probably thinking something's wrong with me."

Emily glanced around. She saw familiar faces, one after the other, and acknowledged a few before turning back. "Is anyone staring? No. And you know they would if they thought something was wrong."

"The surgeon told me to allow six weeks. It's only been four and a half."

"So, there you go," Emily said.

Kay turned to her. "You're chipper. Does that mean things went well with Doug?"

But Emily wasn't ready to talk about Doug. "First, you guys." To Kay, "How's school?"

"Great. The kids are finally getting into the swing of things. Summer vacation sets them back. It takes a full month to get them working up to speed again."

"Hi, Mrs. Arkin," said their waitress, Jenny Yeo. "Can I get you a drink?"

Emily saw iced teas sitting in front of Kay and Celeste. "I'll have the same. Are we ready to order?" she asked the others. She hadn't eaten an actual meal since brunch the day before, and she knew the Eatery's menu by heart. "I'm starved."

Celeste ordered the Southwestern salad, Emily chicken fajitas, and Kay nachos with extra hot cheese and jalapeño peppers, "Because I'm in a daring mood," she explained, and, when Jenny had left, said, "I've been lobbying for it for years, and the go-ahead just came through. We're starting a debate team."

"In eighth grade?" Celeste asked.

"Sure. Okay, so the debates won't be polished, but it's a great introduction to public speaking. We'll be competing around the state on Saturday afternoons."

"We, as in you, personally?" Emily asked.

"I am the adviser."

"Does John know?"

"No, but he won't mind. He doesn't count on me on Saturdays."

Emily wondered if that was by choice or default. Kay always seemed to have something to do on Saturdays that kept her occupied and out of reach. One year it was a community service project, another year a class-wide internship with the local newspaper, now the debate team. As noble as those activities were, Emily didn't know that *she* would immerse herself so totally, if she had as kind a man as John waiting for her at home.

"If we start the kids younger," Kay was saying, "we'll get them involved before they reach that disgusting stage where they're either too self-conscious to speak before a group, or too social to want to bother. Which was it with our kids?"

Emily thought back several years. "For Jill, a little of both. The self-consciousness came from social awareness. She wanted to blend in, not stand out."

"Marilee was self-conscious, long before she was socially aware. She didn't like her hair, didn't like her complexion, didn't know *what* to do with the things growing on

263

her chest."

"Dawn never had that problem," Celeste said dryly. "She is small-busted to this day, but defiant enough not to care."

"That's precisely why she won the Shakespeare competition last year," Kay suggested. "She isn't inhibited. She just went out there and gave it her all."

"Yeah. On two days' notice and with little preparation. I felt bad for those kids who spent weeks rehearsing. It didn't seem fair. I told Dawn that. She's going to want something someday and assume that it'll come just as easily, but it won't. She's in for a fall."

"She's very bright," Emily argued on Dawn's behalf.

"So are the other kids she's competing with now. If she doesn't study, she'll find herself at the bottom of the heap."

"So, is she studying?"

"She says she is. She says she loves it. I told her that if she wants to keep on loving it, she'd better buckle down, or she'll find herself booted out and back home with me, in which case I will be *furious* with her."

"What did she say to that?"

"She says she'd run away first."

"With a laugh, naturally."

"Unfortunately."

"But you have to hand it to her," Kay said. "She has guts."

"She gets those from me." With a flourish, Celeste drew a large manilla envelope from her lap and opened the clasp. "Are you ready?"

"Uh-oh."

"Responses to your ad?"

"My God, that's some pile."

"I'm not sure I want to hear."

"They're interesting," Celeste said and picked up the first. " 'Dear GC403' — that's my mailbox at the magazine — 'I am forty-eight and tall, and I do like fine wine, good music, and adventure. My ex-wives say that I'm no knight in shining armor, but I'm working on that.' "

"Ex-wives, plural?" Kay asked.

Celeste turned to the next letter. " 'Dear Sexy Blond DWF, Everything about you sounds great, only you don't say how much you weigh. If you are at all ashamed of your body, we aren't for each other. I am a practicing nudist.' "

"He's direct," Emily mused. She folded her hands together. "You're right. These are interesting." And certainly a diversion from the rest of her thoughts. "Go on."

" 'Dear GC403, I am a gastroenterologi-cal surgeon at Massachusetts General Hospital. I have degrees from the Choate School, Harvard, and Harvard Medical School. I have served on three different president's commissions and have published fifty-six articles in twenty-one prestigious medical journals in ten foreign countries.' "

"Humble."

"Wait," Celeste said with a grin, setting the doctor aside. "This gets better." She held up the next for them to see. "Hand-typed, single-spaced, at the very top of the page, with *no* letterhead." She read, " 'I am the presedent' — misspelled — 'of a large corperation' — misspelled — 'which has offices in New York, Texas, and San Antonio.' "

Emily laughed. "Celeste, these are *awful.*"

"Don't they get any better?" Kay asked.

Celeste nodded, still grinning. "But you gotta hear these, so you can appreciate the good ones." She waved a torn piece of paper. "Here's my ad. This guy circles it, writes in the margin, 'Send picture,' along with his own post office box. Screw him," she said with feeling and turned to the next. "Here we go. This one is sweet. 'Dear GC403, I am blond, too, and my friends say that I'm sexy, though since I don't turn myself on, I can't know that for sure. I am a SWM, who is six-four and into whitewater

266

rafting. When I'm not shooting the rapids, I am writing articles for a regional magazine. I love sitting by a campfire and making love under the stars. If you don't have a hang-up about dating a younger man, give me a call.' "

"Younger?" Emily asked. "How much younger?"

"He put his age as an afterthought at the bottom of the page, very small, like he really feels it's insignificant."

"How old?" Kay asked.

"Twenty-five."

"And he knows you're forty-three? He must have an Oedipus complex."

Celeste looked doubtful. "He does sound sweet, not to mention honest and interesting. Besides, there is something to be said for young flesh."

"Please, Celeste," Kay protested and turned to Emily. "Tell her she's nuts."

Emily couldn't do that. The man did sound sweet and honest and interesting. Not that Emily would want to date a twenty-five-year-old, if she were free. She would want to date someone her own age.

"Is that the best?" she asked Celeste over the rim of her newly arrived iced tea.

"No. Here's a cute one. 'I am forty-four, tall, dark, and handsome, and definitely sexy. I am a banker by profession. I am also an avid reader who has just discovered poetry and would like someone to discuss it with. I do feel that I have to be up front and tell you that I am currently serving two to five years at the federal penitentiary in Allentown —' "

"Let's hear the *good* ones," Kay prompted.

"You don't want to hear about the guy who says he's been a victim all his life?"

"No."

"Or the guy who says he likes black lace?"

"No."

"Okay." Celeste set down several of the letters. "Here. This one isn't bad. 'Dear Sexy Blond DWF, I am a fifty-year-old widower with three children. Now that my youngest has just left home to go to college, I am looking to form new relationships. I am British by birth, am chivalrous to a fault, and do indeed like fine wine, adventure, and song. If five-ten is tall enough for you, drop me a note.' " She looked up. "Think he might be too stuffy?"

Kay shrugged. "He says he likes adventure."

"But what if he's only saying that because I said it?"

Emily was uncomfortable with the prospect of Celeste actually going out with these men. "Isn't that what you have to ask yourself? How honest will any respondent be?"

"He doesn't say he's drop-dead gorgeous," Celeste reasoned. "He doesn't say he's ultra-tall. And he's certainly at the same stage in life as me. But if he's stuffy —"

Kay gestured toward the letters in her hand. "Read another of the good ones."

Setting the widower aside, Celeste skimmed over the next. "This one sounds straightforward. He starts off by saying that this is the first time he has answered an ad, but that he hates the singles scene almost as much as he hates being fixed up by friends. He says that he doesn't like dancing around issues, the way men and women often do. 'I am in health care management. I am also a marathoner, which means that I am tall and slim, but that I spend much of my free time training, so I don't have time to waste. I am looking for a woman who can be honest with me about things that she does or does not want to do.' "

"Hi, ladies."

"John!" Kay cried. "What are you doing here?"

He shrugged and looked idly around. "There was nothing doing at home. I figured

I'd take a ride. The car brought me here."

"Cute, but you can't eat with us. There are no men allowed at this booth."

He looked lonesome. Emily's heart went out to him.

"Whatcha got there, Celeste?" he asked.

"Here?" Celeste looked at the papers in her hand. "Uh, letters. Letters I wrote to my parents. At different times. Growing up."

He craned his neck. "Anything funny?"

"Nah," she said, pushing the papers aside. "Just girls' stuff."

"Ah." He put his hands in his pockets. "What'd you order?"

"Salads, fajitas, and chips," Kay said. "Did you see Brian over there?"

John looked around. "Huh. Maybe I'll go say hello. Join him for a cup of coffee. Looks like the baby's asleep."

Julia was indeed. Emily melted at the sight of them, her with her head on Brian's shoulder, and him with his back to the wall and his legs sprawled along the booth bench. He looked like he was half-asleep himself, though he gestured John over.

"Close," Kay breathed when he left.

Celeste made a noise. "I hate lying."

"You could have told him the truth."

"Really." She drew the papers front and center again. "So. What's the verdict on the

270

marathoner?"

Emily supposed that he was better than the others. "Not bad."

"A maybe," Kay decided. "How many more do you have?"

"Just two." Celeste lifted the first of those. " 'Dear Sexy Blond DWF, I was attracted to the part of your ad that said your second life was just beginning. I feel that way about mine. My wife of twelve years recently left me for a childhood sweetheart.' "

"Poor guy," Kay said.

Celeste read on. " 'I'm a veterinarian, with a successful practice. Since I've always loved animals, I consider myself fortunate to be doing something that I find satisfying. Many people don't have that. I am not a playboy, but I am a romantic. I much prefer intimate dinners at home, eaten in front of the fireplace, to dinners at fancy restaurants. I like Bach, Beethoven, and Liszt, though I have been known to go on easy-listening binges with the likes of the Eagles, Cat Stevens, or Simon and Garfunkel. I chop my own firewood, by the way. I am interested in meeting someone who will introduce me to new things, at the same time that she values my quiet life. I may be barking up the wrong tree answering an ad that starts with sexy and blond, but if there is

271

substance beneath the looks, please drop me a note.' "

"Whew," Emily said.

Kay agreed. "He sounds the most sane so far."

"Assuming he doesn't have a menagerie living in his house," Celeste cautioned. "But wait. I've saved the best for last. Listen." She read from the final letter. " 'Dear GC403, I'm not sure how to answer your ad. I'm not a hunk, though I am good-looking. I'm not an adventurer, though I enjoy trying new things. I'm a dark-haired, brown-eyed guy, age forty-one, six-foot even, one-eighty pounds, who designs houses for people with lots of money to spend. In the past, business has taken me traveling, but my name is finally established enough so that I can stay more in one place. I'm looking to put down roots, and at the same time cultivate the kind of relationship that my work always made difficult. Money isn't an issue. I want companionship and laughter. If love develops, fine. I'm old enough to recognize it, and young enough to make the most of it.' "

Celeste set down the letter. She raised speculative eyes. "Tempting?"

Emily looked at Kay. "He sounds intelligent, articulate, humble. There must be a catch."

"The catch," Kay told Celeste, "is exactly what *you* asked about Brian Stasek when I first mentioned him. Do you remember? You asked what's wrong with him, if he's forty and single. Brian's excuse is his wife's death. What's this guy's excuse?"

"His work," Celeste said. "As long as it kept him on the move, he couldn't pursue deep relationships."

"You said you didn't want to get married again," Emily reminded her.

"I don't. This guy doesn't mention marriage, and he only mentions love as an afterthought. But I have nothing against deep relationships." She came forward. "Look at it this way. He's a successful professional. He's well-traveled, which means that he has a certain worldliness. I'm sure that he still has to spend some time at whatever site he's designing for, so I wouldn't be stuck with someone hanging on me every minute. But then he works at home in a stunning studio that he has designed himself, and he's his own boss, so his hours are flexible. You heard him. Money is no object. The possibilities are endless."

"Assuming he's telling the truth," Kay warned. "How do you know?"

"I don't, for sure."

"You would make a date with him, not knowing for sure?"

"Yes, I would. I'd arrange to meet him for drinks somewhere very public, and tell him to look for the blond holding the rose. He wouldn't know my name, much less my address or phone number. If it doesn't work out, that's it, the end. He can't bother me further."

"What if he follows you?"

"I'd make sure he didn't."

"How?"

"Kay, there are ways."

"Like what?"

Celeste sighed. "Like climbing into a cab and having the cabbie drive around before delivering me back to my car. If I *really* think the guy's a problem, I'll make a beeline for the nearest police station. I'm telling you. There are ways."

"And you really want to risk it?"

Celeste stared at her. "Yes, I do. I have common sense and solid instincts. I am not getting into trouble with this."

Emily touched her arm. "We're worried. That's all. We don't want anything to happen to you."

"Nothing will," Celeste assured her and sat back, waiting for Kay's capitulation.

Their dinners arrived, a timely buffer. As though calmed by the act of separating a cheese-covered nacho from the pile on her plate, Kay said, "Okay. You're determined to follow through. What happens next?"

"I contact the ones who interest me and propose a meeting."

It sounded very clinical to Emily, but who was she to criticize. She had spent the day systematically taking apart her marriage, step by step, item by item. "Which ones will you contact?"

Celeste started on her salad as she separated letters from the pile. "The architect is the best. No doubt about it. Next in order of preference is the vet, the marathoner, then the widower. For good measure, I may just throw in the doctor and the twenty-five year old."

Kay gave her a pleading look. "Why the twenty-five-year-old?"

"Why not?"

"Because you're forty-three. You look great, Celeste, and not a day over thirty-five, but even then, you have ten years on him. He'll have smooth skin, unwrinkled hands, and firm thighs. You'll feel old beside him."

"If I turn him on, I'll feel flattered. Besides, I'm not ashamed of my body. Are you

275

ashamed of yours?"

"My body isn't an issue. John and I have been married too long for that."

"And John has twelve years on you. Why is it okay for the man to be older, and not the woman?"

"That's just the way it's always been."

"Not anymore. Not nowadays. There are plenty of relationships where the opposite is true."

"In Hollywood."

"Those are the ones we hear about, but there are others."

"Name some."

Celeste threw up a hand. "Uh . . . uh." She scowled. "It happens all the time. I just can't think of names off the top of my head." She looked away. In the next instant her scowl faded. "Yes, I can." She lowered her voice and leaned forward without taking her eyes off the person in question. "Cynthia Berlo. She's been involved with her husband's accountant for years."

"Pure rumor," Kay said.

"She's fifty-eight to his thirty-five."

"There's no proof they're involved."

"I heard it from Enid Hildridge, who does Cynthia's tailoring. Cynthia brought the accountant with her one day. They were all over each other in the dressing room."

Kay looked dismayed. "What in the world would a thirty-five-year-old want with Cynthia?"

"She happens to be in great shape."

"But she's *fifty-eight*."

"So? That doesn't mean she can't desire a man, or feel sexual pleasure, and it sure doesn't mean she can't turn a man on. Sex doesn't end with menopause, Kay."

"I never said it did."

"Guys," Emily broke in, putting a hand out to each. "There isn't any point in arguing, especially about Cynthia Berlo. She isn't a role model, by a long shot."

"I agree," Kay grumbled. "Comparisons to her make me ill."

"There *isn't* any comparison. We're talking apples and oranges. Celeste is smart and sane. Look, I'm nervous about her dating these men, but she's thought it through, and it is her life."

"What about yours?" Celeste asked. "How was the weekend?"

Emily sighed. She *still* wasn't ready to talk about Doug. Then again, she needed to air her angst. "Not great."

"What did he do?" Kay asked.

"Nothing. That's the problem. He comes home and goes through the motions, like going through the motions is enough. I sug-

277

gested we drive to Stockbridge; he shrugged. I suggested we buy lobsters and boil them; he shrugged. I suggested we go to a lecture at the college; he shrugged. It's impossible to get a rise from the man."

"Is he just tired?"

"If he were, he'd spend the weekend sleeping, but he doesn't. He's just not interested in doing things with me. I try to engage him in discussions about what's happening in the world — he prides himself on being out there in the middle of it all — only he won't be engaged. He gives an answer or two, then finds something else to do. It's like I bore him. Well, y'know, he bores *me*."

"Whew," Kay said softly. "That's quite an admission."

"Well, I can't keep defending him," Emily cried in despair. "I have no idea what he wants from our relationship. He has nothing to say to me, which is a statement, but I don't know what *of*. Does he want a dull, boring marriage to balance the other parts of his life? Does he want me to be different in some way I can't imagine? Or does he want a divorce?"

"Have you asked him?" Celeste asked.

"About the last?" Emily couldn't repeat the word. It shook her up. "Not like that."

"Maybe you should."

"What if he says yes?" Her heart thundered. She didn't want a divorce. She wanted things back the way they had been twenty-two years before — which was an absurd notion. She and Doug were different people from the ones they had been then.

Thoughtful, troubled, Kay said, "This isn't any kind of a life for you, Emily."

But she couldn't throw in the towel, not yet. "It's not so bad. I talked with Rod Meany over at the *Sun* last Thursday. He gave me a couple of assignments, little things that are more fun than substance."

"You deserve substance."

"I'll get that from Petra Drovski." Petra was head of the English department at the college. Emily had talked with her, too. "She needs help editing a collection of critical analyses of the works of American writers in the early 1900s. It's an interesting project."

"Won't keep you warm at night," Celeste advised. "Your husband is supposed to do that, on weekends, at least, but he's not here even then. Doug is involved in your marriage in name only."

Emily started to deny it. Only it was true. Name only. They hadn't really talked, hadn't shared laughs, hadn't *made love* in weeks and weeks.

"What are you going to do about it?" Celeste asked.

Emily couldn't exactly seduce him, not if he didn't want to be seduced, which was the impression he gave. "Keep trying, I guess. I can't just chuck twenty-two years. Parents' weekend is coming up. We'll meet in Boston. He promised he'd come. Maybe being together in a hotel will inspire him. Maybe being with me away from *here* will." It had occurred to her that Grannick might be the problem.

"Does Doug spend any time with Brian?" Kay asked.

Emily pictured the two men together, Brian head and shoulders above Doug, and so much more appealing to her that she was frightened. "They say hello in passing. That's about all. Why?"

"I'd think he would be jealous. There you are at home with a good-looking guy right next door. I'd think he would want to rush home and restake his claim."

Emily would have thought so, too. She remembered feeling guilty the first time she had referred to Brian by name. But Doug wasn't jealous. "It doesn't occur to him that I might even be remotely attracted to another man."

"Are you?" Celeste asked.

She was. Very much so. But she still hoped to salvage her marriage, so she said, simply, "Brian is a wonderful man. If I were the type to be unfaithful to my husband, he could tempt me."

"He could tempt *me*," Celeste said.

Kay swatted at her. "Oh, hush."

"Well, he could. Those eyes are something to do a strip-tease for. But he has a child. You can have him, Em."

Emily half-wished she could, more than half-wished it, if the truth were told. She had had a dream or two about Brian, and while her fantasies hadn't involved a strip-tease, neither dream had been pure. Both had awakened long-dormant feelings, both had raised guilt.

Far better, she decided, far safer and wiser, to concentrate on what she had, which was Jill, home in ten days and counting.

ELEVEN

John was leaning against a lightpost, looking idly down the street, when Kay emerged
from the Eatery with Emily and Celeste.
She told herself to be grateful he was there,
given Emily's woes. Still she felt vaguely
piqued. "I thought you'd gone home," she
said and followed his line of sight. "Is
something up?"

John was looking at her now. "Nah. Just
seemed silly for Celeste to have to drive you,
since I'm already here."

"But you left an hour ago." With Brian,
she had thought.

"I've been walking around. Caught some
of your students lighting up behind the
pizza house."

"Who?" An ex-smoker, Kay hated the
smell, sight, thought of the stuff, particularly
with regard to kids. She had every intention
of collaring the offenders the next day.

But John wasn't giving up names. "I

promised I wouldn't tell, in exchange for their handing over the smokes. I lectured 'em good."

She could believe that. It was some solace, at least.

He pushed off from the lightpost. "All set?"

No, she wanted to say. She loved Monday nights. She prized her time with Emily and Celeste. She didn't want to feel chaperoned, much less guilty for abandoning John for the evening. This was her time, and he knew it.

But it seemed foolish to stand on principle. Dinner was done, and John was here. Of course, he would drive her home.

To the others, she said dryly, "My keeper calls. Talk with you tomorrow?" When they waved her away, she set off beside John.

"Are you annoyed?" he asked.

Yes, she was annoyed. She didn't like being tailed. "There are times when I feel like you're checking up on me."

"Why would I do that?"

"Beats me. You're the one with the imagination."

"I wasn't checking up on you. I was bored, that's all."

The car was parked down the block — mercifully Kay's car, not the cruiser. He saw her in, rounded the front, and slid in behind the wheel. When they were on their way, he said, "The house is empty when you're not there. I hate it."

"I've been doing this on Monday nights for years."

"It was different when Marilee was home."

Kay steeled herself for questions. *When did you talk with her last? What's she doing? Who's she doing it with? Is she studying?*

None came. She glanced at him. His eyes were on the road.

"It'll be good seeing her," he said. "Having her around the house again."

Ten days until fall break. Kay was looking forward to seeing Marilee, too. Still, she cautioned, "Don't count on her just hanging around. All of her friends will be home, too. She'll want to see them."

"But we're her parents."

"She'll see us first, then she'll run out."

"But I want to spend time with her."

So did Kay, but she was a realist. "Parents aren't high priority for eighteen-year-olds."

"That isn't right. We love her."

They did, indeed. But that didn't warrant putting her under house arrest. "If we love her, we give her wings. She'll fly off and establish her independence, then fly back to us when it's time."

"When's it time?" he asked in a way that was a little pouting, a little impatient, and oddly endearing.

Kay smiled. "Not yet. She's just discovered how to work the wings. Give her time. She'll be back." She had read about what to expect. "Fall break can be tough for freshmen. They run to each others' houses in triumph, having survived seven weeks as cool college kids, then they race back to high school and discover they've been dethroned. Remember senior spring? Remember the headiness Marilee felt? She's thinking things will be the same, but they won't. It's sad. All rites of passages are. The old has to end to make way for the new."

"Huh. I'm not sure I like the new."

Kay sighed, thinking back to the evening's discussion. "You may not be the only one. The Arkins are having a time of it."

"How?"

"Emily is frustrated. Doug isn't much of a husband, and it's worse with Jill gone. She's wanting to do things, and he's as eager as a wet rag."

"Hard to be eager if you're never there."

"Precisely."

Kay thought about Emily through the rest of the drive. Of the three of them, Emily was the most vulnerable, the one who most

285

needed her husband, now that her daughter had left. Celeste was enjoying freedom, and Kay had her work.

Kay also had John, who, once they reached home, followed her into the house, through the kitchen, and into the hall.

"Will Emily be okay?" he asked.

She turned at the newel post. "For now. In the long run, I don't know."

He leaned against the front door, hands in his pockets, and frowned. "Bad timing. She loses Jill. She loses Doug." His frown deepened. "Things are different when the kids leave. The playing field changes. A new game starts."

Kay was bemused. John had never been one to talk in analogies. She hadn't thought he had it in him.

His eyes met hers.

He had something on his mind. Instinct — or simply his troubled look — told Kay he wasn't thinking about the Arkins. A new game? She didn't like the sound of that, certainly not if he was thinking about *them.*

When he didn't seem to know how to go on, she asked, "What's the new game?"

He shrugged.

"A new game for *us?*"

He studied the floor.

"John, are you trying to tell me something?"

It was a while before he said, "Maybe."

Her mind was scrambling to think of what that something was, but the only thing popping up was unacceptable. John loved her. He wouldn't want a divorce. He wouldn't want *another woman.* Would he?

Wary, she sat down on the stairs. "Is it bigger than a breadbox?"

His shrug was one-shouldered this time.

"John, don't keep me in suspense. Tell me what's wrong. Are you unhappy — with us, with *me?*"

"No," he blurted out, "but I wish we could do more together."

"More, like what?"

He gestured uncertainly. "I don't know. More."

"When? We work."

"We have nights and weekends to ourselves now. But you fill them up with other things."

He was *jealous?* "One night a week with my friends."

"I'm talking about the other stuff. The stuff for school."

"That's my job."

"Do you have to volunteer for committees that meet three nights a week?"

"I have seniority. They need me on those committees."

"Maybe I need you here."

"To do *what?*"

"I don't know. Something. And Saturdays. Why do you have to work Saturdays?"

"Because there isn't time during the week for some things."

"The unions don't bargain for Saturdays."

"Neither do most of my colleagues, but that's their problem. Mine is dedication."

She geared up to defend herself, but he only looked at the rug, shifted his feet, folded his arms over his chest. "You're the best teacher they have. And I know you like what you do." He raised his eyes. "But if you wanted to be with me, you'd make time for that, too."

Was he feeling *sorry* for himself? "Have I ever said I didn't want to be with you?"

"You're always making plans to be away."

Kay was mystified as to the cause of John's mood. She wondered if, at fifty-seven, he was going through the midlife crisis he had never gone through in his forties, or whether he was simply having trouble adjusting to Marilee's absence. In either case, she felt wrongly attacked.

"Remember when we were first married," she asked, "when I stopped working to raise

Marilee, and I was alone here, day after day and then nights, while you were putting in overtime to get your gold shield? Did I ever complain? Did I tell you you worked too much?"

"I was building my career. You understood."

"Yes, I understood. But it wasn't always easy. I was lonesome. I might have liked you home more."

He put his hands on his hips. "So you should know what I'm feeling now."

"I *don't.* You don't need help with a child. Or the house. Or food. You're a big boy."

"That's right. And big boys like big boy things."

"John. What *are* you getting at?"

He looked away. After a minute of scowling at the wall, he said, "Maybe I'm getting tired of working. How long does it go on? Until we die? We just work 'til we drop? Isn't there more to life than that?"

"What, more? What do you want?"

He made a grumbling sound. "It might be nice," he said, glancing at her, then away again, "if once in a while you'd touch me. Men like to know that they're loved."

She was taken aback. "You know I love you. I *tell* you so."

"You say the words."

"Isn't that the best way? Straightforward and direct?"

"It's one way. There are others."

"And I do them. I shine your badge and polish your shoes. I make dinner for you even when I'm going out to meet my friends. Aren't those ways of conveying love?"

He looked straight at her. "I'm thinking about physical ways."

She would have had to be dense not to catch his drift, and in that split second, taking in the whole of him as he stood braced against the door, she was swept back twenty-two years, a new teacher in Grannick chancing upon one of Grannick's finest. He had been striking in his blues, quiet in a way that made him all the more masculine, and so tender in the night that her inhibitions had eased.

She had been twenty-three then. She was far older now. But time had been kinder to John. At fifty-seven, he was an eminently virile man. He was tall, broad in the shoulders, and while not as narrow in the hips as he had been in his prime, tapering still. He had neither a beer gut nor a double chin. He had all his teeth and all his hair. It didn't matter that the latter was gray, it was striking. Likewise the lines fanning from the

290

corners of his eyes.

John Davies was a very attractive man, speaking aloud of physical needs for what Kay believed was the very first time. A self-conscious flush rose to her cheeks. "I can't believe you're saying this."

"I've been trying to say it for days."

"When?"

"I suggested we spend a weekend in Washington."

"To see Marilee."

"And to have time alone."

"We have time alone here."

"Huh. When I come near you, you're either reading or doing something for school. Even tonight. I was hoping you'd be pleased I came by to drive you home, but it didn't turn you on one bit."

Her color deepened. "For God's sake, John."

"What?"

"We've been married for years. We aren't teenagers."

"What's that got to do with anything?"

She opened her mouth, but no sound came out. *Clearly,* they weren't teenagers. *Clearly,* they weren't newlyweds. But as people grew older, they settled into routines, and the Davieses' routine wasn't highly sexual.

The thought that John might want it to be unsettled her. She hadn't married the playboy, but the stalwart policeman. It had been a long time, a dozen pounds, and a slathering of cellulite since she had thought of herself in sexual terms.

Feeling awkward and hating it, she looked at her watch. "It's late. I have to go over my lesson plan." She rose and, without a look back, went up the stairs to the spare bedroom she used as an office. She had put her notebook there when she had come home from school and now opened it and turned to the proper page, but that was the extent of her diligence. Her mind wasn't on lesson plans. It kept returning to John.

He wanted closeness, touching, sex. But she wasn't a physical person. She had been twenty-three when she had married him, and she hadn't been a physical person even then. Not that they hadn't had an active sex life. They had, but over the years the excitement had mellowed into a more relaxed pleasure. If they made love once every few weeks, that was fine. She was satisfied. She had thought he was, too.

After looking over the lesson plan for the third time without absorbing a thing, she closed the notebook and stood for a time at the desk, massaging the tired muscles in her lower back, listening for sounds of John. It wasn't until she moved quietly into the hall that she heard the television downstairs.

Okay. He was set. He would watch for a while, fall asleep, wake in an hour or two, and come to bed. She would be sound asleep, but he would snuggle close, and that would be fine. There was warmth in that. There was *love* in that. Wasn't there?

She asked herself the question all the way down the hall to the bathroom, and was no closer to finding an answer when the tub was filled than she had been at the start. Undressing quickly, she slid under cover of the bubbles.

She didn't have to see her body to know its shape and size, and it wasn't a *bad* body, as forty-five-year-old bodies went. It was straight and, cellulite aside, not terribly overweight. It had pleasant curves, but like an ice sculpture too long in the warmth, those curves had lost their crispness. The end result was lumps.

So she wore blouses that bloused around her waist and skirts that skirted her hips, and she stayed with neutral colors that never drew attention to her body. Her mind was the thing that counted, and it was in rare form, indeed sharper with age. She kept telling herself that. It was some solace for the fact that she had lousy hair, that her skin was thinner with each year that passed, that her hands were veined. She couldn't change those things.

She wished she were petite like Emily or leggy like Celeste. Or had the kind of metabolism that permitted eating french fries without gaining weight, or the kind of bone structure that looked spectacular from birth to death.

Mostly she wished John had never raised the physical issue, because, much as she wanted to be a femme fatale, there was no way in hell she could do it.

Ten days. Celeste studied her calendar. From the start her goal had been to be gorgeous by fall break — and she was going to make it, which meant that the first part of her game plan was complete. The second would kick in once Dawn was back at school.

There were six men on her list. Three of the six had given phone numbers for her to call — the marathoner, the veterinarian, and the twenty-five-year-old. Area codes told her that the marathoner was from eastern Massachusetts, the vet from Vermont, and the boy from upstate New York. The others had given post office boxes, one at the magazine, two at what she assumed to be home. If that assumption was correct, zip codes told her that the doctor was from Maryland and the widower from Connecticut.

She had no idea where the architect was from, but the added mystery made her all the more intrigued.

On her simplest white stationery, she jotted brief notes to the three with post office boxes. In each case she revealed little more than that she lived in western Massachusetts and was interested in meeting centrally for either lunch or an afternoon drink.

That was innocent enough, safe enough. John wouldn't panic.

As she finished each note, she gave it a light spray with cologne before sealing it up and setting it aside for a morning mailing. When the three were done it was after eleven, and while she might have liked to have phoned one of the others, now that she had gotten an okay of sorts from Emily and Kay, she was hesitant. The marathoner was forever in training. He would be asleep. Same with the veterinarian, if he put in as busy a day as she imagined a Vermont animal doctor might do. That left the twenty-five-year-old.

The boy. She had to smile. Kay was scandalized by that one, for sure. Not that

Celeste was seriously interested in him. She wasn't sure how much she would have to say to a twenty-five-year-old. Still, it was flattering to think that she could interest one. And she had to admit to curiosity about the sex. He was young. His body would be fresh, his energy boundless. And he was an expert at shooting the rapids. Talk about undulation.

While she had her money on the architect as the best of the batch, the twenty-five-year-old was a teaser.

She reread his letter — SWM, six-four, a writer. She had never been whitewater rafting, herself. She had never sat by a campfire and made love under the stars, as he said he liked to do. Jackson wouldn't have dreamed of those things. He hadn't been a spontaneous sort.

So why had she married him? At the time, she had been twenty-two and coming off four years of spontaneity to the extreme. She had managed to graduate from college, but barely, and hadn't the slightest inkling of where to go and what to do. Parentless and lost, she had needed a stabilizing force in her life. Jackson fit the bill.

He was a computer genius who programmed every aspect of his life, and he had stabilized hers, and then some. By the time Dawn was born, she'd had it with his directives. It was one thing for her to be organized to the *n*th degree in her own life, but with a baby? She couldn't do it. She didn't want to try. She'd had it with facing tests she was destined to fail.

In a hail of ugly words, no doubt exacerbated by postpartum depression, she had kicked him out — and he went. That had been his single greatest sin.

She had been defiant enough to stick with the decision.

Defiant still, she picked up the phone and punched out the telephone number the twenty-five-year-old had given. It rang twice before a voice on the tenor side said, "Hello?"

For a split second, she was tongue-tied. He sounded young, indeed. Then she steadied herself. "Uh, hi," she said with what she hoped was a certain nonchalance. "This is GC403." She kept her finger on the phone, ready to disconnect in an instant if this wasn't her man. He was tall. She had expected a deeper voice.

But it was a nice voice. "Hi, GC403," it said.

"Am I calling too late?"

"For me? No." She heard a smile. "I wasn't sure you'd call at all."

His frankness was welcome. She relaxed a little. "Neither was I. I'm still not sure I should be." Frankness deserved frankness. "It's possible you have a serious hang-up."

He laughed. "I don't."

"Then why did you answer my ad?"

"Because I was curious. I've dated women my own age. Now I want to try something different."

"Ahh. The adventurer."

"Isn't that what you want?"

"In a fashion," she said, though the age differential wasn't what she had initially had in mind. "I know that you're a rafter and a writer. Tell me more."

"I grew up in Schenectady. My parents still live there."

"Are you in love with your mother?"

He laughed again. "I'm the youngest of six. My mother was forty-one when I was born. That makes her a lot older than you are, nearly another generation. I love her, but she doesn't give me the hots. So, no, I wouldn't be thinking of her if you and I were to date."

"Well, that's good to know. How'd you train to be a writer?"

"I have a degree. Two, actually. BA and MA."

"In journalism?"

"English. Journalism is what pays the bills while I write the great American novel."

"I see. Then this — our conversation — any possible relationship — is research."

"No. It's life."

Celeste's phone clicked. "Hold on a second?"

"Sure."

She flipped into call waiting. "Hello?"

"Hi, Mom."

"Dawn." *Not* who she wanted to hear from just then. "Good God, you're calling late."

"I just talked with Jill. She's worried about her mom. Is Emily okay?"

"She's fine. But I'm exhausted." And otherwise occupied, sweetie.

"Jill was really upset. I was thinking it'd be cool if I went down to Boston to see her this weekend. Can I take the car?"

"No, you cannot. I need it. Besides, you'll be seeing her next weekend."

"But if I can help her now, isn't that what friends are about? She's always been there for me. It's only right that I be there for her. Besides, there is *nothing* going on here this weekend."

"No parties? I'd have thought the place would be hopping the weekend before fall break."

Dawn made a disparaging sound. "Everyone's studying for midterms."

"Shouldn't you?"

"I will. I'll bring books with me."

"You won't get any decent studying done that way. No, Dawn. You can't go."

"But I told Jill —"

"We'll talk about this tomorrow."

"Jill said —"

"I can't stay on the phone now, Dawn."

"But Mom —"

"Call me tomorrow. Good night." She clicked back to the twenty-five-year-old. "Still there?" she asked, wondering if he had given up.

"Still here," he said in his higher-than-expected voice. It struck her then, with the echo of Dawn's eighteen-year-old voice in her ear, that he was probably more suited to her daughter than to her. The thought was discomfitting.

"I'm sorry," she told him, suddenly needing a breather. "I have to pick up the other line. Can we talk more another time?"

"It's your call," he said with the kind of ease that suggested he didn't care deeply one way or the other, and that annoyed her. She wanted a man of conviction, not a wimp. She wanted a man who wouldn't leave, like Jackson had, without a fight. She wanted a strong man. *That* was adventure.

"Sure thing," she said and hung up the phone. It *was* her call. She would send out her notes in the morning and phone the other two within the next few days. With any luck, by the time fall break was done and Dawn returned to school, her calendar would be filled with dates.

Emily was looking forward to fall break with both excitement and dread. She was dying to have Jill back home, but not quite sure how Doug would be. Oh, he would be fine toward Jill. She didn't doubt that for a minute. But if he showed as much disinterest in Emily as he had been showing of late, Jill would notice. Emily didn't want that.

Her solution, reached after much silent debate, was to keep the weekend moving steadily along with events planned before, preferably with Doug's help, certainly with his approval. She intended to take care of that while he was home this weekend.

On Wednesday morning he called to say that he wanted to get ahead by working through the weekend, so he wouldn't be home until Jill was.

Emily didn't plead. She didn't argue. She didn't say a word in complaint, though one part of her wanted to ask what was wrong with her that he didn't want to be with her.

301

The other part was relieved. Weekends with Doug had become increasingly tense. Her stomach was always jangling, her heart thudding, her hopes and needs seesawing.

Okay. He would be home with Jill. This weekend was Emily's.

She took a long, deep, relaxing breath. She wrote up a short piece that Rod wanted on the coffeehouse that was opening at the church, and drove it to the newspaper office, then went out to lunch with Alice Baker, who was the copyeditor for the *Sun*. Halfway through, they were joined by Alice's sister, who worked at the library and insisted Emily return there to see several new books. By the time Emily was back home, most of the afternoon was gone.

Wandering into the yard, she climbed onto the rocks overlooking the pond, lay back, and basked in the sun. Its summertime heyday was done, its shaft lower and weaker, its pale light more precious. Come November, the mornings would be iced, the trees bare, the pond murky. Today, though, there was a lingering warmth enriching the scent of moist earth and crisp leaves.

As precarious as other things might be, her marriage most immediately, nature never changed. It was a comforting thought.

She lost track of time as she lay there. Her

mind whisked over the pieces of her life without dwelling on a one, but, rather, focusing on the breeze that rose to kiss her face and finger her hair. She stretched and settled, and suddenly new thoughts entered her mind.

She was forty and in her prime. Her major responsibility was no longer a major responsibility. She had easily as many years ahead as behind. And she was female.

The last thought came from nowhere, startling her, but she didn't chase it away. It wasn't unpleasant, given her mood. She felt sensitized, as she lay supine on her rock in the slanting rays of the late-day sun.

She heard the Jeep pull into the driveway, heard a door slam, then Brian's, "Hey, you! Where are you going? Come back here, you minx!"

Emily smiled at the sound of an explosive giggle and turned her head on the rock to see Julia barreling toward her, curls bobbing, arms waving. Brian caught her halfway and tossed her over his shoulder, prompting another round of giggles, before setting her down again. She hit the ground running, heading for the pond this time. Emily slid down the rock and headed her off.

"Oh, no, you don't." Wrapping her arms around the child, she bent over her from behind. "That water is cold and wet and too deep for a monkey like you."

"Laloo," Julia said, pointing at the pond.

Emily glanced at Brian, who had come up from behind.

"Water," he interpreted.

"Ahhh. Laloo. How did I miss that?" To Julia, she said, "Want to take a closer look?" She walked her to the water's edge, picked up a pebble, and tossed it in. "Look. See the circles it makes?"

"Laloo," Julia said.

Emily tossed another pebble, let Julia watch the ripples, then offered her a pebble. "Want to try?"

Julia closed her fist around the tiny stone, but when she raised her hand and tossed it toward the water, her timing was off. She didn't open her fist until the toss was done. The pebble fell to the ground by her sneaker.

"Ooops," Emily said and picked up another. "Here we go. Let's try again." It was two more tries before things clicked, and then Emily clapped Julia's hands together. "That was a good one! Good for Julia!"

Julia took over the clapping, grinning triumphantly at Emily, then at Brian. Emily sat beside her and gave her a hug. "Incredible, how they need our approval," she said to Brian. "Can you imagine a parent who doesn't give it?"

He was hunkering down nearby. "I've seen them. Their kids try most everything to get their attention. When they can't do it by fair means, they try foul, and even then the message doesn't always get across. Some parents don't want to hear."

"So what happens?"

"The kids spend time in detention. They mix with other troubled kids and hear about bigger and better stuff, and before they know it, they've forgotten about their parents and are wanting the approval of their new friends. It's a lousy cycle."

"How do you break it?"

"Beats me. Boot camps aren't the panacea some people hoped they'd be. You can give a kid a new self-image in a new environment, but put him back in the old environment, and the old self-image is back right along with the bad influences. So there's your answer. You don't put him back in the old environment. Unfortunately, in a democracy, you can't tell him where to go once he's done his time."

"That must be frustrating for you."

"Very. One of the biggest battles a cop fights is with his own cynicism. That's why changes are good sometimes. Like my moving here. I miss the action, but I don't miss the tension that goes with it. I'm sleeping better."

"The apartment is comfortable?"

"It's perfect."

He smiled at her then, making her feel feminine indeed. "When's Doug due back?"

Emily enunciated each word. "One week from tomorrow."

"Not this weekend?"

"He wants to get ahead, to make up for next week." When Brian looked disappointed for her, she said, "It's okay. Makes things easier, in a way." Feeling guilty and sorry and even, in that instant, angry at Doug, she took a quick breath. "I was thinking I'd do something special."

"What?"

"I don't know. I haven't gotten past something special."

"Julia and I are going exploring. We're heading north, letting the road lead us where it will. Want to come?"

She liked the idea. She liked it a lot. "That sounds nice, but maybe you and Julia should be alone."

"We're alone every night. I think she'd like the change. I sure would."

Emily went. They set off Saturday morning

heading north, had lunch in Hanover, New Hampshire, and walked around the town, then headed east toward the lakes of south-central Maine. They stopped there to let Julia run over paths strewn with pine needles, and then, because she was sleeping soundly in the backseat, and because they couldn't think of any good reason to turn back, they drove on. By nightfall, they reached the coast. They ate fresh boiled lobster in a rustic shack, with a fire going in the hearth to ward off the evening chill, and when the headlands were too tempting to miss at dawn, they took rooms at a nearby motel.

In her own room, nude under the covers, since she hadn't packed for the night, Emily lay awake enjoying her body's warm buzz. She hadn't felt it in a very long time, wasn't sure she had ever felt it before.

She didn't analyze it deeply, simply took it for the pleasure it gave, and the pleasure went on the next day, through breakfast, a morning walk on the beach, and the leisurely drive back home. She was feeling mellow when they passed the town limits and entered Grannick, and when they turned onto China Pond Road, she was wishing the day wouldn't end.

Then she saw two cruisers in front of Myra's house and her serenity took a jolt.

She sat straighter. "Something's wrong."

Brian pulled into the driveway. Emily was out in a flash, running across the cul-de-sac and up to Myra's front door. It was pulled open before she could do it herself.

"There you are!" Myra cried, looking shaky and pale. "I've been so frightened. First the lights didn't go on in your house, and then they didn't go on over the garage, and when the Jeep didn't come back, I figured you'd gone somewhere with him. I kept waiting and watching, but when you didn't come back *today,* I thought something terrible had happened."

"I'm fine," Emily assured her. Her eyes darted past those of three patrolmen to John's.

But Myra wasn't done. "It's so unlike you to leave without a word. I thought for sure he had done something to you."

"Brian?" Emily asked, puzzled. "He wouldn't do anything to me."

"Well, of course, *Brian* wouldn't. I'm not talking about Brian."

"Then who?" John asked.

Myra looked startled by the question. "Why, well, *any* man might have come, any man," she stammered. "*Doug* might have come. He's her husband. Husbands hurt their wives all the time."

"I'm sorry," Emily apologized softly to John. "We started driving yesterday and just kept going."

John raised a hand that said she owed him neither apology nor explanation. He looked less forgiving when Brian came through the door, but before Emily could speak up in his defense, Myra said, "I didn't mean to suggest that the detective had done anything wrong. Thank goodness, you're all right," she said to Brian, then to Emily, "I was so afraid. You *are* coming to my cookout on Wednesday night, aren't you?"

"Of course," Emily assured her. "I'm bringing the grill."

"Ahhh," Myra said with a great sigh of relief. She put her hands together and smiled. "That's good. Very good. Maybe things will be all right after all."

TWELVE

Emily prepared eagerly for Jill's homecoming. Since she didn't have Doug's input — he neither asked about her plans, nor offered any suggestions when she asked him — she decided to simply stock the kitchen with enough food to handle most any situation that might arise. She baked all of Jill's favorites, packed the freezer with goodies, stocked the cupboards. Upstairs, she opened the windows and aired out Jill's room, then dusted, item by item, careful to put each back exactly where it had been. She didn't open a drawer or the closet. Those were sacrosanct for this little while more.

Tuesday night, bored and itchy, she repapered the upstairs bathroom with the wallpaper that Doug had liked.

Midday Wednesday found her looking for something to do, but Kay was working, Celeste was at the hair shop getting streaked, and Myra refused to let her bake for the cookout.

So, Emily set off on foot down the street to enjoy Grannick at its brilliant autumn best. The air was cool, the day clear. Between the sun, and her sweatshirt and leggings, she was pleasantly warm and calmer than usual, but only until she started thinking. Then, like shadows under the sun, the old questions returned.

Who am I? Where am I going?

She took her usual route into town, counting the Victorians on LaGrange until she forced herself to stop. But without counting, what? *What to do? Who to be?*

She stopped at the drugstore to chat with Mary Elizabeth, and at the bookstore to say hello to Connie Yeo. Since the day was so lovely, she walked on into Grannick's college half, passing stores that the students frequented, heading for the college itself.

There was work to do here, even beyond Petra. If Emily was desperate, she could teach writing. She had been offered the job once, but had refused, preferring to work at her own pace, in her own time.

It wouldn't hurt to do another book, if Doug could accept it, but she doubted he would. She wondered if Kay and Celeste were right, that he was threatened by the thought of her success.

Troubled, she turned around at the stone pillars that marked the college's entrance and headed back along the less scenic route, past the auto body shop, the plumbing parts store, and the bus station. As she approached the last, a large bus pulled up and opened its doors to a cluster of back-packed students waiting at the curb. As they climbed aboard, Emily swore she saw Dawn.

She raised a hand to wave, but the girl was already inside. The bus closed its door, shifted into gear with a groan and a noxious expulsion from its tail, and pulled away from the curb. Emily was wondering if it had truly been Dawn, when a horn sounded. Looking around, she saw Brian's Jeep. She broke into an easy smile, went to the lowering passenger's window, and set her elbows on the rim.

"Are you lost?" he asked, smiling back at her.

The eyes, ahhhh, the eyes. They cleared the mind of all else. "Nope. Just walking. It's a nice day. Hey, neat tie." It was covered with little pink pigs.

"I thought it made a statement."

"Definitely. Are you on patrol?"

"Vaguely." He reached across and opened the passenger's door.

"Is this allowed?"

"If I say it is."

Unable to argue with such sound logic, she slid in. Being with Brian was as uplifting as any fine autumn afternoon.

"I'm getting to know streets and faces," he said, starting off. "See those old guys?" There were three, sitting under a worn awning in front of a cement box of a building. "They're always there. Nine in the morning, noon, three — rain or shine — weekday, weekend. That's their life, watching the street." He waved as he cruised by. They waved back. "They know my car now. That's good. Guys like that come in handy. They see everything."

Emily gave the men a token glance before returning to Brian. He was a study in contrasts — New York-knowing, Grannick-feeling; cop-tough, daddy-soft; hard of body, gentle of voice. In his jeans, shirt and tie, and jacket, he was easy on the eye. And then there was his scent. The car held it. It was clean and male.

He shot her no less than three separate looks, while she shamelessly studied him, before asking, "What got you out walking?"

"The sun."

He shot her another look, this one was uncertain.

"Really," she assured him, touched by his

concern. "It wasn't like the nights. I finished everything at home. It was nice out. I wanted to move."

They were circling behind the college, through the section of town known as the kitchen, for the support staff it gave the school. It was an area of aged two- and three-family houses, of skewed porches, packed clotheslines, and rusted pickups. Its shabbiness was heightened when the sun moved behind a cloud.

"I don't like doing nothing," she said.

"What about the *Sun?*"

"Two more articles, done. I write them faster than Rod can assign them. I need more to do. If Doug is going to be away as much as Jill is, I'm in trouble."

"What kind of trouble?"

Oh, God. Where to begin. "Boredom — loneliness — frustration — impatience — envy — hunger." The last tumbled out quite spontaneously, rather like her thoughts on being feminine the other day. The two weren't unrelated.

"What kind of hunger?" Brian asked.

The kind that isn't allowed, she thought but was mercifully saved from having to say it aloud or lie, when the two-way radio made a staticky sound.

Brian listened in. "There's a problem

three streets over," he said and picked up the handset. After logging in his position, he conversed with the dispatcher. Then he put the car into gear. "A woman just reported a peeping Tom. Feel like taking a ride?"

What to do? Who to be? Riding shotgun with Brian was right down her alley. "Definitely."

"Her name's Leila Jones."

"I know Leila. She was several years ahead of Jill in school, but they played town soccer together."

"Were they friends?"

"No. There wasn't time. Leila moved up to the next division. Then she got pregnant and dropped out of school, out of soccer, the whole thing."

"How old was she?"

"Fourteen when the first was born. She's had others since."

He made a frustrated sound as he turned onto Leila's street, and moments later pulled up before the shabbiest house there. It was a three-decker, with peeling paint, windows covered with graffitied wood planks, and broken toys strewn on the lawn.

Brian released his seat belt. "Want to wait in the car?"

"Not particularly." She was tired of being

spectator to other people's sport."

"I can't talk you into it?" His eyes tried.

She slipped out of the car and started up the front walk.

Easily catching up, he reached ahead of her to ring the bell. "Let me do the talking, at least."

"I think the bell may not work."

He knocked. Child sounds, mixed with television sounds, came from inside the house. He knocked more loudly.

"Is this her? First floor?" Emily asked.

"That's what they said."

The door opened. Emily recognized Leila instantly, even with one child in her arms and another clinging to her leg, though she was dismayed at the girl's state. Her hair was uncombed, her clothes worn, her eyes large and tired. She looked nearly as old and rundown as the house — which put things in perspective for Emily. For all her own concerns, her life was far safer, saner, more secure than this girl's.

Brian showed his badge. "I'm Detective Stasek. I understand you're having some trouble."

Leila looked unsurely at Emily, until he said, "Mrs. Arkin is my sidekick for the afternoon," when she stood back to let them come in.

316

The inside of the house was as depressing as the outside, with most everything worn, broken, or patched. In addition to the two children clinging to Leila, two others were fighting over a toy, while a third one sat crying in a wooden crate.

"Shut up, Joey," Leila snapped at the crying one, who only cried louder. "You can't play with the others 'cause you bite."

"Momma, it's *my* turn," screamed one of the squabblers. "Gimme it, Lissie! *Gim*me it!"

"But I'm not done," Lissie cried.

"You had it too long!"

"Lissie, let Davis have it!"

Lissie clutched the toy to her stomach and bent over, at which point Davis began pummeling her.

Leila rushed over, leaving the child who had been attached to her leg staggering on its own. "Davis Jones, don't you hit your sister that way." She hauled the child off by the arm. Behind her, the abandoned child sat down hard and started to wail.

Emily lifted the child. "Hey, hey," she said softly.

"This is all I hear," Leila complained over the ongoing noise. "All they do is scream and fight."

"How old are they?" Brian asked.

317

Leila pointed. "Seven, five, four, two, and ten months."

"How old are you?"

"Twenty-one."

"Is there a father around?"

"There should'a been, for the two littlest ones, but he couldn't stand the noise, either, so he left. They all do. They just leave the babies with me, but how am I s'posed to take care of them? How am I s'posed to do everything they can't?"

"Shouldn't the oldest be in school?"

"They sent her home for lice, so I gotta treat that and make sure none of the others get it, and they will, they always do."

"I thought your mother was helping you out," Emily said.

"She did until the last baby came along, then she said that if I was so stupid as to have another one, I could just take care of it myself, but I'm having trouble getting everything done, and all they do is scream." She turned on the one in the crate, who continued to cry. *"Shut up, Joey!"* She pointed a shaky finger at Brian and encompassed the other children in her gaze. "Do you know who this man is? He's a policeman, and he's gonna lock you up in jail and leave you there, if you don't all *shut up* this minute!"

Emily pressed the head of the child she held to her breast. If the shrillness of Leila's voice upset *her,* she could imagine what it did to the children. Leila broadcast panic. The children were catching it.

Speaking in a voice that was starkly calm by contrast, Brian said, "Tell me about the man who was looking in your windows. Do you know him?"

"No."

"Has he ever been here before?"

"I don't know."

"What, exactly, was he doing?"

"I'm *hungry,* Mama!"

"I wanna go out!"

Leila tried to free herself from the older two, who, having forgotten about the toy they had been fighting over moments before, were tugging at her shirt. "You can't go out," she told the little girl. "It's gonna rain." To Brian, she said, "He was walking around the house, looking in the windows. Don't pull at me, Davis! Lissie, get Davis a cookie."

"I don't want a cookie. I want cheese."

"I don't have cheese. Lissie, get him a cookie."

"The windows are raised off the ground," Brian said. "Do you mean that he was looking up at them?"

"Yes."

"Can you describe him for me?"

"He was dark — dark clothes, dark hair."

Brian made notes in a small notebook. "Caucasian?"

"Yes."

"I wanna go out, Mama," Lissie whined.

"I told you to get Davis a cookie!"

"How old was he?" Brian asked.

"I don't know. He was wearing a hat."

"What kind of hat?"

"I guess it was a baseball hat."

"Did it have anything on it?"

"I don't know. Maybe."

"Writing? A picture?"

"I couldn't see."

"Mama, I wanna watch television."

"No, Davis! It's broken!" Davis ran into the other room. "Joey, stop *crying*."

"Can you tell me how tall he was?" Brian asked.

She raised a hand as high as it would go.

"Was he heavy?"

She frowned, then shrugged.

"Was there anything unusual about him? Any distinctive feature?"

"I didn't see any, I was so nervous. He just kept wandering around the house, looking in at us. It was making the kids scared. He didn't look like he was passing by, I mean, he was looking for something."

Emily was wondering if he was trying to decide what to repair first, when Brian asked, "Do you think he might have been hired to paint the house?"

"He didn't have any stuff with him. He was just looking in at us, walking around and looking in."

"Who owns this house?"

"Ray Telly. He lives on the third floor."

Brian noted that. "This man who was walking around looking in — did he see you looking back at him?"

"He must have, because the kids were looking out at him, and I kept yelling at them to get away, but they wouldn't. He's going to come back. I know he is. Maybe he wants to do somethin' to one of the kids."

Emily felt a shudder of remembrance.

Gently, Brian asked, "Why would he want to do that?"

"*I* don't know, but something awful might happen if he comes back. I can't watch these kids every minute." A crash came from the back of the house. She raced in that direction with Brian on her heels.

Emily followed.

Leila was shrieking even before she reached the kitchen. *"Davis, what did you do? I was heatin' that water to give the baby a bath, and now you got it spilled all over the floor. Why'd you go and do that?"*

Brian put a hand on her arm. "Yelling at him like that won't help."

"What will?" she yelled at Brian. "I've tried everything, but whatever I say, they don't do." Her thin body was shaking. She was on the verge of hysteria.

Emily's heart went out to her. "Isn't there someone who can give you a hand?"

She shifted the baby, took a dirty cloth from the counter and dropped it on the puddle on the floor. "No one'll come. But if I'm all alone here, that man will come in and do something awful."

"You have no idea who he was?" Brian asked.

"No. I told you. I never saw him before."

Brian slipped the notebook back into his pocket. "Tell you what. I'm going to take a look around outside. Then I'll talk with your neighbors about what they've seen." He turned to Emily, but she spoke before he could.

"I'll help Leila out until you're done outside."

She did what she could. By the time he returned, the two youngest children had been bathed and changed, the three others were playing in a fort under a blanket-draped table, and in the marginally cleaned kitchen, Leila was cooking a pot of spaghetti.

She faced Brian apprehensively.

"I didn't learn much," he confessed, "but I'll take what I have back to the station and pass it around. We'll keep an eye on the house for a couple of days. Sound fair?"

Leila swallowed. She looked at Emily, then at Brian, and nodded.

"What did you find?" Emily asked when they reached the car.

"Footprints, lots of different ones in the dirt around the house, and cigarette butts, same thing, different brands. I checked the neighbors on both sides, plus the two living above. No one saw any strange man walking around."

"So what do we do?"

"We?" he asked, sliding her the corner of a smile. "*We* do nothing. *I* file my report and keep an eye on her."

"She needs help."

"She needs birth control. Why do these kids keep doing it, over and over again? She can't handle four, so she has another? It doesn't make sense."

"Maybe sex is her only pleasure," Emily suggested. "Maybe that's the only time she feels loved."

"Okay. *Have* sex. But *use* something, for God's sake." He leaned toward the wheel and peered up. "It's getting darker out there. Think it'll rain?"

"Lord, I hope not. Myra will be distraught."

"When are we due there?"

"Six."

"I'll drop you home, then go back to the station to file my report before I pick up Julia. Okay?"

"Okay."

Julia was quiet when Brian arrived. She toddled straight to him and, when he swung her up, put her head down on his shoulder. He sensed something was wrong, even before Janice said, "I don't think she's feeling well. She may be coming down with a cold."

He felt a wave of panic. She hadn't been sick since they'd been alone. In fact, she hadn't been sick at all. "What do I do for a cold?"

"Start with baby aspirin. She feels warm. If she needs a decongestant, your pediatrician will suggest one."

Brian wasn't taking the chance of needing one and being without. On the way home, he stopped at the drugstore for aspirin and the decongestant that Harold said Julia's pediatrician liked. He bought cough syrup and an antacid for good measure.

Julia lay quietly against Brian while he paid for the medicine, and then, because she felt warm, cuddly, and unusually docile, he strolled toward the back of the store.

He dug quarters out of his pocket and slid into the photo booth. "Grammie will never know that you weren't feeling well. I don't think she believes me when I tell her we're doing fine, so we'll take this picture and send it along. Here we go. Real quick and easy. One quarter, two, three, four. There." He settled himself in and gave Julia a nudge. When she didn't move, he checked her face. Her eyes were closed, her mouth open and moist. She was sound asleep.

He grunted just as the first flash went off, and gave her another nudge. "Wake up, toots. Time to smile for Grammie." He shifted her, but she was like a limp scarf, molding to his shoulder regardless of how he tried to arrange her. The second flash came and went with her breathing heavy against his neck. Her cheek was flushed. He touched it, disconcerted by its warmth. Sighing, he asked, "No picture yet?" as the third flash went off, then said, "What the hell," and produced a broad smile for the fourth.

She didn't wake up when he put her back in the car and slept all the way home, but when he tried to put her into her crib, she began to cry. That made giving her the aspirin easy. Once that was done, he picked her up and sank into the chair. She settled against him, content once more.

Myra scowled at the sky. She didn't understand. It had been so beautiful — bright sun, blue skies, crisp air — all day. Now that the time of her cookout was approaching, clouds had moved in.

Her guests were due at six. The rain might hold off. Maybe there wouldn't be rain at all, just clouds, in which case they could stay out in the yard. She had candles for when it grew dark, white candles in lovely little glass cups that reminded her of the ones in church.

She turned on the radio in the kitchen and moved the tuner up and down the dial, skipping over music, stopping at words until she heard the ones she wanted. ". . . Southbound is clear to the Pike. The weather forecast isn't as promising. Clouds will be moving in —"

"They're already here!" she shouted.

"With rain likely by dusk and continuing on through the night."

She turned off the radio and shot a worried look at the clock. It was five-thirty. Dusk wasn't until six-fifteen. They had a chance.

But if the clouds were already in, Grannick was ahead of the rest of the world, which meant that the rain could come any time.

She tried to call Emily, but reached the machine instead and hung up. She hated machines. A machine couldn't tell her that Emily was in the bath, which was where, no doubt, she was. She had been out walking earlier. Myra had seen her leave. Brian had driven her home, then left. He had just returned with Julia.

She dialed Emily's number again, hung up on the machine, and counted to ten before dialing again, hanging up again, counting again. She repeated the sequence three more times before Emily answered.

"Emily, I *know* you were in the tub, and I'm very sorry to get you out, but you said you would help me with the coals for the cookout, and it's time."

"Myra! Good Lord, I was frightened. I didn't know who it would be, calling over and over again."

"The clouds are already in, which means that the rain may come sooner than they say. I can't let that happen."

"It's no problem, Myra. We can always eat inside."

"But this is a cook*out.* Eating *in* defeats the purpose. I thought that if you could come right over, we might get started. We'll call Brian as soon as the coals are done. Come now, Emily."

"You'll have to give me ten minutes to dress."

"Ten minutes. Oh, dear. I suppose I can start taking things from the refrigerator. You won't be any longer, though, will you?"

She hung up the phone and glanced outside. Beneath the willow, on the grass by the bench, was the beautiful green blanket she had spread, and, on top, the brightly colored paper plates and napkins that she had bought in town. The colors looked brighter beneath the backyard lamps. The sky looked all the darker by contrast.

Hurriedly, she began taking the results of two days' work from the refrigerator. She had made three different salads — potato, carrot-raisin, and the five-bean salad Frank loved. She had baked corn bread and had stuffed mushrooms. She had sliced tomatoes and red onions, had made a fruit compote and mixed up punch. Not knowing Brian's preference, she had bought regular chips, ripple chips, and barbecued chips, not to mention ketchup, green and red relish, brown and yellow mustard, and green and black olives.

She rushed back and forth from the kitchen to the yard, setting bowl after bowl on the blanket. She was just carrying out the platter of meat when Emily arrived.

"And none too soon. Hurry, Emily. Light the grill. There's not a moment to spare."

"Hamburgers, hot dogs, *and* chicken? Myra, you have enough food here to feed an army!"

Myra saw the willow sway. "Oh, dear. The wind is picking up. Hurry, Emily, hurry." But even as she spoke, she felt the first drops of rain. "Oh, *no,*" she wailed. "I've waited *so* long for this. It *can't* rain now! My plans will be *ruined.*"

"No, they won't," Emily said, filling her arms with the dishes that Myra had just carried out. "We'll simply eat in the house. Let's get these back inside."

"But it has to be *here,*" Myra cried. "That was the whole point."

Arms laden, Emily made a dash for the house. Myra stared at the spread on the blanket, so lovely moments before, now growing wet, and she thought of the opportunity being lost.

She looked skyward. Frank had to be there. She couldn't think of any other explanation. He was controlling things still.

"Hurry, Myra!" Emily cried, grabbing her hand. "You're getting soaked."

Myra didn't feel the chill of the rain seeping through her dress, to her skin, as she was led toward the house. All she felt was an old, familiar sense of defeat.

Brian was just as glad that they were eating inside. It was far more comfortable, what with Julia collapsed on his shoulder. Poor Myra, though, remained dispirited, despite every attempt to cheer her up. They complimented her on the food, on the drink, on the paper plates with their large autumn flowers. Brian, for one, ate far more than he wanted to, just to show her how good it was, and he stayed longer than he would have, given Julia's cold.

Inevitably, though, it was time to leave.

"Thanks, Myra," he said at the door. "You were good to have us over."

She looked heartsick. "I wanted us to sit outside."

"Another time, we will."

She considered that for a minute, then

looked up. "Really?"

"Really."

"Soon?"

"If the snows hold off. Otherwise next spring."

"I may be *gone* by then."

Emily put an arm around her. "You'll be here. Thanks for dinner, Myra. Everything was wonderful."

Brian opened his umbrella, while Emily held Julia. He drew them close to keep them dry as they crossed the cul-de-sac.

At her door, Emily said, "I'd invite you in, but Julia needs to be in her crib."

He looked down at Julia. Her nose had started to run. "I've never lived through a cold with her."

"Keep giving her aspirin. If she feels really hot and gets cranky, put her in a tepid tub. That'll bring the temperature down. She may wake up crying from time to time, but that's because she doesn't know why she feels lousy. Just keep reassuring her, and she'll be fine."

Brian clung to those words. He bathed Julia and put her in her pajamas, gave her another dose of aspirin, then held her for a while. Long after she was asleep, he held her, and it wasn't because he thought Gayle would have. Gayle would have been in bed, asleep in anticipation of the next busy day. No, he held Julia because he remembered being held as a child, himself. He remembered being cared for and loved. He wanted Julia to feel that, too.

It was nearly eleven when he finally carried her to her crib, drew bunny close, and covered them both with the blanket. He stood over her for a minute to make sure she was sleeping, then quickly showered and checked in on her again, before returning to the main room, pulling out the sofa bed, and stretching out.

He barely had time to think about feeling lonely or frightened, before he was asleep, but both hit him head-on when, several hours later, he awoke to a godawful sound.

It was coming from Julia's room.

THIRTEEN

Julia was sitting in her crib, crying, but the sound of it was like nothing Brian had ever heard. His first thought was that she was suffocating, but when he grabbed her up and switched on a light, she wasn't blue at all. Her cheeks were pink and her nose running furiously. She looked as terrified by the noise she was making as he was.

Wrapping her in the blanket, he raced into the other room and was pushing his feet into his sneakers at the same time that he picked up the phone and called Emily.

She said a groggy, "Hello?"

"Julia's making horrible sounds when she breathes. Listen." He held the phone to Julia, who wheezed obligingly. "Hear that? I'm taking her to the hospital."

"No, no, Brian. Don't. There's no need. Not yet, at least. She has croup."

"Croup?"

"Laryngitis for babies. She needs moisture

in the air. I have a humidifier that I used for Jill. I'll bring it over. In the meanwhile, take her into the bathroom, close the door, and run the shower hot. Let the room fill with steam and sit there with her. I'll get the humidifier going in her room. Is the downstairs door unlocked?"

"It will be in two seconds."

He hung up, raced down the stairs and unlocked the door, then raced back up and made for the bathroom, holding Julia all the while. "There we go," he told her when he had the shower running. "Full force, on hot." He wiped her nose with a piece of Kleenex. "This will help. Emily knows."

For an instant there, he had imagined a hospital emergency room, with tubes and respirators and doctors taking him aside with their arms around his shoulders and their eyes filled with regret. He had imagined losing Julia.

But she was safe in his arms, looking around the room as it grew misty, seeming alert and aware. The hoarse sound still came when she breathed, but it was less ominous, now that it had a name.

Emily hauled the humidifier down from the top shelf of the linen closet and, pausing only to pull a sweater on over her nightgown, ran through the rain, across the driveway to the garage apartment. She let herself in and hurried up the stairs, passing right through the living room to knock softly on the bathroom door.

Brian opened it enough for her to slip inside. She set the humidifier in the sink and turned to Julia. "Hey, pretty girl," she touched her cheek, "did you give your daddy a scare?"

Julia touched her cheek right back in a way that made Emily's heart melt, all the more when she said in her hoarse little rasp, "Em-mee."

"Poor baby, you sound *terrible,* when you probably don't feel terrible at all. Am I right?"

Julia pointed at the shower. "Dad-dy la-loo."

"Definitely croup," Emily told Brian.

"How long does it last?"

"The worst will be over by the morning. Actually, the worst is probably over now, the panic that first time."

"I'll bet you didn't panic."

"Are you kidding? I thought Jill was choking on something that *I* had left in her crib. Doug was running around, yelling at me. It was a nightmare." She took the top off the humidifier and began to fill it with water.

"I'll get this going in her room."

It didn't take long. Once a fine mist was radiating into the air, she closed the door to concentrate it, and returned to the bathroom. Brian was sitting on the floor with his back against the tub. Julia was between his legs, reading a vinyl book.

"She doesn't seem any worse for the wear," Brian remarked. "I wish I could say the same for myself. That little scare aged me a year."

He didn't look it, Emily thought. She thought he looked wonderful, all sinewy arms and hair-spattered legs. He was the image of the modern father taking care of his child, and there was a sweetness, a gentleness to it that made her ache. The fact that he wore nothing but a pair of gray, slim-fitting, thigh-long knit boxers enhanced the contrast, male with child.

Brian peered down at Julia. "She looks wide awake."

"So am I. Funny how a scare can do that."

He turned warm, tired eyes on her. "I'm sorry I woke you."

"Don't be silly. I'd have been upset if you hadn't. Not that I know all the answers, and if she was sounding worse now, I'd be driving you to the hospital, myself, but if there's the chance of an easy answer, why not take it."

"I'm grateful."

She smiled. "That's why it's so nice to help you out." Thinking that Doug was never grateful for anything, she reached over and turned off the shower. "The moisture will hang in here for a while."

"How long do we stay?"

"Another few minutes. By then her bedroom should be moist." It occurred to Emily to return home, but she truly was wide awake, and then Julia was scrambling to her feet, running to her with the book held high. "What's this? A book? How *lovely.* What's it about?" She turned a page. "A house that talks? What's it saying?" She hunkered down and looked at the book with Julia, who hunkered right down beside her. After a minute, it simply seemed more comfortable to slide to the floor. Julia climbed into the crook of her legs.

"How sociable she is at one in the morning," Brian mused. "Is this a harbinger of the future?"

"Nah. She was frightened, too. This is relief."

"Dog," Julia said in her hoarse way, pointing at the book while she looked up at Emily.

"Actually," Emily observed, "I think it's a squirrel, but that's kind of hard to pronounce, so we'll call it a dog."

"Did Jill get sick much?"

"For a while, when she started spending time with other children. Then she built up her immunities."

"So Julia caught this at Janice's."

"Probably, though croup is her own body's response to a cold. Another child might have the cold without the croup. Jill still gets laryngitis."

Julia climbed out of Emily's lap, leaving the book there, and went to Brian. When he scooped her up, she put her head on his shoulder and a thumb in her mouth.

"This is nice," he said. When she gave a coarse little cough, he stroked her curls. He was calmer now and passed the calm along.

"I should leave," Emily said, but his eyes caught hers, and then, as though to second his protest, Julia coughed again, longer and more loudly. "Do you have cough medicine?"

"On the kitchen counter."

"Have you given her any?"

"Not yet."

Emily rose to get it. She returned with both the cough syrup and the baby aspirin, and knelt beside Brian while he turned Julia in his arms. The aspirin went down just fine. Julia even sucked on the dropper. The cough syrup was another matter. The smell somehow made its way through her stuffy nose even before she tasted it, and then she twisted to escape it. When Brian tried to hold her still, she fought.

In the end, it took four adult hands and two refills of the dropper before a proper dose was inside her, and by then both Brian's chest and Julia's pajamas were sticky with the stuff, and her crying was a hacking sob.

He carried her into her room, and paced the small space, talking softly, rubbing her back to soothe her. Emily took her from him so that he could shower the medicine away. By the time he was done, she had changed Julia and was rocking her in the chair under a dim glow from the lamp.

"Want me to take over?" he asked.

But Emily was content. She was doing what she knew best, what she loved. "I'm fine. You must be exhausted. Go lie down. I'll sit with her a while."

"She's my responsibility."

"So's work. You have it tomorrow. I don't."

"I don't like taking advantage of you."

"Why not, if I offer? Go to sleep, Brian."

He stretched out on his stomach on the

small rug before the crib, reaching, as an afterthought, for the pillow that Emily had displaced when she had sunk into the rocker. She thought to tell him that she hadn't meant for him to sleep on the floor, but he was quickly settled in.

So she rocked in the chair, with Julia's warm weight against her, and though she tried looking anywhere but, her eyes kept returning to his long, prone form. He was damp from the shower, the hair darker than its usual honey on his head and his limbs. His back was well-toned, ropy higher, lean lower. His waist was firm, his backside tight.

She hummed softly to Julia and closed her eyes, but his image lingered behind her lids, and then little things started coming to mind — the comfort she felt when he held her and the pleasure of it, the way his eyes made her insides flow, his calling her beautiful. She remembered the awakening she had felt as she lay on the rock by the pond, remembered feeling luxuriously feminine, talking of hunger even before she realized she felt it.

She didn't have to remember the way she tingled when she was with Brian. She was doing it now.

"She's sleeping," he whispered close by her ear. Her eyes flew open as he slid his arms against her body, lifted Julia, and put her gently in her crib.

Emily was still throbbing from the feel of his arms, when he took her hand and drew her up. She heard a raggedness in his breath, and met his gaze, and suddenly, whether from a trick of the dim light or not, there was nothing otherworldly or super-powerful about his eyes. They were simply human, wholly male, and rich with desire.

"I've been lying down there," he said in a gritty whisper, "telling myself I should be thinking about my daughter and thanking God she's all right, but I'm not thinking about Julia, I'm wanting you." When he drew her close, she could feel how much. With trembling arms wrapped around her and his breath uneven on her temple, he said, "I know it isn't a good time in your life for this, I know you're not free, and I'm not either, really, but that doesn't make it go away. If you don't want it, better leave now."

Emily was as stunned by his bluntness as by his suggestion. It was one thing to fantasize about him, another to be with the man, in the flesh, and hear him ask to make love.

He was right. It wasn't a good time for her. She was married to another man.

But that other man hadn't wanted her in ages, and she was powerfully drawn to Brian. The fact of that draw being mutual, of his wanting her with a hunger that thickened his voice and drew his body taut, was golden. His need excited her as much as everything else about him did. It was a salve on the bruises left by Doug's neglect.

She moved her face against his chest. His eyes might have finally been human, but he smelled divine — not only clean and male, but sexy — such that even if some tiny part of her wanted to leave, she wouldn't have been able to tear herself away. There was comfort here, and excitement and warmth, such warmth. It radiated from his skin and deeper, from her skin and deeper, and that wasn't to mention the knot in her belly, growing tighter, making her shake with the tension of it.

She had such need, *such need.* When she opened her mouth against Brian's skin to breathe that need, he echoed the thought with a guttural sound. He took her face in his hands and began to whisper soft kisses top to bottom. With repetition, the kisses grew less soft and more wet, until his mouth was liquid on hers and his tongue deep inside.

Hunger was one word for what she felt,

desperation another. She ached to be loved, body and soul.

She didn't protest when she found herself on Brian's bed in the next room, and when he pulled the sweater over her head, all she could think of was holding him again.

He busied her mouth with long, caring kisses that said she was precious, and touched her through her nightgown until the knot in her belly began to burn. She writhed against the heat. There was some relief when he drew the nightgown over her head, but it was short-lived. Once his boxers were gone and he was naked against her, the heat rose tenfold.

Emily had never known such a charge from body contact alone. Perhaps it was the newness of Brian, the texture of his body, its scent. Perhaps it was the famine she had lived through. Perhaps the excitement came from the chemistry between them, or the way he moved against her belly and between her legs. Whatever, she was caught up in a need to be closer, ever closer, then part of and absorbed, and when he finally buried himself inside her, she cried out in sheer relief.

Just this once, she promised herself in one of the few fragmented thoughts he allowed, because he had turned her mindless, a

343

creature of sensation. She felt heat and need as she arched to his hands and his mouth, tingled and buzzed and ached as he stretched her and stroked her. She cried out again when he withdrew completely and thrust back in, and when he praised her with hoarse sounds and the imminence of his climax, she soared.

She clung to him while all else around her faded and the yearning inside sharpened, and when he drove into her with a final heightened force, everything hung there, hung there, then burst.

The descent was slow and sweet, moments of pleasure interspersed with ones of shock. When the throbbing inside her eased, when her breathing steadied and her fingers relaxed on his chest over damp, curling hair and a hammering heart, when her limbs rested entwined with his, she pressed her face to his collarbone.

He allowed it for a short time, holding her tightly, as though he were as reluctant as she to let it end. Inevitably, he relaxed his hold and rose on an elbow. "I'm not sorry," he declared.

Just this once. For something so consuming, so uplifting, so rewarding. "Me, neither." She focused on his throat. "Does that make me wicked?"

"Not in my book. He isn't satisfying your most basic needs, and I'm not talking about sex. He's never here. He doesn't help with the loneliness, or the boredom, or the loss you feel with Jill away. He doesn't talk with you, and he isn't here to hold you when you cry, and, *yeah,* let's talk about sex. When was the last time you had it with him?"

Emily couldn't remember exactly when, it was that long ago. "I told myself that it was natural for sexual interest to decline with age."

"You are not in decline," Brian said with a chuckle, and she tried not to join him — the situation wasn't funny at all — but she couldn't contain it completely.

Still, the sound that came out held an element of self-consciousness. "I swear, I wasn't looking for this."

"Don't feel guilty."

"I do. I *am.*"

"You're beautiful, is what you are."

She was a mess — hair rumpled, face naked — but his eyes mirrored his words, making her believe.

"You're also sexy," he said.

"I don't know about that."

"Trust me. You are."

She thought of the dreams she'd been having, dreams of skin on skin, of hands touching forbidden places and breath whispering into private nooks. "Maybe," she conceded with a blush.

"Sexy. Oh, yeah." He smiled, then settled onto the pillow and drew her to face him. Looking at him that way, she felt a whole new wave of desire.

"What?" he asked.

"I'm — uh — I don't know how to handle this." *Just this once,* she had sworn, but that once was over, so what in the *hell* was she feeling?

"Handle what?"

"This. I didn't expect it." Her eyes grew pleading as they roamed his face. "What am I going to do?" she whispered, because that new wave of desire was making her want to melt against him again. "He's my husband. I believe in fidelity. If he was unfaithful to me, I'd be crushed."

Brian brushed his fingers over her mouth, then her cheeks before sliding them into her hair, and all the while his eyes held hers, airing need and desire, even love, if she chose to believe it.

She gasped when he slid a hand low on her belly over the spot where she was still sensitive.

His voice was hoarse. "I love that sound, your surprise when you feel it. You did it wherever I touched you before."

She gasped again when his fingers slid deeper. "Brian."

"Mmmmm."

"I can't do this."

"Does it feel good?"

"Oh, yes."

"Do you want it?"

"Oh, yes."

"Then let me love you."

Being loved was all she had ever wanted. It was why she had married Doug so young, why she had set aside her own pain over the years and made a pleasing cocoon for Jill and him. It was why, she supposed, she was drawn to Brian, who had offered compassion and affection and need right from the start.

She didn't think of Doug or Jill. For once, she thought of herself — something new — and of Brian. She touched him, and found new excitement in the touching, and when he was huge in her hand, she tasted a new sense of power. Rather than being threatened, as Doug would have been, he coaxed her on with low words and the smooth shifts of his body, until she pulled him to her. Their coupling was wild, less gentle than before and shocking, as she thought of it later, not that she would have stopped or slowed the pace or sought anything milder. Fierceness was another new experience. She found it exciting beyond belief.

This time when it was done, breathless laughter mingled with moans. Brian clutched her close, his mouth to her hair. "*Je*sus. What did you *do?*"

"I don't know. I just *did*. What did *you* do?"

"Beats me, but it sure felt good."

Ahh, it had. If she was to be damned for betraying Doug, at least she had enjoyed herself in the process.

Brian's chest was damp, the hair there curled, dark gold and masculine. She looked down his body to those parts that were even more so. When she looked up again, it was in amazement at what she had done and felt, *still* felt.

Suddenly Brian's eyes went wide. "Christ." In the instant he was out of her arms and the bed, and running into Julia's room. He reappeared moments later, resting briefly against the doorjamb, before crossing the room and returning to bed. "She's still sleeping. Some father I am. I forgot all about her."

Emily had, too. "We would have heard if she was worse."

"Not me. I was gone."

"Really?"

"Totally." He looked down at her. "You sound surprised."

"Doug was never totally gone."

He settled her in his arms. "Well, I was."

She felt him relax, felt his breathing slow and grow rhythmic with the approach of sleep. "I should go," she whispered.

"Noooo," he whispered back and drew her closer.

Being wanted was a heady experience. More than heady. Irresistible. Would it hurt to stay the night? Just this once. It had been so long since she had slept wrapped up in a man, so long since she'd had that comfort. One night wouldn't hurt.

Come morning, she would face what she had done. For now, she curled close.

Dawn brought the inevitable guilt and the realization that making love with Brian added another wrinkle to an already over-wrinkled life. But Emily was a survivor. She lived one day at a time.

Doug would be home Friday afternoon.

Jill would be home Friday evening.

Brian would be nothing more than the man renting the apartment over the garage.

Emily was an expert at pushing troubles from mind — first Daniel's disappearance,

349

then Doug's career. So now she refused to dwell on what she had done with Brian.

There would be time. But not now.

Jill arrived on the five o'clock bus. Quite content to leave Doug at the health club, Emily met her and held her and didn't stop grinning once, not during the tour of Grannick that Jill insisted on, nor during the triumphant drive down China Pond Road, nor during the excited exit from the car, the eager entrance to the house.

When the phone rang, Emily fully expected it to be for Jill, but it was Celeste, in a mild panic. "I have no idea where Dawn is. I thought for sure she'd be here by mid afternoon. She told me a friend was driving her home, or I'd have picked her up. No one answers her dorm phone."

"When did you talk with her last?" Emily had seen her on Wednesday afternoon.

"She called Tuesday. Briefly. She's still angry because I wouldn't let her visit Jill last weekend, but I didn't see the point, with Jill here *this* weekend."

Suspicious, Emily put the mouthpiece to her neck and asked Jill, "When was the last time you talked with Dawn?"

Jill looked at her watch. "Five hours ago."

"Where was she then?"

350

"In my dorm room. She's been visiting since Wednesday night." Eyes narrowing, she took the phone from Emily. "She's staying one more day. She told me you knew."

"No, I didn't!" Emily could hear Celeste cry. "She said she'd be home today. How is she getting here tomorrow?"

"She met a guy. He'll give her a ride."

"What guy?"

"He's the friend of a girl on my floor."

"Give me your mother."

With a look that was expectant to the point of parody, Jill handed the phone to Emily.

"She met a guy," Celeste started right in. "Swell. Does she need one in every port?"

Emily remembered the list of five men — or was it six — that had come from Celeste's ad. "He may just be a friend."

"She is an impossible child."

"She's not a child. That's what she's trying to tell you."

"Well, don't *you* think a trip to Boston last weekend would have been dumb?"

"Yes, but she didn't, and she's saying that she's of age and can do what she wants."

"On my dime."

"On Jackson's dime. Give her room, Celeste."

"Do you give Jill room?"

Emily hooked an arm through Jill's. "I don't have to. She isn't a rebel."

"Well, you're the lucky one, then. I have a major problem."

"No, you don't. Just grant that Dawn is eighteen. I thought you *wanted* her to be independent."

"Not when I'm waiting for her to come through the door."

"Then let her know you were worried."

"Yeah, yeah."

"Mom," Jill whispered, "can I run over to the Davies's before Dad gets home?"

Emily nodded and let her go. To Celeste, she said, "You're coming over with her tomorrow night, aren't you?" Jill was having a homecoming party. Doug wasn't pleased with the prospect of young bodies traipsing in and out, but Jill wanted it, and Emily was feeling defiant. Jill hadn't been home in seven weeks. Doug had, for what little he chose.

"We'll be there, if she ever gets home," Celeste said. "How many are coming?"

"How many, Jill?"

Jill turned back at the door. "Twenty, maybe twenty-five." She turned again just as Brian and Julia appeared through the glass.

Emily felt a frisson of excitement. She had

been waiting for weeks to show Jill off to Brian. "Gotta run, Celeste. Stay sweet?"

"Yeah, yeah."

She hung up the phone and joined Jill at the door. "Jill, meet Brian and Julia."

"Hi," Jill said with a bright smile. "So you're the guys who've taken over my playroom?"

"Sure are," Brian answered.

To Julia, in a childlike way, Jill said, "Well hel-lo. You're a pretty little girl."

"Can you say 'hi'?" Brian asked Julia, but Julia just stared at Jill. "It takes her a while. Your face is new to her. Not to me, though. I've seen pictures. You have one proud mother."

Jill blushed. "Of course, she isn't biased."

"Perish the thought."

"Mom says your place is great."

"Want to see?"

"Can I later? I have to see a friend before my dad gets home."

"Sure." Brian held the door wider for her to pass. "Drive carefully." When she looked back in amusement, he gave a sheepish smile and shrugged.

Jill laughed. "If you hadn't said it, Mom would have."

"Drive *carefully*," Emily called for good measure and watched her back out of the driveway.

"She's you," Brian remarked.

"That's what Doug says when he doesn't like what she's doing."

"Doug's a jerk," he said, which was one of the things Emily liked about him. He stuck up for her. He didn't blame her for losing her son. Even aside from the physical, he made her feel good.

Not that the physical was easily set aside. There was a new intimacy in his eyes — those incredibly penetrating eyes — that suggested indecent things. They made her feel naked and hot. They made her blush.

Looking away, she took the baby's hand. "How's Julia?"

"Better than she was."

"Good. Will you come to our party tomorrow night?"

"Both of us?"

"Sure. Doug will be in and out, but John and Kay will be there, and Celeste, and all of Jill's friends." Plenty of people. Perfectly safe. "The girls will go wild over Julia."

He gave her a heart-stopping grin. "Thanks. We'll stop by." He backed away from the door. "Enjoy Jill."

"I plan to."

His eyes held hers as he went sideways down the stairs. "Have a nice dinner."

"You, too."

"What are you serving?"

"Veal piccata. It's Jill's favorite."

"Mine, too," he said with naughty smile.

"You can't come."

"I figured that." He was walking backward across the driveway. "Don't stay up too late talking with Jill."

She grinned and shrugged. When he finally turned, she dragged in a breath. Between his grin and his eyes and that long, hard body of his, she was aquiver. She stood for a minute at the door with her hand on her chest, steadying the beat of her heart, chastising herself for being so susceptible to a man who wasn't her husband.

Then she banished the thought.

Jill was home, Doug was home, they were a family again, having veal piccata for dinner.

FOURTEEN

Celeste was up first thing Saturday waiting for Dawn. She read the morning paper with one eye on the driveway. She threw on a jacket and raked leaves in the front yard. Inside again, she stalked from window to window, chomping on carrot sticks when noon came and went, then stalking some more. By the time a blue pickup deposited Dawn and drove off, she was fit to be tied.

"Hi, Mom! I'm homed!"

Celeste entered the kitchen with her arms on her hips. "Where have you been?" she demanded. She didn't care *what* Emily advised. She couldn't hide her anger.

"Boston," Dawn answered, dropping her bags. "I told you I was going."

"No. You said you were going last weekend, until I nixed the idea."

"So I waited until Wednesday to go. I stayed with Jill. Didn't she tell you?"

"Sure. After I was out of my mind with

worry. She said you said that I already knew. Dawn, I expected you home *yesterday*. You said the *dorms* closed yesterday."

Finally, a note of sheepishness. "Yeah, well, I got in a little trouble sneaking back in just now, but I only had a backpack with me in Boston. I had to get the rest of my things."

"What things?" Celeste eyed the bags on the floor. "You'll only be here for four more days. What is *in* those?"

"Laundry."

"Laundry. Swell. You drive me out of my mind with worry, and you want me to do your laundry? Fat chance!"

"I'll do it," Dawn said with a defensive tilt of her chin, then she frowned. "You look strange."

"Thanks. Well, you look good, at least." Blond hair cascading over T-shirted shoulders, no sign yet of the freshman fifteen on jean-covered hips. "Irresponsibility always did agree with you."

"Mom, come on." She kept staring. "Why do you look different?"

Celeste wasn't about to say. "Maybe because you haven't seen me in seven weeks."

"Oh, I've seen you — in my mind's eye every day, saying, 'Do your homework.' "

"Hah, hah."

Dawn came closer. "You had your hair colored, didn't you. You had highlights put in, like I wanted to do, only you wouldn't let me."

"You're eighteen. I'm forty-three."

"That's no good reason," Dawn said, staring still. "Different makeup? No. It's your nose." With a look of disbelief, she studied Celeste from the side. "You had it done? You *did* have it done. And you didn't tell me! How *could* you, Mom?"

"I did it for me. No one else. Just for me. I didn't see the point in making a big thing of it."

"But I'm your *daughter.* You had *surgery,* and you didn't tell me. Thanks a heap. That makes me feel great. I'm at school right down the street, and you kept me in the dark. What did you think I'd do? Run all over Grannick telling people?"

"What does your being at school in town have to do with anything?"

"I could have helped if you were sick."

"Whoa. You were the one who only agreed to go to school here if you didn't have to come home until fall break. You were the one who said *you*'d call *me,* not the other way around."

"But I was thinking that nothing in the

358

world would be new. I can't believe you had your nose done. Would you have told me, if I hadn't noticed it?"

"Of course. It's not a secret, and it's no big thing, just something I wanted to do."

"So do I. Only you say I can't."

"Tell you what," Celeste suggested. "You graduate from college, get married and have a baby or two, and then when *they* go off to college, you can have your nose done, my treat."

"Whoopee," Dawn said and turned away. She hauled one of her bags to the kitchen table. "By that time I'll be able to afford it myself." She unzipped the bag. "It'll be *so nice* not to have to beg for what I want." She tossed one shirt here, one shirt there.

"What are you doing?" Celeste cried, imagining the house that had been so neat for seven weeks being suddenly reduced to a sty.

"Separating light and dark. Isn't that what you always tell me to do?"

"Do you have to do it now, here?"

"Why not? I have nothing better to do. It's not like you had special plans to take me to lunch or anything. I mean, that'd be too much to ask."

"I'd have gladly taken you to lunch if you'd been home at lunchtime. Dawn, it's two-thirty in the afternoon."

"Well, I'm sorry, if I'd had my own car, I could have left Boston earlier, but I had to wait for someone else, and then I had to stop at the dorm to get my things, so how could I have been here earlier?"

Sweetly, Celeste said, "If you'd come home yesterday, like everyone else, we'd have had time to do things together today."

"So we have tomorrow, and Monday, and Tuesday." She threw a pair of jeans on the dark pile and glared at Celeste. "Three whole days. Aren't you thrilled?"

Celeste sighed. "You may not believe this, but I was looking forward to seeing you."

Dawn went back to her sorting. "Yeah. Sure."

"I've missed you."

"Hah."

"I have. The house has been very quiet."

"You love it that way. You always did." The phone rang. Dawn rolled her eyes. "Ahh, God. Now I'm gonna hear it." She changed her voice. " 'There's the phone. There's the phone again. There's the phone *again*. If that ringing doesn't stop, I'm going to tear the goddamned thing right out of the wall.' "

"Well, it *was* ringing nonstop last year," Celeste said and snatched up the receiver.

360

"Hello?"

"Hi, Celeste. Is she home yet?"

Celeste held the receiver out. "It's Marilee. She's called three times."

Dawn took the phone with a brilliant smile. "Marilee! How *are* you?"

Celeste moved to the other side of the room, which was the only concession to privacy that she allowed. She hadn't seen Dawn in seven weeks. Hard to believe. Seven weeks.

Dawn did look good. And yes — surprise, surprise — Celeste had missed her. Seeing her now was nice. Having her home was nice. Knowing that she was going back to school in four days was nice, too.

Celeste had forgotten the raw energy that Dawn brought with her into a room.

She hadn't forgotten the discord. From the time Dawn was the littlest girl, they had argued about most everything. After seven weeks apart, that hadn't changed. Celeste wondered if it ever would. Some mothers and daughters were like two peas in a pod, others like fire and water. She and Dawn were of the latter bent.

Dawn hung up the phone, her eyes alive. "Everyone's hanging out at Marilee's. Can I go?"

"In other words, can you take the car."

"Look at it this way. If I do, I'll be back sooner. You and I can have dinner together before we go to Jill's party. You are coming, aren't you?"

"Wouldn't miss it."

Dawn's fingers found the car keys like a magnet to steel. She swept them up and made for the door. "This is great, Mom. Thanks. I won't be long."

Celeste listened to the ensuing silence with a surprising sense of regret. She *had* been looking forward to Dawn coming home. So what had she gotten? Five minutes? Ten?

Then her gaze settled on the piles of dirty clothes on the floor, and she sighed. Oh, yes, she had been looking forward to Dawn coming home, but for the life of her, she didn't know why.

By nine o'clock Saturday night, cars lined China Pond Road from the cul-de-sac halfway to Walker. What had started as a small gathering was resembling a class reunion — and Emily didn't mind a bit. Jill had earned this impromptu party, in payment for all the years she had limited herself to the few friends who wouldn't disturb Doug's weekend.

And where was Doug? Talking business

with the president of the college. He had asked Jill if she would be angry if he took off for several hours. Jill had sent him off with a hug.

The stereo filled the house with sounds Emily didn't know, but she knew the kids and moved eagerly from one to the next, listening to their tales, plying them with food. The dining room table was covered with the munchies she had made. When they were gone, she called the pizza house, and when the soda supply thinned, John went out for more.

Eating and drinking their share in the kitchen along with the other parents who popped in to say hello, were Kay and John, Celeste, and Brian. Julia had been part of the younger set, passed from one erstwhile babysitter to the next, until she had fallen asleep in Brian's arms. As often as he said he ought to take her home, he was such a comfortable member of the kitchen circle, that each offer was met with protest by the others.

Once, returning to the kitchen with a bag of empty soda cans, Emily stopped at the door, looking in.

"Someone's pleased with herself," Celeste remarked.

"I *am*." She left the door, set the bag down

by the sink, and came to stand between John and Brian. Her fingers found Julia's baby-silk curls. "I've always wanted this kind of open, happy feeling, with lots of friends milling around. I'm sorry I didn't do it sooner."

She was feeling ebullient, thinking that if Doug was perfectly happy at the college for several hours while she and Jill did what they wanted most to do, then everyone won, when the telephone rang.

It was Linda Balch, Myra's daughter-in-law. "I'm sorry to bother you," she said hurriedly, "but we've been trying to reach Myra and we can't get through, not yesterday, and not today. We thought she might have been out earlier, but I can't imagine she still is. Not so late."

Neither could Emily. "I'm sure that I saw the lights go on before. There may be something wrong with the phone. Let me run over and check."

"I apologize. It sounds like you have a party going on."

"It won't take but two minutes to check, and now that you've mentioned it, I want to know, too." She took down Laura's number.

When she told the others where she was going, Brian started to rise. John put a restraining hand on his shoulder. "Baby's sleeping. Sit."

Leaving the sounds of the party behind, Emily and John went across the street. The lights were on, but when they rang the bell, no one answered. They rang again. They tried knocking. They peered in the front windows, but saw no sign of Myra.

Emily grew worried.

"Let's take a look in back," John said. "Maybe she's having trouble hearing."

The backyard was all murky shadows and pond-damp smells. They went up the steps and knocked on the door. Emily found it unlocked and pushed it open. *"Myra?"*

She heard an answering sound, quiet and indistinct. "Where are you?" she called.

She stepped into the kitchen, but did an about-face when John said, "Out here."

"What?"

"She's out here. Over there."

Emily hurried back down the steps and across the lawn. Myra was a wraithlike figure, pressed against one end of the wrought iron bench. "What are you doing *here,* Myra? It's too dark and cold to be out at this hour." She slipped onto the bench and took Myra's thin hand. When she felt how icy it was, she stood right up again. "Let's get her into the house," she told John.

Myra went meekly. She didn't protest

when Emily sat her in a kitchen chair and wrapped a blanket around her shoulders, and she took a cup of hot tea in her hands.

"Maybe we should get her to the hospital," John suggested under his breath, but Myra heard and shook her head.

"No hospital."

Emily drew up a chair. "Why were you outside?"

"I wanted to be near the willow."

"Laura was worried. They tried to reach you yesterday, and again today." She looked at John, who picked up the phone and listened for a dial tone, nodded, shrugged.

"I heard the phone ringing," Myra said before Emily could ask. "I just didn't feel like answering. I didn't want to talk with anyone."

"Why not?"

Myra drank her tea, one sip after another. She stared broodingly at the cup.

"Why not, Myra?"

"Because people don't listen. They don't hear what I say. I'm just an old lady, babbling on." She set the cup on the table. "Thank you, Emily. I think I'll go to bed now."

"Would you like to sit at my house for a little while?"

But Myra held up a hand in refusal, rose,

and set off for the door. Emily was ready to catch her if she swayed, but she didn't.

"I'll stop in tomorrow," she called, then said to John as they let themselves out, "She's lonely. Her family thinks she's losing it. I never thought so."

"Do you now?"

"No. She's not irrational. Just sad. I guess that's what aging is about?" She looked to John for an answer, but he didn't have it, and once they were back at Emily's, once she had called Laura with a modicum of reassurance, she was swept up in the party again. She was in the living room, surrounded by Jill's friends, when Brian came looking for her. She returned to the kitchen with him.

John was at the back door, ready to leave. Julia's sleeping lump had been transferred to Kay, suggesting Brian was going with him.

Emily's first thought was of Myra, but before she had time to imagine anything horrible, Brian said, "John got a call from the station about an auto theft. They thought we should come."

"For an auto theft?" Emily asked in surprise.

John said, "The stolen auto is Nestor Berlo's Lotus."

"Ahhhh." Enough said. "Will you be long?"

"Depends on what we find and when we find it."

Brian added, "Kay says she'll take Julia back to my place and put her to bed if the party breaks up before."

But Emily had a better idea. "Julia can stay with me. I'll make a bed for her on the sofa. Celeste will drop Kay home."

Brian was comfortable with that arrangement. He liked having an excuse to return to Emily's. He wanted to see what was going on there. He wanted Doug to know that Emily and he were friends.

And from that? Maybe jealousy. Maybe anger. Maybe an exasperated, "Do what you want. I'm outta here."

Brian wouldn't mind if Doug walked out. It wouldn't change Emily's life, other than to allow them to be together without the guilt. It seemed like forever and a day since they'd touched.

John drove to the Berlo estate, turned in at the stone gates, and followed the curving drive to the four-car garage. All four doors were open. The cruiser was parked nearby, its headlights glancing across the bays while its red-and-blues lit the night.

Nestor separated himself from the patrolman and was waiting when they climbed
from the car. "I'd like this handled quietly,"
he told John.

Brian was puzzled.

Not John. "I understand. When did you
find it gone?"

"Just before I called you. I was out for the
evening in the Jaguar," which stood behind
him in one of the four bays. "As soon as I
pulled in, I knew."

"Think your wife took it?"

He gestured toward the small Mercedes
in another bay. "That's hers. She never
drives the Lotus."

"Was she with you?"

"No. She's with a friend."

Brian was wondering why a couple would
go their separate social ways on a Saturday
night, when John asked, "Could her friend
be driving the Lotus?"

"If he was, his car would be parked here.
It's an Olds."

The only other car, also in the garage, was
a shiny new sports car.

"Then it's the boy," John said.

"Damn right," muttered Nestor.

"Think he's gone far?"

"He never does. He'll be cruising around
Grannick. You'll find him fast."

"What do you want us to do?"

"Hold him for the night."

"Huh. You sure?"

Nestor turned and set off. "I'll come by for him tomorrow."

A short time later, combing Grannick for the Lotus, Brian said, "What's going on?"

John shrugged. "He has money. We aim to please."

"The chief of police, babysitting on a Saturday night?"

John shrugged again.

"Is Berlo that important to the town?"

"He gives money. He's also worth watching."

"What do you mean?"

"Whole family's screwed up."

"Screwed up, how?"

"Father has a lover, mother has a lover. There's an older son who went off to college and never came back."

"Never?"

"Maybe for a day or two here and there. Far as I know he hasn't stepped foot in town since he graduated. That'd be two years, now."

"What about the younger one?"

"He isn't a bad boy."

"Funny, that's what Harold said when the kid tried to lift a bottle of vitamin C from

370

the drugstore."

John spared him a brief look. He drove down one street and up the next before he said, "What'd he want with vitamin C?"

"That's not the point. The point is, he had money on him. He didn't need to shoplift. I got the impression from Harold that he's done it before. Know anything about that?"

John thought about it a bit too long.

"So what's the kid's problem?" Brian asked. "Simple rebellion?"

John shrugged.

Brian pushed. "Is the father as tough as he seems?"

"He's tough on his kids."

"Abusive?"

"In a way."

"*What* way?" Brian asked, growing impatient. Of the things he enjoyed about Grannick, small-town protectionism wasn't one. "Spit it out, John."

"The father's gay."

Gay. Brian hadn't imagined that. "How do you know?"

"There was some trouble a while back."

"What kind of trouble?"

"At the golf course over in Melon Falls. He was having a thing with one of the caddies. The boy was from Grannick. Nestor would pick him up to drive to the course, only sometimes they never got there. When the boy's parents got wind of it, they were upset."

"Jesus. I'd think so." He guessed the outcome. "Berlo wasn't prosecuted, was he."

"Nope. They settled."

"His name wasn't on your list of sex offenders in Grannick."

"We owe him that much, after what he's done for the town. The incident I just told you about happened a long time ago."

"How long ago?"

"Seventeen, eighteen years."

"Now, there you go," Brian complained. "There's a sex offender who was in town when Daniel Arkin disappeared, and his name doesn't appear once in the report. Was he ever questioned?"

"Officially, no. I told you, we didn't make assumptions on pedophilia then, like we might now. Besides, he was out of town the whole week."

"Was that corroborated?"

"Yeah. Besides, Nestor was never violent. He never forced the caddie, just promised goodies afterward. That's how the parents found out. The kid started coming home with a new bike and fancy sneakers. There's the Lotus."

John pulled up behind the car. It was one of four parked on the rim of the quarry, Grannick's lover's lane. Brian wondered what they would find in the Lotus.

Richie was alone. He was glaring out the window with both hands on the wheel. He knew he had company.

So did the occupants of the other three cars. They also seemed to know who that company was. With comic speed, heads popped up, and the drivers fired up their engines and took off.

John put a knuckle to the window and gestured for Richie to roll it down. Brian leaned against the hood of John's car.

"How're ya doin'," John said.

"I'm okay."

"Like the car?"

"It's okay."

"Your father thinks it's more than that. He thinks it's special."

Richie made a disparaging sound.

"He's not happy you took it."

Richie said nothing.

John opened the door. "Come on out now. We'll take a ride to the station."

Brian waited for him to protest, and was profoundly sad when the boy only said, "Will he be there?"

"Tomorrow."

373

The hands on the wheel loosened a bit. "What about the car?"

"My partner will return it."

Brian approached. Richie gave him a wary look.

John made the introductions. "Richie Berlo, Brian Stasek."

If Richie recognized Brian from that time in the drugstore, he didn't let on. He simply asked, "Do you know how to drive this?"

Brian eyed the beautiful beast and smiled dryly. "I can manage."

"You'd better not grind the gears. He'll know. He goes apeshit over this car."

"Is that why you took it?"

Richie looked abruptly furious, seeming ready to explode with the reasons why he had taken the car. Then his anger fizzled. "Yeah. That's why."

"Come on now," John repeated before Brian could ask another question. "It's late."

Richie left his car and entered John's. He sat in the passenger's seat, no questions asked.

Brian waited until John drove off before starting the Lotus, but as he drove, it wasn't the sleekness of the car he was thinking of, or its power. He was thinking that Richie Berlo led a troubled life, and that, irrespective of his father's largesse where the town

374

was concerned, someone had to address that. The boy was begging for it.

Brian wondered what he would try next.

Exhausted but content, Emily and Jill sat curled against the pillows on Jill's bed with only Cat between them. Jill yawned into a smiling sigh. "That was fun. Thanks, Mom."

"Don't thank me. I had as much fun as you did. You have nice friends."

"I want you to meet my friends from school. They're nice, too.

"They seem it — at least, the two who've already called here do. Who's Adam?" He was one of those calls. Emily didn't want to make a big thing about it. All she wanted to know was how old he was, where he was from, what he was studying, whether he was a prude or a lecher.

"A friend. He's sweet, but I'm not rushing to hook up with anyone. It'd be too confining, when there are so many great kids there. I've met some *really* nice ones. I'm lucky."

"Luck has nothing to do with it. Nice people attract nice friends."

Jill made a face that was only half comical. "So how'd you attract Daddy?"

Emily touched her hair. "Hey. Where'd that come from?"

"He isn't very sociable. He could have hung around to see my friends."

"You gave him permission to leave."

"Because it was clear he wanted to. Parties make him nervous." She grinned. "But it was a great party. I loved seeing everyone. Brian's cool."

Emily had been wondering what Jill thought of him, but would never have asked. She was doing everything in her power not to think about Brian. Sometimes it worked, sometimes it didn't.

"He has incredible eyes," Jill remarked.

"Quite. And a precious daughter, and nice ways."

"I'm glad he's living here. It makes me feel like you're less alone. The bathrooms look great. What else will you do?"

"With the house? Clean this room."

"No. Not this room. Not yet."

"Jill, it's a mess."

"But it's *my* mess. I like it this way. I was nervous on the bus ride home. I kept thinking I'd walk in here and everything would be changed. It's nice to know nothing has."

Emily felt a pang of guilt. Things had changed. Big things. Like Emily taking a lover. Only it didn't show in ways Jill could see.

Emily didn't know what to do about Brian.

"So what are you going to do with yourself?" Jill asked. When Emily looked blank, she said, "If you're not doing more around the house. Can you and Daddy take a vacation?"

"We are. In two weeks."

"That's Parents' Weekend. It doesn't count."

"Sure, it does."

"You should go *away* away."

It was a thought that had even more merit now than when Jill had first suggested it. Doug wouldn't go willingly. But they needed time alone, good quality time, to work things out. The last thing Emily wanted was to be cheating on her husband, but when basic needs weren't met — no, there wasn't any excuse for it.

"I'll work on him," she said.

"Are you doing more for the *Sun?*"

"Uh-huh. Whatever Rod needs. And Petra, whenever." Emily prayed it would be soon. Jill would be back at school in three days — the thought brought a giant hollowness, still, yet, again. Doug would be back at work, wherever it was he was going this week. Without some kind of diversion, Emily would be thinking about things she shouldn't. "Connie Yeo needs help in her store. I love books. Selling them might be fun."

"What about writing them?"

"I'm toying with the idea."

"What will you write about?"

"I don't know." She had been writing about Daniel for years, small scraps of thoughts packed away. She had a book right there.

"You have an office with a word processor downstairs. I think you should do it, Mom. This time it could be your own book from start to finish. This time we could make a *big* celebration."

"We celebrated last time."

"We went out to dinner with Sam and Donnie. It wasn't much of a celebration." Her voice grew excited. "I'll throw you a party this time."

Emily smiled. "You will?"

"Yeah, like you threw for me tonight. It was super, Mom. Thanks."

Emily's contentment swelled. The future remained an enigma, but as long as she had warm times like this, she would survive.

Marilee flew back to Washington on Monday afternoon. Kay might have called in sick and stayed home from school if John hadn't

378

announced that he was taking the day off from work, himself, to take Marilee to lunch and the airport.

She was surprised. John had always been a stickler for duty when it came to the department. She remembered his taking time off when he had the flu, when his father died, when Marilee was born, when she graduated. He and Kay had driven her to college on a weekend, so he hadn't missed any work then. Amazing, that he was taking a whole day off now.

Amazing, too, that he thought to bring Marilee by to see Kay, for a final goodbye on the way from lunch to the airport. Kay had had trouble saying goodbye that morning. Amazing that he had sensed it.

She didn't know why the parting was more difficult this time. She hadn't had as much trouble in August. Maybe parting was a novelty then. Now it was real. Now she understood its deeper meaning. Now she saw, as she hadn't seen for all her intuitive brilliance, that Marilee's departure left her and John alone with each other for the rest of their lives.

That thought remained with her long after the car was gone from the school parking lot. She was thinking about it still, later that afternoon, when she packed up her briefcase and headed home.

She did love John. He was steadfast and sure. In marrying him, she had gotten the stable home she wanted and the child she had nearly given up hope of having. With that child grown now, she and John were in each other's limelight. She was feeling unbalanced by the glare.

The cruiser was in the driveway. She parked beside it and went inside, half-expecting to find a sex-starved madman waiting to drag her to bed.

But there wasn't any sex-starved madman, just John, leaning against the kitchen counter, holding a bouquet of yellow roses.

"For me?" she asked when he held them out, then murmured, "I guess, they have to be, since there's no one else here."

"Thanks for a nice weekend. From Marilee and me."

Kay was startled. "They're beautiful. You didn't have to."

"I wanted to. I thought they'd cheer you up. She'll be back home soon."

Kay nodded. Oddly tongue-tied, she took the flowers.

He smiled, touched her cheek, and went off to watch the news before she could muster the wherewithal to say a thing.

■ ■ ■ ■

Emily lay in bed, wide awake. Doug had left that morning after a flurry of perfunctory hugs that had left her depressed, but it was Jill's afternoon departure that brought tears. Emily wondered if the pain of parting would ever get easier, if the silence of the house would ever grow less stark.

The furnace kicked on from time to time, shooting heat through the pipes as the house cooled, but Emily wasn't aware of any chill. Beyond the pain and the silence was something else, something distractingly hot and sly. It was lodged in her belly and rose each time she thought of Brian.

Tossing the covers aside, she went to the window. Myra's night light fickered beyond the spattering of leaves that lingered on the front yard maples. Beyond the yard the fence was pale, beyond the fence the street dark.

It was a typical Grannick night. Only nothing felt typical inside Emily. She wanted. Stunningly, selfishly wanted.

She went into the bathroom for a drink of water, but that made her no less restless, so she headed for Doug's den to surround herself with his trappings, sat in his chair with her feet on the desk, and flipped on the television. She went through the channels twice before flipping it off.

She put something smooth and smoky on the stereo, went to the living room window and swayed before it in the dark for a while, but what should have been soothing became sensual. Well before the music ran out, she was in the kitchen, tugging the last of the sweet red grapes from the bunch that Jill had otherwise denuded.

She tried to feel guilty for feeling desire, but the desire was too strong. Neither guilt nor reason could kill it. Shyness didn't even have a chance.

She went to the back door, held the knob for a minute, turned around and leaned against it for another minute. She directed her thoughts to Jill, inviting the pain of that particular loss, but Brian came again in no time flat, filling her mind with all that she had been telling herself she couldn't have.

This is wrong, this is wrong, her mind sang, but her body kept hearing a different tune. Snagged by its beat, she slipped into her jacket and stole out the door. She took the longer, darker, colder way around the back of the garage, giving herself every opportunity to change her mind, but the beat went on and the heat held.

She knocked softly on his door. He couldn't possibly hear, she knew, but she couldn't get herself to ring the bell and wake Julia. So she knocked again, still softly, then put a shoulder to the doorframe and waited.

She figured that either she would come to her senses, turn around and go home, or she would get chilled and forget about sex.

Both scenarios became moot when she heard his footfall on the stairs. Pulse skittering, she waited with her head down, wondering what to say, what to do. The door opened. She looked up, feeling positively depraved.

"I shouldn't be here," she said, but before she could turn and run, he drew her inside, out of the cold that she didn't feel, and closed the door. She settled against it. "I shouldn't be here. I was lying in bed. I couldn't sleep."

"You're missing Jill."

"Some." She focused on his shirt. It was a heavy, faded plaid, open over a pair of jeans. "Weren't you sleeping?"

"No. I was reading. Dozing. Whatever."

The jeans weren't snapped. The sight of his navel upped her heat several notches. Not knowing what to say, but needing, needing, she reached over and caught his waistband. "Make me leave," she begged.

A throaty whisper. "I can't."

"This is wrong. My husband was just here."

"Did you make love with him?"

"No. And I wouldn't have been thinking about him, if I had." She had been praying Doug wouldn't reach for her, for just that reason. The betrayal would have been compounded.

Brian's breathing had grown uneven and his body tight against her fingers. She put her cheek to his chest. "There's this . . . awful . . . restlessness. It won't go away." She touched his middle, then, when desire got the better of her, higher. The hair on his chest was soft by contrast to the firm skin beneath. Her hand was in heaven, knowing what it wanted and taking it in ways that her mind resisted. The loud beat of his heart in her ear chipped at that resistance, as did the elbow he hooked around her neck to hold her close.

He wanted her. That fact alone made her love him.

And then it all seemed so necessary to life — the heat, the desire, the budding of things that were female and too long put down. She brushed her mouth over his chest, pushed at the lapels of his shirt, touched her tongue to one hot, hard nipple. She was someone she hadn't been before, a different woman from the one who was married to Doug.

A different woman. That was better. Easier to accept.

Egged on by the shaky glide of his hands on her back, she moved impatiently against him. She needed to taste more, touch more, but the hunger wouldn't be sated, it seemed, and then, tasting and touching weren't enough, not for her, and not for him. When he urged her hand lower, she unzipped his jeans and let him loose.

Untamed was one word for what happened then. Brian had her nightgown bunched at her waist in no time, had his hands under her and her back to the wall. In no time, he had her filled so full she thought she would burst, but he held that off, stoking her with fierce thrusts that pushed the pleasure up and up, well beyond what she would have thought she could bear. With her arms and legs wrapped around him, she held on for dear life until she was lost, then found, then cradled ever so gently in the damp, dark afterglow, in the stairwell by the garage.

FIFTEEN

Celeste walked into the Sunflower with a rose in her hand and stood quietly in the waiting area just beyond the hostess's post. The restaurant occupied a glass bubble that clung to the side of a hotel in downtown Springfield. She had chosen it for its openness and its brightness, and would have actually preferred to have been there in daylight. Unfortunately, what with work and transportation, her men couldn't meet her for lunch unless they took the whole day off. She couldn't blame them for not doing that. They didn't know her name, or whether they would like her in the least. They didn't know if she would even show up.

She didn't know if they would, either, but the drive from Grannick to Springfield was an easy one, and if she was stood up, nothing but her ego would know it.

So the rationale went. It was seven o'clock,

the very time she was to meet the marathoner for supper. Not dinner, supper. She had
made that clear. The Sunflower specialized
in salads and sandwiches. Anything heavier
would have entailed more of a commitment,
not to mention taking longer. If the marathoner turned out to be a dud, she wanted
a fast supper and a faster escape.

There he was. She knew instantly. He had
said he was tall and slim, and he was slim,
indeed — to the point of gauntness. Not
that he was ugly. Just very angular.

He approached her. "I was told to look
for someone holding a rose."

"You found her." She extended her hand.
"My name's Celeste."

His hand was knobby. "Craig."

It fit him. She moved toward the hostess.
"Did you have any trouble finding the
place?"

"No. I've run races in Springfield."

"Ahhh. Two, nonsmoking," she told the
hostess.

During the walk to their table, Celeste
cursed whatever impulse had made her do
this. She hated small-talk, hated awkwardness, hated first dates. But first dates led to
second dates, which weren't so bad. Not
that she thought she would have a second
date with Craig. Gut instinct told her he

wasn't the one.

Maybe gut instinct was wrong. She supposed she could sit through supper and see.

They sat down at the table. "You're very pretty," he said in a straightforward, almost factual way that took something from it.

"Thanks." She tried to think of something to say back on the same vein. All she could come up with was, "So you're a marathoner. How many have you run?"

"Seven." He listed them, along with his times for each, along with the winners, the first-runners up, and notable also-rans.

"Ahh," she said. She smiled and turned to her menu. "They make a wonderful chicken Caesar here."

"I don't eat eggs."

"No, no, I'm talking salad."

"Caesar dressing contains eggs."

She wanted to tell him that the roll he was reaching for did, too, but she didn't want to sound snippy. So she said, "Take anything in moderation, and you'll do fine."

"I *never* eat eggs."

She closed her menu and set it aside. "What do you eat?"

"Complex carbohydrates. Pasta is a mainstay of my diet."

The waitress materialized. "Can I get you anything to drink?"

"Bottled water for me. I don't touch alcohol."

Celeste looked the waitress in the eye. "I'll have a glass of the house chardonnay. And the quiche, please." She asked Craig, "Do you know what you want?"

He ordered rotini with sun-dried tomatoes and basil, no oil, no cream, no garlic, no salt. It sounded boring as hell to Celeste. *He* sounded boring as hell to Celeste.

But she was determined to give him a chance. So, patiently, she said, "Tell me what you do. You said you were in health-care management."

"I'm in the accounting department of an HMO on the North Shore."

"Ahh. An accountant."

"I'm actually looking for another position. Health care isn't a stable field anymore."

She knew enough not to open that can of worms. "What are you looking for?"

"Something in sporting equipment. My friend is opening a running store. I'd be a natural for it."

"To sell?"

"To manage the books. I'm an accountant."

How could she have forgotten. "Would that be a full-time job?" It didn't sound it to her, and if not, where would he get the money to indulge in the fine wine, good music, and adventure that he claimed he wanted. If he was looking for a woman to bankroll their relationship, he was sitting across from the wrong one.

"I've never worked full-time," he said. "If I did that, I wouldn't have time to run. I do a hundred miles a week."

"Really."

"I have to, to keep in shape."

Celeste didn't see any shape. She assumed there had to be muscle somewhere, but she couldn't see much beyond skin and bones. She couldn't see herself reaching for that in the night.

"Are you into fitness?" he asked.

"I don't run, if that's what you mean."

"You should. You have the build for it."

Celeste had no desire to run. With a dismissive smile, she said, "I wouldn't know where to begin."

He proceeded to tell her. He talked about shoes and singlets, sweatbands and gloves. He talked about starting slow and building up, about keeping a log, about warm-up exercises and cool-down ones. He talked about shinsplints. He named the kind of watch she would need. He even pontificated on jogging bras.

By the time he was done, their food had

come and gone, as had every last bit of Celeste's interest. She glanced at her watch. "I have to leave. I have a long drive home." She put enough money on the table to more than pay for her meal, then rose. "It was nice meeting you."

"If you give me your address, I'll send you a notice when my friend opens his store. We could set you up to get started."

"Tell you what," she said. "I have your phone number. When I get the urge to run, I'll give you a call."

Two days later, Celeste walked into the Sunflower with a rose in her hand and was immediately approached by the hostess. "The gentleman is already here. Right this way."

Celeste followed her to a corner table — valued not for privacy here, but for the lovely sense of being surrounded by glass — and got her first glimpse of the British widower.

He had said he was fifty, and he looked it. His hair was gray and his face lined and round. But it was the kind of warm, friendly face that was perpetually wreathed in a smile.

He left his seat when she approached, thanked the hostess, then held out his hand.

"I'm Michael."

"Celeste. It's nice to meet you."

His face smiled more broadly. "The pleasure is mine." He saw her comfortably seated before he returned to his own chair.

"Have you been waiting long?"

"No. I'm compulsively early." He made a tsking sound. "But I shouldn't use that word, now, should I, when I'm trying to impress someone new." His accent was mild and quite pleasant.

"Compulsive?"

"It isn't a positive trait, or so my children say, and they're usually right."

He respected his children. That was sweet. "How old are they?"

"Twenty-nine, twenty-five, and eighteen. And you? Do you have children, or was the 'second life' you mentioned in your ad to do with a marriage that has ended?"

"My marriage ended when my daughter was one. She's eighteen now, too, and in college."

His face beamed. "Really? Well, we have that in common, although my eighteen-year-old is a boy. He and I are quite close. His leaving home has hit me hard."

"How long ago did your wife die?"

"Five years. It was very sudden. I don't know what I'd have done without my children. They have been hugely supportive. My oldest, a girl, is married with two children. She lives in Bloomfield. That's twenty minutes from Hartford, where I live. My middle is a boy. He works with me."

Lovely. "What kind of work do you do?"

"I make nuts and bolts — or my workers do. I sit at a desk beside a large window that overlooks the plant. Jay — that's my son — has his own apartment. I have to confess that there have been times in the last few weeks when I would have liked him living back home."

Celeste couldn't imagine that. She couldn't imagine anyone welcoming the work, the responsibility, the dissention that a child at home entailed. She had breathed a sigh of relief when fall break had ended.

"My children and I grew close after my wife died," Michael said. "I needed them as much as they needed me. Ahh, here's our waitress. I took the liberty of ordering a bottle of wine. It's a rather interesting Chardonnay. Is that all right?"

His preordering almost made up for the great relationship he had with his kids. "Chardonnay is my favorite," she said with a smile as he poured.

"That's what my youngest always says. Of course, he's underage, so I'm not terribly impressed. For you, it's fine." He raised his glass. "To a lovely lady bearing a rose."

She touched her glass to his. He was either as chivalrous as he had said, or corny as hell. She wasn't sure which.

"I take it you've eaten here before?" he asked.

"Several times."

"Do you have any recommendations?"

"The chicken Caesar is good, although I always love the quiche. It may be more of a luncheon dish, but I think people pay far too much heed to conventions like that. Your stomach doesn't know what time of day it is. I've read articles calling pizza a perfectly appropriate breakfast."

The marathoner would have died. Michael merely chuckled. "My kids have been eating pizza for breakfast for years. Even the two oldest, when they were living at home, before their mother died. She never believed that it was worth a fight, and while I much prefer the great British breakfast, I don't believe in fighting, either."

"What is the great British breakfast?" Celeste asked before he could return to the subject of kids.

"Eggs, kippers and sausage, broiled tomatoes and mushrooms and toast. It's quite large. I can't eat like that anymore, of course. My doctor says *I'm* too large, and besides, I'm not the best of cooks at any time, much less first thing in the morning. So a tradition has arisen in my house. Special occasions are marked by the children coming over and cooking me the great British breakfast. Not that it's often, mind you. But it is fun."

For just a moment, Celeste wondered what it would be like to be part of a large and congenial family. Then she pushed the thought aside. Large families meant more food to cook, more clothes to wash, more misdeeds to monitor. She didn't wish it for the world.

"Have you decided?" Michael asked when the waitress returned.

Celeste ordered the quiche. During the time it took him to order the chicken Caesar, she noted that his hair was vaguely shaggy, as were his clothes, clean but shaggy. He had a distinctly broken-in look.

Once the waitress left, he asked her if she was having the same trouble adjusting to being without children at home that he was. She couldn't lie. To his credit, he didn't look shocked.

"It must be different for a woman to shoulder the responsibility of parenthood alone, than for a man," he said and proceeded to talk about the years since his wife had died as they related to his children.

At one point, Celeste tried to bring the discussion around to what he did in his own time for fun, but his own time appeared to be family time. If he wasn't visiting his grandchildren, he was taking his older son to Whalers' games, or attending parents' weekend at the younger one's school. He took one vacation a year, with both sons, his daughter and son-in-law, and grand-children.

Celeste was *not* ready for grandchildren.

By the time their food had come and gone, she realized that she wasn't ready for Michael, either. She was tired of hearing about his kids. She was still too close to parenthood to want to talk about it all the time. Granted, he sounded like a great father. But she wasn't looking for a father.

Then again, as she bid him goodbye, she felt a twinge of regret. There was something endearing about his smily face. It wasn't an inspiring face, or a pensive one. But it was kind.

Not that he was in serious contention as a suitor, she decided as she drove home to Grannick. There wasn't any chemistry between them, and chemistry was impor-tant.

She might find it with the veterinarian. He had a lovely, deep voice that was definitely a turn-on. Unfortunately he had left to go to a conference the day after she called. They were meeting at the Sunflower the following week.

So there was that to look forward to.

And the doctor, though she had certain qualms about that one. Arranging a date with him had been as complex an ordeal as reading his résumé had been. In response to her note suggesting the Sunflower, he had sent his telephone number. The first challenge, then, had been to reach *him,* rather than his answering service. The second challenge had been to find a suitably accessible meeting place. He was from Baltimore and had no business, whatsoever, he claimed, in Springfield. So they were meeting in Boston, where he had meetings the following week.

He had sounded almost begrudging, as though she was one more appointment to be squeezed into an already overbooked schedule. She wasn't sure why she hadn't hung up on him. Maybe because doctors earned a bundle. More probably because she had just returned from striking out with the marathoner. She might yet call and cancel.

Then, sigh, there was the architect. As she

had done with the others, she had sent him a note suggesting a meeting at the Sunflower. Unfortunately, since she had to write through the magazine post office box, it had taken him longer to respond. The wait had been worth it.

"Dear GC403, I loved your note. Supper at the Sunflower sounds perfect, though I actually had another thought. One of my clients, an artist, is having a showing of her work at a gallery in Cambridge. A large open house is planned for the last Sunday in October. If you were to come, you would not only see a sample of my work, but hers, as well. There will be many interesting people there, including artists and authors from the area, so that even if you think me a total bore and never want to see my face again, the afternoon won't be a waste. On the chance that you find me as interesting, if not more so, than some of those others, there is a wonderful coffeehouse nearby where we can go for drinks and entertainment, before I put you in your car and send you home."

It was the kind of adventure that sounded full of possibility. Her anticipation of it, as she drove home from Springfield with Michael's kind face in her mind, was peppered with heat and spice.

■ ■ ■ ■

Brian looked despairingly in the direction of his kitchen. Pots, pans, and baby bottles filled the sink. Dirty dishes littered the counter. Laundry was piled on the floor by the dryer.

He was exhausted looking at it. He was exhausted thinking about it. It seemed he had been doing nothing but pots and pans and dishes and laundry for two months straight.

If there was a heaven, Gayle was up there enjoying the irony of the do-nothing father doing all. Well, at least he was trying, which was more than *she* was doing. She had let a goddamned car wipe her out.

He should have cleaned the kitchen and folded the laundry last night, but he had been tired. Why? Because he had been up into the wee hours the night before making love to Emily.

So maybe Gayle was enjoying herself out of spite.

Women would be the death of him yet.

"Brian?"

But a sweet death it would be. The sound of her voice, alone, made him jump. He reached the door just as Emily arrived at the top of the stairs and braced his hands on either side of the frame. "You can't come in yet."

"Why not?"

"Because this place isn't ready for viewing. I need ten minutes."

"I'm not viewing."

"Five minutes."

She ducked under his arm and took a look around. "Mmm. You're right. Not for viewing."

"I try to keep ahead of it, but it's impossible. As soon as the clothes are clean, they get dirty again. Same with pots and pans, and I swear I make up that goddamned sofabed ten times a day. Dust the table, and there's more in an hour, so what's the point? It's doing and redoing, doing and redoing. There's never an *end* to it."

She shot him a droll look. "Now you know."

"How do women survive?"

"You get used to it after a while."

"But what do I do before 'after a while' sets in?"

"Listening to music helps. Some women make phone calls while they're folding laundry. Some watch television while they're doing the beds. Unfortunately, if we don't do the work, it won't get done, and we want it done."

Brian stalked to the bed and began pulling at sheets. "You've got it, there. I tried leaving the bed unmade on the theory that no one's here during the day to see, but then *I* had to see when I walked in at night, and when Julia saw the thing open, she insisted on playing there and having supper there, and she spilled food all over the place, so I had to wash the sheets."

Emily nudged him aside. "I'll do the bed. You do the laundry."

"No. It's my bed."

"I've spent some time in it myself this week."

"Not enough," he grumbled. She rarely spent the night. He knew that she was struggling with the morality of their affair, that she came to him against her better judgment, but he was dying to wake up with her. She was, still, that little pocket of calm in his life. Even when they were making love, he felt stabilized.

But he was loath to pressure her, when she was so vulnerable. So he ran a hand through his hair and sighed. "Sorry. I rushed to get Julia to day care so I could come back here and clean before work, but it's not my idea of how to best start the morning."

His idea of how to best start the morning entailed taking Emily in his arms, but something about her said that wasn't why she had come. Suddenly frightened, he reached for her hand.

Emily closed her fingers around his. "We have to stop."

His fear grew. "You don't want to be with me?"

"I do. Too much. I *love* being with you. Then I go back home and feel guilty, and it isn't only the cheating on Doug. When I'm with you, I'm not thinking about him."

"That's the point."

"But he's my husband, and we have a daughter. Unless I'm prepared to ask for a divorce, I need to think about him more. I need to try to make my marriage work."

"Why?"

"Because he's my husband. And because we had a good marriage once."

"That was before Daniel disappeared," Brian said and regretted it when a shaft of pain crossed her face. But it had to be said. "Isn't it true?"

"Yes, but one thing may not have caused the other. Doug has grown. He's changed."

"Do you love him?"

"I don't know him the way I used to."

"That's not a good answer."

"Well, I don't have a better one, and until I do, I have to look for it!" She took a breath. "Being with you clouds the picture."

Brian heard her anguish. It was some solace for what she was saying. Feeling helpless and more than a little inadequate, he drew her close. "When you're with me, you smile. You laugh. You enjoy yourself. You deserve to do those things, Emily."

"Maybe someday."

Inadequate. Oh, yeah, he felt that. Doug was a major roadblock in their relationship, but he wasn't the only one. Daniel was right there beside him. She claimed he was dead, but she wouldn't leave the house, or the town where he had lived. Brian feared she wouldn't leave Doug for the same reason.

He almost told her about the photograph. It had arrived several days before, a computer rendition of a file photo of Daniel. At twenty-one, he was handsome, half-scholar, half-rogue. His blond hair had darkened to a shade of brown midway between Doug's lighter and Emily's darker. His face was more narrow than the child's had been, his eyes intelligent, his mouth gentle. He looked markedly like Jill, except for the shadow of a beard. Emily would have been proud of the young man in the print.

But showing it to her wouldn't help anything. He had sent it out through every channel possible, and could do nothing now but wait. He was also waiting for the fingerprint enhancement to be done, so that he could run a check on it. And he was preparing to question those people who hadn't been questioned the first time around. He had even greater incentive to do that now.

Startling, how dependent on her he had grown. She offered him the kind of guileless devotion no other woman had, and he loved it. He felt pampered. He felt needed. Whereas his relationship with Gayle had been programmed to allow for a wedding, a child, a simple evening together, his relationship with Emily was spontaneous and hot.

She complemented him. She challenged his mind. She brought sun to his day. And *damn it* he brought it to hers. He knew he did. Even now, with her arms wrapped around him and her face burrowing into his neck, he could feel her drinking off his strength, his sturdiness, his love. Rather than being depleted by what she took, he was always enhanced.

"I don't want to let you go."

"I have to do this," she whispered brokenly.

He would have argued, if he hadn't been so loath to cause her pain.

"We'll still see each other," she said.

But not *that* way, and *that* way was what set their relationship apart from the relationships they had with other people. He thought to tell her he loved her, but that would only make things harder. So he simply held her for a while. He waited for her to draw back, but she didn't. So he held her longer. Still she didn't draw back.

Finally, sensing that she needed him to do it, he released her. "I'll be here," he said and managed a smile.

She nodded. "It's good to know."

"Julia loves you."

"I love her, too." She looked around, drinking in the room with thirsty eyes before finding a diversion. "Why are there dishes in the sink? Is something wrong with the dishwasher?"

"Yeah. It's full. Everything inside is clean. I just haven't had a chance to unload it."

She took a deep breath. "Okay. You fold the laundry. I'll do the bed."

"John would kill me."

With a dry, "John's not here," she put Brian's newest jazz revival disc on the player and set to work. It was her way of saying that though they wouldn't be sleeping together, not much else would change.

Brian took heart from that.

At the moment of Daniel's disappearance, there had been four other customers and three employees inside the post office with Emily. The only employee questioned at the time had been the one helping the customers. The other two had been sorting mail in the back room.

One of those had died nine years before. The other was retired and living with his daughter two towns east of Grannick.

"Arthur Terrell?" Brian asked when a white-haired man answered his knock.

"Yes."

He flashed his badge. "Detective Stasek. Grannick Police Department. I understand you were working at the post office nineteen years ago when Daniel Arkin was taken from his mother's car. Do you remember that day?"

"Arkin. Sure do. Ever find the boy?"

"No. We're doing some clean-up on the case. The file says that you were in the back room at the time of the crime. Do you remember how long you'd been there that morning?"

"I was sick about the boy. His picture was on our wall for a long time after. He was a cute-looking thing. My daughter had one just his age. Couldn't imagine something like that happening to him."

"Mr. Terrell?"

"How can I help you, sir?"

"How long were you in the back room?"

"The back room? That's where we sorted the mail. Did it all by hand in those days. The carriers kept coming back to get more."

"Were you in the back room the whole time Mrs. Arkin was there?"

"I didn't know when she was there. We couldn't see anything up front. Didn't know nothing had happened 'til the police showed up."

"You didn't leave the back room at all? Not to poke your head out front? Or go outside for coffee or a smoke?"

"Don't smoke."

"How about getting fresh air?"

"I always stayed inside 'til the job was done. Didn't see nothing outside, seeing as we didn't have no windows." He frowned. "I figured it had t've been someone passing through town. No one in Grannick would'a taken the boy. No one in Grannick would'a *kept* the boy, seeing as Emily was so upset. Such a nice girl. My heart broke for her."

Brian's, too, but he wanted a lead. "You mentioned the carriers coming back for

407

more mail. Did any of them come or go while Mrs. Arkin was there?"

"I just told you. I didn't see her there."

"Okay. I'll rephrase that. The police arrived within ten minutes of Mrs. Arkin's leaving the post office. Did any of the carriers come or go during, say, the half hour before the police showed up?"

Arthur thought about that. "Don't remember, really."

"How about sounds? You couldn't see what was going on out front, but could you hear?"

"Some."

"What does 'some' mean?"

"If there was a ruckus, I'd a heard."

"Did you hear one that morning?"

"No."

"Did you hear anything at all unusual that morning?"

"Not that I recall. I used to stand out back listening to the voices, playing a game, trying to recognize them, just to pass the time, know what I mean? You couldn't always hear the ladies' voices. Oh, you could hear Constance Marret's voice, no one could miss that one, it was all high and whiny. Emily's would'a been softer, like a hum. Once the police came through and said what happened, I remember thinking that the voices were too calm for something like that. 'Course, Constance had been in earlier, and Archie Hickocks" — he upped his own voice — "who made high little sounds, kind of like this," he paused, "and Frank Balch was in, and his voice was the worst. Could always hear Frank. He had a mean voice."

"Was it any meaner than usual that day?"

"No meaner. Just the same. Those were the times when my partner — Horace, he passed on a few years back — my partner and I'd look at each other and be real happy we weren't working out front."

Brian got nothing more. After passing Arthur his card, he returned to the Jeep and considered the next name on his list.

Four patrons had been inside the post office with Emily that day. Archie Hickocks had left on foot, heading down the street to the sandwich shop that had been where the Eatery now was. His arrival had been well documented.

Frank Balch had climbed into his own car without seeing Emily's car or the child. He had been counting out change from the twenty dollar bill he had used to pay for his stamps and thought he'd been gypped of a dollar. He had been ready to storm back in, when he had found it.

409

Selma and May McDougall had left the post office and gone to the dress shop across the street. They hadn't seen a thing.

The owner of the dress shop had been interviewed within an hour of Daniel's disappearance. Not so the two customers who were there when the McDougalls arrived. They were Mary Viola and Susan Boyd, mother and daughter. Mary had moved to a retirement community in Florida, but Susan still lived in Grannick with her husband.

Brian showed his badge and introduced himself. "I'm new to Grannick. I've been reading old files and want to tie up some loose ends regarding Daniel Arkin's disappearance."

Susan looked startled. "Daniel Arkin? That's a very old case."

"This is just housekeeping," he said nonchalantly. "You weren't questioned at the time. Do you remember that day?"

"Very well. I have two boys of my own. My husband and I had nightmares about what happened."

"Did you see Emily's car pull into the post office lot?"

"No. I was trying to help my mother buy a dress. She wasn't the easiest person to shop with."

"Did you look across the street at all?"

"Not until afterward. I didn't know anything had happened until I was paying for my mother's dress. Selma McDougall was the one who noticed the police car. Then we saw people milling around."

Nineteen years hadn't changed the story. It was identical to the one in the files given by Belle Fraser, the owner of the dress shop. Belle's window had the best view in town of the post office lot.

"Where were the people milling?" Brian asked.

"In front of the post office and in the parking lot. I saw two cars — Emily's and a police car."

"Did you see any peripheral movement off to the side or at the back of the parking lot?"

"No."

"Did you *hear* anything unusual, something that might have registered, even while you were dealing with your mother, like the squeal of tires?"

Susan looked apologetic. "You wouldn't be asking that if you knew my mother. She talks nonstop. All the while we were at Belle's that day — I remember, because when we found out what had happened, it seemed so petty — she was jabbering on

411

about how unflattering the dress styles were and how much smaller the dressmakers were making their things, so that she had to buy a bigger size than she used to. She took time off to complain about Frank Balch and his old car and the awful noise it made, but all *I* heard was her voice. I'm sorry. I wish I could help."

Later, sitting in John's office, Brian repeated that thought.

"They all want to help. But they're not telling me anything new. Everyone liked Emily. Everyone feels bad for her. No one knows who would take her child or why. Frank Balch's name keeps popping up. Sounds like he was a mean son of a bitch. Could he have done more than he said?"

"Don't know how. Don't know *why.* He hated kids."

"Maybe that was why."

"Nah. He had just gotten rid of his own. He wouldn't want to go anywhere near Daniel. Besides, we questioned him, questioned him two, three times. His story didn't change. Myra corroborated it."

"She wasn't with him."

"No, but she was at home when he got back, and that was five minutes after he left the post office. So what's he gonna do? Take the kid and dump him in five minutes? Give

412

me a motive."

"Meanness."

"Meanness ain't no crime. The guy never even got a speeding ticket."

Brian sighed. "Well, I'm sorry he's dead. I'd have liked to talk with him."

"No, you wouldn't. Trust me."

But Brian held firm. "Guys like that are sometimes the biggest help. They have chips on their shoulders. They love bad-mouthing other people. They have the guts to say things that kinder people don't. They don't protect *anyone*."

"No kidding. Poor Emily was going through a time of it, and all Frank could do was flay her for leaving the child in the car. Sweet guy, huh?"

Myra sat on the bench under the willow. She was wrapped in the large wool jacket that Frank used to wear to chop wood. Her daughter-in-law, Linda, wearing a more stylish parka, sat beside her.

Myra hadn't invited her over. Linda had just shown up and insisted they talk. So Myra had said, "Fine, but I'm going outside," as she pulled on the jacket.

It was cloudy at midday, and chilly as October days went. The grass had been crunchy that morning, and though it had softened some, crunchy meant winter was at hand.

"We worry about you," Linda said. "Carl doesn't like the idea of your being out here all alone."

"I'm not alone. I have people in town. And Emily and Brian. And Frank."

"Yes, well, we were wondering if you'd consider a move."

"Good Lord, no. I'm not moving."

"There's a wonderful place, garden apartments not a half hour from us. The people are lovely."

"I can't move."

"Why not?"

"I've lived here for thirty-seven years. Everything that matters is here."

"Maybe when Carl, Peter, and Nowell were home, and when Frank was alive, but it's only you now."

"It's more than that."

"These apartments are wonderful, Myra. You'd have a bedroom, a den, and a living room, all carpeted. The kitchen was just redone. It even has a microwave."

"I can't work a microwave."

"You can learn. It's freezing out here. Wouldn't you like to go back inside?"

"No," Myra said. She brushed shriveled leaves from the bench and tipped back her head. The boughs had thinned. Two more weeks, and a good rain would leave them bare.

"Would you just *look* at this apartment?" Linda asked.

"No. You'd only have to drive me right back. I'm not interested in moving." She gazed out over the pond. It was what she had first loved about the house. She couldn't imagine living where there wasn't a pond.

"It's adorable, Myra. The bedroom and den are up a curved stairway. The living room has a separate dining area with a door to the kitchen. And there are sliding doors off the living room that lead to a private patio."

Myra wondered why Linda thought a patio would appeal, when she had all this.

"The closet space is good. There's a window in the bathroom. There's even a ceiling fan in the bedroom."

That gave Myra a moment's pause, but only a moment's. "Frank wouldn't like it," she said. Rising, she went to the water's edge. It was dark where it lapped at the rocks, and, farther out, gray beneath the clouds. She imagined that a world of creatures lay under the murk.

"Myra," said Linda, softly, from behind, "Frank is dead."

Myra didn't bother to argue. Linda couldn't understand that Frank lived on, any more than Carl could, or Peter or Nowell, or Emily or Brian could. But he did live. Myra felt the force of him every day and every night.

As she stood there beside the pond, with Linda going on about an apartment that Myra wouldn't move to, couldn't move to, she dreamed that the creatures under the surface rose up one night, took form, and left the water. She imagined that they came across the grass to the willow.

Sixteen

Emily sat in the attic with her back against a carton labeled JILL'S DOLLS and her legs askew on the aged wood planks. Open before her lay the large accordian-pleated folder that held all the bits and snatches of things she had written in the days following Daniel's disappearance. They weren't in any order. She had jotted down thoughts as they'd come, on whatever material was handy, and had stashed them here. After years of random extractions and returns, they were a jumbled mess.

She drew out a piece of paper and read, "I touch his crib and see him playing with his toys on the floor, then I blink and see nothing, just my mind playing games. I remember him as he was, doing all the things he loved, and I want him to do them again. He's been gone four months, an eternity in such a young life. With each day that passes, chances of things ever being the same grow smaller."

She reached in again and drew out a phone bill with writing on its back. "I lost control again today. We were eating dinner in silence, as seems our way since Daniel, when I started to sweat and shake. I left the table and went outside for air. Doug was annoyed with me, but I couldn't help it. The walls were closing in. I felt that if I didn't *move* I would suffocate. So I started walking down the street and kept going, into town and around and back. At the head of China Pond Road I saw him, or imagined I did. He was wearing the same clothes he had on that day, the little dungarees bulging around his diapers, the red striped jersey, the sneakers, the baby baseball hat with the pin on the front. DADDY'S BOY, it said. Doug bought it for him."

Emily remembered that hat, clear as day. She remembered the dungarees, the jersey, the sneakers. She remembered thinking horrible things about what might have happened to those clothes, picturing them torn and bloody. She remembered coiling into herself on the edge of the sidewalk, hugging her knees, wanting to die there and then if all there was to her future were torn and bloody thoughts. She remembered John coming by, stopping, talking softly.

418

She hadn't remembered those silent dinners until now, though. Once Jill had been old enough to join in, her presence had livened things up. But there had been that silence before.

Her marriage had been good until Daniel disappeared. Much as she had downplayed cause-and-effect when Brian suggested it, she might have been wrong.

She sifted through the folder for the piece of faded yellow construction paper that she often drew out. She had been in the process of making a card for Doug, when he had burst into the room, wanting to know why his partner had seen her car parked at the office of her obstetrician. There had been no point in making a card then, since the cat was out of the bag. Later, she had simply written out her thoughts.

"I'm pregnant again. Still can't believe it. Must have conceived shortly before Daniel disappeared, because Doug and I haven't had sex since. Some would call it a cruel joke, what with the hell of our lives now. I call it a miracle. After so many nights when I honestly didn't care if I lived to see the day again, I do now. A new baby means a second chance."

She tucked the yellow paper in with the rest and stretched a thick elastic band around the accordian-pleated folder. Then she went down to Doug's den. She set the accordian-pleated folder on the desk, pulled up the telephone, and dialed New York.

A receptionist announced that she had reached Renton Press.

"Kate Cerrillo, please."

She looked off toward the pond. Framed by the mullioned window, Canada geese were poking their bills through the backyard grass, three, four, five of them. They would be gone soon, flown farther south, leaving the chicadees and the squirrels to fight for the feeder's seed.

"Kate Cerrillo."

"Hi, Kate. It's Emily."

"Emily! Good to *hear* from you! I've been thinking about you. How's Jill?"

"Jill is great. Back at school after fall break, and liking it a lot."

"Do you like advanced parenthood as much?"

"I'm not sure yet. It's different. I'm still adjusting."

"Emily." All business. "I need a book."

Emily smiled. It was a familiar line, delivered by Kate each time they talked. "What is it now?"

"A juicy scandal brewing in Washington. One of the president's top aides is involved with the wife of a senator from the opposition party. No, you haven't read anything about it yet, mainly because there is bipartisan opposition to a leak, but the leak is coming. We want a book. It has your name written all over it."

Emily didn't think so. "Not good timing for me."

"Why not? Jill's away. Doug travels. You're young and energetic. I'd do it if I weren't so old."

"You're not old."

"For running in and out of corridors and up and down marble steps? I'm nearly sixty. Besides, too many people know me. Not you, though. You're low key enough to slip through doors that would be shut in my face. It would mean spending time in Washington. Don't worry about money. We'll cover all your expenses —"

"It's not that. I'm kind of involved in something else."

"Something to do with writing?" Kate asked.

"Possibly."

There was a pause, then a hopeful "Are you serious?"

"I'm getting there."

A quietly excited "About Daniel?"

Emily's smile was skewed. "How'd you guess?"

"I can hear it in your voice. It's your Daniel tone. You're terrified, but you're thinking of all those notes you've kept all these years, and you know that you won't be able to write anything else until you've done this."

"But can I do it? That's the question."

"Sure, you can. Writing was an outlet for you after Daniel disappeared. It kept you sane. You told me so."

She had indeed, during one of several lunches that had gone on for hours and hours. From the start, there had been a rapport between Kate and her — not quite mother and daughter, not quite best of friends, but a tight connection nonetheless.

"Okay, it'll be tough reliving things," Kate went on, "but you have all the raw materials right there."

"Would you be interested in publishing it, if I did it?"

"I've been wanting it for years. Give me a month, and you'll have a contract."

But Emily wasn't ready to commit. "No contract. Not yet. I said I was *getting* there. I didn't say I was there."

"Do it, Emily. Please?"

Kate's plea was still echoing in Emily's ear

when Brian called. "How about lunch?" he asked.

She brightened. Lunch was innocent — a broad daylight rendezvous between friends. "Can you take the time?"

"Sure. It's a quiet day. Want to?"

"Yeah."

"Great. I'll be there soon."

When he pulled into the driveway five minutes later, she was wearing a fresh sweater and slacks, and a pleased smile. She ran out to the Jeep and slipped inside.

"Hi," she breathed.

"Hi, yourself," he said with a grin and started off.

"This is a treat."

"My treat. You're the prettiest thing I've seen all day."

"That may or may not be a compliment."

"It is. I wasn't sure you'd come."

"This is safe, isn't it?"

"Depends what you'd call safe. If you mean we can't make love at the Eatery, you're right. But I won't promise that my eyes won't give it a try, and if you feel a wandering hand under the table —"

"You won't."

"Why not?"

"Because I asked you not to. Right?"

He didn't answer the question, simply said

a soft, "I'm glad you came."

Over sandwiches, they talked about his morning's interrogations of one drunk driver, one obscene phone caller, and one victim of a spray-painted car. Emily told him about her talk with Kate, but it wasn't until they had been there for nearly forty minutes, that Brian said, "This is the first time we've been out together in public."

"We've eaten here before."

"Not without Julia. It's different without Julia. What if people talk?"

"If? Make that when. And it won't bother me." She had sworn off sex, not friendship. "Will it bother you?"

"No. Will it bother Doug?"

Emily wasn't sure. It was actually an intriguing thought. "He thinks you're great. He tells me he's glad you're next door. He feels better leaving me alone, knowing you're here." She found the irony of it amusing. "He should only know."

"Detective Stasek?" It was their waitress. "Chief Davies just called." She passed him a slip of paper, along with the bill.

Brian read it, took money enough from his wallet to cover lunch and a tip, and drew Emily out of the booth. On the sidewalk, he said, "Something's come up. I'll have to drop you home."

"What is it?"

"Another visit to Leila Jones."

As he settled her in the Jeep, she asked, "What's up?"

"She's having trouble with her kids." He shut the door, rounded the hood, and slid in behind the wheel. "I won't know what 'til I get there."

Emily accepted that for all of thirty seconds. He had barely swung a U-turn when she decided that he knew more than he was letting on. Most everyone in Grannick knew Leila Jones better than Brian did. Yet John wanted Brian there.

She reached over and pulled John's note from his pocket.

"Emily —"

The words she read tied her stomach in knots. "One of her kids is *missing?*"

He sighed. "That's what it says."

"I'm coming."

"You're not." He continued along LaGrange in the opposite direction from where Leila Jones lived.

"I'm coming," Emily insisted.

"You can't. This is police work."

"I came once before."

"That was different."

But Emily wasn't giving up. Who *better* to be in on the search for a child than one who knew firsthand how it felt? "I know Leila. I know what she's thinking. I can stay with her and help keep her calm while you look for the child."

"No. It's too close to home. I don't want you upset."

She let him have it. "I'll be *more* upset sitting home waiting for word. I'll be imagining that the child was kidnapped by some perverted stranger who is doing the same kind of unspeakably terrifying things to it as someone did to Daniel. I'll be thinking that the first few hours are the most crucial, and that if I could be there with Leila, I could maybe pick up something from her that would give a clue as to who took the child and where they went. I can be a *help,* Brian," she begged, needing the redemption of it. "Don't deny me that."

His mouth was set, his eyes firm ahead, but when he reached China Pond Road, he swore, made another U-turn, and started back toward town. "This is not good. I just know it. I don't know why I listen. Either you are the most persuasive woman in the world, or I'm just such a sucker for a sweet thing that common sense goes right out the window." His finger pointed at her, while his eyes hugged the road. "If this upsets you, don't come crying to me. I've warned you.

I've tried to protect you. You are *impossible.*"

"But you do love me."

He sighed, his fight gone. "Ain't it the truth."

It was a light moment, that dissipated the closer they came to Leila's street and was forgotten completely when the flashing lights atop the cruisers at Leila's house came into view. Neighbors were standing in small clumps, keeping their distance. A bald-headed man in an undershirt was watching the goings-on from the sill of the third-floor window.

Memory, and the smell of tragedy pulled the knot in Emily's stomach tighter.

Leila was on the front steps with the baby on her lap and the three other children looking out from the door behind her like caged beasts, eyes wide, noses flattened on the misshapen screen. The children were silent. Leila was the one making noise this time, a wailing sound, halfway between a whine and a sob.

Immersing herself in Leila's grief, Emily sat and slipped an arm around her shoulder. John and another officer were hovering, with two more officers wandering around the house.

Leila's eyes went to Brian. "I was out back

427

hanging the wash. I had the baby, but th' others was *s'posed* to stay *in*side. Travis followed me out."

"Travis is the two-year-old?" Brian asked.

"I *told* him to stay inside, but he's *never* listening to what I say. I *told* him to stay with the others, and that if he didn't something bad was gonna happen to him, but what was I s'posed to do, stay inside watching him *every* minute? I had to go out to hang the wash, and then when I came back inside, he wasn't there, and th' others told me he was out, so I went back out, and he was there, and then he *wasn't.*"

"Did you see anyone around the house?" Brian asked.

"I didn't see *no* one. I was hanging out the wash. There was so much of it, nothing stays clean for long, they're always spilling stuff all over the place. I try my best, but I can't do *everything,* not with them *squalling* all the time."

Brian turned to John and said in a low voice, "Has someone searched the house?"

"He isn't *in* the house," Leila cried. "He came *out,* after I told him not to. I told him *so many times* to stay inside with Lissie and Davis and Joey, but they're always doing awful things to him, *even when I tell them not to,* so he wanted to come out."

"Sam's in there now," John told Brian. "Hooks and Munroe are out back. We got a description of the boy. I put it on the horn."

Brian made to lean against the stair rail near Leila, but caught himself when it started to give. "Did you actually see Travis outside?"

"He was right there, walking all through my clean laundry, pulling on things so I had to slap his hand."

"What did he do then?"

"He sat down and *screamed.*"

The baby started to cry. Leila put it to her shoulder and began a convulsive rocking. Emily offered to hold her, but Leila didn't respond. Her eyes were fixed on Brian.

"What did you do then?" he asked.

"I went back to hanging the laundry. He got quiet, and I didn't hear anything else."

"He didn't cry out, maybe when someone snatched him up?"

"I couldn't *hear.* The baby had been sleeping in the basket and woke up and was crying then, too, so I couldn't hear *nothing.*"

"Do you remember the last time I was here?" Brian asked. His eyes had grown demanding.

Emily would have told those eyes most anything.

Leila answered, "Yes."

429

"The man you saw hanging around the house?"

She nodded.

"Was he back again after that?"

"I don't know. I think so."

"Did you see him?"

"I guess. But as soon as I get a look out the window, one of the kids is needing something or other, and by the time I'm back there, he's gone."

Brian's eyes were steady. "Same guy, dirty blond hair, kinda short, wearin' a wool cap?"

"I guess, but I don't know if he's around. Like I said, one of the kids is always wanting me for something. I don't get a minute of free time to be looking around."

Brian left them and took John out of earshot, but Emily knew what he was saying. He was saying that Leila had described the first man as tall, dark, and wearing a baseball hat. He was saying that something wasn't right, and while nearly every other impulse in Emily was crying, *Look for the child, get a description, put out an APB, there isn't any time to spare,* a small one was agreeing with him.

"We're taking a look around," Brian called and set off with John.

Leila looked miserable. "I can't be a mother to these kids the right way."

From behind came a high-pitched, "Where's Travis, Momma?"

"I'm hungry."

"Momma, can *we* come *out?*"

"No," Leila shrieked without turning, *"you can't come out until I say, and I'm not saying it yet."*

"They aren't bad kids," Emily coaxed softly.

"But I can't take care of them by myself. One wants something, and then the other wants something, and then the baby is crying and wet and spitting up. I can't do everything, not by myself."

"Didn't someone come to see you, after we were here last?" Brian had arranged it. Emily had insisted. "Someone from Social Services?"

Leila nodded. "She didn't stay long."

"What did she say?"

"She said I was doin' okay." Leila started shaking her head hypnotically. "But I'm not. I'm all alone here. I need help." The head shake outlasted the words.

At this stage nineteen years ago, when Daniel had disappeared and the police had arrived, Emily had been in a panic looking for him. She had been running around the parking lot, looking under and behind shrubs, under and behind the employees' cars. She had been asking nearly as many questions as the police.

Leila wasn't in that kind of panic. She seemed more overwhelmed by her children, in general, than worried about Travis.

It struck Emily that Leila knew about Daniel, just like the rest of the town did, and that if she was looking for an attention-getter, Emily's presence last time might have put a bug in her ear.

"Where do you think Travis is?" Emily asked.

"I don't know."

"Would he have wandered off by himself?"

"Maybe."

"Has he ever done that before?"

"Well, he plays out here with all the other kids. When they go across the street, he goes, too."

Brian returned. He put a foot on the stair and an elbow on his knee. "Do you have any idea why someone would take Travis?"

"No."

"What about his father? Could he have come and taken the boy?"

"I keep asking him to do it every time I see him, but all he says is he's going to Boston to find work and he can't take Travis, so I have to keep him. That's what they all say, but they're not the ones stuck with

432

the kids."

"We can get you help," Emily said softly. "The first woman must have misunderstood. There are ways to help young mothers like you."

"There are?"

"Of course."

Leila looked at her as though she was afraid to hope, but wanted to more than anything.

Brian's voice gentled. "Tell me about Travis. Does he play hide and seek?"

Leila began picking tiny wool balls off the baby's dirty sweater. "He runs after the bigger kids sometimes."

"Where do they hide?"

She went on picking. "I don't know. Under the porch. In the Henzis' shed. Sometimes behind the trash cans."

"Anywhere else?"

"The dig."

"Where?"

Even Emily had had trouble catching the words.

"The dig," Leila repeated, frowning at the sweater. "Down the street. Where they're building."

Brian caught Emily's eye for an instant before asking Leila softly, "Do you think I should check there?"

Leila didn't look up. She hesitated, then nodded.

The following Monday night, Emily discussed the experience with Kay and Celeste. "They found the little boy in an empty appliance box that someone had dumped off there. He had a little pile of dirt with him and was happy as a pig in you-know-what. One of the neighbors confirmed seeing Leila carry him there."

"Is she being charged with anything?" Celeste asked.

Kay said, "John couldn't get himself to do it. Leila has problems enough without. Technically, she put him there like it was a playpen, with every intention of going back for him later."

"But she reported him missing. She got half our police force out looking for him. Isn't that false something or other?"

"Technically," Emily echoed Kay, "and if she were living in a big city, she'd probably have been taken into custody for it. But we all know Leila. She isn't evil. She is simply and totally overwhelmed by the portion that's on her plate. So she's doing what she has to do to get attention. It's a classic cry for help."

"Will she get it?"

"Hopefully. I talked with her mother. Not much by way of sympathy coming from that front, but the woman did agree to stop by. Brian also raised a stink with DSS. They're sending another worker over this time, one with more stamina than the first."

"Will they take the kids away?"

"I hope not. Leila loves them in her way, and they're not being mistreated, at least, not yet. DSS may suggest a temporary placement while she pulls herself together. Can you imagine — five children, and she's just twenty-one?"

Celeste snorted. "I couldn't handle one child at twenty-five."

"Was it difficult for you?" Kay asked Emily. "Being with Leila when they thought her little boy might have been kidnapped?"

Emily remembered arriving at Leila's house, the neighbors milling, the cruiser lights flashing. "At first. I was back in the post office parking lot. The scene had the same panicky feel." She waved the image away.

"How's Doug?"

The missing-child image was gone, but not the unease — different cause, same intensity. "Doug is Doug."

"The weekend was a bust?"

"By my standards. He refuses to talk."

"About *anything?*" Celeste asked.

"Anything substantial." Emily had tried so hard, had been solicitous and easygoing, had modulated her voice to sound innocent and nonthreatening, just curious. "He won't talk about his work. He won't talk about mine. He won't talk about Grannick, couldn't care less what's happening here. He'll talk about Jill. He'll talk about the weather and how it may affect his flights. That's it. He certainly won't talk about Daniel." She studied her fork. "Brian thought there might be a connection between Doug's attitude toward our marriage and Daniel's disappearance. So I asked Doug if he ever thought about Daniel."

"What did he say?"

"He said no. Then I asked if he thought Daniel's disappearance had shaped his life any. He looked at me like I was dumb." Which was nothing new, but still hurtful, particularly given the subject matter. "He said *of course* it had shaped his life, *anything* that serious shapes a person's life. When I asked in what ways, he rolled his eyes and said he wasn't in the mood to give a lecture in elementary psychology, and walked off." She looked at her friends. "I don't think he likes me anymore."

"Jerk."

"The man doesn't know what he has."

Emily's insides were jangling. Thinking about Doug set it off. "Yeah," she sighed, "well, he doesn't seem to care. I can't make him talk. I can't make him listen. He has his own agenda and won't deviate from it. Do you think he's trying to tell me something?"

"Like what?" Kay asked.

"Like he wants a divorce." She hated the word, but it kept coming to mind.

"Your husband is a self-centered man," Celeste argued. "If he wanted a divorce, he'd ask for it."

"Does it follow, then, that if he's not asking for it, he doesn't want it?" Emily asked. She was trying to reason things out, trying to get a grip on this man who had grown so elusive. "Should I keep fighting to find something worth saying?"

"Do you want to?" Kay asked.

"I think so."

Celeste looked mystified. "Why?"

"Because I'm married to him, he's my husband, we have a child."

"At some point, those things become secondary."

"Maybe. But I'm not there yet."

For several minutes, no one spoke. Emily picked at the remains of her sandwich, wondering if she was foolish clinging to something with so little substance, wondering why it *had* so little substance and whether it could ever have more.

"What are you going to do?" Celeste asked.

"Keep at it, I guess. We'll be together in Boston for Parents' Weekend. I may get the opening I want."

Oh, she would get the opening. The question was whether Doug would take it. Emily knew the others were thinking the same thing. She could see it on their faces.

"Back up a little," Kay said. "How did you come to be discussing Doug with Brian?"

Emily felt her cheeks warm. "Brian lives over the garage. He sees how little time Doug spends home."

"You and he talk about things like that?"

"Sure. He's a cop, like John." It was a good point, she thought. "He asks lot of questions. He does it in a way that makes it hard not to answer."

"It's the eyes," Celeste said. "I warned you about those." She raised her soda to her mouth and remarked around the straw, "I hear you had lunch with him the other day."

"He was free. So was I."

"I hear you made a nice couple."

"Who said that?" Emily asked, evading

the issue.

But Celeste had a one-track mind. "You do make a nice couple. Would you be interested in him?"

"I'm married."

Celeste held up a hand. "If you weren't, would you be interested in him?"

Emily made a show of deliberating. She finally shrugged. "Why not? He's a nice guy."

"Nice? Those eyes alone can make a woman melt."

You should only know the half, Emily thought with another, even greater rush of warmth.

"Hypothetically," Celeste went on, "if you weren't married to Doug, would you be looking at other men?"

"I don't know." But she did. Brian would be first on her list, if she weren't married to Doug.

"Would you be interested in sex?"

"If you're asking," Emily said with a sigh that she hoped sounded bored, "whether I think it's all right for you to be wanting sex, I think it is. I just think you have to be selective about who you have it with."

"Do *you* want sex?"

"This minute, no," she snapped, annoyed that Celeste persisted. "In the future, yes."

"You don't think people outgrow it?"

Emily gave her a look. "You don't believe that. Why are you asking me?"

"I want to know if I'm strange. Am I oversexed, looking for a lover at my age?"

"You're only forty-three."

"Forty-three isn't twenty-five."

That struck a familiar note. "Ahhh. You're thinking about the boy who answered your ad."

"He isn't a boy. He's a younger man. I've talked with him on the phone twice now. He's nice. Sounds very mature. Seems totally comfortable with the idea of having sex with an older woman."

"He talks about it?" Kay asked. It was the first thing she'd said in a while.

"Yeah. It's kinda racy. But safe. Phone sex is."

"What happens when you meet him?" Emily asked.

"I doubt I will."

"Why not?"

"Because *I'm* not comfortable with the idea of his having sex with an older woman. Besides, there are enough others closer to my age to keep me busy for a while, even with the marathoner and the doctor crossed off the list."

"You crossed off the doctor?" Emily asked

in surprise. She had thought Celeste was meeting him later this week.

"He sent a message through the magazine — urgent, he said, so they actually called me on the phone to tell me that he won't be in Boston this week after all."

"Why don't you just reschedule?"

"Because, A, he had his secretary call the message in, and, B, when I tried to call back, I got his answering service three times. I don't need that. I don't care *how* wealthy he is. I don't want to be dealing with a secretary, or an answering machine, and I *don't* want to be squeezed in between meetings. I have no idea why he placed his ad in the first place. That was one thing about the widower, Michael. He made me feel like he had all the time in the world just for me. Okay, so there weren't any fireworks, still, I liked that feeling. Besides, I'm meeting the veterinarian on Wednesday. And then," she grinned, "on Sunday," she sighed, "the architect."

Emily had been hearing about the architect for days. "I hope you're not setting yourself up for a fall."

"I'm not. I'm telling you, he is going to be *the* best. I just know it."

Kay hung behind a bit when they left the

441

Eatery. When Celeste climbed into her car, she attached herself to the nearby parking meter, and when the car pulled away from the curb, she didn't move.

Emily joined her. "You were quiet back there."

"I was uncomfortable."

"With Celeste's men?"

"More than that." It was late. She had school tomorrow. But there were things on her mind that would keep her awake anyway, and, awkward as it was to express, she needed feedback. "Are you in a rush to get home?"

"Me? For what?"

"I don't know. A call from Jill. Doug."

"Jill knows I'm with you guys," Emily answered, "and Doug's only been gone for a day. He won't call." She sat down on the curb and patted the spot beside her.

Kay took it. She wrapped her arms around her knees. "I feel bad about Doug."

"I know."

"Do you still love him? The truth, Em."

It was a minute and several cars rolling past before Emily said, "I don't know. I don't feel a rush when he walks in the door, just a lot of nervousness, and hope, hope that things will be better this time. Only they never are. Our relationship stinks."

442

"Do you sleep together?"

"We sleep in the same bad."

"Do you miss the other?"

After a minute, she said, softly, "Yes."

She sounded like she wasn't entirely comfortable talking about sex, which helped Kay, since she wasn't either. The darkness helped, too. She didn't feel quite so exposed.

"Did you mean what you told Celeste? About sex? About wanting it with another man, if you and Doug split?"

"This is an awkard discussion."

"I know."

They sat for a time before Emily said, again softly, "I'm not ready to shrivel and die."

Kay looked out across the street. "You don't think sex is overblown for women our age?"

"We're not terribly old."

"I'm older than you are."

"By a few years. That's not much. Do you think sex is overblown for *men* our age?"

"They're different. Society assumes they'll keep on going. They don't reach menopause."

"You haven't, have you?"

"No." She hugged her knees. Menopause scared the living daylights out of her. She felt less than sexy now, but at least she was

fertile. She couldn't imagine not having
something so female as a period. "Was sex
with Doug good?"

"In the beginning." Emily watched her
fingers steepling. "It changed after Daniel."

"How?"

"Became mechanical."

"Could that have been marital blahs setting in?"

"Possibly."

Kay didn't know why she had asked. Her
problem wasn't the blahs. When it was dark,
when John touched her, she liked it.

Emily came forward to hug her knees, too.
In a gentle voice, she asked, "Are you having trouble with John?"

"Actually," Kay sighed, "he's having
trouble with me." She blurted it out. "He
wants more, and I'm not even talking about
all-the-way sex. He wants touchy-feely
before dinner. He wants sweet talk and
kisses here and there, for no reason at all.
Isn't that weird?"

"No. It's nice."

"He wants me to take the initiative. I don't
know if I can."

"Why not?"

"It's just not me."

"Aren't you attracted to him?"

"Yes, but I don't define myself in sexual

terms. I just don't *think* that way. It doesn't *occur* to me to do little physical things. I thought our marriage had gone past that point."

"Slid into a kind of elderly status?" Emily teased, nudging her, thigh to thigh.

"You know what I mean."

"Slid into a pattern."

"Yes." But John was amenable to most anything she wanted, and he always saw her satisfied. So why was she having trouble giving a little on her own? "I feel like a fraud," she blurted out. Emily remained silent beside her, their legs bumping comfortingly. "When I think of myself pretending to be sexy, I'm mortified. I'm not sexy. I'm not attractive."

"You are so."

"Not like a Sharon Stone or a Geena Davis."

"John isn't leaving town to run after either of them. He's staying right here with you."

"I'm fat."

"You're not fat."

"Compared to when I was married, I am. My body is getting older. In a few more years, I'll look like my mother did."

Emily gave her thigh a knock. "I loved your mother. She was the sweetest woman in the world."

"She was obese. I used to come home from school, and there she would be at the kitchen table, eating candy." Kay let her memories out of the bag she had kept them stashed in. "Know what she used to say? She'd say, 'Look at your mother, Kay. Look long and hard, and make up your mind right now that you won't ever grow up to be like her.' Then she'd pop another candy into her mouth. It was like she was absolved of overeating as long as she warned me against it."

"You don't overeat."

"Not like she did. But every ten years a few more pounds go on. When I look in the mirror, I see my mother. How can I feel sexy?"

Emily swiveled to face her. "John loves you. He isn't seeing your mother when he looks at you. He's seeing *you*."

"But I don't *feel* attractive."

"Then *do* something about it."

"Like what? I don't want to have my nose done like Celeste did, and if I ever had my hair colored that way, I'd feel like even more of a fraud. Can you imagine having gorgeous hair on a blobby body?"

"If your body's the problem, do something your mother never did. Exercise."

"I do. I run around school all day."

446

"Join an aerobics class."

"Emily, I'd make a *fool* of myself at one of those."

"Okay, then an exercise class."

"Wearing a leotard? Right."

"Okay, then walk. Get a warmup suit that covers everything up, put it on every morning, and go for a half hour walk before school. Do that for a month, or two, or three, and you'll feel different about yourself. Think about it. Your mother never exercised. She was too heavy. So as long as you get yourself out there, you're different from her."

Kay wanted to argue. But she wanted to believe even more. "You really think I'd feel different?"

"I do."

"Just half an hour?"

"That's all."

"What if it rains?"

"Skip a day."

"What if someone stops and tells me I'm rushing Halloween?"

"Kay."

"What if John laughs at me?"

"He won't."

"What if he does?"

"Tell him that for every day you walk, you add a day to your life, and that he can laugh

447

all he wants, but when he's dead and gone, you'll be going strong and having a ball without him."

"If I tell him that, he may just walk *with* me."

"For protection. Sweet."

Kay laughed. Her smile stayed.

"Do it," Emily urged softly. "You have nothing to lose, nothing but something that's been haunting you for years. Put it to rest, Kay. It's time."

SEVENTEEN

Brian was acutely aware of Halloween's approach, not because the department had been hitting the schools with safety tips, or because every store window in town sported pumpkins and witches, or because Grannick's vandal had started in with raw eggs, but because this was his first Halloween as a single parent, and he was taking the role to heart. Julia needed a costume. So he left work early one day, fetched her at Janice's, and drove to the mall.

"Well, look at this," he announced when they were standing before the largest display of costumes in the place. "You can be a witch, or a ghost, or Snow White." He moved on. "You can be a dinosaur. You can be a Ninja turtle. You can be Aladdin. You can be Princess Jasmin. Or a ballerina. Or a mermaid. Or a ladybug." He gave her a little squeeze. "What'll it be, toots?"

Julia was staring wide-eyed at the mannequins.

"Okay, let's simplify things here. These are the little girl choices. Not politically correct of me, but what the hell, you are my little girl. You can be Snow White, Princess Jasmin, a ballerina, or a mermaid."

"Dis," Julia said, pointing.

"Which? The mermaid?"

"Dis."

"The ladybug?"

"Bug."

"That wasn't one of the choices. Look at Snow White." He approached that one. "Isn't she beautiful?"

"Bug."

"Let's see what sizes there are." He bent to study boxed Snow Whites. "Large. Large. Medium. Large. Large. Swell. Okay, not Snow White. How about the princess."

"Bug."

"The bug is weird. It has a green face and funny things sticking out of its head. The princess is you." He bent at the princess pile. "Medium. Medium. Large. Large. Large." Straightening, he looked up and around until he spotted a salesgirl two aisles over. "Miss? Excuse me, miss? Could I have some help here?" When the girl arrived, he said, "My daughter wants to be Princess Jasmin, but there aren't any costumes in her size."

"Only the big sizes are left," the girl said.

"Well, I can see that, but I was thinking that there must be some in back."

"Everything we have is on display."

"How can you run out two full days before Halloween?"

"These have been on sale for a month. Most people come early."

"Bug," said Julia.

The girl glanced at that pile. "There's a small."

"I don't like the ladybug."

"*Bug,* Daddy."

"Why do you want the bug?" Brian asked, spearing her with a look.

She speared him right back. *"Daddy, bug."* She reached toward the costume and began to squirm. By the time he had her shifted and securely anchored again, the salesgirl was holding out the proper box.

"Thanks," he grunted and strode gracelessly toward the front of the store.

A short time later, in a nearby McDonald's, he put Julia in a booster seat, slid in across from her, and began to tear apart her meal. "What was so appealing about the ladybug?"

She stuck a piece of hamburger in her mouth.

"You'd have made a pretty Snow White. Or a ballerina. Why a ladybug, of all things?"

Julia offered a string of garbled words.

"Okay. It's cute. I suppose." He put his weight on his forearms and questioned her in earnest. "But why the bug? Why not the ghost? Or Aladdin?" He was intrigued by the fact that she'd had such a definite opinion. She was very little to be having definite opinions.

She reached for a fry. "Emmy."

"Emily did not suggest a ladybug. She said she had a worm in the attic. A worm is not a ladybug."

Julia offered him a piece of meat. He took it.

"You really liked the ladybug?"

The look on her face, incredibly, said that she was surprised he would ask, when clearly, the ladybug was the best costume there.

"Okay," he conceded. "It may not have been the one I wanted, but I'm not the one wearing it, right? If you like it, that's what counts. You'll make an adorable ladybug."

She grinned, ear to ear, and his heart melted. It struck him that Gayle should see that grin, that she should see her daughter forming definite opinions — God, so like *her!* He missed Gayle, in the same way that he would have missed a good friend, because she had been that, and a part of his life for so long. He would have liked being able to sit down with her and tell her everything that had happened since she had died.

He would even tell her about Emily. Gayle would like Emily, would like the idea of someone with a heart of gold spending time with her daughter.

Brian missed Emily, and not just the sex. He missed lying together, talking softly, being on the same wavelength in ways that Gayle and he had never been. He missed discussing problems. He missed having fun and feeling peace. Emily had helped him through a rough time. He would love her forever for that alone.

They were far from finished, Emily and him. That thought raised his spirits. And he was doing okay with Julia. And he was doing okay with his new job. So he might just make it after all.

Suddenly in a better mood and ferociously hungry, he went back to the counter and bought two Big Macs for himself, and then, when Julia seemed done with her meal, he bought an ice cream cone for them to share, and *then,* when the opportunity seemed too good to pass up, he stopped on the way home at the drugstore, grabbed Julia and the ladybug mask, and went straight to the photo booth at the back.

Studying the mask for the first time close-up, Julia was preoccupied enough not to notice when he fit his quarters into the slot. She was still staring at it when he propped it beside the camera's eye. She was startled when the first flash went off.

"Look, toots," Brian cajoled, bobbing the mask up and down. "Smile at the ladybug."

Julia's eyes were growing larger when the second flash went off, and even larger when the third one came. In a last ditch attempt to get a smile, Brian put the mask to his face and made what he thought would be a ladybug sound.

Julia let out a blood-curdling scream.

"Jesus Christ," he muttered, dropping the mask. "It's me, it's Daddy," he pleaded, but she was sobbing hysterically, so he scooped her up, stuffed yet another pathetic quartet of photos in his back pocket, and left. It wasn't until he turned onto China Pond Road that he remembered the mask.

"No problem," Emily said when he told her what he had done.

"Easy for you to say. You're not the one whose kid will be the only one without a mask. How could I have left it in the god-damned booth, after all that?"

Emily was trying not to laugh. He was adorable in his distress, so earnest in wanting to do things right. "You were shaken," she reasoned. "Julia was screaming. You wanted to get away from the scene of the crime, so to speak."

They were on the floor in Brian's living room, with their backs against his sofa and their legs outstretched, denim to denim. Those legs were actually similarly shaped, Emily noticed, straight and lean. Only his were longer. And the bare feet sticking out of his were larger and more knobby. And his toes didn't have Sensuous Burgundy on the nails.

She wished she could have said that she had painted her toenails for Doug, but Doug wasn't coming home that weekend. He had called to say he was working straight through to be entirely free the following weekend for Jill. Not for Emily. For Jill.

Emily wondered if there was a message in that. She wondered why so many companies suddenly wanted him on Sundays. She wondered how much golf he was playing.

She had painted her toenails *after* he called, in defiance that he would pick golf over her.

She wasn't with Brian in defiance, though. She was with him because she wanted to be. They couldn't make love, though Lord knew she ached to, with her insides abuzz and his warmth running up her side. Oh, yes, she was trying to be good. But she couldn't deny herself completely.

"So what do I do?" he was asking. "I called the drugstore, but the night girl went looking and couldn't find it, which means that some little kid has a ladybug mask with no costume. What'll I do for Julia?"

The little lady in question was sleeping soundly on his chest, the book that Brian had been reading to her prior to Emily's arrival discarded on the floor nearby.

Emily thought back to Jill's earliest Halloweens. Then, because she felt safe when she was with Brian, she allowed her thoughts back farther, to the two Halloweens she had had with Daniel. "Daniel hated masks, not to look at, only to wear. He wouldn't let me put anything over his face. So I put him in the body of the costume, got a little wool hat and pinned ears to it, and drew whiskers on his face. He was a mouse." So sweet to remember. Not as painful as it used to be. "I took my lesson from that when it was Jill's turn. The worm costume was a little tube of reddish-brown fabric that I stitched together. I made a bonnet out of the same material for the head, but her face was free. I put lipstick on her and darkened her nose and drew in exaggerated eyelashes. Not that worms have eyelashes. But she looked cute. So would Julia. A little nose, some eyelashes, some whiskers. I can pick up a little plastic headband at the drug store, and attach pipe cleaners for the antennae. She'll look precious."

His eyes relaxed and warmed. "You're good at this."

"I love it. And I've had practice. Years of Halloweens. Years of Valentine's Days. Years of teacher conferences and PTA meetings. My life has been geared to kids' things for so long, it's weird being without."

"You were a conscientious mom. I'll bet *you* wouldn't have lost a mask."

"Maybe not. But I lost a child."

"Emily."

"It's true."

"No, it's not. A child was *taken* from you. There's a difference."

Emily might have argued that she had left the child alone, except that she was tired of taking the blame for something that happened so long ago. She was *tired* of feeling guilty. Oh, she still ached for Daniel. But she needed to smile. She needed to relax.

Daniel was gone, but she needed to *live.*

She planned to tell Doug that when she met him in Boston the following weekend.

Celeste arrived at the art opening in Cambridge on Sunday afternoon, holding a rose in her hand and her poise by a thread. She felt she was dying of foreplay, teased by expectation to the point of implosion. It was all she could do to look calm and sophisticated, which was the image she had chosen for the afternoon.

She was wearing a suit in ivory wool, a black-sashed ivory hat, and sexy black heels. Being dressed up for the first time in so long added to the fantasy, as did the airy, near-brilliance of the modern gallery into which it seemed she had fallen.

She needed this, after the fiasco that Wednesday evening with the veterinarian had been. He turned out to be shy to the extreme, talking only in reponse to what she asked, avoiding her gaze. He hadn't been kidding when he'd said, "I may be barking up the wrong tree answering an ad that starts with sexy and blond." She felt bad for him. He was lonely. He wanted human companionship. But she was no martyr.

She looked slowly around the room, passing over artsy types and business types until her eye found a man who was a combination of both. He was conservatively dressed in a dark suit and held a glass of champagne, but the way his curly dark hair framed a tanned face and striking brown eyes suggested a wildness that set him apart from the rest.

Those eyes held hers in ways that the veterinarian couldn't have even begun to comprehend, much less do. He was the right age, the right height, the right weight. He was the one. No doubt about it. He was the reason she had had her nose done and her chin tucked. He was the answer to her prayers.

She didn't move, but waited for him to come to her. He sipped his champagne. He conversed with those around him. His eyes rarely left hers for long.

Finally, murmuring something to his companions, he wove his slow way to where she stood. His lips twitched, male and satisfied. "And they said it couldn't be done through an ad."

She allowed herself the smallest of smug smiles, but said nothing.

"My name's Carter."

"Celeste."

"Celeste." Again, the twitch of the lips, then the tiniest break in his voice. "That's lovely. As you are." He stared at her for another minute, before catching himself and looking around. "Come. Let me introduce you to my friends."

With the lightest touch to her back, the whisper of a palm over the closure of her bra — sweet, private, intimate — he guided her around the room. She met the artist whose work was being shown. She met the owners of the gallery. She met other artists. She met Carter's partner.

The scene was as much a dream as Carter, worlds away from any other date she had ever had, worlds away from anything she had ever experienced in Grannick. For an instant she imagined herself an imposter here, outclassed and ill-prepared in spite of her clothes and her dreams. Then she looked at Carter again. As smooth as he was, he was reassuringly down to earth. When he found her a glass of champagne, took a fresh one for himself, and said, gently, "To new people," her qualms dissolved.

As she had known he would, he took the lead. From a quiet shaded corner with a view of the angular lines of the building, he told her not about his children or grandchildren, as the widower had done interminably, but about the people she had just met, about each one's work, each one's life. He made no assumptions about her knowledge of art, but spoke in plain terms, with neither arrogance nor condescension.

Celeste was enthralled. He was articulate and learned where art and architecture were concerned — and intuitive enough to judge her level of understanding perfectly, neither exceeding it, nor underestimating it.

"But I've been doing all the talking," he finally said with a rakishly diffident smile.

"That's fine. What you've said is far more appropriate to the setting than anything I might be saying."

"Then we'll have to change the setting." His gaze touched her mouth before it returned to her eyes. "There's still a little sun left to the afternoon. Would you like to walk?"

Harvard Square was filled with people. Most were far more casually dressed than they were, but that was part of the fantasy, too. Sunday afternoon strolling was the epitome of romance. They walked in a bubble of elegance, aware always of something simmering at its core.

It was outwardly innocent, walking and talking, but there were periods of walk without talk, when Carter held her hand or hooked her arm through his. At those times she realized how in step with each other they were. There was no impatient striding, as she imagined there would have been with the marathoner, but a comfortably matched gait. It felt right to Celeste, the prelude to a destined something, even sweeter than she had dreamed.

In time, they found themselves in a cafe with cappucino royales, and when they began to feel the liquor, Carter suggested stopping at a small restaurant several blocks over for something to eat. The restaurant was Indonesian. Celeste was content to hide her ignorance by letting him do the ordering.

Afterward, she couldn't have said what it was that she ate, because the place was dark, their corner intimate, and her thoughts a long way from food. She nibbled on whatever arrived, and watched Carter do the same, but all the while she was remembering the marathoner and his neuroses, the doctor and his scheduling, the vet and his shyness, and she gloated silently, thinking, "I knew it would be like this, I *knew* it would."

At the end of the meal, when he offered a husky, "My place is right down the street," she didn't think twice. She had been waiting too long. She wasn't waiting a minute longer.

Darkness had fallen by the time they reached the house, a small frame structure that proved to be nearly as spectacular as the art gallery had been. It had been gutted and rebuilt with a dearth of walls and a keen eye for angle and line.

Guided only by the glow of the street lamps spilling through windows and Carter's hand on her back, Celeste climbed the open stairway to a landing that extended far enough to allow for a huge platform bed.

The only pause she felt had to do with the magnitude of the moment. Carter was a dream, the embodiment of everything good and strong and caring in a man.

Piece by piece, he removed her clothes until she stood naked before him. He didn't touch her then, or kiss her, but simply looked at her body while, piece by piece, he removed his own things.

Celeste felt the chill of the air on her skin, but it only heightened her arousal. Her body was swollen, her insides throbbing and wet. By the time he discarded his shorts and applied a condom, she was dying for what she had seen.

"Lie down," he whispered.

Breathing fast, she did, and raised her

knees when he came between them. The reward was golden. He filled her with a pulsing strength that took her from one orgasm to another, dream upon dream, pleasure after pleasure. It didn't occur to her that she didn't know his last name, or where he had grown up, or what he did to keep his body in shape. He inspired trust, and she gave it.

The moon played in and around the clouds over China Pond Road. It splintered through Brian's windowed wall and fell in silvery shards across everything in sight. Brian had long since put Julia to bed and was sprawled on the sofa, wishing Emily were there, when the telephone rang. He bobbled the receiver before getting it to his ear.

"Yeah."

A high voice, alarmed but distinctive, said, "Detective? Detective, I need your help. Something's coming out of the pond. I don't know what it is, but it keeps lifting its head, higher each time. Something's out there. I know it is, but I don't know what it's going to do. You have to come. Come *quickly.*"

Brian sighed. This wasn't the first such call he'd had. There had been three in the past week, each one a false alarm. "Is it the Haffenreffers' dog again?"

"No. It isn't a dog. It's something else."

"Maybe a deer. I saw one in the woods the other night."

"It is not a deer. I know what deer look like, and this isn't that."

"What does this look like?" he asked, patient in deference to Myra's age.

"It has a long neck, a very long neck and a very small head and eyes that glow."

"That glow."

"Green," she said.

Brian scrubbed at an eye with the heel of his hand. The monster had never glowed before. "Someone's playing a Halloween prank."

"No, no, no. This isn't a costume. It's real, and it's dangerous, and it's after my willow. I have to go outside and do something to stop it. I'd wake up Frank, but he had a very long day. Will you come, Detective?"

The last thing Brian wanted was to go out in the cold. But Myra was old and widowed, like his mother, and although his mother was more lucid, more social, and more active, he still made the link.

He sighed. "Sure, Myra. I'll be right there."

He stepped into his sneakers and pulled

on a jacket, then checked on Julia. She was dead to the world. So he trotted down the stairs, and jogged down the driveway and across the cul de sac to Myra's front door. When she didn't answer his ring, he went around back. The moon appeared long enough to show her on the bench under the willow.

He sank down on the other end and tucked his hands in his pockets for warmth. "It's a chilly night, Myra. You shouldn't be out here." She was wearing a coat. Still.

"I have to be."

"Why?"

She seemed taken back by the direct question. "Because."

He studied the pond. Its surface was a glassy reflection of bulbous, moon-fringed clouds. "I don't see anything here."

"No. It's below now."

"A monster."

"It's been here for years. I kept telling Frank, but he wouldn't listen. But it's *there,* and I can't *stand* it."

"A monster. With glowing eyes."

She took a breath and seemed to steady herself. "Well, I don't know if the eyes are glowing. It just seems that way sometimes."

In a soft voice, he asked, "Myra, is Frank buried here?" It seemed one logical explanation for her fixation on the area, particularly if she had been so controlled by the man in life that she couldn't accept his death.

"Here? Oh, no. He's on the other side of town. The *monster* is buried here."

"Buried?"

"In the water."

Brian's eyes skated over the water's surface to the trees at the far side. He didn't see a thing. "You said it was after the willow. Why do you think so?"

"The willow's roots go right to the water. The thing will pull and tug until it sucks the willow right underground."

"But why would it want the willow?"

"Because the willow protects us."

Brian turned sideways. He looked Myra square in the eye, giving the emphasis to his words that he kept gentle in his voice. "There isn't really a monster."

She stared at him.

"Nothing's going to dig up your willow."

"Someone *has* to."

"Why?"

She looked confused. "I don't know."

"Come." He drew her up. "It's too cold for you here. Let me bring you inside."

"But I'll only have to call you another night. He's out here. I saw him."

"Well," Brian said, "you'll call me another

467

time, then."

"But you won't be able to do *anything* once the ground freezes."

He slipped an arm around her shoulder and guided her up the stairs. "I'll be here, Myra. You'll call me, and I'll come right over."

With that promise, she allowed herself to be shown into the house.

EIGHTEEN

Emily drove to Boston with the highest of hopes the following Friday. She was thrilled to be seeing Jill, and nearly as excited about meeting her friends and learning her favorite haunts. She wanted to be able to put faces with names, wanted to be able to visualize the reading room of the library, the dining hall, the student union. She wanted to be able to picture every little detail when Jill called on the phone.

Doug was another matter. She was nervous. Much rested on the weekend, on the precious little time when they would be alone. She needed to see if there was any feeling for her left in him. If not, their marriage was doomed.

When the skyline of the city appeared on the horizon, she remembered the last time she had made the trip. She and Jill had been holding hands, fearing the unknowns ahead, dreading the moment of parting. They had been focused on Jill's college experience. Emily hadn't had a clue about the shifts her own life would take.

This time around, Jill was waiting outside the dorm, running to the curb with a huge smile when Emily pulled up. Emily was teary with happiness at the sight of her daughter the college student, laughing, holding Jill tightly. Then there were the introductions, because no less than five friends had been waiting with Jill, and a mini-tour in advance of the full one for Doug.

Emily had arranged to meet him at the hotel at five. He didn't arrive until five-thirty, and if it hadn't been for Jill's nervous looks at her watch, Emily wouldn't have minded. She loved being alone with Jill, without having to be alert to Doug's needs.

Doug was buoyant enough when he arrived to compensate for the delay. After a brief stop upstairs while he changed clothes, they headed back to the campus.

Friday night consisted of dinner in the dining hall, a concert by the college's three singing groups, and a reception at Jill's dorm. It was late by the time Emily and Doug returned to the hotel. High on the goodwill of the evening, Emily was perfectly happy to climb into bed and fall asleep.

When she awoke the next morning, Doug was out.

"Gone running," said the note he left on the pad by the phone, though it didn't say when he had left or how long he would be.

Emily showered and dressed, then sat in an armchair and waited anxiously. They were meeting Jill at ten. She didn't want to be late.

It struck her that Doug was late a lot. He never used to be. She wondered if he was late for work, too, or whether it was just home things that he had grown so lackadaisical about.

She didn't ask, because he returned sweaty and out of breath, with just enough time to get ready, and then they were swept up in the day's events, so that she didn't think about it until later that night, when it no longer seemed critical. He had been with them for the entire day. He had been a good sport through tours, lectures, a luncheon, a football game, dinner at a restaurant with Jill's closest friends and their parents, and several hours of dorm-hopping to meet and spend time with others. He had been friendly. He had been personable.

Granted, he didn't spend much time talking with Emily. She suspected he knew more about the daily lives of some of the

471

people he had met that day than he did about hers.

But Jill was happy having him there. If she was aware of his lack of attentiveness to Emily, she didn't let on.

Emily lay in bed that night, curled on her side with her back to Doug. She didn't know if he was sleeping and neither asked nor slid back until their bodies touched. She was quiet. She kept her breathing low and even. Though the weekend was supposed to be a time of marital regeneration, she did nothing to suggest she wanted to make love. And she felt guilty as hell.

It was hours before she fell asleep. When she awoke, Doug was out running again. She was relieved and, therein, felt more guilty than ever.

Doug was her husband. She should want him. But she didn't. He was a stranger to her. If he had been one of the fathers she had met yesterday, she would have smiled and exchanged surface pleasantries, then moved on without a backward glance.

Jill was their only link.

The more Emily thought about it, the more frightened that made her. People who liked each other as little as she and Doug did, usually ended up divorced.

Divorced. God, she *hated* that word.

But it made sense for them. Particularly in light of Brian. If Emily, who prized fidelity so highly, had slept with another man, something was *really* wrong with her marriage.

Divorce made sense.

Still, she fought it.

Feeling jittery, she bolted out of bed and hurriedly dressed and packed. Doug returned just as she finished, as sweaty and breathless and short of time as he had been the morning before.

Wishing she could put it off, but knowing it was now or never, she followed him into the bathroom. "Can we talk?"

He set his running watch down by the sink. "I'm late."

"We never talk, Doug. I think we need to do something."

To his credit, he didn't start in with condescending looks, or ask why she was trying to ruin a fine weekend. He didn't pretend not to know something was wrong. Instead, neutrally, he asked, "Like what?" and, bending over, began washing his face.

"Like see a counselor." It was a last ditch effort. She couldn't think of anything else.

She had to wait until he had straightened and was reaching for his shave cream before

he said, "Why do you want to see a counsel-
or?"

"Because our relationship stinks. We can't
talk."

"We can talk. We just don't."

"Okay. Same thing."

"No, it's not. If we choose not to talk, we
choose not to talk. There's nothing wrong
with that."

"There is if we're both innately social, and
we are, Doug. We talk with everyone else,
just not with each other."

"That's the nature of our relationship."

"I want to change it."

"Fine. Go to a counselor."

"I want *us* to."

He finished lathering his lower face and
reached for his razor. "I'm not seeing a
counselor."

"Why not?"

"It's a waste of time and money."

"Not if it improves our relationship. Don't
you want to do that?"

"I don't think our relationship needs scrutiny."

"You think it's good?" she cried. "Doug,
we go separate ways. We rarely even pass in
the night. We share Jill. Period."

He systematically stroked away one strip
of shave cream, then another.

"Is it Daniel?" she asked with her heart in her throat.

"No."

"It's natural to be thinking of him, with Jill gone."

"I'm not."

"Then what?"

"How the hell do I know?"

"What's on your mind?"

"Right now? Getting ready in time."

"Doug. This is important."

He rinsed the blade. "Don't nag. There's nothing I hate more than a woman who nags."

Emily closed her mouth, but the injustice of his criticism had her reopening it the next minute. "What's happening with us isn't right. Life should be opening up, not closing down, now that we don't have the everyday responsibility of kids. Don't you want something more out of life?"

"Like what?"

"Like *living*. Smiles. Laughter. Fun." She pictured Brian, with whom she had all of that, and felt guilty. Her guilt intensified when she realized that she was looking at Doug in only the skimpiest of running shorts, and feeling nothing.

"I have those things," he said in an off-handed way.

"With work, but what about a woman?" she blurted out. "Don't you want a woman?" He was a normal, red-blooded male. At least, he used to be. Now he wasn't even asking for sex.

He hadn't in a while, and even then, Emily had had the feeling that he wanted it when she didn't to punish her. Now he had lost even that urge.

She hadn't lost the urge, as Brian had so eloquently pointed out.

"I have you," Doug said illogically.

"But we don't have fun together, not just us two. We don't touch. We don't make love. Don't *you* want that?"

He rinsed the blade again. "If you were that desperate for sex, you could have told me." He shot a look at his watch. "It's a little late now."

"God, Doug," she breathed, amazed at his coarseness, his *ignorance,* if he thought she still wanted him, what with the lack of love.

The lack of love. That was it in a nutshell. She didn't love Doug. He didn't love her. They had no business staying together.

Except for Jill.

Except for the fact that Doug did rely on those few hours home between trips.

Except for the house they shared.

Except for Daniel.

Emily turned and left the bathroom, wondering if Doug ever thought about those things. She wondered if he ever thought about divorce. She wondered how he could *not* think about it.

She was still wondering hours later, heading west on the turnpike, toward Grannick. She was feeling blue, anyway. Leaving Jill had been hard, even knowing that Thanksgiving was only eighteen days off. Leaving Doug had been easy. That was upsetting Emily no end.

The familiarity of Grannick failed to settle her. Nor did the haven of the dark house at the end of China Pond Road. She saw lights on above the garage. It was all she could do not to go there.

But being with Brian meant closing her eyes to problems that had to be faced. She wished she knew what to do.

Flipping lights on as she went, she carried her suitcase up to the bedroom and unpacked. Then, wanting to lift out and savor the weekend's good times, she took refuge in Jill's room. There was comfort here, a sense of love, at least. She sat on the bed and hugged Cat, remembering not so much the weekend just done, but fun times she and Jill had had here at home in years past.

Her eye roamed the room. It was a teenager's room, messy as was a teenager's way. Yes, she had dusted — gingerly — but the mother in her itched to sort through the basket of magazines and toss out the oldest, to do something with the single red prom rose that stood dead in its bud vase, to wade through the papers and books piled on the desk. But Jill wanted things the same, and Emily knew that was going to be a tall order when it came to Doug.

So she kept on hugging Cat, swaying a little in time to a lullaby that drifted back from years before. She remembered singing it to Jill. No. To Daniel. It had been his favorite. She had sung it to him every night, sometimes three or four times when he cried for more. His eyes would grow heavier with each round, until the final, "Mo-a, mo-a," was little more than a dazed murmur. Daniel sleeping, had been a hauntingly in-nocent sight.

Feeling chilled, she went to the closet, reached into Jill's sweater basket, and pulled on the first one she touched. It was a ratty cotton thing that had been wisely left behind, but it was fine for Emily. She wasn't fussy. She much preferred sweaters with his-tory to ones with panache.

The basket was filled with such time-worn sweaters, tossed in with a general abandon.

Thinking that there might be others to borrow — no, she was not cleaning the closet — she took out the next one, shook it straight, and gave it a onceover. She held it close for a minute, breathing in Jill and the comfort that brought, before folding it neatly, setting it aside, and reaching for another. She didn't think she would use this one either, so she folded it and put it carefully on top of the first. The next one in the basket, a teal heather, looked more promising. She pulled it out. That was when she saw the folded paper that lay on the bottommost sweater.

Setting the teal heather aside, she unfolded the paper. It was something Jill had written for English class the spring before. Emily didn't see a grade at the top, didn't see any marks on the page. For that matter, she didn't see the wear and tear that usually came with being crammed into a notebook and carried to and from school. The paper looked clean and crisp, as though it had just emerged from the Image-writer.

"Seeing Things," was the title. Emily began to read.

"All my life I've been looking forward to going to college. My parents met there and always talked about the fun they had. After looking at lots of different schools, I applied to the ones I liked. I was lucky. I got into my first choice. Same with my best friends. We were all excited. In April my college had an open house for the students who had been accepted. I signed up to go and was matched up with a girl there who would take me around with her."

Emily remembered it clearly. A nervous, but very excited Jill had taken the bus into Boston on a Thursday afternoon.

"The girl, Jessica, was cool. She met me at the admissions office and took me to dinner with her at the dining hall. That night, there were parties in the dorm. The college kids had been told they weren't supposed to drink with the pre-frosh, but there was some beer anyway, not enough to get drunk on, just enough to feel like we were in college. I had a ball."

Clever Jill. She hadn't told Emily about the beer.

"The next morning Jessica took me to classes, but by lunchtime we'd had enough. She suggested we walk to a favorite cafe of hers for lunch with some of her friends, and we did."

Yes. The Harvard Bookstore Cafe.

"After lunch, we walked on Newbury Street. It was neat. I loved the shops and the people. I come from a college town and never thought of Boston as being one, but it did feel like it there, because there were college students all over. One of the other prefrosh bought some things in one of the stores, and then we all went for yogurt. Finally we had to start back, so that I could get my things and take the bus home. We crossed over Commonwealth Avenue, walked another block, and were crossing the next street when I saw him."

Emily frowned.

"He was coming out of one of the townhouses, wearing a business suit that I had seen many times before, and I thought that it was an awesome coincidence that he was doing business here at the same time I was visiting, because I wouldn't have to take the bus home after all. 'My God,' I told my friends. 'There's my father!' I was just about to call out to him when a woman followed him out of the townhouse. She was carrying a little boy. As I stood there watching, my father took the little boy from her and held him. He wrapped his other arm around the woman."

But Doug had been in New York that day — Emily remembered because she, too, had thought it would be wonderful if he could drive Jill home, only he had ruled it out.

Pressing a hand to her chest, she read on.

"Jessica asked if the woman was my mom. That was when I realized I'd made a mistake. My father knew I was in Boston. If he was going to be there, too, he would have arranged to meet me and drive me home. Besides, my father wouldn't be holding another woman that way. He wouldn't be kissing her that way, or hugging the little boy so tightly before unwrapping his arms from his neck and handing him back to the woman. The man on the steps couldn't possibly have been my father. He belonged to that family, not mine. He just looked a lot like my dad."

Emily was breathing shallowly.

"I still think about that man. The other day I started wondering if it was possible for a man to have two families. If he traveled a lot, like my dad does, he could. He could see one family during the week and the other on the weekends. My own father wouldn't do that, but another man could, I suppose."

The writing ended. Emily whipped the page over, but it was blank. Same with the one after it. Flipping back to the first, she reread the last paragraph, then reread the whole piece, breathing faster with each page until her whole body shook. "Oh my God," she whispered. "The *bastard*."

Heart pounding, she set aside the paper and, not knowing what else to do, took out the last sweater. Trembling wildly, she folded it as best she could and replaced it. She put each of the others on top, slid the basket back into the closet, and shut the door. Then she took the paper and went downstairs.

"The *bastard,*" she murmured, returning a hand to her chest in an attempt to check the tumult inside, but her fury needed an outlet. So she began to pace the floor, back and forth, trying to accept that he had actually done the one thing she had positively *refused* all these years to consider, even *after* Brian, because just *considering* it had seemed a betrayal of Doug!

"How *could* you?" she cried as she paced, hurt now, as well as enraged. "A woman and a *child?* How could you betray *us* like this? It must have been going on for *years!* And *I* felt so guilty. I don't believe this!"

Needing to vent the ugliness churning inside, she dropped the paper, swept out the front door, and set off into the night. She walked at a furious pace, then broke into a run. Breathless by the time she reached Sycamore, she stopped, bent at the waist to put her hands on her knees, and tried to catch her breath.

Stupid, starry-eyed Emily. Refusing to see, to imagine, to accept. But it made perfect sense!

Panting, she resumed her stride, as oblivious to the snap of the dried leaves underfoot as she was to the spectral arms of the trees, the shadows, the November cold. Driven by more adrenaline than she could handle, she stormed all the way through town and back. She was home before she felt the first inkling of fatigue, and when it hit, it was overshadowed by grief.

Sickened, she stumbled into the backyard. At the edge of the pond, her legs gave out. She fell to her knees, then her heels. Her hands went flat on the grass for support, but the ground was cold, the grass ungiving. Everything around her was dark. She felt bereft in ways she hadn't since the day she had accepted that Daniel was gone. Doug's betrayal was a final twist in that same, seemingly endless tragedy.

Tears came in a rush, then. She couldn't stop them, couldn't slow them. All she could do was to hug her middle and try to hold herself together against the pain that threatened to split her apart. She cried for herself and for Jill — and for Daniel and all the many things that had been lost that day at the post office. She rocked a little, but the motion didn't ease the pain, so she slid to her bottom, hugged her knees, and buried her face.

Suddenly she felt a hand on her hair, then her shoulder, and in the next sobbing breath she was being gathered to a chest that was solid and warm. He didn't ask why she was crying, didn't beg her to stop, didn't say anything at all. He just held her and let her cry, which she continued to do as though she had been granted permission, finally, deservedly, to be weak.

In time, the tears slowed. Embarrassed, she eased her hold on his sweater.

"We have to stop meeting this way," he teased, but his arms remained looped around her.

She made a sound that might have been a laugh, and nodded.

"The weekend was bad, huh?"

"Some."

"Want to talk?"

She shook her head. Her thoughts were too raw. She had to let them sink in.

He chafed her arms. "You're freezing. Want to come up to my place?"

She gave a tiny headshake.

"For a brandy?"

She repeated the headshake.

"Maybe you shouldn't be alone."

With a choppy sigh, she said, "I have to be. I have to work out some things in my mind." She wiped her cheeks with the heels of her hands.

He rose, drew her up, and walked her to her kitchen door. "Are you sure you're all right?"

She nodded, even managed a small smile. "When you hit rock bottom, there's no-where to go but up." She liked the idea of going up. It seemed forever that she had been dreading that fall to rock bottom. But she had survived.

"Thanks, Brian," she whispered, knowing that she owed him more than two words, but unable to do more for now.

She caught his acknowledging smile in the dark. He touched the tip of her chin, turned, and left.

Emily actually slept. She woke up early the next morning, rested enough to be able to handle the storm of emotion that immedi-ately hit her. Seeking an outlet in activity, she filled the house with the sound of Miles Davis and tore off the new wallpaper she had put in the upstairs bathroom such a few short weeks before. She crushed it, crammed it into a trash bag, and took it to the dump with the rest of the garbage. On the way home, she picked up wallpaper far more suited to her own taste than Doug's, and spent the morning putting it up.

Because that felt good, she drove to the mall and bought new sheets and a comforter in a pale blue and white floral pattern that was feminine and fresh, plus extra sheets to make curtains, plus a slew of throw pillows with ruffles. Caught up in her statement of self, she bought blue paint for the walls, and then, because blue made her think of sun, sand, and surf, she bought several large seaside prints. Then she stopped at the local garage and made an appointment for a new muffler, new fan belts, and new tires.

Riding a wave of bravado, she came home and called Jill. When the answering machine came on, she left a light-hearted message about how much she had loved seeing Jill. She didn't mention finding the paper. She didn't know what to say about it yet.

Likewise, to Kay and Celeste. Monday meant dinner with them, and though she would have liked to pass that night, she knew she wouldn't be allowed to cancel without an explanation. So she simply told them about the weekend and shrugged when they asked about Doug. Any slack in the conversation was picked up by Celeste, who raved on ad infinitum about Carter.

Kay looked uncomfortable with it all.

Emily felt uncomfortable with it all. She tried to be happy for Celeste's sake, but every Carter-miracle that Celeste cited reminded Emily of Doug's treachery and her own very sad, very deep humiliation. Thinking about the latter made her angry again, because, damn it, she hadn't done anything to deserve what he'd done, certainly not the extent of it, such deliberate betrayal over so long a time. He should have spoken up if he was so unhappy. He should have asked for a divorce himself if he was in love with another woman.

There was no message from him on the machine when she arrived home. But he was in New Haven, just as he had claimed. She called to check. The hotel confirmed it, and not surprisingly. She assumed that some of what he said was the truth, but there was a pattern. During each week on the road, he went to one, maybe two cities, with plans to be back on Thursday or Friday. Increasingly, he called midweek to postpone his homecoming a day.

Playing a hunch, she waited. Sure enough, he called on Wednesday night to say that he had been late getting to Bridgeport and wouldn't be home until Saturday. The tiny part of her that still held out hope against her suspicions twisted and writhed, but the rest of her was vaguely gratified.

She might have been blind for years, but she wasn't stupid, or as small-town naive as Doug wanted to believe.

Nor was she dependent on Brian in any way, shape, or form. To the contrary, she was trying to keep her distance and make independent decisions, but she needed feedback now, and he seemed the best one to ask.

So, soon after Doug called, she knocked on Brian's door. He opened it wearing sweatpants, a sweatshirt, and a warm, sleepy look. She nearly backed away, not because she feared she had woken him, but because the sight of him made her weak at a time when she had to be strong.

Halfway into the room she paused, listening to a jazz piano, something by Jelly Roll Morton, but new.

"Marcus Roberts," Brian said. "Know his work?" She shook her head. "I heard him play in the city last year. He's good. Want coffee or something?"

"No coffee. Just a little of your time." She took Jill's paper from her pocket and passed it across, waiting until he read it before explaining how she had found it. "Jill must have meant me to. She kept telling me not

489

to clean her room, but she knew I wouldn't be able to resist straightening up, especially when she didn't do any cleaning herself when she was home, and there it was, lying all crisp and clean."

His eyes asked if she did believe that Doug was the man on the steps.

"Jill surely wants me to deny it," she said, "but it makes too much sense. The minute I read that paper, I knew. It's so simple, and explains so much — his short tempers, the kinds of clothes he buys, his taking up new activities like golf. It explains all the traveling, and the last minute calls to say he won't be home for another day. There was the time he told me he'd be in Baltimore and he wasn't. He was furious when I asked him about it. He was furious that I had tried to *reach* him. What kind of husband would react that way?"

She began to walk around the room, touching things for the comfort of it but seeing little. "There are other things that never made sense until now. He doesn't like my asking about work, doesn't like talking about his life at all. He won't *hear* of my traveling with him. He wasn't wild about Jill going to school in Boston, either. He kept trying to steer her to other places. For all I know, when he was running last weekend he went to *her* place."

Brian leaned against the back of the armchair. "That's a heavy accusation, a long-term affair."

"But it *makes sense,*" Emily insisted. "It explains his relationship with me, or lack thereof." She had passed the point where pride was an issue. Anger had eclipsed embarrassment. "It also explains where the money he earns goes. He did well when he sold his share of the farm, and he poured it back into the new business, but what did he need? His overhead is next to nothing! He must have stashed the surplus away. He kept Jill and me thinking we were hard up, but he always spent on himself. I'll bet he has money we know nothing about!"

"Don't you sign tax returns?"

"Sure. Do I read them? No. Stupid of me, I know, but I *trusted* Doug. Even when I received royalties from the book, I just signed the checks over to him to deposit in our account. I don't pay the bills at the end of the month, so I don't even know how much comes in and goes out."

Something struck her then. "Y'know, I offered to do it once, to pay the bills and save him the time. Without giving it two seconds' thought, he said that I wouldn't know what was business and what wasn't, and would only mess things up." Something else struck her then. "He was *always* doing that — putting me down. Instead of saying that it would be easier for him to pay the bills himself, he'd say that my doing it would mess things up. Or that my getting a job would hike our taxes. Or that my traveling with him would be a burden."

"It's a form of abuse," Brian suggested quietly.

Emily was disgusted with herself. "Well, I didn't think anything of it. I assumed Doug knew better than I did, on money matters, certainly. He was always telling me things were tight. The economy and all. Jill's expenses and all." Her anger was returning to Doug, growing with each realization. "So when he said I could get a few more miles out of the tires on my car, I figured I could. I figured the bill would be better coming later, than now. Only *he*'s been buying all along. I chalked it up to the image he needed to be successful, but looking at it, it's bizarre. His clothes, his car, his whole lifestyle is so far above my world —"

"Fancy clothes don't mean a good goddamn."

She stopped walking and took a breath. "I know. Still, you've met him. Would you have put the two of us together?"

"No. I'd have put you with someone of greater substance."

"Oh, Doug has substance," she said sadly, "just not in the same sphere I do. He used to. When we first moved here, we were of like minds about everything. Then Daniel was taken." She thought of Jill's paper again.

Quietly, Brian asked, "What about the little boy in Boston?"

Precisely. She studied her thumb. "I don't know. It might be hers. Or theirs. That's the part that hurts most, I think."

"I would think *all* of it would hurt."

It did. But there was something else. Going to him, she clasped his hands. "I've been confused for so long, not understanding why Doug was growing more and more distant, thinking that maybe I *was* imagining it. This would explain so many things, that there's a kind of relief. And more anger than hurt, actually, and even then, as much on Jill's behalf as mine." She felt it rising again. "He missed a good deal of her childhood, Brian. Damn it, he couldn't even stick around to drive her to college, and there he was, in the same city where she's headed. Can you *imagine* her seeing him on the street that way?"

"She may have convinced herself that it wasn't him."

"No. She knows. Otherwise she wouldn't have written what she did and left it *where* she did. She needed to tell me, and she didn't know how else. Can you *imagine* her having to grapple with a thing like that?" Emily fought for control. "She always asked about him when she called. She wanted to know where he was and when he was coming home and what we were doing then. She told me she thought Doug and I should take a vacation, go somewhere together, like Bermuda. No. She knows. And she's afraid. How can a father do that to his daughter?"

"Have you asked him?"

She took a shaky breath and shook her head. "I won't do it on the phone. He called a little while ago to say that he wouldn't be home Friday night after all, but Saturday. I assume he's spending Friday night with her." Her eyes held Brian's. "I want proof."

He looked wary. "What do you mean, proof?"

"I want to see with my own two eyes, maybe even take pictures."

"Tail him?"

"If possible. The problem is that since I don't want to tell Jill, I can't ask her exactly where it was she saw him, so I don't know where to look." This was what she had come for. No. Maybe she had come to tell Brian the story, too. Maybe she had come to touch his hands and feel his warmth. But this was where he could help her the most. "I checked the Boston phone book, but Doug's name isn't listed. I want the address. Is there a way to get it? Local records that tell who owns what, where?"

"The Registry of Deeds. I could make a call."

She had known he would offer, but she was doing this herself. "I want to do it. Are those records open to the public?"

"Yes." His eyes moved over Jill's paper. "Do you know the name of the street?"

"I checked a map. Given what Jill said, it's Marlborough Street. What if the house isn't in his name?"

Brian was still searching the paper. "This is pretty vague. If you don't get a specific address, you'll have to position yourself on the most likely street and sit and wait and watch. I'm not thrilled with that idea, Emily. You could be sitting forever on the wrong street. After a while, it would be unsafe."

"Detectives do it."

"Yeah, with a gun handy. You got a gun?"

She shivered. "I hate guns."

"That's good, because someone who doesn't, who takes one look at a wisp of a thing sitting in a car in the wee hours of the night, would have it out of your hands and pointed at you before you could even *think* about the mace in your bag. Besides, detectives don't sit blindly in cars. At least, they don't do it often."

"So how do they find people?"

"They get an address."

"How?"

"Public records. Tips from informers. Phone bills."

"But if the phone isn't listed —" she stopped when what Brian had said sank in. "He may not have the house in his name, but he would be paying the phone bill, wouldn't he. Or the electric bill. Or the gas bill. Or writing checks to her." It was so simple, right in front of her, really. Doug's office was filled with records, all neatly filed, all ready and waiting. "And he didn't want me to work with the checkbook," she muttered and made for the door. Halfway there, she did an about-face, returned to him, and gave him a hug. "You are a love."

"I could make calls. I could get you your address."

But she shook her head, as sure about this as she was about anything. "He kept me impotent, and I let him do it. He belittled me. He humiliated me. And I'm furious. I need to do this now. It's a matter of my own self-respect."

Doug's office was a Pandora's box that, once opened, gushed with condemning information. Emily was nearly as stunned by the ease of her access to it, as by its quantity. He hadn't camouflaged anything. It was all there for the taking. Apparently it hadn't occurred to the bastard that she would look.

She pored through bank books, paid bills and canceled checks, and the tax forms that she had so naively signed. She booted up the computer, turned to his calendar, and printed out his work schedule and lack thereof on certain days when he had told her otherwise. She studied the airline's frequent flier statement, detailing dates and points of departure and arrival far different from what she had been led to believe. She found certificates of deposit and money market accounts.

For the most part, she was dispassionate, approaching the task as she would research for a book. The satisfaction of being proved right in her suspicions, of having solid evidence and feeling clever for a change, helped her through the inevitable moments of humiliation and fury. And there were both, in abundance. For years, it seemed, she had been blind to the extreme.

She thought of Celeste at one odd moment, and felt a glimmer of understanding. Celeste was taking control of her life. She had defined her goals and was steering herself their way. Emily didn't necessarily agree with her methods, but she could identify with the motive. Control was important, all the more so after such a long time without.

By dawn, Emily had two folders containing duplicate copies of the damning data, made on the machine that Doug had so cleverly bought for the business. She stood one of the folders in the kitchen between the cookbooks that she had used over the years in her efforts to please Doug. She wanted it handy, should he opt for denial when she confronted him.

She tucked the other away for safekeeping in Daniel's room. That was the one place in the house that Doug would never look.

NINETEEN

On Friday morning, Emily gassed up the car, with its new tires, new fan belts, and new muffler, and drove to Boston. She was there by noon, earlier than necessary, if the information on Doug's calendar was correct. He had appointments in Bridgeport at nine and eleven. She figured he would be on the road by noon and in Boston by three. But she wasn't taking a chance on missing him.

It took her half an hour of driving around the block before someone pulled out of the kind of parking space she needed. It was diagonally across the street from the address she had, an easy view past her front windshield.

But the view was where easy ended. There was pain in looking at that townhouse, a lovely brick three-storied thing, with tall windows and a carved oak door flanked by whiskey barrels filled with flowers. Even from outside, the draperies looked elegant, certainly heavier and more elaborate than anything Emily had ever sewn. Not that the woman of the house had sewn them. One window to the next, all the way up, spoke of a designer's touch.

She tried to keep her mind blank as she sat there with her stomach in knots and her eyes on the front stoop of the townhouse, but all she could think was that this was Doug's other home, the one in which he invested the energy and emotion that should have been hers. Maybe she was wrong, she tried to remind herself. Maybe there were explanations for the phone bills and the gas bills and the furniture bills. Maybe the woman who lived there had paid for the draperies. But Emily didn't believe it, and as she sat, she began to simmer.

She had brought along sandwiches and a thermos filled with coffee, but she didn't touch either. She kept her eyes on the townhouse and Jill's camera in her lap. She was determined to get a picture. If Doug dared suggest that her allegations were crazy, she planned to whip out something to wash out his tan.

That tan was *another* thing. He hadn't gotten it spending time with her, but playing golf at the nice little country club on the outskirts of Boston, where, according to his records, he had been a member in good standing for the past three years.

She wondered who the other members of the club thought was his wife. She wondered what would happen if she showed up there looking for him. She wondered what it would be like to cause a scene.

Not that she would. She couldn't be ugly that way, didn't have it in her. Nor, though, would she be lied to again.

She took her eyes from the townhouse only to dart quick looks at the clock or the occasional passerby. As one-thirty inched its way toward two, the leisurely lunch crowd merged with a more directed afternoon one. She saw students who might have been Jill, and businessmen who might have been Doug, but no one climbed the steps of the townhouse with the elegant drapes and the carved oak door.

By the time three o'clock arrived, the knots in her stomach were twisting. By four, she was thinking that Brian might have been right, that maybe she had made a mistake coming here blindly, without proof that Doug was on his way. She wondered if she should have just asked him, without coming at all. The file she had was incriminating enough. She didn't need a photograph.

What she needed was self-confidence, which was the real purpose of the trip. She needed to know that she had taken Jill's clue, found proof of its claim, and backed that proof up. She needed to know that she could beat Doug at his own game.

That was one way to fight the anger. As for the hurt, the humiliation, the profound sadness, she needed time.

Then she saw him. He rounded the corner on foot and approached the townhouse, Doug, bold as brass, looking dazzling in casual clothes — not even a *business suit,* the *bastard* — and totally oblivious to the possibility that she was lying in wait.

Trembling, she rushed the camera to her eye, but it was a minute before she could get her fingers to work right. She took one picture, jerked the film ahead, and took another. She advanced, refocused, and kept shooting, thinking, absurdly, that Doug would die if he knew what good use she was making of the camera he had so nobly bought Jill for a photography course junior year.

She wrenched the focus knob, too late realizing that her tears were what blurred the picture. Whimpering, she fought the devastation she felt, struggling to shoot, advance, and shoot more quickly as Doug climbed the steps of the townhouse.

She got shots of him standing at the door, reaching into his pocket, unlocking the door, and stepping inside. She took one picture of the door after he was gone, then another and another until the camera slipped on her tears. That was when the absurdity of what she was doing hit her. Sitting here, witnessing firsthand the existence of Doug's other life, was pure masochism.

She grabbed a tissue and tried to stop crying, but the tears kept coming. Her marriage was done, her life forever changed. The finality of it was heartbreaking.

Then she caught her breath. Standing on the sidewalk staring at her, barely two cars down from where she was parked, was Jill.

Emily made a sobbing sound when her heart hit her ribs. She swiped at her tears with both hands, praying that she had seen wrong, but Jill remained. For a split second, Emily was paralyzed by a fathomless grief. In the next instant, the mother in her was out of the car.

Jill's face was pale, that of a child whose bottom had fallen out of her world. Knowing just how she felt, Emily took her in her arms and held on. She wasn't crying now. Motherhood demanded she be strong.

But when Jill whispered, "I love you,

Mom," she lost it and burst into a fresh bout of tears. She held Jill for her own sake then, taking every bit of the comfort her mature woman-daughter offered.

It was a minute before she had the wherewithal to ease back and say a sniffly, "I love you, too, sweetheart."

"You read my paper."

"Mm."

"I didn't know what to do," Jill rushed out, "I wasn't sure if it was him, but like, there were so many reasons why it could be, and then I felt guilty for thinking he'd do that. I wanted to tell you but I didn't know how, so writing seemed the best way, since I *knew* you'd do something with my closet."

Emily was wiping her eyes with her fingers. "Only the sweater basket. I haven't touched anything else. And writing it down was fine." Though she would have done anything to spare Jill this, she was relieved to have it out in the open. Misery loved company. She needed to be with someone she loved. "Have you come here before?"

"No. I told myself you'd do whatever had to be done. But I kept wondering anyway."

"Why today?"

"Because the first time I saw him here was a Friday. And because he was strange last weekend. Nice to everyone but you. Who is she?"

Emily drew in a shaky breath. She had a name. But Jill was asking about the nature of the relationship. "I don't know."

"Maybe he had a business friend who died, and he's checking up on the widow."

It was a romantic notion that Emily had herself entertained in one delusive moment, but it didn't explain why he had a key to the place, why he hadn't told Emily about her, and it certainly didn't explain what she had found in his files.

"How long has he been coming here?" Jill asked.

"I don't know."

"Who is the little boy?"

Emily's throat tightened. She wasn't ready to think about the little boy, and besides, she didn't know how much to tell Jill about *any* of this. She was so frightened of making a mistake. She needed time to regroup. "Let's go someplace where we can talk."

They returned to the car and drove to a cafe close to Jill's dorm. Once settled in a booth with warm drinks on order and their hands linked, Jill started in with questions again. "How did you know where to wait? I didn't know the address."

"I found it in your father's den."

"Just written down?"

"No. There were bills."

"He's *supporting* her?"

"Maybe not. I really don't know, Jill. There could be a perfectly good reason for everything he's done."

But Jill was shaking her head. "When I saw them that first time, there was something about them together. They looked like a couple. They looked like a *family.*"

Emily felt the pain of that. *They* were a family. Emily and Jill were alone.

If the little boy was Doug's, he was Jill's half-brother. She wondered if Jill had thought about that.

"Will you ask him about it?" Jill asked.

Would she ever. She took a steadying breath. "Yes. I need to know what we saw."

"When?"

"When he gets home."

"Tomorrow?"

"Most likely."

"Unless he calls to say he won't be home until Sunday," Jill grumbled, and her composure slipped. "I hate him for this. He calls to say he's working, but he's not, he's doing something with another family."

"Don't," Emily pleaded through new tears. Her greatest fear had always been having Jill hurt. She had done everything in her power to prevent it. But it was happening, inevitably and irrevocably. "If anyone should feel those things, it's me, not you. The problem is with your father and me, not your father and you."

"When was the last time he spent a week at home? He couldn't even stay around the week before I left. Do you think he was really in Pittsburgh?"

"Yes." His frequent flyer account had confirmed it. "Most of the time he tells us the truth."

"You're defending him," Jill charged.

Emily was trying hard to be fair. More than anyone else, she had a right to distrust Doug, but being spiteful wouldn't help Jill. "He *was* in Pittsburgh. And earlier this week he was in New Haven, like he said."

"And tonight? Where did he say he'd be?"

Emily was caught. She sighed. "Bridge-port."

"Aren't you *furious?*"

"Of course, I am!" she cried, letting go a little. "I've been raging all week. I'm furious and hurt and confused and embarrassed — the list is endless. I go through periods of disbelief, then shock, then out-and-out nausea. I've been married to your father for twenty-two years. *Twenty-two years.* This isn't easy."

Jill quieted. "I'm sorry." She frowned. "It's just that I don't understand. Is something wrong with us? Why does he need to be with them?"

Emily took a deep, shaky breath. "That's one of the things I have to ask him."

Their drinks arrived, espresso for Emily, mocha latte for Jill. Emily put her fingertips to the cup, but she couldn't take her eyes off Jill. Her daughter was beautiful, but that was nothing new. What was new was an expression that spoke of illusions dashed. It was the last thing Emily had ever wanted to see.

"What?" Jill asked.

"I'm sorry, so sorry for all this."

"It's not your fault."

"Maybe if I'd been a different kind of woman, or if I'd grown more along with your father —"

"Don't *say* that. There's nothing wrong with you. *He*'s the one with the problem. He cheated on his wife. *And* on his daughter."

"We don't know that for sure," Emily cautioned, trying hard, *so hard,* to be fair. "He walked up a set of steps and into a townhouse. That's all we saw. We don't know what goes on inside. It might be innocent."

"You're doing it again, Mom. Don't defend him. He lied to you. And *keeps* lying to you. You're too good. You let him get away with too much. I think you should divorce him."

"Shh." Emily doubted Jill had considered the effect a divorce would have on her life. She had barely started to consider it, herself.

"Will you?" Jill prodded.

"Not if there's an explanation for what we saw today."

"There isn't."

"How do you know?"

"Because," she said, looking at Emily with something so sad and sure that Emily couldn't possibly doubt her, "this has been coming. You and I both know it. We've been walking on eggshells around Daddy for years. We coax him into doing little things with us, and then rush to smooth things over when he gets antsy. We act like nothing's wrong and that this is just the way things are when a man has to travel the way Daddy does, but he never says, 'Wow, am I glad to be home.' He doesn't plan things for us to do. He doesn't seem to care if we do anything. You two won't take a vacation together. We three won't take a vacation together."

"We don't have the money," Emily said

out of habit, but Jill was knowing, even in that.

"*We* don't," she replied dryly and studied her drink. She took a breath, seeming ready to say more on that score. Then she closed her mouth and frowned. "He calls me sometimes at school, really talkative. He asks questions about my friends and my classes, and listens to the answers and then asks more questions. I can't get him off the phone sometimes."

"He loves you." Emily did believe that, at least.

"It's guilt. Do you know how far that townhouse is from my dorm? Fifteen minutes by foot, three by car. How often do you think he's been there since I started school? Once a week?"

"No. He was in London for two weeks." When Jill shot her a skeptical look, Emily insisted, "I saw the tags on his luggage."

"Was he with her?"

Emily suspected he was, though she didn't know for sure.

Jill wilted. "What am I going to say to him, Mom? I could play the game before, because I wasn't sure that was him on those steps, but now that I know it was, what am I going to say when he calls? I don't want to talk with him. Not after what he's done."

Emily took her hand and squeezed it while she searched for an answer. *Tell him to go to hell,* was what she wanted to say, because Doug didn't deserve Jill. But Doug wasn't the one who mattered. Jill was, and Emily wanted only what was best for her. "He's still your father."

"He's treated us like *shit.*"

"If he didn't love you, he wouldn't be calling."

"He feels guilty, that's all."

He's not feeling guilty about me, Emily thought. *He's not calling me. He's not asking me dozens of questions about my life, and keeping me on the phone for hours.*

Wearied by the length of the day and the weight of her thoughts, Emily sighed. "I have to talk with him, Jill. We have questions now, you and I, that can't be answered until then. We only have one side of the story. We need to hear his side."

"Do you think he'll tell the truth?"

Emily thought of the folder that stood between her cookbooks, and the identical one safely stowed upstairs. "He'll tell the truth," she said with quiet confidence and an undercurrent of unspoken rage.

That unspoken rage had Emily planted in a corner of the living room sofa when Doug

511

pulled into the garage on Saturday night. She didn't move when she heard the rev of his car's engine — never understood why that last rev was necessary before he turned off the engine, other than to give him a sense of power — or the silence that followed, or the slam of the car door, then the trunk, or his footfall on the back stairs.

The kitchen door opened. "Emily? I'm home!"

Her rage grew. Calling out that way, he might have been the conquering hero returning from war, fully assuming that she was waiting, just dying to see him.

Oh, she was dying to see him, all right, but not, she warranted, for the reasons he expected.

"Emily?" he called again.

He crossed through the kitchen into the hall, and set his luggage by the foot of the stairs. He looked up them, then turned and caught sight of her.

"Why in the world are you sitting in the dark?"

"I'm not in the dark."

"Practically." He switched on the hall light to supplement the small lamp lit by her side, and made a show of shrugging out of his blazer with a tired shift of his shoulders, the weary businessman, home at last from a week of nonstop work.

She wanted to gag. But she didn't. Nor did she speak or move. She sat and watched, seething — but sad, and in spite of everything, vaguely intimidated by what she was about to do. Once her words were out there would be no taking them back.

"Sorry I'm late," he said, rubbing his back. "I was hoping to be home for dinner, but my last meeting didn't finish until six, and I-91 was a nightmare. You didn't cook, did you?"

"No. I had a feeling you'd be late." She spoke evenly, but since she was usually upbeat, even that was out of character.

"You're angry," he charged. "Like it was my fault."

"I didn't say that."

"You didn't have to. I can feel your censure. Christ, Emily, do you think I didn't want to get out of there at noon? But the meeting dragged on. They kept asking me questions. I couldn't just get up and leave, not with what they're paying me."

Not with us desperate for every last penny, she added silently. "What company was this?"

"Eldridge Tire. I'm their last resort, before they file for bankruptcy."

"That explains their willingness to work

on Saturday. What made I-91 a nightmare?"

"Accidents, one in New Haven, one in Windsor Locks. Traffic was down to two lanes."

"I hope no one died. I'll have to check the paper tomorrow."

"Actually," he backpedaled, "it looked more messy than tragic. I probably hit it at the worst time. An hour before or after, and I would have been fine. How're things here?"

"Fine."

He slipped his hands in his pockets and looked around. "What have you been doing? Listening to music?"

"No."

"Reading?"

She shook her head.

He stared, then sighed. "Well, something's on your mind. Come on, Emily. I've been gone all week, and I'm tired. Do we have to play twenty questions, or will you just blurt it out?"

"I spent yesterday in Boston."

He didn't blink. "Visiting Jill?"

"Well, I did that, but it was accidental. I didn't see her until after I saw you. Until after *she* saw you."

Emily felt a moment's satisfaction when he blanched, but as quickly he reddened in anger. "Were you following me?"

"No, I was just sitting on Marlborough Street."

"Checking up on me. Waiting for me to appear. Tripping me up just now by talking about Bridgeport, when you knew damn well I wasn't in Bridgeport at all."

"Oh, you were in Bridgeport. I called the hotel. You checked out yesterday morning."

"You called the hotel," he echoed. "What in the hell is this? An inquisition? And who in the hell are you, judge, jury, and executioner? What is it, boredom? You don't have anything to do, so you've decided to stir up a little trouble? Or revenge, getting back at me for being away so much?"

She marveled at his self-righteousness. "It's incredible how you do that, turn things around so that I'm the bad guy. But, why not? It's always worked for you before. I've always accepted your argument and run off with my tail between my legs. Only I'm not doing it this time, Doug. I'm not the bad guy here, not by a long shot."

"And I am? Me? The one who's out there earning a living?"

Irate, she burst from the sofa. "The one who's out there earning far more than you ever let on and spending the excess on another woman, another child, a three-story townhouse in the Back Bay, clothing that has never seen the inside of *this* house, a country club membership, plus a slew of other things that come from stores I sure don't shop in."

Absurdly, he said, "I need clothes."

"Women's clothes? Children's clothes? Are you personally benefiting from enrollment at the Back Bay Montessori School? Or days of beauty at Elizabeth Arden? Or the interior decorating services of a firm called Dayton and Webb?"

He put his hands on his hips. "You've been through my files."

"Well, what did you expect?" she cried. "I'm not stupid, Doug. I may have given you the benefit of the doubt for far longer than I should have, but I knew something was wrong — and I have asked you about it, but you keep putting me off, telling me that this is the way things are and that I'm selfish. Not selfish, Doug. Human. How many times did you think you could call and say you'd be delayed another day, without my growing suspicious? How long did you think I would sit here alone, without wondering why you weren't lonely, too?"

"I have my work."

"Yeah, that's what you said last weekend, your stock answer, only the truth is that you have far more than that. You have for some time. How long has it been going on, Doug?"

"How long has what been going on?"

"Oh, please. The game's over."

"How long has *what* been going on?"

She sighed. "Rebecca Mills. Doug, I *know.* I've seen canceled checks and morgage statements."

"You had no right to go through my den."

"Your den?" She nearly laughed, because he was doing it again, sidestepping an accusation by making one of his own, only she wasn't having it. "This is *our* house. I didn't pick any locks. I simply looked through papers that were lying right there. It's a miracle I didn't stumble across them sooner."

He stared at her for a long minute, then said with a look of disgust, "No miracle. You're such an innocent."

"I was. But I've lost my cherry, so to speak." She played her hand. "I have copies of everything I found, and copies of those copies, put away for safekeeping. I also have pictures of you letting yourself into that townhouse with a key yesterday afternoon."

Lips thinning, he nodded. "So you poisoned Jill's mind. You told her I was having an affair."

"I didn't tell Jill a thing." It had more or less been the other way around, though Emily wouldn't say that. She didn't want to turn Doug against Jill. "She saw you let yourself into that townhouse. She was there on that street totally independent of me."

"You've turned my own child against me."

"No, no, no," Emily cried. She didn't know who he was trying to kid. Then again, she did. But she was done taking the fall. "If she's turned against you, it's your own doing. It's one thing to treat *me* like a poor, pathetic halfwit, but when you do it to kids, they smell it faster than a wife who's trying to hold things together. Jill knew things weren't right. You're *never here* — and don't say it's your work," she said before he could. "People choose what they do. If they're unhappy, they change things. But you aren't unhappy, are you?"

For a minute, he didn't say anything. Then his eyes grew hard. "What's to be unhappy about? I have the son I've been wanting for nineteen years, ever since the day Daniel was taken from our car because *you* left him there alone."

Emily felt she'd been hit. Short of breath, she took one step back, then another, hating herself for retreating but needing to sit. She had always known Doug blamed her, but hearing the words, hearing, seeing, feeling his *hatred* was something else.

"Is the little boy yours?" she asked brokenly.

"Damn right," came Doug's taunt. "Four years old and smart as a whip."

Emily thought of Daniel, who had never reached the age of four, and felt her eyes brim. "I didn't know you wanted a boy so badly. I might have had another one, if we had tried."

"Are you kidding?" he shot back, stronger with her weakening. "You had your chance the first time around, but you blew it."

"I didn't kidnap Daniel."

"You left him alone. He was in your care, and you blew it. Face it, Emily. You blew it."

That was what she had always thought, too, until someone recently had said it wasn't so. "I didn't do anything that other parents don't do all the time," she argued as Brian had, then as Brian hadn't, "I didn't do anything *you* didn't do yourself. *You* left him alone in the car a time or two. I *saw.*"

Doug jabbed a thumb at his chest. "But I didn't lose the kid. You did. You lost my child. My Daniel. *God,* I adored that little boy." He pushed a hand through his hair and turned away. "I had dreams of our

519

working the farm together — the father and son team that *my* father and I could never have been because he was such a mean bastard — and then when Daniel wasn't there anymore, I didn't feel the same way about the farm. It became no more than a money-making scheme, and a mediocre one at that, so I built it up and got the hell out, and I've never regretted it once. That farm held memories. I couldn't escape them. I never go past the place now. I think it'd be painful still."

"You never talked about the pain."

"Yeah, well, what good would it have done?"

"We might have shared it. We might have grown closer, rather than farther apart."

He snorted. "I had my pain, you had yours. Then you turned up pregnant, and I thought there might be another chance. But Jill wasn't Daniel."

"Because she was a *girl?*"

"Because she was *yours*. You two were inseparable, right from the start. You poured everything you had into her. She became your clone. So why would I want her work-ing with me? I'd only look at her and see you and think of Daniel."

Emily shrank away, feeling unwanted, unloved, alone, and scared. She hugged her stomach. "Do you do that anyway?"

"No. Not as long as I separate Jill from the rest."

"From me."

He didn't deny it. "It's easier now that she's at school. I like calling her."

Emily nodded, relieved for Jill, at least. "But she thinks you call her out of guilt. We'll have to address that, Doug. Children suffer when a marriage ends. Just because she's eighteen doesn't mean there won't be pain."

Doug looked up the stairs, then down at his shoes. "So you want a divorce."

"Don't you?" she bit out. She couldn't *imagine* continuing on like this.

He kept his eyes on his shoes.

"Doug, you have another woman, another child, another home! You hate me! I'd think you'd be *dying* to get rid of me. Frankly, I don't know why you stayed around so long. I don't know why you haven't asked for a divorce yourself."

He was quiet for another minute. Then he raised his eyes and said in a petulant voice, "Oh, I want a divorce, but if you plan to soak me, think again. You didn't help me build my business. I did it *in spite* of you."

Emily was speechless. She hadn't given a thought to money. Besides, his accusation was absurd! If she had been a golddigger, she would have been at his throat long ago. But no, she had been a prudent little mouse, watching her pennies, accepting their financial straits without complaint.

Taking her silence for a declaration of war, Doug vowed, "I'll fight you, Emily. You have a secure little life here. You don't need much. I'll give you only what you're used to. God knows, you haven't even earned that."

Indignance drew her spine ramrod straight and more, brought her to her feet. "Oh, I have," she told him. "I've earned it through sweat and tears, through every imaginable effort to please you, and years of slights and put downs and doing without when there was no reason for it at all. Were you punishing me? Did you make like we were broke just to worry me? Did you cancel out on me at the last minute just to annoy me? Did you tell me over and over and over again that I couldn't get a decent job, just to make me feel stupid? What about my book? Was that stupid?"

"That book was a one-time thing," he scoffed with the wave of his hand. "You had the right material in the right place at the right time. Most anyone half-literate could have gotten it published."

Once upon a time Emily would have agreed. But times had changed. "Not according to my editor. She wants me to do another. I always turned her down, because you didn't want me to work, but that doesn't make any more sense to me now than before. The issue of having to pay taxes doesn't hold water. Last time, on one book, I earned enough to cover those taxes and have a tidy sum left over — a tidy sum that you squirreled away into our bank account, ostensibly to keep us solvent, more probably to keep me in the dark as to just how much was accumulating." She remembered what Kay and Celeste had always said. "But that's what you want, isn't it? You want me in the dark. You want me unaware of my own potential. You don't want me to earn money, and become stronger and more independent of you. If I become a person in my own right, I won't be quite so naive. I won't let you walk all over me. I may just tell you to go to hell."

She drew in a hard breath, egged on by the dislike she felt for her husband just then. "Well, I'm doing it now, Doug. I'm telling you to go to hell. I want a divorce. And don't tell me you won't give me a cent, because I have paperwork to show a judge that I've been lied to and cheated on for years. I have proof of the existence of assets I never knew about. I'll come out of a divorce far better off than when I went in."

"No, you won't. Women never do."

"I will. And if I don't, so what? You aren't the same person I married. I don't want you anymore." Her eyes went to his luggage. "That means tonight, too. I don't want you warm from another woman's bed. You can check into the Grannick Lodge. Or drive back to Boston. There shouldn't be any traffic tie-ups this time of night."

"You're kicking me out of my own home? Try again, Emily. You can't make me leave."

"No?" She was angry enough to bluff. "One call to the police, and you'll be spending the night in jail."

He made a disbelieving sound. "On what charge?"

"Assault. Battery. Threat of bodily harm."

"I have never theatened you with bodily harm."

"Right," she said without a stitch of remorse, "but I'll claim that you have until Monday morning, when I formally file for divorce, and when I do that, I'll get a restraining order keeping you away from this house."

"I *own* this house."

"And I *live* here, far more than you do.

Any member of the Grannick Police Department will testify to that. Besides, you own another house. Go stay there. Be with the little boy you've wanted for nineteen years. Be with his mother. Let *her* wash your socks for a change. I'm done."

She stormed to the front door and opened it wide, intent on pointing him out, but once started, the words wouldn't stop. "Our marriage has been over for years, only neither of us could admit it. But, *God,*" she put a hand to her chest, "there's a relief in saying it now. Our marriage has been a *strain.* I never *realized* how much, until now. I've been grasping at the remnants of what we had once, but they're so tattered and torn that I barely recognize them, and they aren't even what I want."

"What do you want?"

"What I want doesn't matter. What I *don't* want is feeling small and inadequate and *guilty* all the time. I'm tired of making excuses for your absences. I'm tired of trying to please you, when you won't be pleased."

"I'm not that hard to live with."

"You are *very* hard to live with!" she cried, because he was doing it again, making her feel *wrong,* and she was tired of it! Then she realized he was goading her. So she leveled

525

her voice and steadied her gaze. "Leave, Doug. I'll be talking with Shep Hubbard on Monday. Have your lawyer call him. If you want to stop by for some of your things tomorrow, call first."

He stared at her for a long time. When she refused to look away, refused to *blink,* he said, "You're tough."

She sighed. "No. But I'm learning." She gestured him into the night and stood back while he passed.

TWENTY

Emily spent Sunday morning emptying Doug's den. She had a frenzied need to be active, and couldn't think of anything more appropriate. His den was symbolic of the life he had made without her, and she wanted it transformed.

She crated up Doug's books and papers, emptied desk drawers and file cabinets, and began carting boxes to the garage. Brian drove up halfway through, his tires crunching on the dusting of snow that had fallen at dawn and frozen where it lay. He scooped Julia from the Jeep and tucked her inside his parka so that only her face showed. "What are you doing?" he called, walking into the garage.

Emily wiped her hands on her jeans. "Cleaning."

"Need any help?"

"Nope." She wiggled her fingers at Julia. Julia wiggled her nose back.

Softly, Brian asked, "Are you okay?"

Emily nodded.

"Are these his?"

"Uh-huh."

He grinned. "Please. Let me help."

She gave him a nudge and left her shoulder against his arm. "You're bad."

"Just selfish. I miss you."

She missed him, too. But her hands, her mind, her needs just then were focused on Doug. So she simply leaned in closer for a minute, before stepping away.

"Really," he said, serious now. "I can carry boxes."

But she shook her head and sent him off. She needed to do the work herself, needed the exertion, the therapy of it. She made trip after trip to the garage, until the whole of his office, minus furniture, was relocated there.

Back in the house, staring at bare shelves, a naked desk, and all the machines that she would need for her work, she marveled at her nerve. She had never dared defy Doug — had never before had conscious cause — but it felt good. This was her declaration of independence. It went a small way toward boosting her self-esteem.

Cleaning the room went another small way, as did gathering her own possessions, previously stashed in random out-of-the-way places, and neatly arranging them in drawers and on shelves. She brought an elegant old lamp from the basement, one that she had bought at an attic sale years before but that Doug had hated on sight, and stood it on a corner of the desk. She nailed her diploma to the wall. She filled the shelves with her favorite books, and set up photographs of Jill and, yes, Daniel. She stood a copy of the book she had written face out at eye-level.

By then it was four in the afternoon. She had fully expected Doug to have come by for clothes, papers, something. Naturally, because she expected it, he wouldn't do it.

So, wearing leggings, thick scrunchy socks, and a huge sweatshirt, rolled several times at the wrists, she sat at the desk and made chronological piles of the contents of her large accordion-pleated folder.

There her discipline ended. She couldn't concentrate the way she needed to. Her mind drifted. She kept looking off toward the yard and rehashing the week.

The back door slammed. *"What in the hell did you do with my things?"*

Her stomach cramped. For a split second she regretted what she'd done. Then she thought of the woman, the child, the townhouse, the country club, and the repeated lies and denials, and she tucked her legs under her and tipped up her chin.

Angry Italian loafers slapped across the kitchen floor and into the hall. *"Emily?"*

She sat back in the chair and waited. He knew where she was.

Within seconds, he was at the door, looking very Armani, in slacks, a sweater, and a jacket with the collar pulled up just so, but fired up and, to her satisfaction, a bit unsettled. "I nearly drove into the garage just now! Do you have any idea what would have happened if I had? I'd have lost reams of files *and* damaged the car. Don't you have *any* brains? Why in the hell did you put my things *there?*"

She'd had many a curious moment in the hours just past, wondering what it would be like, seeing him for the first time after she'd asked for a divorce. If he had shown up all apologetic and sweet, shocked to his senses, wanting to try to work things out for Jill's sake, she might have had a qualm. His outrage solved that problem.

Why had she put his things in the garage? Because there was a poetic justice to it. The garage was where he kept his most prized possessions, wasn't it?

She tucked her legs up. "I thought it

would be a help. Now all you have to do is load them in the car."

"*All?* Christ, you messed everything up! I'll have to re-sort every goddamned thing. Those were important papers you were tossing around!"

She didn't know how important they could be, stashed in a room where he hadn't spent any significant time in weeks. "Relax, Doug. I didn't 'toss' anything around. I put things in boxes, exactly as they were organized here. Everything's labeled. Nothing's been lost."

He put his hands on his hips and snorted, then shook his head and snorted again. "You are incredible."

Emily wasn't asking if that was good or bad. She knew what he would say, and didn't want to hear it. She had sworn off masochism. "If you came back for clothes, help yourself. I haven't touched them."

He stared at her for another minute, before letting his hands fall to his sides. "How did Jill come to see me on Friday?" There was no anger now. Just concern.

Emily softened. How could she not? Jill had always been her own major worry. She wanted Doug to be sensitive to Jill, and for that, he needed the truth. "She saw you there once before."

531

"When?"

"Last spring. Pre-frosh weekend. She was walking down the street with girls from the school and saw you on the front stoop. With them. She kept telling herself it wasn't you, but it haunted her. Then she saw how we were together last weekend."

"How were we?"

"Distant. She's a big girl, Doug. She sees. She understands."

"Did you talk with her about it, after last weekend?"

"Only Friday, after Marlborough Street. She was upset. I tried to smooth things a little."

"How?"

"I told her there might be explanations for what we saw. I said she had to talk with you. You're her father. She won't have another one in this life."

"Does she hate me?"

"Maybe a little. But love, too. She's confused."

"How will she react if I call her?"

"I don't know. But the longer you wait, the harder it will be. She's wondering what place she has in your life. She needs to know you love her. She needs to know you care about how she's taking this."

He scowled for a long minute, then

grunted and looked away. Wearing his elegant clothes like a shield, he wandered around the den, glancing from bookshelf to bookshelf to wall to lamp, taking stock of every change she had made. She wondered if he noticed the pictures of Daniel. She wondered if he noticed her book. She wondered where he had spent the night.

"You move fast," he finally said.

She hugged her knees. "I always had to go looking for space when I wanted to do something for myself. You had your own space. Jill had her own space. I never did. Now I do."

"To do what?" he asked, craning his neck toward the desk.

"Organize my thoughts."

"Thoughts on what?"

She looked him in the eye. "Daniel. These are the notes I made over the years."

"About Daniel."

"And me. My feelings about what happened. What it's like to lose a child that way."

"If you're writing a book, you'd better let me know. My lawyer's going to want to know if you're earning any money."

"I'm not."

"Will you be?"

"You'd be in a better position to tell me

that," she said. "You kept better track of the money I made on the last book than I did. To hear you, it was next to nothing, more a hindrance than a help."

"Slander me in your book, and I'll sue."

Such an inflated ego. Such a distrustful mind. "I'm not interested in writing about you."

"Won't it be inevitable? Our marriage is falling apart because of Daniel. The two are closely related. You can't go into any kind of depth on one, without mentioning the other. Why do you want to write about Daniel, anyway?"

"Because he happened."

"But how can you relive it?"

"How can I *not?* He was my son. We never did put him to rest."

"Buried him, you mean." He turned to the window, slipped his hands into his trousers pockets, and stood there for a long time before, quietly, reluctantly, self-consciously saying, "I've been thinking about Daniel, too. I guess it's natural. I've been driving around; all the places I swore I wouldn't go. I keep telling myself to get the hell outta here, but it's hard." He grew silent again, staring out the window, his back stiff. Finally, he took a breath. "It's like I'm being disloyal to Daniel if I leave. Pretty stupid, huh? The kid's not here to see what I do." He paused, then added in a low voice, "But it's like he is."

Emily knew what he meant. That knowing forged the first truly honest connection between them in years. "This is where we saw him last," she offered, because it was the only explanation she had. "It's our only link to him — Grannick, this house, our marriage." She focused on one of the pictures of Daniel. "Is he why you didn't ask me for a divorce yourself?"

Doug didn't answer.

"If you hated me so much," she added. "If I was a constant reminder of what you lost, I'm surprised you didn't leave me years ago."

He shifted a shoulder. She took it for an admission. There was some solace in knowing that she wasn't the only one whose life's course had been steered by a ghost.

Doug turned, his face tired, for once unadorned by pride, resentment, or machismo. "Where does it end?"

Seeing him then, vulnerable as she couldn't remember him being before, Emily had every opportunity to regret what they were about to do. And she did regret it, but only in an intellectualized way. She regretted his suffering. She regretted leaving Daniel in the car that day. She regretted the failure of her marriage.

But she didn't regret that she wouldn't be planning her life around Doug's short stops home. They had grown painful. For nineteen years, her life with Doug had been defined by Daniel's absence, every step aimed at compensating for the loss, apologizing, doing penance in the most subtle and subservient of ways. Leaving that life was a first step in putting Daniel, finally, to rest.

Where did it end? She shrugged and shook her head, as anxious for that ending, but befuddled, as he was. Then a sound came from the direction of the kitchen, and she looked sharply toward the door.

The footsteps were quieter this time around. Sneakers hit wood far differently than loafers did. Within seconds, Brian had a hand on the doorjamb. "Am I interrupting anything?"

Emily's insides rocked. She felt the familiar warmth that came with Brian, along with an awful awkwardness.

Doug folded his arms over his chest and put a hip to the window sill.

"We were just talking," she told Brian, then, frightened for Julia, asked quickly, "Is everything all right?"

"Everything's fine. I'm putting together

an order for pizza. Want some?" He extended the invitation to Doug with the arch of his brows.

Doug didn't say a word.

"Maybe another time," Emily said.

Brian rapped his hand on the jamb. "Okay. But if you change your mind, give a call. Julia will probably sleep for another half hour. I'll go when she wakes up." With a hand up to Doug, he was gone.

The back door had barely made its distant slap when Doug turned curious eyes on Emily and said, "It didn't take *you* long."

"What didn't?" she asked, though she knew what he meant. She knew exactly what Brian's entrance looked like, thank you, Brian. It looked familiar and practiced.

"Hooking up with him. Boy, you took me seriously when I said I liked him."

Emily unfolded her legs. She didn't know who to be more irked at, Brian for setting the scene or Doug for playing it out. "You have no right to make accusations, Doug."

Looking smug — leering, even — he pushed off from the window. "Tell me you're not sleeping with him."

"What I'm doing, or not doing, is none of your business."

He approached the desk. "That's why you're kicking me out, isn't it? You're sleeping with *him.* Funny, I was thinking about that last night, too. I couldn't understand why you did it so quick, with no discussion, no forewarning, nothing. I came home, and, boom, you wanted me gone. Now I know why."

Emily felt a flare of anger so hard and strong that she flew to her feet. "You — know — nothing," she seethed. Forget Brian. She would deal with him next. Right now, she was furious at Doug. "I wanted you gone when I learned that you have a whole other life, a whole other family, a whole other set of possessions that you've been supporting while you cry poor-mouth to me. And there was nothing sudden about it! You've been carrying on with her for at least four years and nine months, and all the while our marriage has gotten weaker and weaker. Sudden?" she cried, caught up in the fury. "*Forget* sudden! I've been asking you for *months* what's wrong, what you want, why we can't be together, and you couldn't give me the truth. I went so far as to suggest counseling, because I *did* want to save the marriage. *Sudden?* There's nothing *sudden* about this. I tried to make it work. I tried *hard.* So what did you do? You said you wouldn't waste the time or money on counseling. Far better to be a member in good standing at the country club."

"You're jealous."

"Of a country club membership?" She would have laughed, had she not been so angry. "Not quite. What I want — wanted, past tense — was a meaningful marriage. I wanted a companion. I wanted to spend time with someone who cared, but you didn't. You don't. You've been lying to me for years, so that you could spend time with your mistress and her son."

"He's *my* son," Doug said.

"Yes, so you told me last night. And I kicked you out. You can call that quick if you want. I call it appropriate."

"Appropriate, my foot. You wanted me out so you could shack up with the cop. Did he choose the colors for the bedroom?"

Emily bristled. "I chose them. Neither he, nor any other man but you, has ever seen that room. It's mine, and only mine, and I plan to keep it that way for a while. Know what I've discovered in the last few weeks?" She thumped her chest. "There's a *me* in this world. There's an individual inside this body who isn't anyone's slave. That individual is tasting freedom for the very first time in her adult life."

He smirked. "Now, that's devotion for you, the woman who equates motherhood with slavery."

She held up a hand. "Oh, no. I wasn't referring to motherhood, and you know it. I was referring to marriage to you. You held me down, Doug. It's as simple as that."

"And he doesn't? Baby, the only man who gives a woman total freedom is one who doesn't care where she goes or what she does. So. Is he good?"

Damn good, she thought. *Much better than you ever were, you self-centered oaf.*

She strode toward the door. "I think you should leave."

He followed her. "Why? Because I'm putting you on the hot seat?"

"Because you're *way* out of line." She turned on him in the hall. "Once upon a time you had the right to question me about my life. You don't any more. *Especially* not with what you did to me. Talk about the pot calling the kettle black!" She whirled back around and headed for the kitchen.

"I have every right to question you. It's *my* money you're asking for."

"It's *my* money," she yelled. "Hard-earned and long overdue."

"Keep your voice down."

She opened the door and hollered, "I'll raise my voice as high as I want. It's my life, my turf, my voice." She stood back and in an abruptly quieter way, one all the more emphatic for it, said, "I want you to leave, Doug. This discussion is done."

As he walked past, close enough to brush her with his arm, he murmured, "Racing up there for a quick bang?"

"Get out," she said. A quick bang? *Not quite.* The instant the shiny black car disappeared from sight, she stormed from the kitchen, crossed the driveway, and ran up the steps to the apartment.

Brian had papers spread on the coffee table, and while he didn't look exactly guilty, he had the good grace to appear unsure.

"Why did you do that?" she asked without preamble. "You saw his car. You knew he was here."

"I wanted to make sure you were all right."

"You could have called. Or rung the bell."

"I was worried he was pulling something mean."

"Come on, Brian."

"I'm serious. I've seen domestic violence. Men don't take kindly to being thrown out on the street."

"He's hardly on the street. He has a perfectly good place to go."

"So what was he doing back here?"

"Talking with me. He'll have to do that

sometimes. He's Jill's father. Any time he wants to talk with me about Jill, I'll listen."

"Was that what he wanted?" Brian asked.

"Not once he saw you. Once he saw you, walking in there like you do it all the time, all he wanted to talk about was when we started sleeping together."

"Did you tell him?"

"Certainly *not.* I didn't confirm *anything.*"

"Why not?"

"Because what I do with my nights is my business, not his."

"Are you embarrassed?"

"By what?"

"Our relationship."

"Of *course* not." Secretive of it, perhaps, and rightly so, given that it had preceded her separation from Doug. Protective of it, certainly, and excited by it, even now, when she was incensed. Embarrassed? Never. "Why would you ask that, much less think it?"

He shrugged. "I'd have told him, if it were me."

"Obviously. That's the real reason you barged in there just now. You wanted him to know. You couldn't have made it clearer, if you'd hired a skywriter."

"Damn right," Brian said, leaving the sofa. "I'm not ashamed of what we have. It happens to be a very fine, very noble, very beautiful thing. I love you. I'm not ashamed of that. Are you?"

"That's not the *point,*" she insisted, steeling herself against those pale blue eyes that could swallow her brain. He loved her. Oh, God, the words were sweet, so sweet. But she had spent a lifetime being lulled by words into hiding her thoughts. She had to be more honest, more assertive. "The point is that it isn't *your* place to tell him what I'm doing with my life. It's *my* place, and no one else's."

"Why don't you want him to know?"

"I don't *care* if he knows," she cried, frustrated to the extreme. "But I had a right to tell him in my own way and time. I didn't need you rushing in there, so blatantly possessive that a blind man would have seen it. I don't *belong* to you, Brian."

He stood a foot from her and held the distance. "I never said you did."

"Maybe not, but that's the feeling that came across back there. I belonged to Doug, once. I *let* myself belong to him. I let myself play second fiddle. I let myself be *subjugated.* So look where I am."

"Where are you?"

"I'm forty years old and starting from scratch."

"I wouldn't say that. I'd say that you're forty years old and blossoming in ways you couldn't have done before. You didn't have the roots when you were twenty or thirty. Now you do. Now you have a grip on your life."

"Well, that does sound poetic, but it doesn't describe some of the feelings I've had in the last few months, the last few *days*." They tumbled out then, so many things that had been germs, now coalescing into thoughts. "It doesn't describe fear or shock. It doesn't describe the awful upset of losing my underpinnings, of having the rug pulled out from under my feet. It doesn't describe the sting of being betrayed, or the knowledge, deep down inside, that I let it happen, *let* it happen, and it *doesn't* describe the stark realization that I have no one to depend on in life but myself, and that I'm not terribly well equipped to take on the responsibility. That is scary stuff, and what's *most* scary, is that I set myself up for it. I let Doug keep me in the dark about finances, and about his feelings toward me. Want to be poetic? I can be poetic. I let myself be crippled. Now I'm learning how to walk."

"Do you love me?"

"Yes, I love you!" She never would have had an affair with him if she didn't. "But I

544

won't use you as a crutch! I won't just stumble from one relationship into another. I won't be dependent like I was before. If we have a future, you and I, I want it to be *different*. I want there to be respect."

"I respect you. I have from day one."

"I need to respect myself. That's what I'm working on now."

"By writing. I can buy that."

"There's more to it," she said and spoke with a confidence that felt new and so, so good. "I'm finding my voice. I'm deciding what *I* want for dinner, not what Doug wants, or Jill wants. I'm sleeping in a bedroom decorated to *my* tastes. I'm using the bathroom when *I* want, not when no one else wants it."

"I have no problem with that. But what does it mean for us?"

"It means," she said with a sigh, feeling a great release, a catharsis she had never known with Doug, "that I need my space. It means," she said with a smile and, reaching up, curled her hand around his neck, "that as sweet as it is for you to run to my aid, I need to deal with Doug on my own. I need to sleep alone sometimes. I need to get to know *me*."

"But you do love me?"

"Yes." She sighed in resignation this time.

How could she *not* love him, when his eyes worshiped her that way. "I do love you."

He slid his hands down her spine, and lifted her, fitting her thighs to his hips as he backed her to the wall by the door. "Will you sleep with me those times when you don't need to sleep alone?"

She nodded.

"Will you eat what I decide to cook sometimes?"

She nodded again.

"Will you have sex with me right now?"

"No."

"Why not?"

"Because it's too soon. I'm too newly separated."

"We made love before you were separated at all."

"Shhh."

"I need you, Em." His breath was hot against her forehead, his arms enfolding her with exquisite care and incredible strength. "I've been in agony, waiting for something to happen. I was afraid you'd patch things up with him."

"How could I, if I'm in love with you?"

"You'd have done it for Jill, and I love you for that, too, only I've missed you something awful." His voice broke into a gritty groan, with the deepening of his embrace. "Oh, babe, do I ever need you."

The feeling was mutual. She didn't want it, indeed, had every intention of working to make herself more self-sufficient, but, Lord, she had missed him. Her body remembered the intimacy of his, the love-every-part-of-me need, and cried for it now. Did that mean she was weakening? Or just realizing what she wanted and taking it? "I came here to make a point about independence."

"So make it," he whispered. "Take the lead all you want. My body's yours."

It was tempting. His body was magnificent — long, hard, leanly muscular, properly haired. "What about Julia?"

"Sleeping." He moved against her in hungry ways, then, with her back to the wall, took her face in his hands. "It's so swollen inside me, all I want to give you, and it isn't only sex, it's all the other stuff."

"I know," she said. He had been giving her the other stuff since the first day she'd met him, and while a part of her wondered if she should refuse sex on principle — she wasn't being anyone's physical outlet, not ever again — another part couldn't fathom why she would want to deny herself the pleasure. Wasn't the pleasure a product of that other, more soulful stuff?

Deciding that being independent didn't

have to mean living stoically or chastely, she gave a wonderfully replete sigh and sought his mouth.

TWENTY-ONE

Brian was feeling thwarted. He gave Emily love, great sex, even space when she needed it. But the one thing that he wanted to give her, more than anything, continued to elude him.

The fingerprint that his contact had produced, the one that enhanced the two-year-old Daniel's print, hadn't matched up to a thing. So Daniel Arkin didn't have a criminal record. He hadn't been enrolled in a military school, or any other school that fingerprinted its students. He wasn't a Green Beret, a Navy Seal, or a government employee with high-security clearance — the last understandably, since he would have only been twenty-one, but Brian hadn't left anything to chance.

"Give it up," John said more than once. "You're not gonna find anything this late."

"What do you think happened to him?"

"A drifter. A gypsy. Christ, I don't know.

But he's gone."

Gone, but far from forgotten, which was why Brian persevered. Not that he wanted Emily to forget Daniel. He would never, ever ask that of her. But he wanted a resolution, just as she would, if she knew there was a chance.

Maybe there wasn't. But he had worked on cases that had looked to be dead in the water, when a single bubble broke the surface. He couldn't give up yet, particularly now that Emily's life was starting to change. She had ended her marriage and begun to write, and she was giving herself to Brian in ways that suggested forever and a day, but he wanted more than a suggestion.

That was why he drove two hours to Lower Hadley, the small town to which he had traced the woman who owned the candy store in Grannick at the time of Daniel's disappearance. The store had been down the street from the post office, with a view of the place that was oblique at best and, at worst, as had been the case that day, obscured by the truck owned by one of two customers in the shop at the time. Moreover, a taffy-pulling machine had been on, creating a noise of its own that would have drowned out most any sound from the street.

The woman hadn't seen a thing, hadn't heard a thing, didn't know a thing.

He wasn't surprised. But he was discouraged. He had already talked with four others — the owner of the bakery, a client in the real estate office, and the two customers in the candy store that day.

Nothing.

Driving back to Grannick, he agonized over where to turn next. He had gone through the list of known sex offenders, had talked with those who had been in town at the time of Daniel's disappearance, had even — quietly, gently, and without John's knowledge — checked out Nestor Berlo's story.

When he learned nothing there, he turned to the computer, using it as cold case squads often did, generating a list of child-snatchers from Daniel's time give or take five years. Pulling strings with every contact he had ever developed, he tracked down each one.

Several were dead. Most were in jail. He interviewed three of the latter with no luck, and as for those who had been on the streets at the time Daniel was taken, all had alibis placing them far from Grannick, alibis corroborated by either law enforcement officers, or by friends, relatives, or employees. Brian knew how easily a friend or relative could lie. But he couldn't open an investigation without a germ of suspicion, and he didn't even have that. None of the child-snatchers from Daniel's time had taken children that young, from cars or homes, without asking a ransom. None of the *known* child-snatchers, at least. Which left the ones who weren't known. Which left Brian right back where he'd begun, way out in left field.

He stared at the computer, reading and rereading files so often that he knew their contents by heart. Names, profiles, rap sheets — he had been hoping upon hope to find something, hoping that if he looked long enough, he would see a clue or a pattern.

He wanted Daniel solved. He wanted Emily to be able to close the book, literally and figuratively, on that chapter of her life. Mostly he wanted her to know that he had done it for her, wanted her to look up at him in the adoring way that made his chest swell and his throat grow tight with thoughts of how much she mattered.

There had to be an answer. Okay, so he was emotionally involved. Okay, so he wasn't being as realistic as officers of the law were supposed to be. But his emotional, unrealistic, involved-with-Emily self insisted that someone, somewhere had to know what happened to Daniel.

For lack of other direction — and because Emily was thinking about Daniel more, because she had all those notes spread before her, because Brian thought there might be a clue in them, in *her,* that she had been too close to the case to see — but mostly because Doug was gone and Brian felt freer to love her, he started stopping by in the middle of the day to see how she was doing.

He brought sandwiches with him on Monday. On Tuesday, because snow was falling and the world was cold and crisp, she made soup. On Wednesday, because he felt she needed a break, he dragged her from her computer to the Eatery.

They were on their way home when his radio crackled. He picked it up and conversed with the dispatcher. Cursing the timing, he stepped on the gas.

"What?" Emily asked.

He should have left her home, where things were safe and Daniel's disappearance was the only one she had to suffer through again and again and again.

"Brian?"

"You don't want to know."

"It's another missing child, isn't it?"

He figured she had made out at least part

of the dispatcher's message, and careened around a corner, muttering, "Missing doesn't mean kidnapped. Christ, what *is* it about this town?"

"The dispatcher said the end of LaGrange. That's a wealthy area. Did she say Hammelman?"

"Sounded like it. Do you know them?"

"Not well. They own movie theaters. They're friends of the Berlos."

Brian grunted. "Is that friends of his, friends of hers, or friends of lovers somewhere along the way?" The Berlos were definitely unusual. He slowed when he approached their stone wall, not because it was theirs, but because it marked the way to China Pond Road. "Am I dropping you home?"

"No."

He reaccelerated. "Didn't think so." He continued down LaGrange until he reached the large brick house with a cruiser parked behind a small Mercedes, which was parked behind a Jaguar, which was parked behind a larger Mercedes on the circular drive. "Wait here," he told Emily, but she was already out of the car.

Munroe had his forearms on the roof of the cruiser. He pulled them off to fill Brian in. "Three-year-old girl. Mother left her with a sitter. They're both gone."

"No note left behind saying where they went?" Brian asked.

"Nope. The child has a bad cough. The mother was real clear about coming back at one to take her to the doctor."

"Maybe the sitter got scared and took the little girl to the hospital herself."

"*Him*self. The sitter was Richie Berlo."

"Richie Berlo?" Brian asked in dismay.

"His mother and Mrs. Hammelman are best friends. They were going to Hartford, and when the little girl couldn't be with her playgroup because of the cold, he was filling in."

"Why wasn't he in school?"

Munroe shrugged. "Gotta find him to ask him. Half the department's out looking. No one's seen him."

"Did they put out an APB?"

"Not yet."

"Why not?" Brian demanded, foolishly. No APB had been issued for the same reason that Harold had looked the other way when Richie had tried to shoplift from his store. Money talked. Nestor Berlo was to be spared embarrassment at all costs.

To Emily, Brian muttered, "That kid is a disaster waiting to happen."

"They won't touch him," she confirmed.

"I will. I know some of his hiding places. Come on. Let's join the chase." But before he could reach the Jeep, the dispatcher had told Munroe that the chase was underway, high-speed, on the outskirts of town. Munroe passed the word to Brian.

Brian put a flasher on the roof and his foot to the floor.

"I've never been in on a chase before," Emily said.

"And you won't be now," he informed her, listening to the radio with one ear as the others reported their positions. "I'm going fast. That's one step slower than speeding, which is three steps slower than chasing."

"Go faster."

"Not with you in the car and slush on the road."

"Don't you want to catch Richie?"

"No. All I want is to be there once he's caught. I want my turn questioning him. I'm not intimidated by his father, the way most of this town seems to be." He turned up the radio. Excited reports were coming in, one after the other.

"How much do you know about Nestor?" Emily asked with the tact of a loyal Grannickite.

"I know that his lover is the same sex as his wife's lover, if that's what you're getting

556

at." A quick look told him that it was. He frowned at something the dispatcher said. "Ridge Road?"

But Emily was more familiar with the town. "River Road. It's a little beyond." She leaned closer, because the voices were coming fast and furious. *"What?"*

Brian started to speed. "Accident," he said.

"Who?"

"I don't know."

"John."

"Let's wait and see."

"John's hurt."

"We don't know that."

"They just said so. They're calling an ambulance."

"Stay cool," Brian said, feeling anything but. He hated it when any officer was hurt, hated it even more when he knew the officer, and when he knew the perpetrator, when his gut told him the whole thing could have been prevented, he hated it the most.

He whipped around corners as fast as the Jeep would take them, fishtailing around a few on the remants of yesterday's snow, hitting his horn more than once when an unsuspecting driver threatened to intrude on his path. He was wired by the time he reached River Road. His nerves sparked hotly when he saw John's cruiser wedged on its side against a tree.

"My God," Emily cried, tugging at her door.

Brian wanted to make her stay in the Jeep, but short of tying her down, he didn't know how, and then ambulance sounds came from behind, and it seemed pointless. He ran forward just as a crew of others righted John's car. Emily was among the first to get to John, but she, too, had to stand aside when the EMTs came through.

"He's alive," she told Brian. "He's talking."

But Brian could see John's facial expressions. "Looks like he's hurting. His legs?"

"Yes."

He put his hands on her shoulders, and said, "Stay here until they get him in the ambulance. Want to go with him?"

"Yes."

He passed that word on, then turned to the side. There, standing by his slush-spattered sports car, looking for all the world like a spectator, rather than the object of a manhunt, was Richie Berlo. The Hammelman child knelt like a forgotten bag of groceries on the front seat of his car.

"What was this all about?" Brian asked with a tired sigh. Before Richie could answer, he walked past him and lifted the child from the car. "Hey, you," he teased, "where you been?"

"We went riding," she said in the kind of sweet, little-girl voice he imagined Julia would have at three. "We went fast. It was fun."

"Your Mommy's worried."

"But I didn't cough once."

With a look at Richie that forbade him to move, Brian carried the child to Sam. "You take her. I'll take him." He returned to Richie with a pair of handcuffs.

"What're those for?"

"They're what we use when we don't trust that the people we're taking in for questioning won't turn tail and run."

"Questioning? For *speeding?*"

Brian snapped on the cuffs and set off, hauling Richie along.

"Where are you taking me?"

"For starters to get a good look at the guy they're laying out on that stretcher over there. In case you don't recognize him, he's the chief of police in this town. He's someone's husband and someone's father and a friend to lots and lots of people around here. He's the guy who might have died just now, thanks to you." He took Richie by the back of the neck. "Look good."

John was sickly pale. Blood ran from a facial cut. His features were twisted with pain.

When Richie started to turn away, Brian tightened his hand. "Watch, goddammit," he muttered under his breath, though, in fact, his own eyes had found Emily's. She was frightened for John, but there was something reassuring in the look she sent him. It calmed his nerves.

He waited until she climbed in behind the stretcher. None too gently, he ushered Richie to the Jeep and shoved him inside.

"I didn't make him hit the tree," the boy protested once they were on the road.

Brian held the wheel with both hands. "You knew he was behind you, you knew he wanted you to stop, you led him on a merry chase. He wouldn't have hit the tree if you hadn't done that."

"He skidded on ice. It wasn't my fault."

"What were you doing with the little girl?"

"Nothing. She was bored, so we took a ride."

"With her mother coming back at one?"

"I forgot. And anyway," he added, sounding petulant and wise, "they're never back when they say they'll be. Brunch takes hours. It's the most important thing they have to do with their lives."

"Yours is school. Why weren't you there?"

"Because I had to babysit."

"You didn't have to. You don't need the money."

"I was doing her a favor. I was doing my mother a favor. Besides, I'm a senior. School is irrelevant at this point."

"Not if you want to get into college."

Richie made a sputtering sound.

"Ahhh," Brian interpreted. "Getting into college isn't a problem. Not with Daddy greasing the right palms. So you were doing Mrs. Hammelman a favor. Why would she think you'd kidnap the child?"

Richie looked appalled. "*Kidnap?* I didn't *kidnap* the kid. Is that what she says?"

"Yeah. I want to know why."

The boy's expression soured. "Go ask her."

"I'm asking you. You're the son of her best friend. Her first instinct should be to trust, not accuse."

"She doesn't like my father."

"Why not?"

"Three guesses. The first two don't count."

"Why *not?*" When Richie didn't answer, he said, "I'm new to town. Make like I don't know a thing."

"She doesn't like my father," the boy

enunciated slowly, "because she doesn't turn him on."

"So what does that have to do with her not trusting you?"

"Come on, man. I'm the guy's son. Use your imagination."

"I'm law and order, black and white. I got no imagination. Tell me what you being Nestor's son has to do with her not trusting you."

"Shit." He looked away.

"Spit it out, Richie."

"She thinks I'm *like him.* Duhhhh."

Brian wondered if he was, if his lashing out stemmed from the angst of sexual confusion. But he wasn't touching on that, not until he had something more going with the boy. "If Mrs. Hammelman thinks that, why did she leave you with her child?"

"She probably figured I was safe with a girl. Where are we going? This isn't the way into town."

"I feel like taking a drive." He dropped one of his hands from the wheel. "Relax a little, y'know."

"You better take me back. They'll be wondering where I am."

Brian pointed to the radio. "They know where you are. They can reach us if they want. This way we can talk. We won't be

562

able to, back at the station."

"We won't have to," he grumbled. "I'll be out in five minutes."

"Not if I can help it. Kidnapping's a serious charge."

"I did not kidnap Sara."

"Then there's always driving to endanger, or flight with intent to escape arrest. There's my chief, probably getting to the hospital right about now, with injuries that may be life threatening, and then there's the matter of vandalism, just a little, enough to annoy, and I wouldn't dismiss the kidnap business so fast. Mrs. Hammelman was worried enough to call the cops, and your mother let her."

"My mother was scared. She knew if she went home without me, my father would be mad. He likes to know where I am."

"Is he rigid about it?"

Richie snorted his confirmation.

"I suppose," Brian reasoned, "that that's a small price to pay for living such an easy life. You go to school when and if you want. You lift a little Vitamin C from the drugstore, tool around in Daddy's Lotus, spray paint cars, toss eggs, take off with a three-year-old and joyride at breakneck speeds, and you never get punished."

"Shows how much *you* know," Richie

mumbled.

"You break laws, but you count on your name getting you off."

Richie turned on him. "So punish me. Lock me up. Fuckin' *do* it already."

"Nah. I think I'll take you home."

"Charge me with something! Put me away! You said it yourself, you're the new guy in town. You don't owe my father jack shit. Go ahead. Charge me. Get me the fuck *outta* here."

Brian eased the Jeep to the side of the road. It was a quiet street, beautiful, with the sun setting the snow on fire. If there were houses, they were hidden behind trees. There wasn't another car in sight.

Leaving one loose hand on the wheel, he turned quietly to Richie. "That sounded like a plea."

Richie faced the windshield.

"Want to talk about it?"

"Talk about what?"

"What it's like, living at home? Why your mother goes out all the time, why your big brother never comes back?"

Richie shrank in his seat.

More gently, Brian said, "You don't have to confront him, y'know. I can understand why that would be tough."

"No, you can't," Richie spat, but there

were tears in his eyes. "You can't understand what it's like having a father who does — who does — who does things like that." He looked away.

"To you?" Brian asked quietly.

Richie didn't deny it.

Brian felt sick. "I'll bet it's been going on since your brother left."

"He knew it would, but he left anyway. He didn't care about me. He was only thinking of himself."

"Does your mother know?"

He hesitated again. Then, as though there was so much bitterness he couldn't hold it in, he blurted, "She *has* to. But she looks the other way. She has a good thing going, and she knows it. She's not giving it up for me." He turned adamant eyes on Brian. "I'm not like him. I *hate* it."

"So what will you do? Go off to college like your brother did, and never come back?"

"I wish I could," he cried with an hysterical edge, "but he wants to keep me around. He says he's sending me to college here!"

"And you'd rather go to jail." It explained his attempts to get arrested, or, at the very least, noticed by the police.

"I'd rather *anything*."

Brian knew enough not to touch the boy,

though he wanted to, in reassurance, in acceptance, in understanding of his pain. The kid was crying for help, loud and clear. Granted, his voice was off-key. "You don't want jail, Richie. That'd be worse than your father. But those don't have to be your choices. I can give you others."

"No, you can't. My father controls everyone in Grannick. He does what he wants and gets away with it."

"He won't get away with pedophilia."

"You don't *understand*. They'll never *charge* him with that. *I* sure won't accuse him. He'll kill me if I do."

"There are ways to handle it. Quiet ways. Private ways."

But Richie was shaking his head. "He'll *kill* me."

"He'll never know you said anything."

"Yeah. Sure."

Brian held out his arms. "Do you see a wire? I'm not recording anything. That's one of the reasons we're driving around. What's said here is between you and me. If anything goes farther, it's because you take it there. You call the shots."

The boy still looked doubtful, but there was an element of tentativeness that hadn't been there moments before.

Brian pressed his advantage. "Look,

Richie, your father's preferences are no secret in town. The police have known them for years. If we were to talk with him as your parent about our concern for you, about the shoplifting and the vandalism and the joyriding — without saying anything about what he does at home — if we were to recommend that you stay with your brother, or another relative somewhere else for a while, he'd buy it."

Richie was glum. "He wants me here."

"He doesn't want a scandal."

"There won't be one. His money keeps people quiet."

"Yeah, and that's what he wants. He wants people to keep quiet about his preferences. His beneficence is hush money. Think about it, Richie. Sure, Grannick wants the money, but your father wants his privacy just as much. He pays big bucks for it, which should tell you how bad he wants it. He can threaten us about what he'll do if you're sent out of town, but we can threaten right back about what *we*'ll do if you aren't."

Richie was quiet. He stared out the window. He chewed on his cheek. He looked at Brian. "Would that work?"

"I'd put money on it. He isn't invulnerable. Few men in his situation are."

"What if I went away and he followed me?"

"Did he follow your brother?"

"No."

"He isn't a fool. He has a successful business to run and a reputation to uphold. Trust me. He won't do anything to risk disclosure of what he's been doing. Being gay is one thing. Being a child abuser is something else entirely."

Richie was staring at the windshield again, again looking close to tears. "I didn't mean for anything to happen to Chief Davies."

"I know."

"I stopped as soon as I saw him flip. Will he be all right?"

"I don't know. Want to take a ride to the hospital with me?"

There was a pause, a darting look to see if Brian was serious, then an appreciative, "Yeah."

Kay was midway through her last class of the day when the principal appeared and sent her to the phone. It was Emily, saying that John had been in an accident and was hurt, which was a totally absurd concept. He was the halest, hardiest man Kay knew, not to mention the safest driver.

"Surgery?" she repeated in echo of Emily.

"There's possible internal bleeding, and damage to his legs."

Kay couldn't picture it. "What kind of damage?"

"Broken bones, whatever, I don't know the details, Kay, you'll be the better one to ask the doctors."

"*John?* But how did it happen?"

"He was in a high-speed chase. The cruiser hit a tree."

Kay flinched, but the image she conjured came from Hollywood, not real life. "He's never been in an accident before. How come you're there?"

"I was with Brian when it happened. We got to the scene just as the ambulance arrived."

"They took him in an *ambulance?*" It did follow that if he had been hurt badly enough to require surgery, an ambulance would have been involved, but she couldn't picture John on a *stretcher,* much less an operating table.

"Want me to come for you, Kay?"

Something of Emily's urgency finally got through. "No. I'll drive there myself. I'm leaving right now." And she did, thinking all the while that injuries in the line of duty happened to cops in other towns, bigger towns. Many a time John had marched with

569

police contingents in funerals around the state, but the cops who died were never from Grannick, Grannick was a sleepy town. It was a peaceful town. High-speed chases were little more than macho rushes of adrenaline on deserted country roads.

She was still skeptical when she pulled up at the hospital, but the atmosphere of the place couldn't be ignored. Even then, it took the concern on Emily's face — such real concern — to drive the message home.

Emily guided her to a waiting room. "They promised they'd come tell us as soon as there's word."

Kay lowered herself to a pink vinyl sofa. As if validating everything she had been thinking about small, sleepy towns, she and Emily had the room to themselves.

"Tell me the truth, Emily. Are we talking life and death?"

"No. No, no. Not unless he reacts badly to the anesthesia."

"Why the rush to surgery then? Was he shot?"

"There were no guns involved."

"Did he hit the other car?"

"No. Only the tree. There was ice on the shoulder of the road from yesterday's snow. He hit a bend and skidded making the turn."

Kay took that in with a chill. "Was he conscious in the ambulance?"

"Yes. He was talking to me."

"What was he saying?"

Emily smiled wryly. "He was swearing mostly. He couldn't believe he'd wrecked the cruiser."

That was the first thing Kay had heard that sounded at all like the man, which made things just that little bit more real. "How bad are his legs?"

"He has multiple fractures in both."

"Both? My God, how will he walk?"

"He won't, for a while."

"How will he get around?"

"He won't, for a while."

"I can't picture it." Absolutely not. "How long did they say he'd be in surgery?"

"They didn't."

She tried to analyze the meaning of that, then, when she couldn't, tried to organize her thoughts. "Maybe I should call Marilee. No. That's silly. She'll only worry. I'll wait until I know more. Until he's awake. Until I talk with the doctor. Afterward." She was frightened. John had never been disabled in any way, shape, or form. "I feel like I'm talking about a stranger."

Emily took her hand. "He'll be all right."

"I know. It's just," she tried to articulate

it, "John is so — perfect — physically. Everything works. He doesn't have allergies, doesn't have high blood pressure. He's never sick." She was feeling shaky. "I'm not prepared for this."

"I'll help all I can, you know that. John is as close to a brother as I've ever had."

But he was Kay's husband, and he was going to need her. Prepared or not, she had to be there for him.

It was nearly seven before he was wheeled into his room. Kay was already there.

She had sent Emily home, assuring her that she would be fine, insisting that she had done enough for the Davies for one day. The truth was that, much as she loved Emily, much as she appreciated the concern of members of the department who came by in a steady flow, she needed time alone with her thoughts — to accept that John was hurt, to rejoice that he would recover, to deal with the sour aftertaste a brush with mortality had left.

Besides, she wanted to be the one John saw when he woke up.

She waited, heart pounding, eyes wide on poles, bottles, tubes, and casts, while the attendants finished arranging him to their satisfaction. Then she approached the bed.

His eyes were shut, one swollen, with stitches above it. His gray hair was mussed, his skin ashen, his lips pale and dry.

She touched his arm with the back of her hand. He stirred. One eye came open, poorly focused. She positioned herself in its range. "Hi," she said softly.

His voice was scratchy. "Kay?"

"Uh-huh. How do you feel?"

"Lousy."

"That's about how you look," she said because humor seemed the best approach. "You've got a good shiner."

"Huh." He closed his eyes.

Kay studied the casts on his legs. They were suspended on slings, and looked to weigh a ton. The doctor had explained that the elevation was temporary, but that John would be bedridden for a time. One broken leg was manageable; two complicated things.

"Kay?"

"Right here." She leaned closer.

"What happened to the boy?"

She smiled, feeling oddly calmed. She might have known that his mind would be back at the scene of the accident, piecing together events. There was normalcy in that. "He's fine. He feels awful about what happened. Brian brought him by before."

"Gotta get him out of that house."

"Brian's working on it."

He tried to raise his head and look at his legs, but with only one good eye and a neck like rubber, he couldn't make it. Kay caught his head when it wobbled and eased it back to the pillow. "You have to rest. Lie still."

"What about my legs?"

"They're on the mend."

"How long?"

"Depending on how the healing goes, two or three months."

He groaned.

"Does it hurt?"

"Huh." Neither question nor answer. "Mouth is dry."

She hurriedly reached for a glass of water and held it while he drank through the straw. Then she pushed at the pillows to give his neck better support. "Can I do something? Get you something?"

His eyes were closed, his mouth barely moving. "Just stay here a little."

She sat on the edge of the bed. "I called Marilee. She wanted to fly right home. I told her to wait until she talked with you. She told me to tell you she loves you." Her throat grew tight. She raised a hand to her neck, but it quickly fell to his arm. "So do I," she whispered. "Do you hear me, John? I

574

don't like it when things like this happen to you." Tentatively she touched his hand. Lightly, furtively, she slipped her fingers through his as he slept.

TWENTY-TWO

On a seriousness scale of one to ten, John's accident had only been a four, but it affected Emily deeply. It made her think about the fragility of life, and its randomness. Two feet to the left, and John would have missed the patch of ice and been fine. Two feet to the right, and he would have missed the tree, tumbled into the gulley, and died.

Two paces, give or take, and Gayle Stasek would have made it safely home from her run.

Three minutes, give or take, and Jill would never have seen Doug on the stoop of that townhouse in Boston.

Four minutes, give or take, and whoever had taken Daniel from her car that day, would never have seen him there.

"Scary," she whispered, lost in her thoughts as she stared at the flames that licked the logs in the hearth.

"What is?" Brian asked.

She sat against him with her elbows on his bent knees. Turning her cheek to his throat, she said, "Hmmm?"

"What's scary?"

"The suddenness of things. The *finality* of things. What if I hadn't gone to the post office that day? Or if I had gone earlier or later? Daniel's abduction was a impulsive thing, I'm sure of it, someone deranged just happening by. If I hadn't left the car when I did, my life would have been very different. Same with Gayle. If she hadn't gone running that day, or had gone a little earlier or a little later, you'd be back in New York with her now."

She faced the fire again. "Do you miss New York?"

"Only when I talk with my old buddies. From a distance their stories are all excitement and success. Then I hang up the phone and remember the endless hours and the danger and the cases that fall apart. I don't miss that part."

"You aren't bored here?"

"Nah. I missed the action, at first. Missed the camaraderie. But I know people here now. They accept me. So there's camaraderie. And action, too, just of a different sort."

"What sort?"

"Personal. I was involved in more cases there, but here I have a greater impact on each one. There's more follow-through. Like Leila. Ritchie. I like that. It's gratifying. Why do you ask?"

She asked because she wanted him to stick around. High-speed chases notwithstanding, a policeman had a better chance of staying alive in Grannick than in Manhattan. Emily shuddered to think of Brian being shot or stabbed.

"I was wondering if you're restless," she said.

He turned her until she was cradled between his arms and knees. "Do I feel like I'm restless?"

"Right now? No." His pale eyes held her, intrigued her. "But I don't know what you're feeling when you're heading down here for yet another day in the good old Grannick Police Department."

"Not restless," he assured her with a glint in his eyes. "Sleepy some mornings. Relaxed. Looking forward to what's coming, in a laid-back kind of way. Work in the city is intense. It eats you up. I never could understand why so many cops had marriage problems — well, I knew the reason, but I never really *felt* it until I got away. How can you give to a marriage when you're consumed by high-tension stuff ten, twelve, fourteen hours a day? How can you be an attentive parent?"

He looked down at Julia, who slept on a blanket beside them. Emily watched him watching her, watched the play of emotion on his face, gilded from the fire, the protectiveness, the love.

"I made the right decision leaving," he said. "Julia is doing well here. She doesn't scream the way she used to when she hears a loud noise or a cry or, God forbid, a siren. She sleeps through the night and wakes up glad to see me. She's growing. She's talking. Okay, unintelligibly. But *I* know what she's saying."

Emily was content, just listening to his voice. She liked what it said. She liked the rumble of it above and behind her.

"My mom is disappointed we're not coming for Thanksgiving. I told her I didn't want to wrench Julia up so soon. She needs sameness for a little while more. When does Jill get home?"

"Wednesday afternoon. The forecast is for snow."

"Snow for Thanksgiving? Whoa! That's great!"

"Not if I can't drive in for Jill."

"She can always take a bus."

"I know. But I wanted to be there at her dorm. She's feeling unsettled about Doug."

"Angry still?"

"And sad. She's torn. She wants to hate him, but she can't. She's struggling with her loyalties. I keep telling her she doesn't have to choose, that she can have both of us, but the situation is still very new."

He put the pad of his thumb to her lower lip. "She'll do fine. She has you. You're level-headed."

"How else can I be? I want what's best for Jill. I don't want her hurt."

"Is she nervous about the holiday?"

"A little. How about you? It's your first without Gayle."

"I think about her. I wish she could see Julia. Am I dreading Thanksgiving? No. We always went to Gayle's parents' home in Westchester for formal sit-downs. They lasted forever. I was ready to leave halfway through. What did you and Doug do?"

"Had it here. Friends came over. This'll be the first time I haven't cooked the turkey in twenty-two years."

"Will you miss it?"

Slowly, deliberately, she shook her head. "I couldn't do the same thing this year. Not with all that's happened. I need something different, so I won't be making comparisons." She smiled in anticipation of what was in the works. Everyone was descending on the Davies — Brian and Julia, Emily and Jill, Celeste and Dawn and Celeste's new heartthrob, several of Kay's colleagues, several of John's — all bringing food. It would definitely be different. "I can guarantee you nothing will be formal this year."

"That's good. I'm not a formal person. That part of New York didn't fit me real well."

"Tell me you used to go to the opera."

"Nuh-uh. I drew the line there. But theater. Symphony. Fancy parties thrown by Gayle's firm."

"I can't picture you in a tux." The most dressed she had seen him was in a shirt, tie, and jeans. Usually at home he wore sweats. At night he wore nothing.

"I look dashing in a tux."

"No doubt. But confined."

"That, too. That a *lot,* which is why I gave the tux away before I moved. It was symbolic. Giving up one life for another."

Emily wondered if he would ever come to miss it, if he would tire of Grannick one day, and want to leave. It could create a problem, if they were together. She couldn't leave. She couldn't.

She shifted again, so that her cheek lay on

his chest and her ear timed his heart. There was something about resting against Brian like this, something soothing about his scent and reassuring about his bulk. There was something comforting, in the sense of not being alone. The fact of Julia being inches away only added to the moment. Emily had known moments like these for a short time with Daniel and Doug. She had hoped to live them again after Jill was born, but that hadn't happened.

"I love you," Brian whispered.

She nestled closer.

"Did you hear me?" he asked, whispering still.

"Yes," she whispered back.

"I want to marry you."

"Shhh. I can't think about it now."

"Why not?"

"Too soon. I just want to enjoy this." She turned her face into him. Her voice grew muffled in his warmth. "I don't want to plan. I just want to *be*."

She felt a large, protective hand on her back, sliding around and up under her hair.

"Okay," he said at last. "I can live with letting you *be* for a little while. But can I say the words when I am so moved?"

She smiled. "You can say the words."

"Good," he said.

Still smiling she waited, fully expecting that he would say them again before long. When he didn't, she let out a slow, soft breath. She didn't need to hear the words. She could feel the caring coming from him. It was more than she'd had in so long. It was more than enough for now.

Doug called Emily that night. She had just put a chocolate cake in the oven. "How're you doing?" he asked with the kind of enthusiasm he hadn't directed her way in years.

She was quickly wary. "Not bad."

"What are your plans for Thanksgiving?"

She told him about the group heading for the Davieses'. "Since John can't go anywhere, it makes sense."

"Is Brian going?"

"Yes," she said without apology.

"Is it serious between you two?"

"Kay wouldn't hear of his doing anything else, since he's new in town and alone with Julia."

"You didn't answer my question."

"No. I didn't." She had no intention of answering his question.

"Well?"

"What are you doing for the holiday?"

He persisted. "Is it serious between you

and Brian?"

"That's none of your business."

"Does Jill know you're involved with him?"

"Jill likes him. She feels comfortable knowing he's here."

"She might not, if she knew you were sleeping with him."

Emily let out a breath. "Doug. Please. You're beating a dead horse."

"How so? What you do affects her. I'm concerned about her."

"Oh, my God!" she exploded. "You are incredible! You're worried about what *I* do? *Nothing* I do could be half as hurtful as what you've been doing for the past five years."

"Eight years."

"Excuse me. Eight years." *Eight* years. She felt the blow of that revelation in her gut, felt stung, dirty, cheapened. "You didn't think much of me at all, did you?"

"I blamed you for Daniel," he said, as though to excuse it.

"You didn't have the guts, Doug. You were fooling around behind my back for *eight* years, you knew we had no future together, but you didn't have the guts to make the break yourself."

"I kept thinking of Daniel," he repeated, but without pride.

"You hated me because of Daniel, but couldn't divorce me because of Daniel."

"Something like that." There was a pause, then a tentative, "Do you think he's alive somewhere?"

Oh, God. "No."

"Why not?"

"Because if he were, he'd have tried to contact us. He would be twenty-one."

"What if he was told that the people who raised him were his biological parents? He wouldn't have known there was anyone to contact."

Emily had considered that possibility. "I still think he'd have known, somehow."

"What if we'd gotten him back?"

"When?"

"Anytime. Say after four or five years."

She wasn't sure what he was asking. "Yes?"

"Would things have gone back to how they were?"

"Between us?"

"Yes."

"I don't know. It would depend on how he had lived during those four or five years. Anything negative, and you'd have blamed me still."

She held the receiver through another long stretch during which the only sounds coming from Doug were those of breathing and

585

the occasional false start. He sounded to be struggling with the issue of Daniel in ways she hadn't thought him capable, and while it didn't excuse what he'd done, or the fact that he continued to blame her, she was relieved to know that at least he remembered his son.

His *first* son.

"I wonder if they could find him now," Doug said.

"No. Too much time has passed."

"Lots of cases are solved later."

"Not ones like this."

"Don't you want to know what happened to him?"

"Yes! My God," she cried, "I was the one who fought to keep the investigation open. I was the one whose emotions seesawed for years, while you just put it all aside. When they closed the investigation because there wasn't anything to investigate, even *then* I tried, but there was nothing. I can't get my hopes up again. I just can't. He's dead, Doug. One way or another, he's dead."

"Is that what you'll write in your book?"

"*If* I do a book, it'll be about my feelings about Daniel, before, during, and after. It'll be about years of torment and the struggle to find an ending. Our divorce may help. The other thing that will help is accepting, finally, that I'm not getting Daniel back."

"You're a lousy mother if you do that."

"But I have to survive!" she cried. He was at it again, making her out to be the bad guy, when she *wasn't*. "I can't go looking for him again. Don't ask me to do that."

"What if I ask your good friend, Brian?"

"No! Don't!"

"Why not?"

Because Brian is pure, where Daniel is concerned. He's my present and future. I don't want him tainted. "He won't be able to find anything. John couldn't, and God knows, he tried."

"John isn't very bright."

"He *is*."

"Couldn't solve *this* case."

"And you resented him all these years for it." She had known it, of course, had seen it in Doug's slow but steady distancing of himself from John. "He's a cop, not a miracle worker." She took a fast breath. "I have to go now, Doug. I'm baking for Thursday."

"So you're eating at the Davieses'. I might drop in and say hello."

Her heart rose to her throat. "That's not a good idea."

"Why not? Jill's my daughter. I have a right to see her on Thanksgiving."

"Before or after. Not at." At was a *terrible* idea. It would upset *everyone!*

"I want to talk with Brian," Doug insisted, prodding where he had found her weak.

"If you do, it's without my consent. Before or after," she repeated, "not at."

"I want the mystery solved once and for all."

"Before or after. Not at. Goodbye, Doug." She hung up the phone with an uneasy shiver.

Emily kept waiting for Doug to show up. He was obsessed with Brian, obsessed with Daniel, neither of whom he had had much interest in until after she had learned about *his* indiscretions. But she didn't want him touching Brian in any way, shape, or form that might have to do with Daniel. She had lived and breathed false hopes for years. She just couldn't do it again.

She didn't fully relax until Thanksgiving dinner was done and Jill, Marilee, and Dawn had taken off to visit friends. In the kitchen, drying platters and pans as Kay washed, she said, "I thought he'd show up here, just because I told him not to. He's trying to keep me off-balance."

"What does he know about Brian?"

"Nothing. He guesses." She met Kay's

gaze with a sheepish shrug. "He doesn't see us together like you do."

"Lucky for that. Brian's eyes give it away. Yours, too, sweetie."

"How can I help it? He's so different from Doug. Doug and I were totally swept up in being young and in love. But everything with Brian is deeper."

"More mature."

"Positively speaking," Emily agreed, but she was looking at Kay, thinking of subtle changes there, too. "How're things here?"

Kay blushed. "Interesting. It's been different with John around. Nice. Maybe we all need a shock once in a while. Yours was learning about Doug's other family. Mine was John's accident."

The kitchen door swung open. Celeste breezed in. "Okay, guys. What do you think? Is he great, or is he great?"

Emily said, "He's definitely handsome."

"And charming," Kay added.

"Not that we saw any of the others you met."

"He's different from what I thought you'd get with an ad."

Celeste waited. After a minute's silence, she asked, "Why do I hear 'buts'? Tell me what's wrong with him. I can't find a thing."

"Neither can I," Emily said. That was what

bothered her. Carter was smooth, almost too much so. She didn't want to breathe the word slick, though it was the one that came to mind. He had been the perfect guest, bringing flowers to Kay and a book to John, talking law enforcement with those in law enforcement and college with those in college. He had smiled and teased and drawn people in. He hadn't gone near Julia, but then, neither had Celeste. Maybe that was what bothered Emily, though she knew it shouldn't. Just because she found Julia irresistible didn't mean everyone did.

"Where did he grow up?" Kay asked.

"All over. He was an army brat."

"Where do his parents live now?"

"They're dead."

"Does he have siblings?"

Celeste shook her head. "He's all by his lonesome."

"No wife at any point?"

"No. I read you his letter. His work kept him on the move too much to allow for a wife."

"Statements like that aren't definitive. He could have had a wife, but abandoned her."

Emily cleared her throat. "Yes, we do know that happens."

"He is not like Doug," Celeste declared. "Since we met, he's been here in Grannick more than he's been away."

"What about his work?" Kay asked.

"He's the idea man, the concept guy. He creates the initial drawings and leaves the drudgery to his assistants."

"Is he working, while he's here?"

"Of course not. Good God, he's earned a vacation. He's been working nonstop for years."

He didn't looked overworked. He was tanned. He seemed rested. Emily would have pegged him as a playboy, not a workaholic.

"Come on, guys," Celeste was plaintive now, "don't rain on my parade. He treats me like a princess. He even treats *Dawn* like a princess. Would you believe, he showed up yesterday morning with flowers and gifts for both of us? He's incredible."

Emily thought about the yesterday morning part, which implied a last night and this morning part. "Is he staying at your house?"

"Of course."

"Dawn knows you're sleeping with him?" Emily hadn't told Jill about Brian and her. She wanted to. She had thought to broach it a dozen times during the drive from Boston to Grannick, but had lost her nerve each time.

Celeste's situation was different. She had

been divorced for years.

"Dawn *adores* him," Celeste was saying. "She actually behaves when he's around. I don't think she and I have fought once. He's a good influence on her. Would you believe, the two of them made me breakfast this morning? Dawn, cooking? Dawn, waiting on me? Dawn, *smiling* in my presence? I didn't know what that smile was the first time I saw it, she's usually so sullen."

"Absence makes the heart grow fonder," Kay said.

Emily was pleased for Celeste, far more with regard to Dawn than Carter. "Moments like those are special. They're the ones we keep forever. Jill and I were out in the snow yesterday afternoon after she got home." There hadn't been enough to mess up the drive, just enough for fun. "We took Julia out. She had never played in snow before. It was priceless watching her. We made angels, and teeny snowmen, used up just about all the snow there was."

Brian had been there, too, and the four of them had had a ball. Jill had been caught up enough in Julia's excitement not to be looking for things between Emily and Brian. That was how Emily wanted it, a gradual getting to know one another, that would make something deeper perfectly natural, when and if it came.

Playing there in the yard, Emily wasn't thinking of Doug. She wasn't thinking of Daniel. She was thinking of Jill, Brian, and Julia, thinking how much all three meant to her. They were laughter-filled, light-hearted moments when the problems of the world seemed eons away.

It was late before the last of Kay's guests left, and a while after that before she had the house in order, but as she worked, she, too, was thinking about special moments. The past few days had been full of them.

First came Marilee, out of the blue, home for vacation early to help with John, insisting Kay shouldn't be alone.

Kay hadn't had the heart to tell her that she wasn't alone, that between Emily and Celeste and half the police force and their wives, John had more babysitters than he wanted. The fact was that with Marilee there, Kay felt less stressed. In a few short months away from home, Marilee had grown up. She had become an individual in her own right. She didn't shy from responsibility, as she once had. Kay found that decidedly rewarding.

Then there was her own work, which suddenly seemed of less significance. She took sick days until John was discharged from the hospital, and once he was installed in a hospital bed in the living room, she rushed home during free periods and lunches. Yes, others were there. But she wanted to be there, too. After years of being the last of the teachers to leave, now as soon as classes ended, she was gone from school.

John had always needed her on some level, but it was largely a custodial one — cook, keep house, wash clothes — and there was that now and more, what with his physical limitations.

But there were emotional needs now, too. He was a terrible patient. If his being laid up was a shocker for her, it was all the more so for him. He grumbled and fussed. He complained. He didn't like what he was wearing, how he was lying, what was on television. His ribs hurt. His legs ached. He was in a constant state of irritation that only eased when Kay was home. She was the only one who could make him smile.

She was surprised at how much that meant to her. For years, they had shared a house and a child and the activities tied to each. But John had his work, and Kay had hers. There hadn't been much sharing of that.

Now Kay was present when Brian or Sam

or one of the others came by at the end of the day with a rundown of activity at the station. John insisted she be there, seeming calmer when she was. Likewise, claiming boredom, he made her tell him about her day at school.

They grew closer, and not only in matters of the mind. There were physical chores, intimate chores, that he allowed only Kay to perform. As a result, she touched him more in the course of a day than she had touched him in months before. Initially awkward, she grew increasingly at ease, and it wasn't only that John was wounded and, hence, less intimidating. It was that he wanted *her* to touch him, wanted *her* to help him, wanted *her* to sit on the edge of the bed, within reach of his hand when whoever it was from the department was there.

He was being possessive, acting proud of her, and she liked that — which appalled the professional person in her, until she realized that she didn't *need* his approval, simply *enjoyed* it. She felt more complete, more confident, even thinner. She didn't know whether it was nervous energy burning off calories, or the walking she did early each morning, and she hadn't lost much more than a few pounds, but she felt better about herself.

Encouraged by John's need, she grew bolder. She bathed him more slowly. She gave him back rubs. Safely clothed while he was bare and vulnerable, she looked at his body in ways she had never dared do, and he loved it. They joked about his arousal, until joking gave way to sweetness. Kay pleasured him, alternately watching the pulsing in her hand, the bunching muscles of his arms in the grip of sexual tension, the pained etch of ecstasy on his face at the moment of climax, and after such times, it seemed only natural to fall asleep beside him in the big hospital bed downstairs.

On Thanksgiving night, he asked her to take off her nightgown.

"Here?"

"I can't go upstairs."

"John, this is the living room."

"Huh."

"Marilee might walk in."

"She's at Jill's for the night."

"People can see in."

"The lights are out. The shades are drawn. I'm stark naked. Why not you?"

"Because . . . because it's different."

"How's it different?"

"You're a man."

"What's different about that?"

"Everything." He was firm all over. Men

596

were that way. They were also more sure about their bodies than women were.

"I haven't touched you since the accident," he said.

"Yes, you have."

"Not that way."

She was sitting beside him in the dark, thinking that things were so lovely *this* way. Then his hand moved. It touched her chin and slipped lower. She tried to stop it, but his fingers worked under the shoulder of her gown.

"You shouldn't," she whispered.

"Why not? I love you."

"I'm fat."

"Who says?"

"Me."

"Not me." He pushed the gown off one shoulder.

"John."

He freed the other shoulder, then her breasts. The darkness didn't hide a thing — not her fullness, not the way his eyes held her, not the self-consciousness that had her hands clutching at her nightgown and cover.

He pushed the nightgown lower and touched her. Self-consciousness didn't keep her from feeling a tug inside, still she wanted to slip under him. That was the way it usually happened. When he covered her, she felt less exposed.

But he couldn't cover her, what with his casts. "Take it off all the way," he said thickly.

She shook her head. "Another time."

"I want to see you now."

"John." It was enough that his fingers were stroking her breasts, drawing helpless sounds from her throat. "This is embarrassing."

"Why?"

"Because . . . because —"

"Why is it embarrassing?"

They were in the living room. He was lying there, watching her. She felt on display. "I told you. I'm fat."

"You're not fat. Take the nightgown off."

"You'll see everything, if I do."

"I want to."

"I don't."

"You see me. I want to see you."

"But you're good to look at. I'm not."

His fingers lifted. "Are you kidding?"

"No."

"You think I don't like the way you look?"

"Women don't age as gracefully as men. We get hippy and lumpy and crepey." She tugged the nightgown up.

"But I like the way you look."

"Well, you have to, in a way. I'm your wife."

"I don't *have* to. I just do."

"I'm like that soft old cardigan that you love slipping into. It's shabby and stretched, but it's familiar, and it's warm."

"I *like* the way you look."

"You don't have to say that, John."

"But I mean it. And I like the way you feel. So I want you naked. I want to see you and feel you."

She wanted to believe, wanted it badly. "You do?"

"How many times do I have to say it?"

"Lots, I guess. You don't usually."

"Can't you tell, from how I touch you?"

"No. Men are physical. They touch. It doesn't say anything about *me.* Only words do that."

"Huh."

For all the times she had let that ride, she asked now, "What does that mean, 'huh'?"

"You just jerked me off, and I want it again. Look at me."

She did. He was hard.

He slipped the nightgown to her waist. "That's from being close to you. It's from touching this, and remembering the way the rest of you feels. I like the way you feel, Kay. I like looking at you."

"I'm getting older."

"Well, hell, so'm I, but I don't want someone who's younger or skinnier. I want you."

He smiled then, a cocky-crooked smile in the night. That smile hadn't changed over the years. It still snowed her.

"Come on, baby," he said with the hoarseness hardons gave him. "Lie naked with me. Give me a thrill."

Kay left the bed only long enough to slip out of her clothes, then she crowded in beside him to hide. But he said the words. He said them over and over, while he touched her, and between the two, she finally found the courage to rise above him and take him in.

Ahhh, yes, she gave him a thrill, but the thrill was hers, too. She needed words. He needed deeds. It seemed an even exchange, for passion.

Myra pushed herself out of bed with a great effort. She made her slow way to the bathroom, wearily performed her ablutions, then, with the hem of Frank's old flannel robe dragging behind her, turned toward the stairs. She had barely put a shaky hand to the newel cap when she felt a wave of dizziness. Clasping the worn wood, she slid down to the top step and leaned heavily against the post.

Thanksgiving had drained her. Oh, she had loved seeing children and grandchildren, but the strain of being on her best behavior had taken its toll.

It had been necessary, though, because they were watching her. There were little looks when they thought she wouldn't notice, and closer scrutiny when she was talking with others. They were looking for signs of madness. They were looking for excuses to put her away.

She hadn't given them any. She had been sweet and lucid and perfectly agreeable. Except when they raised the matter of moving. Then she had put her foot down.

She wasn't moving. She didn't care *what* manner of housing they suggested. She wasn't leaving this house.

She opened her eyes, then closed them again when the world continued to spin. It was pure exhaustion. She wasn't young. Tension took its toll.

So did frustration, and she felt plenty of that. People didn't hear her. They didn't see her. She had tried and tried, but they didn't get her message.

And now there was snow. Well, not very much, it was nearly gone, but the next snowfall would be greater, and the air was brittle. Worse, the grass in the backyard was dead, the ground beneath it hard and ungiving. Months were lost now. She didn't know if she could hang on for the thaw.

Discouraged, she opened her eyes. She wanted tea, perhaps, with a biscuit and jam. That would make her feel better, give her a bit of strength. Painstakingly she drew herself up, and holding tightly, went down one stair at a time. At the bottom, exhausted, she let herself sit again. She put her head to the post again, closed her eyes again.

Slumped there like a pathetic pile of bones, she felt closer to the end than ever before. Never mind all that she still had to do, her strength was dwindling fast. She might well die before . . .

What, then, was her choice? If death was the inevitable outcome, what did any of it matter? If she defied Frank, she would die. If she kept her silence, she would die.

She was going to the grave for sure. The question was what awaited her there. If it was Frank — angry and betrayed — she knew what sort of hell she would meet. But if Frank was in hell himself — and she was headed for heaven — but no, she wasn't headed for heaven.

Silence.
Just a little longer.

TWENTY-THREE

Celeste was on top of the world. She had had the best weekend ever with Carter, the best weekend ever with Dawn. Now they were both gone, Carter off to Cambridge, then on to Paris for a week's work, Dawn back at school. Carter had sent flowers, delivered an hour after he'd left. Dawn hadn't sent anything. But that was all right. Her pleasantness over the weekend had been a gift in and of itself.

On impulse, because his happy face seemed the perfect companion to her mood, and because even though she was sold on Carter, Carter wasn't there, she called the widower. "Hi, Michael. It's Celeste. I was wondering how your Thanksgiving went. *Do* you celebrate Thanksgiving?"

He chuckled in the comfortable way she remembered his being, like a fuzzy old slipper. "Yes. I'm the only Britisher in my clan. The children are entirely Americanized. We had a lovely Thanksgiving, thank you. And you?"

"Me, too. My daughter and I actually got along. I'm too hard on her, I think. But we had such a nice time."

"What did you do?"

"We had dinner with friends, not many of us related, but still like a big happy family. That's how I imagine yours must have been."

"Yes and no. My daughter's husband just lost his job, so that put something of a damper on things."

"Oh dear."

"I would be happy to give him work, but his field is very different. He does medical research. Unfortunately the company he was with is folding. It seems there have been irregularities in some of the studies done there, and though my son-in-law wasn't involved in any of those, the company lost one too many contracts. It puts rather a cloud over his immediate future."

"I'm sorry."

"Well," he said, up again, "he'll find something. It may entail a move, which none of us wants, but if that happens, we will cope. Haven't much choice, have we? But I am happy about you and your daughter. Dawn, is it?"

Such a nice man, to remember. "That's right."

"Is she liking school?"

"Very much."

"Then she feels good about herself. That makes all the difference."

The words stayed in Celeste's thoughts long after she hung up the phone. She knew what feeling good about one-self meant. Thanks to a nose job by her surgeon and a snow job by Carter, she felt better about her own self than she had in years. It did make a difference in one's outlook on life.

Carter called from Cambridge Monday night. Celeste had just returned from dinner with Emily and Kay, abbreviated, what with John hurt, and was tickled to hear his voice. They didn't talk long. He was leaving for Paris the next day and had hours of work to do before that. His apologies and sweet words of missing her more than made up for a lengthy talk.

She lay in bed thinking about him that night and the next. He had said that he wouldn't be calling her, what with the time change and the attention he owed his client, still, whenever the phone rang, her eyes flew toward it and her pulse sped.

That was what happened late Wednesday

afternoon. She had just returned from driving the church van and was feeling satisfied thinking of that, when the peal of the phone set her little heart to racing. By the time she dropped her purse on the table and reached for it, she had calculated that it would be approaching midnight in Paris. Carter would have finished his work and be lying in bed, thinking of her.

But it wasn't Carter. It was Dawn's roommate, Allison. "Is Dawn there?" she asked, sounding hesitant.

Celeste's disappointment at not hearing Carter's voice was offset by amusement at the thought that Dawn might have stopped by. She had religiously avoided drop-in visits, part of the precondition of her attending college in town. It was interesting to think that a pleasant holiday had softened her up on that score — unless, of course, she wanted something.

"I don't see her, Allison. Was she planning on coming over?"

"I thought she was there."

There was no sign that Dawn had been by. The kitchen was exactly as Celeste had left it. "Hold on." She covered the phone. "Dawn? *Dawn?*" She heard nothing. To Allison, she said, "Sorry."

"Is everything all right?"

"With Dawn? You'd know that better than me. I haven't talked with her since she went back."

There was a silence on the other end of the line. Celeste felt a twinge of something eerie. It took form when, nervously, Allison said, "She hasn't been back, Mrs. Prince. Not here, at least."

"What do you mean?"

"I haven't seen her since before the holiday."

"Since last *week?* But she went back Sunday night. I dropped her there myself." But Celeste had a thought. Dawn hadn't been wild about rooming with Allison. She claimed Allison was too neat, too studious, too prim. "Might she be staying in another room?"

"No. No one's seen her. I've been asking. Besides, her stuff is all here. If she moved out, she'd have taken something, wouldn't she have?"

Celeste would have thought so. "This is strange," she said aloud. "What about a guy?" Dawn hadn't mentioned anyone over the weekend, but it would have been typical of her to keep a secret like that from Celeste. It certainly would have explained her good mood. "Is there someone special she was

608

seeing there, someone she may be staying with?"

"No. I asked guys, too. No one's seen her since before Thanksgiving."

Very strange, Celeste decided. Maybe even alarming.

Allison said, "I thought for sure she was at home sick or something, but when she didn't come yesterday or today, and didn't call, I figured I'd call there."

Celeste curbed her alarm. Dawn was known for her antics. "Have you spoken with anyone — a dorm head or anything?"

"No. I didn't want to get her in trouble."

Celeste barked out a laugh. "Oh, she does that on her own, thank you. Listen, Allison, I'll make some calls. Do me a favor, and keep asking around. If you hear anything, call me back?"

Remembering fall break, when Dawn hadn't shown up, Celeste quickly called Jill, but Jill hadn't seen her. Nor, a second call revealed, had Marilee.

Still, Celeste wasn't panicking the way she had done then. Dawn pulled stunts all the time. This one, no doubt, was in compensation for having behaved over the holiday.

Telling herself that, Celeste downplayed the concern of the dean of students, even the campus police. Jackson was another matter. The instant his voice came on the phone, she felt the full weight of responsibility for Dawn.

"You have *no* idea where she is?" he asked.

"I thought she might be with you." It was possible. Dawn did see him every few months. "We had a great time over Thanksgiving. I thought maybe if she felt guilty about it, she might have wanted to give you equal time."

"Dawn doesn't feel guilty about much," Jackson said with what Celeste found to be surprising perception for a man obsessed with the innards of computers. He ruined it by asking, "If you dropped her back at school, where did she go?"

"If I knew *that,* I wouldn't be calling!"

"No one's seen her there?"

"No."

"Has there been any recent trouble on campus?"

"You mean, like a serial rapist? Come on, Jackson. We're talking Dawn here. She's up to something."

"She hasn't ever done anything like this before."

"Yes, she has." Celeste told him about fall break.

"Well, you've already called Jill, and you've already called Marilee, and those are her two best friends, and since neither of them has heard from her, I repeat — she hasn't ever done anything like this before."

Around her thumbnail, Celeste said, "I suppose." She was annoyed as hell with Dawn, and, against her better judgment, just that little bit worried.

"Shouldn't you call the police?" Jackson asked.

"Not yet. She's over eighteen. There's no sign of foul play. I can't call them in until I've done some looking myself."

"Like where?"

"More friends, I guess."

"Call me back later, Celeste?"

"Sure."

Celeste spent the next hour calling others of Dawn's friends besides Marilee and Jill. It took some doing, since many were away at school, and even then the effort proved futile. Celeste herself had apparently been the last one to see Dawn.

She ran out of calls to make at nine o'clock. Not knowing whether to sit back and wait until morning, or panic then and there, she drove to Emily's.

Emily felt a churning at the pit of her stomach when she heard Celeste's tale. She immediately thought of Jill, of the years and years she had fought down panic at the prospect of something happening to her. And she thought of Daniel. She was thinking about him more and more.

Daniel touched every part of her life — Doug, Jill, the house, the town, her friends, even potentially Brian, and now Dawn. Dawn was different, of course. She was eighteen — and, granted, striking enough to attract attention, but she was tough.

Still, tough people got hurt sometimes, too.

Anxiously, Emily led Celeste across the driveway and up the far side stairs to the apartment over the garage. Brian was watching the Celtics, and looked as wonderfully disheveled to Emily as anyone could look, given her own distraction.

He sensed that distraction instantly, drew them in, and made them sit down. Emily found solace in watching him as he listened to Celeste. He would know what to do. She was glad he was there.

"Do I panic now?" Celeste asked when she finished telling Brian everything she had told Emily moments before.

Emily saw through her dry little quips. It didn't matter how many times Celeste insisted that Dawn was playing games, or how many times she insisted that Dawn was an adult and on her own, Celeste was worried.

Brian sensed that and spoke calmly — though Emily suspected some of the soothing was directed at her. He knew why she had dragged Celeste over to see him, rather than waiting for morning. She tried to tell him she was all right, but her insides wouldn't help her out. They insisted on quivering, just faintly, enough to betray themselves to Brian, whose leg touched hers.

"Don't panic yet," he told Celeste. "There's still more to consider." They were grouped at his coffee table, Emily and Brian on one side, Celeste across. He had jotted names on a yellow legal pad as Celeste had tossed them out. Beneath those was a list of possible motives for Dawn's running off. At his elbow, Emily could easily read that list. It assumed Dawn's willing flight.

The alarmist in her wanted to argue, but the realist couldn't. There was no sign of mayhem. And Dawn had a history of getting into trouble.

He put the tip of his pen to the list and looked at Celeste. "You've called friends from school and friends from home. None of them claim to have seen her. Do you think any are lying?"

"I don't know why they would."

"To protect Dawn."

"From me? My disapproval is nothing new. She's used to it."

"What if she's done something unforgivable this time?" Emily asked. She couldn't begin to count the number of times Celeste had sworn she would kill Dawn if she ever did such and such.

Celeste's memory faltered. "Like what?"

Brian picked up. "Like commit a crime — or, forget that for now, like flunking out. Do you think she is?"

Celeste guffawed. "Not quite."

"Dawn is brilliant," Emily explained. "She understands things with the first run-through. She remembers everything. She *speed*reads and remembers everything. She studies very little for very good grades."

"If she studied that little bit more," Celeste injected tartly, "she'd be at the top of her class. She has her father's brains."

"Okay." He put a line through FLUNKING OUT. "Is she pregnant?"

"God, no."

"Are you sure?"

"Yeah, I'm sure, unless her stealing my tampons when she got home last week was for show."

He crossed off KNOCKED UP. "How's she

set for money?"

"Fine."

"She wouldn't be trying to scrounge up more — selling something illegal, prostituting herself?"

Emily saw Celeste pale. But the question was necessary. It had come up in the earliest stages of the Demery case, before the ransom note had arrived. While Susan hadn't wanted for money, some coeds did. Hooking offered fast cash.

"Dawn's father is paying for college," Celeste said. "He gives her a generous expense account."

"Maybe she's gone through it."

"The bank statements come to the house. I read them. She has a healthy balance, at least she did as of last week."

Emily watched him put a line through SEX.

"Has she ever done drugs?"

"No."

He put a line through HABIT. "Does she drink?"

"Not much," Celeste said. To her credit, she slid a look toward Emily, then sighed. "Well, maybe much, but only at parties. I've never known her to have anything during the day or alone. Aside from the wine she had with Carter and me last week, I don't think she had another thing to drink, and she wasn't suffering withdrawal."

"Has she ever had a run-in with the law? Disturbing the peace? Disorderly conduct? Drunk driving?"

"No."

"So if I boot up my computer at the station, I won't find her name?"

"No."

"Nothing formal. What about informal? Was she ever picked up by anyone in the department, given a good talking to, and sent home?"

"No."

He crossed off RECORD and moved on to BOYS. "What about the guy she was with when she didn't show up for fall break?"

"As of last week, a total loser. That's a quote."

"Have you called him?"

"I called Jill, who called the friend whose brother he is, and he hasn't seen her in five weeks."

"What about other guys? Someone else's brother?"

"She didn't mention anything to either Jill or Marilee when they were home, and they're her best friends."

Emily watched his pen move to cross off BOYS, but it stuttered and came to a rest somewhere beyond the word, and, guilty as she felt, Emily agreed. Dawn had boys high up on her own list. Brian was right to put boys on hold now.

"Does she get along with her father?" he asked.

Celeste waggled a hand. "They aren't best of friends, but they're not enemies either. He lives in southern New Hampshire."

"Would she be trying to get his attention?"

"If she is, she's wasting her time. He doesn't see beyond his own desk, his own work, his own daily schedule."

"Does she resent him for that, or for not being around more?"

Celeste certainly did, even after all these years. Emily could hear it in her voice. It would have been a miracle if Dawn hadn't picked up on it.

But Celeste said, defensively, Emily thought, "Not terribly. We've done fine without him — well, as fine as two people can do who don't get along, but last weekend was so *nice,* really it was." She included Emily in her bewilderment. "We *did* get along. I actually *liked* it. And I honestly think that if she were bothered by something, I'd have detected it. We spent more time together than we have in the last three years combined."

"You, Dawn, and Carter," Brian said, which, in the wake of Thanksgiving, was how Emily saw them, too. They had been a tight threesome at the Davieses'.

Celeste smiled. "Dawn liked him a lot. He knew just how to handle her. He treated her like a person, like a grown-up. I have to take a lesson from that."

Emily wasn't sure she wanted Celeste taking lessons from Carter. There was something about him. Emily couldn't put her finger on it. He was too good, too smooth, too perfect.

"Where's Carter now?" Brian asked.

"Paris, until Sunday."

"When did he leave?"

"Yesterday."

"Would he have any idea where Dawn is?"

"I don't see how, if I don't know."

"She might have talked with him."

Celeste shook her head. "If it was about anything sneaky, he'd have told me. And he'd have given her hell."

"They were on close enough terms for that?"

"We were together for the better part of five days."

"The three of you?"

"Yes."

Surprising, Emily thought. Interesting,

actually, coming from a woman who professed to be thrilled to have her daughter
grown up and out, who professed to want
nothing more than to have fun in the second
half of her life.

"Did that get on your nerves?" Brian
asked.

"No. She was reasonable for a change. We
didn't argue. It's the first time in my adult
life that I've been part of a family unit."

Emily hadn't thought Celeste wanted that.
Interesting, indeed.

"Only Carter isn't family," Brian reminded her.

"You know what I mean. It was the closeness. He was a father figure for her. She's
never had that around here. She ate it up."

"Did she have trouble saying goodbye to
him on — what was it — Sunday?"

"Sunday. No. No trouble. She was fine."

"Smiling? Hugging?"

"Yes. What are you getting at?"

"Does she have a crush on him?"

"She wouldn't dare."

"Daring has nothing to do with crushes."

"He's mine. It wouldn't be appropriate."

"Try to explain 'appropriate' to impres-
sionable young women," Brian remarked.

Emily agreed. "If Dawn went ga-ga over
Carter's looks and his manner and the at-

tention he paid her," which, to her eye, Dawn had done, "that's halfway to a crush. There's nothing wrong with it."

But Celeste was insistent. "She didn't. She just liked him."

"Can you reach him?" Brian asked.

"Now? No. I told you. He's in Paris."

"You don't have a phone number there?"

"No."

"Can you get one?"

"I could call his office here. They must have a number. But I don't want to do that. I might embarrass him, chasing him down that way, and besides, he doesn't know anything about Dawn. Believe me. If he knew *anything,* he'd have told me."

To listen to her, Emily might have thought she was talking about her sweetheart of umpty-ump years.

"How long have you known Carter?" Brian asked.

Celeste hesitated. "Four weeks."

"Not very long to be so sure about what someone would do."

"We're very close." To Emily, she said, "Why's he attacking me?"

"He's not," Emily said as gently as she could. "He's trying to narrow the field down to those people who may either be with Dawn or know something about her. Your relationship with Carter has been a whirl-wind affair. Realistically, Celeste, there's a lot you don't know about him."

"You're jealous."

Emily choked on a breath, shot a quick look at Brian, and said, "No. No, I'm not." But she wasn't arguing that point. "You haven't known him long, Celeste. You haven't lived through enough with him. You haven't seen him in different situations."

"I trust him."

"Yes, trust him, but realize that since he didn't raise Dawn, and since he's spent even less time with her than he's spent with you, he may not know the rules. He may not know that if she shares certain kinds of plans, he's supposed to tell you."

"He may not want to betray her."

"Exactly. So, with the best of intentions, he may know something about Dawn right now that would explain where she is."

A full minute passed before, begrudgingly, Celeste said, "I suppose." She faced Brian a bit more humbly. "Even if his office has the Paris number, no one will be there to give it out until morning. Maybe I should be waiting at home in case he calls me there. He said he wouldn't. He said he'd be running around so that he can get back in a week, instead of the ten days he originally planned for the trip. But there's always a chance. Same with Dawn calling. Not likely. But possible."

"Wait at home. That's best."

"She's off somewhere doing her own thing. Isn't she?"

"Probably."

"You don't really think she's in trouble."

"Nah."

But Emily's mind was off in a heartbeat, imagining all *sorts* of trouble at the mere mention of the word.

"Em?" Brian asked softly.

Her eyes flew to his. She wrapped her arms around her middle and propped her upper body on them. "I'm okay."

"Sure?"

She nodded. When Brian asked Celeste for a recent picture of Dawn, she said, "I have one on the corkboard in my kitchen."

Brian looked at his pad, frowned, then, diplomatically, asked Celeste, "If her roommate is right and the closet at the dorm is intact, and if she's been running around somewhere for three days now, what might she be wearing?"

"When I dropped her back on Sunday night, she had on jeans and two sweaters, layered, with flats, but she had a dufflebag full of clean things. She could have put any

622

of them on — the short skirt she was wearing at the Davies's, the shirts and vests, the black stirrups, the Doc Martens."

Brian made the appropriate notations, then dropped his pen on the pad and rose. "Let's assume she's gone of her own volition. If we continue to strike out tomorrow, we'll rethink things."

Emily walked Celeste to her car. "Dawn will be fine," she said in an attempt to be encouraging.

But Celeste was past encouragement, into fury. "No, she won't. She's in deep shit. She'll catch hell for this one, Emily. That's a promise."

Emily supposed that anger was easier to bear than the awful thoughts that kept flitting through her mind, fragmented images of bits of clothing, of Susan Demery's finger, of Daniel's empty car seat.

Brian was just hanging up the phone when she returned.

"Who was that?" she asked.

"The campus police. I want them to know I'm on the case."

"You asked them to search the campus, didn't you?"

He folded her in his arms. With her head pressed to his chest, things didn't look quite so bleak. "It doesn't hurt to cover the

bases," his voice said. "Not that I'm expecting a problem. I'm really not, Emily. This
isn't the case of a two-year-old who can't
talk or fight or recognize danger when he
confronts it, and it isn't the case of an
eighteen-year-old heiress. There are lots of
credible reasons why Dawn isn't where she's
supposed to be." He turned his wrist to see
his watch. "It's after ten. Think Myra's
asleep?"

"Her light's still on." Emily had made a
point of noticing, because therein lay another immediate source of worry. "Why?"

"Think she'd come over and sit with Julia
while we run down to the station?"

"I'll stay with Julia." It was a safer idea.

"But I want you with me," he said. Beauti-
fully intense silver eyes drove home his
earnestness. "You know Dawn. You know
how investigations work. I want you helping."

"Helping, as opposed to sitting here,
growing depressed."

"That, too, and I won't apologize for it.
Will Myra stay? Julia is sound asleep. She'll
sleep through 'til morning, not that we'll be
nearly that long. An hour, maybe two. Can
she handle it?"

"Yes. I think. She's been subdued lately.
Listless. Her family is thinking of forceably

moving her, if she won't move to a nursing home herself."

"They'd actually go to court?"

"No. They'll just sell the house, pack everything up, and *move* her. They won't win in court. When she wants to be, she's fully lucid."

Brian released her with a squeeze. "I'll go get her."

It was a full ten minutes before he returned, and Emily could see why. Myra was moving slowly, seeming to lack the strength that she'd had several weeks before.

"Are you sure you don't mind doing this?" Emily asked.

"I don't sleep lately anyway," Myra said and allowed her coat to be slipped from her arms. "The detective says your friend can't find her daughter."

"Dawn. That's right. But she's probably off with friends."

"I've written the number of the station over there by the phone," Brian told Myra. "If there's any problem, call us. Better still, I'll call you. I'll let you know what's happening." He moved toward the door.

Emily moved with him. "If Julia wakes up, check for the rabbit. It falls out of the crib sometimes."

"Help yourself to food and drink."

"If you can't find Brian's number, dial nine-one-one."

"The furnace clangs twice when it fires up. Don't be alarmed."

Myra followed them to the top of the stairs. Glancing back every few steps, Emily felt a twinge of uneasiness. Then the door closed, and they were on their way.

Brian put out Dawn's description over the Boston area network, putting sixty different departments in Massachusetts, plus the state police, on the lookout. He faxed her photograph to the same departments. The reproduction wouldn't be great. But five-five, one-twenty, eighteen-year-old blonds weren't unique. Something was better than nothing. He could improve on it if she remained at large for long.

On his way to the computer, he called Myra. It took five rings and several weeks off his life before she answered. "How's my Julia?" he asked on a deliberately light note.

"Did you find the girl?"

"No. We won't find her tonight. I'm just establishing the basis for a search. Is Julia all right?"

"She's fine. I keep peeking in. She hasn't woken up."

There was a lift to her voice that hadn't

been there earlier. Brian found it a comfort. "Ahhh," he said. "Good."

"Where are you looking?"

"Locally. We don't think she's gone far."

"You have to look under the willow."

He might have known it would come, and while he was uncomfortable with Myra talking nonsense at the same time that she babysat Julia, he did believe she was harmless. So, appeasingly, he said, "Well, that's an idea for tomorrow. Can't see much in the dark. Call me, now, if Julia gives you trouble."

"She won't," Myra said.

"How is she?" Emily asked when he hung up the phone.

"Julia? Sleeping. Myra? Awake and aware." Actually, quite jaunty, in that last parting note.

His confidence in Julia's safety restored for the time being, he plugged CARTER DEMMING into the computer.

Emily was at his shoulder. "You didn't like him, huh?"

"I liked him okay. But she doesn't know him real well, and he and Dawn were nearly as chummy as he and Celeste at the Davies's that day. I keep asking myself if it's pure coincidence that they left Celeste's one after the other last Sunday."

"But Celeste dropped Dawn at school herself. She watched her walk into that dorm."

His eyes were busy on the screen while he talked. "Then she came back home, spent less than an hour with Carter, and kissed him goodbye. He drove off. She didn't see where he went."

"You're thinking he may have circled back and picked up Dawn."

"Can't rule it out."

"Would he have harmed her?"

He couldn't rule that out, either. He had known some Dr. Jekyll and Mr. Hydes in his day. But he didn't want to alarm Emily unnecessarily, and he really didn't think Carter was manic. "I just think the two of them may have decided to play around a little."

"But if he's in Paris now, wouldn't she be back at school?"

"Do we know for sure he's in Paris?" He hit *escape* with a twack. "He doesn't have a criminal record, at least, not in Massachusetts." He hooked into the federal system, but found no sign of Carter there, either. Nor when he plugged into individual state police files for the entire New England and Midatlantic regions.

He had a thought, but it was a while and

several phone calls before he had what he needed to gain computer access to the files he wanted.

"Taxpayers?" Emily asked when the list came up.

"Real Estate. Celeste said he lived in Cambridge." He scrolled through the alphabetical listing until he reached the *d*s, then the *de*s, then the *demm*s. "If he does, he doesn't own the place, at least not under his own name."

"I don't like this, Brian."

He reached for the phone and called information. "For Cambridge. I'd like a listing for Demming, that's *D* as in David, first name Carter." He waited.

"I'm sorry, sir, but I have no such listing."

"Is there an unlisted number under that name?"

"No."

He hung up. "Something stinks."

"We warned her when she placed that ad," Emily cried, "but she was determined. She said she could sort out the good ones from the bad."

Brian sensed her growing upset. "Don't assume the worst. He may be more shady than bad. Dawn may be perfectly fine."

"Should we call Celeste now?"

"Nah. Won't do any good. Come morning, she'll try to track Carter down. We'll see if she has any luck." He reached for the phone and called home. "Hey, Myra. How's it going?"

"Did you find her?"

"No. Really, we won't have a chance of that until morning."

"Well, that's good. Then you'll look under the willow."

"I told you I would. How's my little girl?"

"She's such a sweet little thing, sleeping so soundly. I was just standing there looking at her, and she turned over and made the cutest little sucking sounds, like she was drinking from a bottle. She still drinks from one, doesn't she? I could give her milk, if she wakes up. I did it before, do you remember, the time she was sleeping in the car when you got home, and you didn't want to wake her up, so you left her there, and I sat with her. She's just a darling little girl. I almost wish she would wake up so that I could play with her. But I won't wake her. No, I won't do that. You will look under the willow tomorrow, won't you?"

"Sure will, Myra. Give us another twenty minutes?"

"Take your time. Take as long as you want. I don't think I could sleep anyway if I had to go home now. This is too exciting. No, I couldn't sleep. You do everything you have to do there. And keep Emily with you. If I know her, she's thinking she has to run back here so that I can go to bed, but you tell her what I just told you. I'm not tired at all. I'll stay here all night and into tomorrow, if you need. Take your time, detective. Please. You're a good man. Take your time."

Emily sat cross-legged on top of the covers. Beneath them, from the waist down, was Brian. His head was propped on the pillows, his body, like hers, shower-damp. Their fingers touched, quiet, soft.

He gave hers a squeeze.

She smiled.

"We'll find her," he whispered.

She nodded. She brought his hand to her lap, measured her fingers against his, stroked his palm.

He said, "I hate it that you have to relive this again."

Her smiled was crooked. "It's my fate in life, I think." The smile faded, because none of those other cases — no, not even Dawn — meant to her what Daniel did, and Daniel's case was the one that wouldn't be solved. "Has Doug called you?"

"Me? No."

"He threatened to. He said he wanted to

ask you about Daniel. After all this time, he wants to know what happened to him."

"It's hard, not knowing."

Emily knew that. Oh, she did. "That's why I tell myself that he's gone." She studied Brian's arm, tawny hair on a roping of flesh. She brushed the hair one way, then the other. "What if Doug calls you? What would you do?"

"About Daniel?"

"Would you reactivate the case?"

He was so quiet that she raised her eyes to his face. The angst there made her heart pound. "I did it," he said without pride. "I took the case apart and studied everything that wasn't studied the first time around. I haven't come up with a clue, Em."

Her breath came out in a shaky wisp.

"I'm sorry. I wanted to do it for you."

She nodded. She should have known he would try.

His fingers circled hers, then carried her hand to his chest and anchored it there. "If I could do anything I wanted, anything at all, I'd take you someplace where you wouldn't have to stare that pain in the face all the time."

"Pain is part of life," she said. "So is loss. The better the life, the greater the pain of the loss. Daniel was special." She looked up at the window over the bed. The moon was there, in the woods, rimming leafless trees with silver tracings, as delicate as they were eerie, almost surreal. "He's out there," she whispered with a sudden fierce yearning. "Dead or alive, he's out there, and maybe I want to know, too. Maybe then there wouldn't *be* the pain."

Brian kissed her fingers and returned them to his chest.

"I thought I had come to terms with him, really I had, but he's suddenly coming back. Why *now?*" But she knew. Jill's leaving home had set off a chain reaction of emotional happenings that had led Emily to a fork in the road. Daniel was there, unfinished business from the road behind her, standing in the way of the road she wanted to take. "I'm locked in here, Brian. I want to grow, but I can't, because things that happened nineteen years ago are holding me back. Nineteen years. I should be past it. Something's wrong with me."

"Nothing's wrong with you. You just love long and hard."

"It's a curse."

"No, a strength."

"I don't feel strong."

"You are. You're one of the strongest women I know."

"So, why does it *hurt* so much?"

It didn't take more than a tiny tug to bring her forward. Lying across him, she put her cheek to his shoulder. Her hands found a needed warmth between their bodies.

He didn't speak, didn't try to explain things for which there weren't good explanations. He didn't offer platitudes or pollute the night with diversionary talk. He simply held her, allowing her to feel the pain that she had suppressed too often, and she let it go, let it go in great gasps and keening wails that were the soul-deep expression of a mother's worst fears and most dreaded grief.

Drained then, finally, she slept.

TWENTY-FOUR

Brian was putting Julia into her car seat the next morning when Myra scurried across the cul-de-sac. Her eyes were bright, her voice a breathless flutter carrying easily into the car. "I've been counting the minutes since dawn. Will you come now?"

It was barely seven, earlier than Brian usually left, but he wanted to get Julia settled in at Janice's, pick up coffee at Nell's, and hit the station in time to work with the computer before he went to Celeste's.

"This isn't the best time," he said and fastened Julia in.

"But you promised," Myra said.

"I haven't forgotten."

"You haven't found the girl, have you?"

"Not yet."

"Then you have to come look in my yard!"

He backed out of the car and closed the door. "First things first. Now, the station. Later, the yard." He took Myra gently by the arm and walked her down the driveway. "Besides, it's freezing. There's no need to look under the willow until it warms up a bit."

"Good Lord, you can't wait until spring, if she's missing now!"

"Not until spring," he guided her toward her house, "just until later this morning, maybe noonish. It'll be warmer once the sun breaks through."

"What if it doesn't break through?"

"Then I'll look anyway. Give me a few hours. I promise, I'll be back."

"But what if you find her first?" Myra asked with such horror that Brian had to wonder if her obsession hadn't gone bad.

He opened her door and saw her inside. Then he gave her his strongest, most re-assuring look. "I'll be back. I'll go out to the willow with you, whether we find Dawn or not. But I can't do it unless you stay warm. Will you stay inside here until I get back?"

Myra looked up at him without blinking. Slowly, obediently, she nodded.

It struck Brian that his own mother wasn't much younger than Myra, that she could deteriorate in the future, that he might have to grapple, as Myra's children were doing, with painful decisions.

Saddened, he put a gentle kiss on Myra's brow, before closing her door and heading back across the street.

Celeste started calling Carter's office at eight the next morning. Carter often called her that early from there, and he wasn't working alone. More than once he had put her on hold while he gave instructions to one of his people.

Today no one answered the phone. She tried every five minutes, pacing between calls, impatient beyond belief, wanting things cleared up. It was bad enough that she didn't know where her daughter was, but the shadow that Brian and Emily cast over Carter made things worse. She couldn't believe that he was anything but wonderful, she just couldn't.

Shortly before eight-thirty, Kay breezed through her door. "I just heard about Dawn! Why didn't you call me last night?"

"There didn't seem any point. I had already talked with Marilee, and she didn't know anything. I'm very confused, Kay. Is Dawn off somewhere, pulling a Dawn? Or am I supposed to worry?"

"Have you reached Carter?"

Celeste grew wary. "How did you know I was trying?"

"Brian stopped by. He'll be over in a little while. He had to do a few things at the station. Did you reach him?"

Celeste knew what Brian was thinking, but he was dead wrong. She intended to prove it. "No one's at his office yet. Someone should be in by nine."

"Carter told you he was going to Paris?"

"He *is* in Paris." She dialed the office number again, let it ring eight times, hung up.

"You'd think they'd have an answering machine," Kay mused. "Ahh, there's Emily. With *coffee,* bless her."

Celeste was more concerned with Kay's suggestion than with coffee. "Why would you think they'd have an answering machine? It's not a prerequisite for success."

"I would think they wouldn't want to miss any calls."

"Clothes shops don't have answering machines. Neither do restaurants, supermarkets, or schools — speaking of which, don't you have to be running along?" If Kay was going to be negative, the sooner she left, the better.

"I'm not teaching today, not with Dawn missing." She opened the door for Emily. "You are a lifesaver."

"How is she?" Emily asked softly.

"I'm fine," Celeste said, "or I would be, if everyone around here weren't so suspicious. *I'm* worried about Dawn. *You* all are worried about Carter."

Emily handed her a cup of coffee. "Have you reached him?"

"I'm waiting for his office to open. This is going to be so embarrassing. What am I supposed to say," she sugared her voice, " 'Hi, sweetie, just wanted to make sure you are where you said you'd be.' " She pulled the top off the coffee, spilled some in the process, and swore. Her scowl encompassed both of her friends. "It's sour grapes. That's all. You guys didn't want me putting an ad in the personals. If Carter turns out to be great, you'll be proved wrong."

That said, she stuck her hands in the back pockets of her jeans.

Emily uncapped her coffee. She sipped it for a minute, then said, "The good news is that he doesn't have a criminal record."

Celeste bristled. "You *checked?*"

"The bad news is that he doesn't have a house or a phone in Cambridge."

"Emily, I've *been* to his house. I've *used* his phone."

"Are you sure they're his?"

"Whose *else* would they be?"

"A friend's, maybe?"

"To what end?"

"To impress you."

Celeste felt betrayed, not by Carter but by Emily, Kay, Brian, John, and every other ugly skeptic in the world. "And his career is a hoax, too? His *designs* are a hoax? Sorry, but I've seen samples of those designs. I've been inside them. No, his career is real. I've met his friends. I've met his clients. I've met his *partner.*"

Emily focused on her coffee.

Celeste found that to be as much an expression of doubt as the spoken word might be. "So now you're thinking that the word 'partner' can be used loosely, that maybe the man he introduced me to is his golf partner, or his poker partner, or his partner in *crime.* How can you be so negative? What's the line about a person being innocent until proven guilty?" She turned to the phone, dialed Carter's office, picked at her thumbnail while the ringing went on and on.

She slammed the phone back onto its hook in time to see a tall shape materialize at the kitchen door. The shape knocked. It turned the knob and let itself in.

Celeste wondered what else could go wrong. "You didn't have to come," she said. "Kay, Emily, you remember Jackson."

She studied him while they said the kinds of brief hellos that Jackson could handle. She hadn't seen him in several years, since Dawn had started driving to meet him herself. He looked well — tired and over-worked, perhaps, but that was nothing new for workaholic old Jack.

His gaze fell on her and stayed.

She folded her arms on her chest and refused to look away. If he had come to berate her for Dawn's misbehavior, she would walk out of the room. Ditto, if he was joining the campaign against Carter.

He surprised her by simply asking, "Has she called?"

Celeste shook her head. "She'll show up. I know she will. You really didn't have to drive all the way down."

"You were worried enough to call me."

"I only called because I thought you might know where she was. I didn't mean for you to drop everything and rush over."

"Didn't you think I'd worry, too?"

"Actually," Celeste said, remembering all the lonely years when she had been over-whelmed by single parenthood, "no. There's no history of that."

"Maybe because you never shared much about her. If there were problems, I never knew. I only heard about the good stuff, the stuff that said what a great mother you were."

"Uh, we'll be in the other room," Kay murmured and, dragging Emily along, was gone.

"I *was* a great mother," Celeste told Jackson, "or a good one, at least. I'm not saying I didn't make mistakes, but I tried, and it was *hard.* I didn't have anyone to consult. I didn't have anyone to share the blame when things went wrong."

Jackson was backed to the counter. His hands curved around the edge flanking his hips, and while his long, lanky frame wasn't exactly slouched, it wasn't straight either. Nor was he arguing with what Celeste said.

So she went on, venting the resentment that she didn't have room for inside, what with concern over Dawn and nervousness — yes, there was that despite her protests — over Carter. "I was alone with Dawn from the time she was one. I had every single responsibility for her right smack dab on my shoulders, and she wasn't an easy child, even back then. She was as headstrong and contentious as she is now."

"Like her mother," Jackson said with a strange smile.

"I *never* challenged my parents the way she did me."

"Maybe not, but you were a wild child when we met." Still, that strange smile. It spoke of memories, fond ones, and softened Celeste, making her feel, oddly, more exposed. For all their years apart, Jack had seen shades of her that others hadn't.

"Okay," she admitted. "I let loose for a time. But I never rubbed my parents' noses in it. And Dawn knows nothing about those days, so she couldn't have been following my example, and even *then* she bucked me at every turn. She tested every limit I ever set."

"She did well in school."

"Well, she had the brains. She's your daughter. But she wouldn't have done well, if I hadn't been on her back to study. So say I'm a nag of a mother, but someone had to do it, and you weren't around. You had the easy part. It didn't take any effort to send that check each month, because you earned it doing what you were good at, but I wasn't good at being a mother. I didn't have the natural aptitude for it that some mothers have. I wasn't good at playing little games and decorating cookies and shopping for clothes. I didn't have the patience. But I stuck with it, because once she was born, she was mine, and there was no one else to take care of her. So if I made mistakes, tough. I tried. That's more than *some* in this room can claim."

She turned her back on him and dialed Carter's office. It was five minutes before nine. Surely someone would be there. But the phone rang and rang.

"Who are you calling?" Jackson asked.

"I'm trying to reach the fellow I've been seeing. He may have an idea of where Dawn might be."

Jackson crossed his ankles. "Who is he?"

"His name's Carter. He's an architect."

"Is it serious?"

"We see each other a lot, if that's what you're asking."

"Does Dawn like him?"

"Of course, she does. Why wouldn't she like him?"

"You haven't had any serious relationships before. Maybe she's jealous of your time."

"I doubt that. When she went to college, she left specific instructions. Don't call me, I'll call you. Does that sound like a girl who covets my time?"

He shrugged, and in the next beat looked at the door. Brian was there.

"Well, why not," Celeste exclaimed, crossing the room to let him in. "Join the crowd. Kay and Emily are in the other room, cowering from domestic violence. This is

Jackson, Dawn's father."

She resumed her place by the phone while the men shook hands. Brian came to her side. In a voice that offered as much privacy as it could in a room as small as her kitchen, he said, "I'm having trouble finding anything on the man."

"Surprise, surprise. He's clean."

"No. I mean, I can't find any record of a Carter Demming existing. Not as a federal taxpayer. Not as a credit card holder. Not as an architect."

Celeste swallowed hard. "You must be spelling his name wrong."

"I tried different spellings."

She held up a hand. "Just wait. I'll locate him." It was after nine. She pressed in the office number and waited, praying silently, fighting panic. She breathed a mammoth sigh of relief, actually did it aloud, when a man's voice answered.

"Hello."

"Hi," she said with a smile. "This is Celeste Prince. I'm Carter's friend. Is this Mark?" He was the partner she had been introduced to that very first day in Cambridge.

"No. Jared."

"Ah." Her smile held. "Jared. I'm trying to reach Carter. Do you have his number?"

There was the sound of rustling papers, then a graceless, "Hold on," and a clunk when the phone hit the desk.

"He's looking for the number," she told Brian on a triumphant note. She imagined Brian had been doubting that Carter's firm existed, yet here she was, talking with one of his colleagues.

Jared returned with little fanfare and reeled off a number.

Celeste wrote it on a pad by the phone. There were seven digits, just like in the States. "Is there an area code? Country code? International something?"

"International? This is in Cambridge."

"No, no. I need to reach him in *Paris*."

"Paris? He's not in Paris. Who did you say this was?"

Celeste swallowed down an awful fear. She was acutely aware of Brian at her elbow, of Jackson across the room. "It's important that I reach him. Will he be calling in later?"

"I doubt it. We talked with him last week. He doesn't call more than once a month."

She chewed on her lower lip. "I see. Well, if he does call, would you ask him to call Celeste? It's urgent." She hung up the phone before Jared could ask for her last name or phone number, either of which would humiliate her.

"Well?" Brian asked.

She continued to face the phone. "He's not there." She didn't know what to do, didn't know who to call. Something wasn't right. Carter was supposed to be there a lot, and if he wasn't there, where was he, and if he wasn't there, *who* was he, and why had he lied, and what was he doing with Dawn? She felt sick to her stomach.

Brian came close and spoke softly. "He's not in Paris?"

She shook her head.

"Where's this number?"

"Cambridge." She met his eyes, pleading. "He told me he was going to Paris. Maybe this guy — this Jared — just didn't know. He said he hasn't talked with Carter since last week." But Carter had told her on Monday that he was calling from the office. So if he hadn't been there, where had he called from. And *where was Dawn?*

"Want me to try this number?" Brian asked.

She nodded and moved aside. She wrapped one arm around her waist, propped an elbow on it, and chewed her thumbnail.

After a minute, Brian hung up the phone. "No answer."

She felt a wave of relief, but it was short-lived. Little things were nudging her, little details she didn't know, details that hadn't mattered because Carter had made her feel so good. "This doesn't make sense," she said to Brian. "You met him. Okay, you weren't wild about him, but did he strike you as a phony?"

"No, but that's the skill of a con man."

"Why would he do it? Not that I believe he did, mind you. Mix-ups happen. Just because I can't reach him doesn't mean anything. But for the sake of the argument, if he isn't what he said he was, why would he have *said* it? I don't have money. It's not like he could bilk me out of much."

"How often does he stay here?"

"Several days a week. More over the holiday."

"Who bought groceries?"

She hesitated for just a minute. "Me."

"Did you ever eat out?"

"Here? No. He said he loved having me all to himself." She had loved hearing that. Now the words were dirtied.

Brian touched her arm in a way that was meant to be reassuring. "It could have been a game, nothing more."

She wasn't feeling reassured. "For sex."

"Possibly."

She wrapped a second arm around her middle. "I don't want to think this, really I don't. He was so much better than the others." She thought of Michael, the widower with the smiley face, who was so sweet and even-keeled and unromantic. Carter was made to order.

"What about Dawn?" Jackson asked.

Her head swung around. She had forgotten he was there. Her hackles went up. "Dawn is fine. Carter wouldn't hurt her." She had to believe that. The alternatives were unthinkable. "Say what else you want about him, but he isn't cruel. I'm not stupid, *or* unobservant. In all the time I spent with him, I never once saw him lift a hand in anger or raise his voice. I never saw him grit his teeth. I never saw his muscles clench, or his knuckles go white, or the little vein throb at his temple the way yours does when something ticks you off." She pointed. "There it is."

"I'm worried about Dawn."

"Carter is kind and considerate. He was *wonderful* with Dawn. She had the best time with him. He wouldn't hurt her. Just the opposite. He bent over backwards to include her in things. He gave her nearly as much attention as he gave me. He *adored* her."

A thought intruded, taking those words that had been offered in praise and casting them, too, in a different light. Her gaze flew to Brian's. Her head moved from side to side in denial. "He wouldn't touch her," she whispered. "He wouldn't. She's my *daughter,* for God's sake."

"I think," he said, "that we have to find her before we jump to any other conclusions. Do you have the address of the place in Cambridge that you thought was his?"

Celeste gave it to him.

"The car he was driving on Thanksgiving Day — his, too?"

"I thought so."

"White BMW. License plate?"

"I have no idea."

Brian picked up the phone. "Let me get this out on the wire."

"She's over eighteen," Jackson said. "What can you charge him with?"

"Nothing at all, assuming she's with him willingly."

"We don't know she *is* with him," Celeste felt called upon to insist. She didn't want Dawn to be with Carter. Not that way. But now that the bug had been put in her ear, more than mere words were taking on a new light. Looking back over the holiday weekend, she saw things differently. She saw Dawn flirting and Carter encouraging it. She saw casual touches that possibly weren't so casual. She saw hugs. She saw a playfulness between them that might have been either innocent or naughty. "I trusted him," she said to no one in particular. "I trusted *her*."

At the same time that Brian spoke into the phone, he held up a hand that told her not to assume the worst, but, once planted, she couldn't shake the idea that her lover might have become her daughter's lover. It made her feel old, blinded by desperation, and very foolish.

It was Jackson who took her hand, led her to the kitchen table, and gently pushed her into a seat.

It didn't take long to find them. They were thirty miles south, in an even smaller town than Grannick, in a motel that rarely saw BMWs, much less looked at the same one for three straight days. The local police, who had eyed the car with longing for as many days, called Grannick the instant the APB came over the line.

The descriptions fit. No question about that, either. The manager of the motel confirmed Dawn's stats. His wife confirmed Carter's.

Jackson drove Celeste, following Brian and Emily in the Jeep. Once they had parked beside the BMW, Celeste jumped right out. Clutching her parka closed, she went to the designated door and knocked.

It was an agonizingly long minute before Carter opened it. She barely had time to note that he was wearing nothing but old jeans and a shocked expression, when Brian pushed past her, badge aloft, hauled him outside and pinned him to the wall.

Celeste stepped into the room. Dawn was kneeling on the bed, clutching the blankets to her chest. She looked tousled but intact.

"Mom!"

Celeste was furious, hurt, and sickened, all at the same time. She opened her mouth to yell at Dawn, but her eyes filled with tears instead. So she closed her mouth, pressed her fingers to it, and stood there, unable to say a word.

"We were worried," Jackson said, coming up behind Celeste.

"Daddy!" This cried in horror.

It struck Celeste that Jackson's presence carried a weighty message to Dawn, and while that infuriated Celeste, given that she had been the one who had sweated and trembled and fought her way through Dawn's upbringing, she was grateful enough to have him finally bear some of the weight, to overlook the injustice of Dawn's response.

"No one knew where you were," he said. "You could have left a message with someone. They've been looking all over campus for you. They've been looking all over the state. Why didn't you let anyone know where you were?"

Dawn was glancing nervously from him, to Celeste, to the door, looking as though she badly wanted Carter to do the talking. But Brian was keeping Carter outside. Celeste blessed him for that. She had plenty to say to her daughter, but not a word to waste on Carter.

Funny, Carter hadn't looked half as attractive just now. He hadn't looked sexy in the least.

"Why didn't you?" Jackson repeated.

"I didn't know where I was going."

"You've been here for three days. Why didn't you call?"

"I was busy."

"It didn't *occur* to you to call."

"I didn't have to," she said with a defiant tip of her chin. "I'm eighteen. I'm a consenting adult."

"Didn't you think your mother would worry?"

Celeste still had her hand pressed to her mouth. She was feeling ill, succeeding more in stemming tears than settling the tipping of her stomach.

"Didn't you?" Jackson prodded.

"No. I didn't. She's been waiting, just waiting to have me gone. She never calls me at school."

"You told me not to!" Celeste cried.

"Only because I knew you wouldn't, and I didn't want to be sitting around expecting it, but you could have, if you missed me."

"I was following *your* instructions."

"Which suited you just fine. You were pleasing yourself, like you always do. You couldn't wait for me to leave, so that you could start living it up. I was a burden, all those years. I held you down."

Celeste was stricken. "I never said that."

"You didn't have to. I felt it. It's true, isn't it?"

"Not the way you think."

"Then what way?"

Celeste swallowed. "I was trying to set a good example."

"Well, that must have been a strain, because what came across was you wanting your freedom."

"Not freedom from you. Freedom from the responsibility. It frightened me."

"Frightened?" Dawn mocked.

"Yes, frightened. The older you got, the less frightening it was in some respects, because you could do things for yourself. But then there were the other problems, parties and drinking and dating, and that's *terrifying* for a parent. So I argued with you about things, maybe yelled and nagged, because I was afraid that you'd make major mistakes and it would be all my fault."

"Isn't it?" Dawn had the gall to ask.

"No," Jackson answered. "Your mother didn't tell you to run off with her boyfriend. You did that all on your own."

Celeste was struck by the enormity of it. "How *could* you? My own daughter! How could you *sleep* with him?"

"He protected me. He wore a condom."

"That's not the point, but since you've raised it, who was he protecting you from? Me? All the other women who came before? Don't kid yourself. He wasn't protecting you. He was protecting himself."

"He loves me," Dawn insisted.

"He loves *women* — you, me, someone else next month."

"You sure liked him enough."

"Yes, I did, stupid me. I thought he was the answer to my prayers, and you knew I thought that, still you came here with him." She pressed a hand to her chest. "Dawn, didn't I teach you *any* values? How could you *do* this?"

"You were the one who took me for birth control."

"That's not the *point!*" she cried, and when tears started again, she let them flow. "Okay. You didn't do this alone. Carter is ten times more wrong than you are, because he knew what he was doing, but you — you — you're my *daughter,* flesh of my flesh. How could you hurt me this way? You knew I was crazy about him. Whether it was stupid of me or not, I was." She sobbed out a sigh. "Damn it, I really *was* good while you were growing up. Did I subject you to a string of 'uncles'? Did I force any male friends on you? No. I always put you first. So how could you do this to me now? Was I *that awful* to you that I deserve this kind of betrayal?"

To her credit, Dawn didn't answer.

Celeste fished a Kleenex from her pocket and pressed it to one eye, then the other. She was feeling battered, suddenly tired, without energy, still nauseous. To Jackson, in a faint voice, she said, "I'm going to the car. I don't feel very well."

Without another look at Dawn, crouched there with the bedclothes crushed to her throat and Carter's scent permeating the room, Celeste left. She walked across the motel porch, went down the steps, keeping her back to Brian and the filth he was with, and leaned against the trunk of Jackson's car.

Emily joined her there. "Is she all right?"

"Oh, yeah."

"Contrite?"

"Fat chance."

"She's probably feeling ashamed, but she's been pushed in a corner, so she'll stand by what she did for a little longer."

"And then what?" Celeste asked, looking blindly off. For the life of her, she didn't know what to do. "She thinks he loves her."

"He may tell her differently once Brian's done."

"What can Brian say? Dawn was a willing accomplice."

"To whom? Who *is* Carter? He sure isn't who he told you. Think of all the things that didn't add up. When people hide their identities that way, they're usually hiding something more. If Carter is, Brian will find it."

That was small solace to Celeste. Pressing the balled Kleenex to her nose, she started crying again. "Oh, Emily, I'm so embarrassed. I believed everything he said. He fed me a line of bull, and I ate it right up, because I wanted to believe, so badly."

Emily slipped an arm around her. "I know."

"I may have acted like it didn't matter all those years, like I was doing just fine, like I didn't want to have to bother with any man, but the act was as much for me as it was for everyone else. It's not like I *need* a man —"

"Celeste," Emily interrupted, "anyone who knows you knows that. Whether or not it was an act, you did it. You raised Dawn on your own. You made a life for yourself, on your own."

"But I missed having more. I missed the fun. I missed the company. There were times when I was so lonely I nearly died of it."

"You could have called me," Jackson said.

Celeste put the Kleenex to her eye. She took a minute to compose herself before drawing away from Emily. "We're divorced, Jackson. We didn't get along. I couldn't call you."

"We could have been friends. Hell, I could have fixed you up."

She laughed in spite of herself. When she looked at him, she saw an endearingly self-conscious smile. She draped her wrist over his shoulder. "Now, would I have been able to communicate with your friends, any more than I could with you?"

658

"Maybe," he said with a shrug. "Some of them aren't too bad."

"So why aren't they married?"

"Probably for the same reason I'm not. Because we're not social beings. It takes a saint to stay married to the likes of us."

"Either a saint or nerd." Her smile waned. "What's Dawn doing?"

"I don't know. There wasn't much more I could say."

"Is Brian still with that scum?"

"He's talking with him."

"I feel like an imbecile."

Jackson settled beside her against the trunk. "Tell me one thing," he said in an indulgent tone. "Was it fun, at least, while it lasted?"

Celeste sighed. "Yes. It was fun."

"Then it was worth it."

"Was it? It destroyed my relationship with my daughter."

"Destroyed?"

"Well, maybe not destroyed. Eroded, certainly."

"For good?"

Celeste wasn't sure she could see beyond the hurt and fury she felt. "I don't know."

"Maybe you have to look at her differently from now on."

She wasn't sure she liked Jackson giving

her advice, not after he had opted out for so long. But there was the matter of sharing the responsibility, and, besides, she was curious. "Like how?"

"Like an adult. Tell her what it was like raising her. Tell her about the fears. She should know."

Celeste pictured Dawn, back in that bed, with the covers to her chin. "When? Do you think she'll come home after this?"

"Where else would she go? You're her mother. You made a mistake. So did she. You can learn from it. Maybe together."

Celeste felt a flash of the old fear and insecurity that she had lived with during those years of raising Dawn. "God," she murmured, "I'm not good at this."

"You're better than me," Jackson said. "And you're better than lots of other mothers. Look at it this way. You didn't have to bail her out of jail. You didn't have to pick her up off the sidewalk. You didn't have to sleep with the president of the college to get her accepted there."

"For *God's* sake, Jackson."

"See? You're not all bad."

Celeste grunted again, but the truth was that her stomach had begun to relax for the first time in a very long twenty-four hours. That Jackson was instrumental in it was

660

remarkable. Then again, not so. As Dawn's father, he was the only one who could have helped quite that way.

She sighed. "You're as good for me now as you were in my wild child days. What happened to us, Jack?"

"We're good in a crisis. That's about it."

"Too bad."

"Yeah."

"So. What do we do about Dawn?"

His voice thinned. "Let the cop drive her wherever she's going — home, school, she'll decide. Or she can take a cab. She has money. If she hasn't, it's because she spent it on the motel room, because Cassanova there forgot his wallet. It won't hurt her to sweat it a little."

"I have to talk with her, don't I?" Celeste asked, but she wasn't eager for it just then. She was too angry. Besides, she refused to go running after Dawn. Dawn was, by her own declaration, an adult. She could come to Celeste.

"You'll talk with her at some point," Jackson assured her.

"So what happens now?"

He checked his watch. It was the oversized kind that offered all sorts of information above and beyond hour, minute, and second. "It's past lunchtime. We'll stop for

661

something. Maybe the answers will come while we eat."

TWENTY-FIVE

"Thank heavens she's all right," Emily told Brian after they had dropped Dawn at her dorm and set out for China Pond Road. She shifted under her seat belt to face him. "I wish she would have let us drop her home. Do you think Carter will go back for her?"

"Not if he has any brains. He knows we're on to him. I'll write up a formal report to have on file in case he shows up again, but he isn't the type to take risks. He'll just go find another woman to latch on to."

"Think he's married?"

"I plan to check."

"Think he's an architect?"

"Possibly. But if so, he isn't as successful as he lets on. He doesn't have any fancy office in Cambridge, or, I'd wager, half the clients he told Celeste about, and if he travels around, like he said when he answered her ad, it's to skip out when women catch on to his game. He carries a Min-

663

nesota driver's license. The BMW belongs to a friend."

Much as Emily had been against Celeste's ad, much as she wanted to say, "I told you so," she couldn't. "Poor Celeste. Her heart's in the right place. I often wonder what she would have done with her life if she hadn't gotten pregnant so soon. Maybe had a career. Maybe divorced Jackson and married someone she was more compatible with and had a child by him, who knows."

"Who knows about life, period. What ifs can drive you crazy."

If they had to do with the past, they could. How well Emily knew that. On the other hand, if they had to do with the future, they would offer up interesting possibilities.

What if she were to write her book and it was published? What if she were to establish a name for herself as an author? What if she were to become self-supporting?

But what if Daniel kept haunting her?

No. What if *Brian* kept *wanting* her? What if she moved in with Julia and him, or they moved in with her? What if she became a wife and mother for a second time? What if Brian wanted *more* kids?

Would she write, too? Would she have the time and energy for it, after giving of herself to a husband and child? Did she *want* to be a full-time wife and mother again?

She had been looking at nothing in particular. Then the Jeep went far enough down China Pond Road for the house to come into view, and she straightened. "Oh, dear." Myra was standing all bundled up at the white picket fence, waving an eager hand as they approached. She was crowding in on Brian even before he opened his door.

"Getting later," Emily heard, "and you said we would do it around midday, so I decided to wait right here until you got back. Now? Can we now?"

Brian had climbed from the Jeep. Holding her shoulders to keep her still, he said, gently, "We found her, Myra. Dawn is safely back home."

Myra looked stricken.

Emily tried to soothe her. "She's with Celeste, and she's fine. It was something of a false alarm."

"No false alarm," Myra cried. "I *saw.*"

"Dawn thought she was in love," Emily explained. "Eighteen-year-olds do that. After Celeste dropped her at the dorm last Sunday, she turned around and left again."

Myra wasn't listening to her. She was clutching Brian's hand, trying to draw him down the driveway. "You have to look under the willow. You promised."

Emily felt a rush of sorrow. Poor Myra.

"But we found her," Brian repeated. "The case is solved."

"It *isn't* solved, no, it isn't!" Myra's voice rose. "You have to look in my yard!"

Emily moved to free Brian by unclamping Myra's hand and found startling strength in her hold. "It's all right," she said softly, steering Myra home. "It's all right."

"No, it isn't, and I can't wait much longer, I can't, and no one listens. You have to look under the tree. *Under* the *tree!*"

Emily shot a worried look at Brian. She had never understood Myra's obsession with the willow. It might have been understandable if Frank had adored the tree. But he hadn't. He had cursed it like he cursed everything else, cursed it for the mess it made in the yard and the work it caused.

Brian was looking puzzled. "Myra, what, exactly, is under the tree?"

Myra shook her head. "I never said anything was under it."

"But you want us to take a look."

"You think I'm crazy," she cried. "I know. My children think it, too, but I'm not. They want to stash me away like old clothes, but there's nothing wrong with me, I swear, there *is not.*"

Emily wanted to believe that. She couldn't

see Myra in a nursing home, not when she so desperately wanted to stay here at the house — not that Emily understood why she did. The place was bigger than she needed, and more work to keep up, and she was alone here, with nothing for company but Frank's ghost.

Then again, Emily wasn't one to talk. She couldn't leave China Pond Road, either. But Daniel was unfinished business. Frank was not.

She had one odd thought, then several more in quick succession. All involved Daniel and Frank. Frank and Daniel. In the post office parking lot at the very same time. Under the willow.

She choked on a stray breath, coughed, put a shaky hand to her chest. She didn't like what she was thinking at all.

"Uh, I think I need to go inside for a minute," she said when the thoughts kept coming. Dropping her hold of Myra, she turned and half-walked, half-ran back across the cul-de-sac, but not to her house. She didn't want to see the backyard, didn't want to see where it bordered on Myra's, didn't want to see *anything* of the stringy winter willow. She ran to the far side of the garage, past the door to Brian's place, and slid down the clapboards to the ground.

Brian was there in seconds, squatting before her. "What, Em?"

She locked her arms around her knees. Her voice came out high and wavery. "Weird thoughts. Weird thoughts."

"About Frank Balch."

She nodded. Frank Balch and Daniel. It couldn't be. Not right next door. Not all these years. "He was questioned. His story checked out. But Myra. Myra."

"Stick to Frank. What do you know about him?"

"He was the kind of man one avoided at all costs."

"Mean."

"What do *you* know about him?" she shot back.

"Only that people keep mentioning his name when we ask them about Daniel. I've been trying to get more, but I can't."

She put her chin to her knees. Her stomach had started to roll. She rocked to counter that movement, welcoming the bang of her back on the wood.

"Myra's obsession with the willow," Brian asked, "how long has it been going on?"

"As long as I can remember. It got worse after Frank died. That was when she started picking the lint up by hand and planting flowers nearby. That was when she put the

668

bench there. *Oh God.* I always just assumed that she was a little nuts when it came to the yard, but the persistence of it, the way she said, so clearly just now, that she wasn't crazy —" her voice was rising, rising on a wave of hysteria, "I believe her, so I ask myself why she keeps trying to drag us over to see what's under that tree."

Emily rocked harder against the wood. She wanted to think *she* was the crazy one entertaining mad thoughts, only they didn't sound mad but like the answer to the puzzle, making horrible sense in the same way as Doug's other life had.

Brian took her face in his hands. He wasn't talking to her, as much as speaking his thoughts aloud. "A method to madness. People do things that seem crazy, only they aren't. Like Richie, needing to get away from his father. Like Leila, needing help in caring for her kids. Even like Dawn, needing to let Celeste know that she wants love or attention or recognition or whatever. Cries for help."

Emily's chest felt ready to explode. She straightened her back against the clapboards and took several deep breaths, but they didn't help.

Brian's hands were a link of warmth when all else was cold. They balanced the urgency

669

in his voice. "Frank and Myra were interviewed at the time. Frank said he didn't see a thing. John grilled the guy. He had his story down pat. So did Myra."

"What if . . ." She couldn't put the thought into words. It was too hideous.

"Frank was finishing up in the post office when you arrived. He went to his car and drove home. Witnesses corroborated that."

"What if . . ."

"They heard his car leave the parking lot. Big car, lousy muffler, lots of noise. But no one actually saw him get into the car. The noise was the thing that made them look, and he was driving off by then."

She forced her eyes to Brian's. "It *can't* be. He wouldn't have been able to live across the street from me all those years if he'd been lying. Neither would Myra." She swallowed down a fast-rising bile. "Tell me we're wrong, Brian, it's too awful, there isn't any why to it."

Quietly, he said, "I need to look there."

"Dig, you mean." She started to cry. They were going to dig for her baby. "Don't you need — need — warrants — or something?"

"I'll get one just in case. I should have weeks ago."

"You had — no cause."

"I still don't, not really." But he was as

670

convinced of it as she was. The gravity of his voice told her so. "I have to alert John. And Sam. He'll help. Want to go to Kay's for a while?"

But Emily wasn't budging. She was Daniel's mother. She was the one who had left him alone in the car, rather than unbuckling him and carrying him into the post office that day. She wasn't making the same mistake twice, wasn't walking away from him now.

Sam and several others from the department came with shovels. Kay was already there, holding Emily, who shook in spite of a parka, gloves, and a hat. Myra was huddled on the back steps, her eyes riveted on the widening hole.

They started digging directly in front of the scrolled wrought iron bench. Once past the brittle top layers, the earth was more pliable. They dug down two feet, but found nothing.

Brian had expected something shallow. He couldn't imagine Frank digging six feet down without arousing suspicion. There had been cops all over the place in the hours and days immediately after the disappearance.

Granted, the backyard couldn't be seen

from the street. Granted, the Balch sons had all left home by that time. Granted, Frank would have dug at night.

Brian went to Myra. His breath wisped white in the cold. "Is this the right place?"

She looked as frigid as those top layers of soil, but she had resisted Brian's suggestions that she wait inside. Now she said, "I didn't say anything was here."

"Should we be digging closer to the pond?"

Her eyes glanced over the water. "You don't know Frank, or you wouldn't be asking. He can dig a hole four, five feet deep without breaking a sweat. He chops wood. It's the same kind of work."

They dug until the hole was three by three, then four by four. The light of day was beginning to fade, the temperature to drop, when they headed for five by five.

Then they hit it, a small disk covered with dirt and rust, that turned like a stone but made a more shallow sound against the tip of the shovel. Brian picked it up, removed the dirt with his thumb. It was a pin, like the kind affixed to a lapel, or a child's hat.

DADDY'S BOY, he read and felt a thickening in his throat. His chin fell to his chest, dragged down by dismay and an overwhelming sense of grief. Only with the greatest effort, knowing that he wore that sorrow on his face but unable to hide it, did he raise his eyes to Emily.

She shook her head, backing away as he approached. She didn't want to see what he held, didn't want to believe Daniel was there . . . there . . . under . . . dead . . . all this time.

"Emily," he said, reaching for her.

"No-o."

He drew her close and held her as if he could protect her from something, but the something was within. All the cushioning in the world couldn't keep her safe. Nineteen years — months of fruitless investigation — dozens of possible scenarios packed into innumerable nightmares and daydreams — all wrong and the truth too cruel to bear. Her baby.

"Right next door!" she wailed against his chest.

"Kay's taking you home."

"No! I'm staying!"

"Em, Em." He held her tightly, moved his hands on her back in an attempt at comfort, but comfort wasn't possible, not then, not yet. In a voice by her ear, he said, "This could go on for a while."

"I know." They would be looking for

bones, bits of clothing, *Oh God,* the remains of her baby. "I'm staying."

She watched from the side, again with Kay, waiting for the cold to numb her, in vain. The pain was as raw as it had ever been, grated now by the horror of the truth.

Right next door. It was unthinkable.

The digging went on for another hour. Between dusk and the ten long feet between her and the hole, Emily couldn't see what they were placing in their bags, but her mind saw. She was there with Daniel, remembering the last time she had held him as though it were hours before, smelling the Sugar Smacks he'd had for breakfast, feeling the silk of his hair, the baby butter of his skin.

"We've done as much as we can now," Brian said, coming up. "We'll take another look in the morning, but I think we're finished."

Finished. Daniel was found. Emily pictured a tiny coffin, pictured a tiny grave with a marker on top, and felt the tiniest inkling of comfort in a world of lies.

Brian took her in his arms and turned her away. "Will you go home now?"

"Where are you going?"

"I have to talk with Myra."

To ask why. To ask how. Questions she had

been agonizing over for nineteen long years. Her baby, dead and buried in her neighbor's backyard. "I'm coming."

"I'd rather you didn't."

"I'm coming."

His eyes said he feared for her emotional state. Her eyes said she wasn't leaving his side.

He sighed and looked at Kay. "We've been through this before, Em and me. She always wins."

It was a light touch, a little reference to their everyday lives, so much kinder than Daniel's fate that, absurdly, Emily started to cry again.

"Don't punish yourself, Em," Brian moaned, putting his face close to hers.

"I have to hear."

"I can tell you later."

But she clung to him, even as she wiped her eyes and told Kay, "Julia's at Janice Stolski's. Will you pick her up?"

"Don't worry about Julia now," Brian protested. "She can stay late."

But there was another inkling of comfort in the relationships and responsibilities that gave meaning to her life. "I want to see her. And Jill. Doug can pick her up in Boston before he drives out." Her eyes asked the added favor of Kay.

"Done," Kay said. "I'll call him. Where do I find his number?"

Emily told her. "And Celeste. Tell her what's happened."

"I will." Kay hugged her around Brian's arms for a final minute. "Do what you have to. We'll be waiting."

Emily had been in Myra's house countless times over the years, but it had never been as difficult as it was now. Her imagination was running circles around itself, defying her attempts to stop it by flashing visions of mayhem in each room they passed through.

Myra. Myra and Frank. And Daniel.

Emily felt sick. She willed herself not to vomit. She wanted to hear, *needed* to hear.

Absurdly, once they were settled in the living room — Brian and Emily, with two patrolmen in the background — Myra offered them tea. They refused.

Quietly, Brian began. "What happened, Myra?"

"What happened, when?" she asked.

"The day Daniel Arkin disappeared."

She frowned. "Well, we were here and the police came, and we said we hadn't seen him. There was a question, because Frank was in town at the same time as Emily, but he left without seeing a thing." She nodded.

"We told the police that."

"Yes. That's what the file says. But we know now that's not the truth."

"Who said? I certainly didn't."

"No. But we found evidence outside which suggests that your husband, and possibly you, too, were involved in Daniel's death."

"I *never* said that. Frank would be furious if he thought I did." She dared a look over her shoulder toward the rest of the house, and whispered, "Please. He has a temper."

"Is that what happened that day?" Brian asked. "Did he lose it?"

Emily remembered the yelling she had often heard and wondered how much of it had had to do, over the years, with Daniel. "This is important, Myra," she cried when Myra didn't answer Brian, and though Myra looked startled by her tone, she didn't soften it. She felt betrayed. Daniel had been murdered by people she trusted. She had no sympathy for Myra. "Frank was hard on you, but he's *dead.*" Like Daniel. Oh God. "He can't hurt you now. You have to tell us what happened."

Myra told the floor, "They think it's only the mothers who have trouble when their children grow up and move out, but it isn't. Sometimes men have the problem. Sometimes they have it worse."

"Did Frank?" Brian asked.

"Some men are angry when their children leave," Myra advised, as though telling a story about someone other than Frank. "They feel like the children are deserting them. They feel like the children aren't grateful at all for the things they did."

"Men like that," Brian prodded, "what do they do?"

"Oh, they get cranky. They get mad at their wives for little things that aren't bad at all. They yell. They even hit, sometimes. Now, Frank never hits me. He never raises a hand. But men like that do. They see people who still have their children at home, and they get mad."

"Mad?"

"They don't understand why others still have their children, if they don't. So they kick things, and they curse. Sometimes they see children left alone in cars, and that makes them *really* mad, so they borrow those children. Just for a little while. Just to have a child around again. Can you *imagine?* My Frank would *never* do that. He's a decent, law-abiding man."

Borrow them? *Borrow* them? Emily was appalled.

"Borrow?" Brian asked.

"Just for a little while."

"But *why?*" Emily cried. "Frank *hated* children."

"*My* Frank?" Myra shook her head. "Not my Frank."

"I heard yelling all the time!"

"Well, when children misbehave, a parent yells, but that doesn't mean he doesn't love them. My Frank loves his sons. He is a wonderful father."

"He was strict, and demanding, and abusive!"

"He counted on them to do chores. He was upset when they left home. To this day, he wants them here with him."

"Did he think *my son* could do those chores? He was only *two*. What in the *world* was Frank *thinking?* What *possessed* him to take my child?"

"Who? Frank? Frank never took anyone's child."

Emily let out a shuddering breath.

Brian took her hand. "These men who borrow children," he said to Myra, "what do they do with them?"

"Oh, they drive them home, and carry them in the house, and their wives are *furious.* Their wives tell them that they can't just wander off with other people's children. They argue until they're blue in the face, but all it does is get everyone upset." Her eyes met her fingers, which were snaking around each other. "They don't mean to make things worse. They're trying to fix things, only they can't."

"Where are they?" Emily asked in a high voice.

Myra seemed detached. "In the kitchen."

"And the boy?" Brian asked. "Where was he?"

"With them." She grew silent.

Emily saw Daniel there, saw him frightened by Frank's booming voice, rushing to the door, pressing his face to the screen, crying for her. She saw his cheeks growing red with his screams, saw the streaming tears, heard the hiccuping howls, coming harder and louder.

Her heart broke. She flew to her feet, unable to sit still.

Shrilly, Myra wailed, "He wouldn't be quiet! I tried to get him to be quiet! He was making things worse! But he wouldn't stop crying because he was scared, and the more he cried the madder Frank got —"

She stopped abruptly. Her eyes flew from Brian to Emily to the floor, but if there was upset in them, Emily was beyond caring. Brian reached for her, only it wasn't his arms she felt, but smaller ones that had clung to her in the wake of a scraped knee, a measles shot, a Halloween mask. She *felt* those smaller arms clawing at the Balchs' back door, groping frantically for a knob, for Emily, for air, for help. Caught up in the terror, she gasped aloud, then said, "I'm okay, I'm okay," when Brian tried to take her from the room. She held up a hand to reinforce her words.

For another minute, his eyes expressed concern. Then he ran his hands up and down her arms, sat her on the sofa again, and, after a last look to make sure she was all right, turned to Myra again. "What happened then?"

She seemed confused. "When?"

He paused, rephrased the question. "What happens, in situations like that, when the child is crying and making the man madder and madder?"

"Why," she began as though it were obvious, "he keeps telling the child to be still, but the child is so frightened that he doesn't hear, so the man slaps him to get his attention."

Emily made a sound. Again she held up her hand to assure Brian that she was all right. The hand curled into a fist and settled against her mouth. She didn't want to cry out, didn't want to interrupt. She had to

681

hear the story, had to know, finally.

Myra turned to her. "The wife tries to get him to stop hitting, but he throws her off to the side with one more big sweep of his hand, and by the time she has herself back on her feet the child is quiet."

Emily began a convulsive rocking. "Dead? Dead then?"

"Well, yes, most likely, because his head has hit the table, and he isn't moving. The wife tries to wake him up, but he isn't breathing."

Emily bolted up and staggered toward the door. One of the patrolmen caught her, then Brian.

"If that was the end," she whispered, "if he didn't know anything after that, I don't need to either, it isn't important." She thought of her baby's terror, cut with a knife-sharp pain into nothingness. Only that wasn't the end. There were years of agony that had followed, a marriage destroyed, the subconscious searching of faces for a familiar one that might have been misplaced, the guilt, the anger, the energy spent in trying to find answers that were under her nose all the time, and she whirled on Myra, hating the woman, crying, "Why didn't you *tell* me? All those years, you *knew,* and I was going through *hell.* You saw me all the time, you

682

saw my husband all the time, you saw my *daughter* all the time. You let that — that *barbarian* near her. How *could* you? How could you *not tell me* what he'd done?"

But she knew — maybe not the details of the threats, but she could guess them. *I'll kill you,* he might have said, or, *I'll kill your sons,* or, *Say one word, and I'll get you in hell, you old bat* — and, whatever, Myra had been so terrified that not even Frank's death had freed her. So she had carried the secret with her, haunted by it, obsessed with it, trying in her pathetically evasive way to get anyone and everyone to sit with her under the willow, as though whoever sat there would know, and she would be relieved of telling them, and thus safe from Frank.

"I have to go," Emily whispered seconds before her legs gave out. She was distantly aware of being carried, then deposited on something soft, then held, but it was a long time before she felt any warmth, and an even longer time before she slept.

The next morning Celeste was in her kitchen dropping batter by the spoonfuls onto baking sheets. She was making butter cookies for Emily. It was a small gesture, but she needed to do it. Emily had been a loyal friend, sticking with her through many an ordeal with Dawn. This latest with Carter had been the worst, but it was petty compared to Emily's own.

Celeste had to keep reminding herself of that, lest she wallow in self-pity. Okay, so she had lost Carter. The man was less of a loss than the fantasy.

Dawn was something else. She was back at the dorm. Celeste didn't know much more than that.

Dropping the spoons in the empty mixing bowl, she wiped her hands on her jeans and dragged open the oven door. One cookie sheet went in, then the second. She closed the door and set the timer.

"Hi."

She whirled around.

Dawn stood just inside the kitchen door wearing a guarded look. Celeste's heart was pounding, but only in part from being startled. She hadn't known when Dawn would show up, hadn't expected her this soon, didn't know what to say or think or feel.

"I heard about Daniel Arkin," Dawn said. "I thought I'd stop over at Emily's."

This isn't Emily's, Celeste thought. *Why are you here?*

"How is she?"

"Okay."

Dawn nodded. She looked at the mixing bowl. "Are the cookies for her?"

They sure aren't for you, sweetie, not after what you did. "Yes, they're for Emily. She's been a good friend to me."

"Does that mean she hates me, too?"

"I don't know. You'd have to ask her."

"Do you hate me?"

"I haven't decided yet."

"But you're disappointed."

"Very."

Dawn grappled with that for a minute. "After Jill called me last night, I was thinking about what happened to Daniel and thinking that something like that could have happened to me with Carter. But how could I know he was a louse?"

"He went from mother to daughter. That should have tipped you off."

"It didn't tip *you* off."

"It sure did. The minute I learned he was with you, it did. You should have vetoed his little escapade the minute he suggested it. You should have known right then he was no good. Good men don't do things like that."

She shrugged. "I was angry."

"Because I had my nose done? Because I was having a good time while you were at school? Because I was happy?"

She shrugged again, looking guilty now.

"Ever hear the expression, bite your nose off to spite your face?" Celeste asked. "That's what you did, Dawn. Boy, you may be book smart, but when it comes to common sense, you get an F."

"I'm sorry!" Dawn cried.

"Why? Because you're worried that I won't let you use my car? Or that your father might cut down your allowance, or, worse, *reneg* on his promise to pay your tuition? He doesn't have to pay it, Dawn. As you love pointing out, you are an adult."

"I know."

"Adults have to take responsibility for their actions."

"I *know.*" She sank into a chair by the table and said in a quiet voice, "I was wrong. I shouldn't have done what I did." She raised sad eyes. "But he was unreal. Handsome. Sexy. He made me feel like I was special. It's nice to feel that way sometimes."

Pointedly, Celeste said, "Isn't it."

"I was *wrong,* Mom. Are you going to hold it against me forever?" She sounded so young that Celeste remembered the child she had once been — yes, stubborn and willful, but so full of spirit, so like Celeste once, that Celeste had been green with envy.

"Remember the awful fights we had over curfews?" she asked.

Dawn nodded.

"You thought I was trying to control you. Maybe I was. And maybe not for the best of reasons," if jealousy had been the case. "But there were valid reasons, too. I've been your age. I got into more than my share of mischief, so I know what teenagers can do. Only things were different in my day, more innocent, less random. I wanted you home safe and off the streets before the roads filled with crazies. I really did worry, Dawn. Would I have done that if all I'd wanted was to get rid of you?"

"I didn't say that was all you wanted."

"You said I was dying for you to leave so I could have my freedom, but if that was so, why wouldn't I ever let you stay out all night? Imagine the freedom I'd have had *then.* If freedom was all I wanted, I wouldn't have cared where you went. But I did. Because you are my daughter, and I do love you, even if right now that's just a word. I don't feel love right now. Just disappointment."

"I'm not seeing Carter again."

"You can have him. I don't want him."

"I don't *either.* He's not a nice person."

"That's not the point."

Dawn looked at her lap. "I know."

Celeste remained silent.

"Nice or not," Dawn admitted, "he was seeing my mother. I was wrong to have gone off with him. I'm sorry."

The buzzer rang. Slipping her hands into mitts, Celeste took the cookie sheets from the oven. When they were set safely on the burner grates, she tossed the mitts aside and turned off the oven.

"What now?" Dawn asked.

"Now they cool."

"What now with us?"

"I don't know. Don't call me, I'll call you, you said."

"I wanted you to call."

"That wasn't what you said."

"It was what I wanted."

"You have to *tell* me then."

"I am. I want you to call."

"Okay. I can."

Dawn nodded. She moistened her lips. "I keep thinking of Emily not knowing Daniel was dead all those years. I keep thinking that something might happen to you and I wouldn't know about it."

"Nothing's going to happen to me," Celeste said, but she was touched.

"Carter told me how you two met. What if the next guy is a *real* crazy?"

"Carter *told* you?" Celeste was embarrassed, until she had a thought. "How did he explain *his* placing an ad?"

"A friend placed it for him."

"Do you believe that?"

"Not anymore."

"Thank you."

"You didn't have to place an ad. There are men in Grannick who'd love to take you out."

"I wanted to meet new people."

"Do you still?"

Celeste considered that for the first time since the fiasco of Carter. "Yes. But I've been burned. I'll be more careful." She would see the widower again. And even the vet, whose shyness might be hiding awesome things. And there were two new, interesting responses that had come from her ad while she was seeing Carter, so she hadn't done anything about them. She would. She might even put in a new ad, using "intelligent" instead of "sexy," as Kay had wanted her to do the first time. It might be interesting to see what that would yield.

She was tempted to tell Dawn about the twenty-five-year-old, but decided against it. Sharing was sick. Besides, Dawn needed to be with college guys. Twenty-five was too old for eighteen — and, ahhhh yes, too young for forty-three.

Fishing a spatula from a drawer, she began freeing cookies from the baking sheet and slipping them into a dish. She felt better — not exactly exuberant, but not depressed over Carter. Life went on. There was hope for her yet.

The cookie on the tip of the spatula was warm and soft, lightly toasted and tempting. Turning, she offered it to Dawn.

TWENTY-SIX

The funeral was held two days later, on a frail yellow December morning, at the cemetery on the outskirts of Grannick.

Emily had been dreading it. She had spent those two days steeling herself, crying softly with Jill, even with Doug, clinging to Brian during those other hours when she simply couldn't be without. She hadn't slept much. Though her tears exhausted her, she kept waking to terror and lies and bloody thoughts. She had thought that the funeral would be the worst.

She was wrong. Everything that came before was heart-wrenching, but the inkling of comfort she had felt that horrible night by the willow, when she imagined Daniel finally being buried, took root. The lowering of the little coffin into the ground was more a benediction, Daniel's long-overdue send-off to a kinder place. Just as Myra had finally relinquished the load she carried, so

Emily buried Daniel, with love.

What was to have been a private rite brought out better than half the town. Emily saw friends and acquaintances. Their presence delivered the kind of comfort that the living needed, along with food to the house later, and gentle words, expressing their sorrow in an endless stream of goodwill.

It wasn't until the next morning that Emily was able to take her first deep, relatively steady breath and sit alone over breakfast with Jill.

"It's strange for me," Jill said. "I never knew him."

"Me, neither, in a way. He was only two, barely formed as a person."

"I still don't understand how Frank could have taken him. You can bet I'll look twice at my neighbors when I buy a home someday."

"Look twice," Emily begged, "but don't agonize. You can't live like that, Jill. If I had second-guessed everything after Daniel, you'd have grown up neurotic. There's the quality of life to consider. Be positive."

"Like you. You always are."

"I've always tried."

"For my sake?"

"Yes. And your father's. I think now I'm

going to try for me." She watched Jill eat, savoring all the little familiar motions, the things she loved and would miss. "It's been nice having you home."

"I'm sorry it was for this."

"Me too. But it's good. We needed to know. Try to get your father to talk about it during the drive." Doug was returning her to Boston later that morning. "He's having a hard time."

"More than you. How come?"

"For a long time he refused to think about Daniel. I've been mourning for years. He's just starting."

"When is it done?"

"I don't know that it's ever completely done, but the wound heals in time. I thought mine had. I was wrong. I guess I got so used to living with the mystery of Daniel's death that I didn't see it, only it was there, affecting everything. I didn't realize how much I needed closure on this." She thought of how she had clung to her marriage, clung to the house, clung to Grannick, even clung to being a homemaker, so that she would be mothering when Daniel returned. She hadn't realized she was doing any of it, until Daniel was found.

"I'm thinking of selling the house."

Jill's eyes grew large. "Selling it?"

"How would you feel if I did?"

"Uh, strange."

"Is that a veto of the idea?"

"No, it's just so sudden." The words were barely out when a look of understanding crossed her face.

Emily smiled a sad confirmation. "I'm having trouble looking at the Balchs' house. I see it every time I drive down the street. Then I look in our backyard and see the pond, and my eyes go to their part of the pond, and their backyard, and the willow. I'm not sure I can stay here. What's done is done. I can't change it. Daniel is buried somewhere else now." She pictured the grassy spot where he was. It was a minute before she could speak again. "I don't think I want to be forever reminded of what happened here. I don't see what good it would do."

"Where would you move?"

"Not far. I like Grannick." The support she had received in the past few days had been convincing. She couldn't see turning her back on friendships that had been two decades in growing. She did like Grannick. She just didn't want to see the Balchs' backyard.

"What about Brian?"

Emily kept her voice slow and easy. "What

about him?"

"If you sell, he'll be without an apartment. You want to stay with him, don't you?"

"Yes."

"He loves you."

"Did he tell you that?"

"He didn't have to."

"How do you feel about it?"

"You and Daddy aren't getting back together?"

"No. There's too much hurt."

"You have a right to be happy. I want you to be."

Emily slipped from her chair, wrapped an arm around Jill's neck, and held on tight. "I love you," she cried, tears, emotions so close to the surface.

"But you love him, too," Jill said.

Emily had to pull back to see her grin. "I do."

"Are you sure you want to take on a baby?"

"No. I'm not sure I want to take on a *man.* I think I need time to find me."

"So what about him?"

Emily blotted her eyes, sighed, and smiled. "I'll let you know when I find out, okay?"

Brian took the day off from work. He wanted to spend time with Julia. Well, what he wanted, actually, was to spend time with Julia *and* Emily, but he knew that Emily would be with Jill for most of the morning, and he respected that need.

So he addressed his own need, the one driven by the raw feelings that the past few days had left. He played with Julia while she was still in her crib, ducking under where she couldn't see him, then popping out and making her laugh. He let her paint his face, then hers, then the bathtub with shaving cream. He let her help him rinse everything off.

Normally of a morning he was distracted, thinking of the day ahead. This morning he was thinking of Julia and took his time.

"Which outfit?" he asked, crouching beside her, examining the pile of clothes that were clean, folded, and waiting.

"Dis." A little finger dabbed at the one she wanted, then retreated into a fist by her bare belly.

"The red shirt?"

She nodded.

"What about pants? Or a skirt? Wanna wear a skirt? Give the guys at the station a thrill?"

The little finger dabbed again, retreated again.

"Green jeans. Red and green. That's rushing the season a little. Why don't we wait on green. Try again."

"Dis," Julia said, pointing to red jeans, looking expectantly at Brian.

"*Good* choice, Julia. Hooray for Julia!" He clapped her hands together, whipped out the pants and dressed her up.

They had breakfast at Nell's, Julia sitting on his lap, while he sat on a stool at the counter. She loved the donuts; everyone loved her. Brian left with a warm feeling that had to do with fresh brewed coffee and new friends, with small-town comforts and the sense that something was right in his life, and the feelings stayed warm through a stop at the police station. Everyone who knew Brian knew Julia. She was the center of attention, and she ate it up, going off with the animal officer to see a lost dog, racing back across the room and into Brian's arms with a high giggle when they were done.

Back in the Jeep, she fell asleep, which was fine. Brian wanted to drive around some. She was still sleeping when he pulled up at John's. He climbed out and started up the front walk, intent on letting her sleep longer. Then he stopped and thought of Daniel, and it wasn't that he worried she would be kidnapped, not from the driveway of the chief of police, just that he wanted to hold her. Returning to the car, he eased her out so smoothly that she didn't even wake.

John was in the living room, talking on the phone, his casts the only remaining sign of his mishap.

He hung up and grinned. "Huh. What tired her out?"

"Me. We've been playing. This is our day together."

"She'll remember it when she's grown."

"I'm doin' it for me as much as for her," Brian cracked. "It may be what *I* remember when I'm in that old rocking chair at the nursing home. How're the legs?"

John batted at one of the casts. "Dead weight. I need these off. I need to be walking again." He glanced at his watch. "I need to be back at work. Reading reports isn't the same as being there when things happen. Did you hear about Hooks?"

"Yeah. I just came from the station."

"So he's going back to school?"

"That's what he says. He says he wants to be a lawyer."

"Think he'll make a good one?"

Brian considered that with his chin against Julia's warm curls. "I don't know. He's a by-the-book cop. I suppose he could be a by-the-book lawyer. That's good for us, I guess. By-the-book lawyers are easier to handle. It's the creative ones who stump us. I don't think Hooks will be one of those."

"Well put," John said. He shot another look at his watch. "Can I talk to you about something?"

Brian was swaying from side to side, enjoying Julia's warmth, feeling content. "Sure."

"What do you think of Grannick?"

"I like it a lot."

"Are you planning to stay?"

"I was." His swaying slowed. He wondered if John was trying to let him down easy. "Is there a problem?"

"No problem. You're good for the department. You have skills some of the others don't have. I'm going to be awhile longer getting these legs working. It's nice knowing you're around with two good ones." He paused, pushed his lower lip out, finally said, "What I was worried about is that you might leave if Emily does. How's she doing?"

"Not bad. As painful as the truth is, it's good to know it after all this time."

"I should've seen something," John muttered.

It wasn't the first time he had told Brian that. He had been agonizing since the body had been found. As always, Brian tried to ease his guilt. "You questioned Frank. You questioned him more than once. He didn't budge. There wasn't anything to see."

"You saw something."

"Only after Myra nearly hit me over the head with it. Emily's like you. She keeps saying she should have guessed it. But that's crazy. Frank might have been mean, but who would have thought he would take a child."

"Borrowing was the word Myra used. I hear she's leaving town."

"Now that Frank's secret is out, she can."

"I wouldn't blame Emily if she did, too. Think she will?"

"No."

"Have you talked with her about it?"

"Not yet. It's on my list of things to do today."

"Huh." John seemed to relax some. "Well, I don't want her leaving, any more'n I want you leaving. You can tell her that." He slid a third look at his watch.

"Are you waiting for someone?"

"My wife. We have a date."

"Yeah?"

"For lunch. She'll be along."

"Want me to wait here 'til she comes?"

"Nah. I have more calls to make. Go enjoy Julia."

Brian wasn't sure he would, given what he had to do next, but there was no avoiding it. It was cold. Winter was here. He figured it was now or never.

He drove to the mall, parked outside Lord & Taylor, and found the children's department without any fuss, but that was the easy part. The hard part lay ahead.

He was feeling slightly daunted confronted with a thousand pieces of clothing, not knowing where to start, when a grandmotherly type approached.

"Julia needs a snowsuit," he blurted out. "I have no idea what size, style, color, nothing."

Esther Nelson took him in hand. She asked him how old Julia was, had him stand her up, showed him the options, gave him the pros and cons of each. It turned out that the hardest part of the purchase was deciding between two that were equally adorable, one pink, one lime green. In the end, he simply set Julia in front of the two.

"Which one do you want, toots?"

"Dis," Julia said, going for the green one without a moment's pause.

Esther set them up with a hat, mittens, and mitten clips, and then, because Brian was riding high on the fact that it had been painless, he let Julia pick out some new winter clothes, again from a prenarrowed selection. Pushover that he was, he even bought the teddy bear that she couldn't keep her little hands away from.

Best of all, he left with Esther's card, a list of the hours she worked, and the assurance that he could call her and she would be there the next time Julia needed clothes.

Grandly buoyed, he took his daughter to the Eatery for lunch. They knew everyone there. Julia babbled to the waitress, proudly waving her bear. She chomped on pieces of chicken, tomato, and olive from Brian's cobb salad. As far as he could detect, she was in as fine a mood as he was.

So they strolled down the street from the Eatery to the flower shop, where he found a small basket lined with a blue and white fabric that reminded him of the bedroom Emily kept to herself. To the florist's horror, he made him cut down a beautiful white lily and arrange the blooms with water picks in the basket. Then he set off for the drugstore.

He held Julia while he browsed through the greeting cards. When she began to squirm, he set her down. He picked the card he wanted, one with a barn-and-meadow scene that was as serene as the way Emily made him feel, and paid for it plus half a dozen Butterfingers, at the register. Then he looked around.

"Julia?" he called out. He crossed the front of the store, looking down each aisle. He hurried past the toys and paced the back of the store, searching the aisles from that end. *"Julia?"*

"Daddy daddy daddy."

It was a minute before he saw a pint-sized person with red pants, a denim jacket, and soft brown curls below the curtain of the photo booth.

"Who's in here?" he asked, parting the curtains.

Julia had her arms on the seat. She grinned up at him.

"What are you doing?"

She slapped the seat with both hands. "Daddydaddy nagoo."

"Yeah. Remember we sat there? Remember *all* the times we sat there? Julia didn't want to sit. Julia didn't want to smile. All Julia wanted to do was cry."

She brought her pointer around, touched the black patch of the camera's eye, and looked questioningly up at him.

"Right on. There's the flash. You don't like that flash."

Her eyes held his.

"Yeah?"

She tried to climb up on the seat but had neither the height nor dexterity for it. Her eyes returned to his, iridescently insistent.

"You want to try?" He sat her on the seat and waited for her to cry.

She looked at the black patch. When it didn't do anything, she pointed. "Daddy dis."

He pulled change from his pocket and showed it to her. "I have to put quarters in the slot. It isn't easy. I don't want to do it, unless you're gonna smile. Are you?"

"Daddy *dis.*"

He hoisted her up, folded himself into the booth, onto the bench, and stood her on his lap. He waited for her to pucker up.

She wrapped an arm around his neck, pointed at the camera, and said something that he chose to believe meant, "Put in the damn quarters and get this show on the road."

He put in the quarters. He tapped the patch. The first flash went off. "Boom! There's one! Smile, pretty Julia — boom! There's two! My God, we're actually getting this right — boom! There's three! Whoa, is Grammie going to be *psyched* — boom! There we *go!*"

Emily was in the den, listening to the strains

of a mellow trombone, feeling a little lonely, a little pensive, a little unsure, when Brian opened the back door and called, "Hello?"

"In here," she called back, but she didn't move. She sat in the chair behind the desk, with her arms cinching her knees, waiting with a lift in her heart. When she saw them, father and daughter, the loneliness eased. "Hey."

Brian set Julia down. She ran to Emily. "Emememem."

"Hi, sweetie." Emily unfolded herself, scooped Julia up, and settled her on her lap. "Whatcha been doin'?"

"This and that," said Julia's father.

A beautiful basket materialized on Emily's desk. It was lined with a fabric not unlike the comforter on her bed, and filled with white lilies and Butterfingers. An envelope followed the basket down. She reached around Julia, drew out the card, and after immersing herself in the picture on the front, read what Brian had written inside. His handwriting was atrocious. Mercifully, there wasn't much to decipher.

Two words. "We'll wait." That was it.

It was enough.

"You are," she said, deeply touched, "an incredible man."

He came to sit on the edge of the desk,

his legs angled to the floor by her chair. "You know what I want."

She did. He wanted to marry her. "Part of me wants it, too, but there's the other part that needs to recover from all this, that needs to breathe a little, needs to think about who *I* am. Sound selfish?"

"No."

"I love you." She drew Julia back against her, strapping her in with her arms. "I love this one, too."

"I saw a barn this morning."

"Like the one on my card?"

"A little. Yeah, actually, a lot. It's over on the hill, off Creighton Path."

Emily knew the one. There was a farmhouse, too, a sprawling structure of wood and stone. Farmhouse, barn, meadows, and woods had belonged to the Fosseys of Grannick for generations. It had been years since the barn had housed anything but cars, years since Fossey children had returned as adults.

The senior Fosseys were packing it in. Farmhouse, barn, meadows, and woods were for sale.

Emily knew that, indeed. The property was one of the prettiest in town. The look in Brian's eyes said that he agreed. It also said something else.

"Well, you can't stay here," he protested as though they had discussed it dozens of times, when in fact she hadn't mentioned it to him once. "You can't punish yourself for the rest of your life having to see the Balch house every day."

"I know."

"You do?"

Nodding, she reached for his hand. When he gave it to her, she brought it to her throat. "Think we can afford the farm?"

"If we do it together. Will you live with me?"

"Not yet." Not until she was sure enough of herself. Not until they were married. But there were other choices. "I'll take the barn."

"I'm taking the barn."

"Brian, it's little more than a shell!"

"Exactly."

"So, you can't have Julia living in a shell."

"I can't have you living in one, either."

"How long would it take to insulate it and put in utilities?"

"Could be livable in a month."

"Yeah?"

"Yeah."

She imagined a large skylit space with separate areas for sleeping, eating, and writing. She imagined a loft space for Jill that could one day be used as a playroom for Julia, if things worked out. She imagined trysts in the woods and love in the meadow, and all sorts of other fun things that were as different from her past as night from day. She imagined going to the cemetery on the outskirts of town and telling Daniel about the place where she lived.

That thought choked her up. She figured it would, for a while.

"What do you think?" he asked, beyond the house versus the barn. The question went deep.

Emily took a breath and swallowed. She could handle deep. She had come to an abyss, crossed it, and survived. A different world was open to her now, with many of the same joys as before and then some.

She kissed his hand and returned it to her neck. "I think, I think," when she couldn't find the words, when her throat tightened again, for love of Brian this time, she simply sighed, smiled, and said, "Yeah."

POSTSCRIPT

Emily sat alone on the low stone wall. Her elbows were on her knees, her hands linked loosely between them. She wore linen pants and a blazer from the same New York designer, a silk blouse open at the throat, and wonderfully bright gold earrings. She still looked about sixteen years old. Her hair did it to her every time. But she felt older. Better. More savvy. Successful.

Behind her were the trees that God had artfully arranged, before her the camera, reflectors, and light that the photographer had artfully arranged.

Beyond the photographer were Brian and Julia.

Julia giggled a five-year-old's giggle. "Smile, Emmy."

Brian didn't have to say it. All he had to do was to look at Emily with those satisfied silver-blue eyes of his and she couldn't have kept a smile from her face if she tried. Not that she would have. As though compensating for the sorrow she had known, life was treating her well.

Another book was about to be published, hence the need for a photograph. It wasn't the book on Daniel; that one had hit the stands eighteen months before. This one dealt with cries for help of the kind she had seen in Grannick, though she had gone far beyond those. She had taken cases from all over the country, gleaned from weeks of travel and interviews.

The book on Daniel had been a private necessity, a summing up of the great anguish of her life, a final gift to her son. She still picked it up and read random parts when she wanted to be near him, but the need for that was diminishing. She could think and talk more freely about him now. Emancipated, she carried him with her wherever she went, a little bump on her heart that, like a beauty mark, neither disappeared nor hemmed her in.

The new book had been far more of an independent intellectual exercise. It was being touted as a must-read for those in law enforcement, social service, even education, and while no one pretended it would be a commercial bestseller, it would establish Emily's name in the field, not to mention add to her nest egg.

Its actual publication would be anticlimactic. Far more momentous to Emily was the day she had put a period to its final sentence, printed out the manuscript, and turned off her computer. That was the day she felt whole. That was the day she had gone to Brian and, with a glowing smile, offered a softer, more confident, "Yeah."

They had been married the weekend after that in what was to have been a small ceremony, but Grannick-style, had swelled to include not only Jill and Julia, Brian's family, and Emily and Brian's closest friends, but all those others whose lives theirs touched daily.

It was rich life. Emily had her career. She had Brian. She had Jill. She had Julia. She had Kay and John, who grew closer with each passing year. She had Celeste, who dated widely but more wisely.

Jill had graduated from college, was working for an advertising firm in Boston, and visited Emily and Brian often. The farm was a breather from the busy pace of her life. In turn, always, she brought Emily joy.

"That's good," the photographer invited. "Give me another like that."

Emily wasn't sure what the first one had been like, but she continued to think happy

711

thoughts, and before long, after several shifts of pose and scene, the photographer was putting his light meter away.

"One of my family?" she asked in a rush.

Brian answered before the photographer could. "No way. This is your day, your picture. Besides, we have more than enough."

She pictured the living room of the farmhouse with its fieldstone hearth, flanked by pine shelves that were covered with photo after framed photo. There were ones of Julia, ones of Jill, ones of Jill and Emily, Emily and Brian, and Emily, Brian, Julia, and Jill. There were ones of Jill's college graduation, next to ones of her high school graduation. There were Halloween ones, Christmas ones, birthday ones. There were ones taken by professionals, by amateurs, and ones taken by the photo booth in town. There were, older but no less treasured, ones of Daniel.

As far as Emily was concerned, there could never be too many photos when it came to documenting the meaning of life. But she didn't argue with Brian. This was her day. A small reprint of this picture would join the others flanking the fieldstone hearth. It would be the very first of her alone.

Alone, but not lonely. Never lonely again.

ABOUT THE AUTHOR

Barbara Delinsky, a lifelong New Englander, was a sociologist and photographer before she began to write. There are more than 30 million copies of her books in print. Readers can contact her c/o P.O. Box 812894, Wellesley, MA 02482-0026, or via the Web at www.barbaradelinsky.com.

The employees of Thorndike Press hope you have enjoyed this Large Print book. All our Thorndike, Wheeler, and Kennebec Large Print titles are designed for easy reading, and all our books are made to last. Other Thorndike Press Large Print books are available at your library, through selected bookstores, or directly from us.

For information about titles, please call:
  (800) 223-1244

or visit our Web site at:
  http://gale.cengage.com/thorndike

To share your comments, please write:
Publisher
Thorndike Press
10 Water St., Suite 310
Waterville, ME 04901